THE
GATHERING
STORM

CROSSWAY BOOKS
by W. E. Davis

Valley of The Peacemaker
Book One—The Gathering Storm
Book Two—The Proving Ground

A Gil Beckman Mystery Series
Suspended Animation
Victim of Circumstance
Black Dragon

VALLEY OF THE PEACEMAKER
BOOK ONE

THE GATHERING STORM

W. E. DAVIS

CROSSWAY BOOKS • WHEATON, ILLINOIS
A DIVISION OF GOOD NEWS PUBLISHERS

The Gathering Storm

Published by Crossway Books
         a division of Good News Publishers
         1300 Crescent Street
         Wheaton, Illinois 60187

Cover illustration: Steve Chorney

Cover design: Cindy Kiple

First printing, 1996

Printed in the United States of America

Library of Congress Cataloging-in-Publication Data
Davis, Wally, 1951-
   The Gathering Storm / W. E. Davis.
      p.   cm. — (Valley of the peacemaker ; bk.1)
   ISBN 0-89107-887-8
   1. Frontier and pioneer life—California—Fiction. 2. Young men—California—Fiction. 3. Sheriffs—California—Fiction. I. Title.
II. Series: Davis, Wally, 1951-   Valley of the peacemaker ; bk. 1.
PS3554.A93785G3 1996
813'.54—dc20   95-47118

04		03		02		01		00		99		98		97		96
15	14	13	12	11	10	9	8	7	6	5	4	3	2	1

DEDICATION

To my sons

PART

ONE

CHAPTER

ONE

JUNE 2, 1863

A Union infantryman hunkered behind a tree at the edge of the clearing holding his rifle close to his body with a tight grip, his face set, eyes staring at the ground but not seeing. He was gaunt with uncombed, matted wet hair and dark, sunken eyes. Beads of sweat cut crooked tracks through the dirt on his face.

His age couldn't be guessed by looking at him. He needed a bath and a shave, his uniform was ill-fitting and dirty, and his eyes betrayed his fear. His hands were those of a farmer.

Although unwounded, he had seen men on both sides of him fall when bullets fired by Reb soldiers ripped through them. He was scared—like everyone else there—and took several deep breaths as he prepared to jump out from behind the tree and charge across open ground to confront the enemy—men he didn't know, much less hate, who were trying to kill him.

He thought of the wife and young son he had left back in Illinois and the farm he had carved out of the countryside for them. He had worked his forty acres for fifteen years, growing corn and wheat, and raising a small herd of dairy cows and had looked forward to his son growing old enough to take over running the place.

The soldier caught his breath as he gazed at the blue mist that hung over the clearing, the smoke from cannons that were still being fired by both sides. The bodies of the dead and injured lay scattered about the wild grass, their uniforms caked with bloody dirt, the near-dead moaning for help that would not come in time.

He was startled by the sudden charge of his company, led by a bearded, sabre-waving lieutenant with wild eyes. They ran past him, their rifles cracking. He abandoned his thoughts, ignored his fears, and spun out from behind the tree, following the other men. Those who fell in his path with fresh bullet wounds he leapt over or dodged, waiting for the chance to raise his rifle to his shoulder and return fire.

That chance came, and not knowing or caring if his bullet found its mark, he fired on the run, then threw himself down behind a dead body to reload. As he stood back up and started forward, he heard the roar of a nearby cannon. Seconds later an unseen cannonball hit him in the arm, taking it off.

The soldier was spun by the force of the blow and knocked hard to the earth. His mind reeled. The pain scorched his right side. He struggled to breathe and heard himself cry out for help.

But none came. He was conscious, and the pain was unbearable. He looked down at what was left of his right arm. He knew he must stop the bleeding to live and managed to take off his pants belt. He looped it around his biceps, just below the shoulder. There was just enough arm left to accommodate the makeshift tourniquet, and as he tightened the belt, he saw the flow of blood slow and finally stop.

As he lay in his own blood, he cried. Again his thoughts turned to his family. He couldn't go home like this, he thought. A man has to take care of his wife and son. He couldn't plow a field or milk a cow or hug his family with only one arm.

He opened his eyes and looked up at the man-made fog that obliterated the sky.

"Why, God?" he shouted. *"Why?"*

He sobbed.

His wife was a good, Christian woman. He never felt much need for it himself, but he couldn't understand why God would let this happen to *her*. What kind of life could half-a-man make for her? *She'd be better off if I'd been killed.*

He lay still, crying silently for awhile, when an idea struck him. At first he rejected it.

"No!" he said aloud. Then he thought of what life would be

like for her: always tending to him, taking over the chores he wouldn't be able to perform. The more he thought about it, the better the idea sounded to him.

He crawled over to a nearby dead man and felt his pockets. He found the only papers the man carried and removed them. There were a few letters and the man's orders. He slid them into his own coat and stuffed his papers into the pocket of the dead man.

He fell back on the grass, exhausted and in intense pain, and passed out.

CHAPTER

TWO

SEPTEMBER 11, 1871

The roan horse plodded lightly up the rocky, winding dirt road through a narrow, shallow canyon. The saddle creaked pleasantly under the weight of the rider, a young man wearing woolen trousers and a cotton shirt, blue suspenders, a flat-brimmed gray hat and gum-soled boots. His Colt Peacemaker single-action revolver was stuck into his waistband, and his left hand rested casually on the saddle horn.

He sat erect, his steel-gray eyes scanning the road ahead for the highwaymen he had been warned about before he left Aurora, Nevada, bound for California. He wore a full mustache, grown since arriving out West just a few months before, and was in need of a shave, giving him the appearance of being older than he actually was.

This wagon trail he rode on was loaded with hazards. Rocks and potholes and brush made travel slow and purposeful. He let the horse find its own way and didn't push him. He was in no hurry. Since coming West he had drifted from one gold camp to another, eking out a meager existence when he could, doing odd jobs or a little placer mining in the streams that cut their twisted beds through the Comstock and Esmeralda mining districts.

He had been in Aurora a few months, spending some of his time with a funny, little man from Missouri who told him some interesting yarns about Mississippi riverboats. The man wasn't much of a prospector, and the drifter urged him to try his hand at writing, putting his stories down on paper and selling them. Who knows, he had told the man, a few people might just read them. The man from Missouri just laughed at the notion.

The drifter on the roan left Aurora in the morning, headed for Bridgeport, California, at the foot of the Sierra Nevadas. He had heard it was magnificent country with snow-capped peaks even in summer, green grass covering the meadows, brilliant orange aspen groves in autumn, and blue skies broken by white, billowy clouds.

Bridgeport was a thriving community, and he hoped to find a job he liked—or even start a business. He'd been careful not to dip into his savings that he had brought with him, living off whatever money he could earn. Bridgeport had a bank, and he was anxious to put his life savings away, where it would be safe. He'd sewn the cash into false bottoms in his saddlebags, but it was a lot of trouble keeping them in sight all the time. The time had come for him to settle down. He could feel it.

As he rode, he hummed an old song his mother had taught him and chewed a piece of tough, seasoned jerked beef. He marveled, as he did almost daily, at the countryside. Even the desolate parts were a wonder: the colors imbedded in the rock, the smell of the sage in spring and summer, the speed of a jackrabbit, the ferocity of a thunderstorm that abated as abruptly as it had arisen.

He was pondering the intricacies of detail in the skin of a large lizard that was sitting on a rock nearby when something up ahead, off in a gully, caught his eye. He pulled up the roan.

What's this? It's not a natural color, and the shape isn't right.

He suspected a robber hiding in the brush and gently eased himself down from the horse, the saddle creaking slightly as his weight was lifted off of it. He kept his eyes fixed on the thing in the brush, the jerky still hanging from his mouth. He pulled the Colt from his waistband and cocked it slowly—the two clicks alarmingly loud—and kept the gun at his side, ready, his finger resting safely on the trigger guard as he crept closer, leading his horse.

Whatever was in the brush didn't move. He got to within twenty yards of it and took a quick inventory of the jagged canyon walls on either side of him, and the road behind. He was alone. He dropped the reins and continued toward the object. He could see more of it now. It appeared to be a man. Still it remained motionless.

As he came within a few feet he swung his gun up and pointed it at the man, but it was quickly obvious the man was not going to move.

He was on his side, his arm tucked under him and his legs drawn up, and his hair was matted with dried blood. He wore an old military coat, dirty, tattered and torn, and gray with age.

The drifter kneeled next to the soldier and felt the side of his throat. There was a pulse, but his breathing was shallow and labored. The only visible injury was the blow to the head. He looked as if he had been here for at least a full day, maybe two. The sun had burned his exposed flesh and it was red, swollen, and blistered.

He pulled the injured man to a sitting position and moved him carefully a few feet, leaning him against a rock. He whistled for the roan, which walked slowly to him, and he retrieved his canteen off the saddle. He wet his neckerchief and dabbed the man's face and neck, then wet it again and put it to the man's puffy, red lips. At first there was no response, but slowly the man's lips began moving and sucking out some of the water. He groaned but did not awaken.

The drifter stood the man up and then bent over, putting his shoulder into the man's stomach and hoisting him up and carrying him to the horse. With great difficulty he managed to lay the man across his saddle, then cleaned and dressed the wound on his head.

"Looks like you got clubbed with a gun butt," he said out loud to the unhearing man. He took a drink himself from the canteen and led his horse up the trail, ever aware that whoever had waylaid the man was possibly somewhere up ahead.

As they passed a stake that marked the California border the drifter thought he heard the sound of distant thunder, then soon realized it wasn't thunder at all, but something man-made. He was all too familiar with the pounding of a stamp mill—where gold-bearing quartz was beat into dust so the gold could be extracted—but hadn't realized there was a mill way out here. He kept moving.

About three miles inside California the canyon receded into

rolling hills and finally broke out into a long valley. In the distance he could see the snow-capped Sierra Nevadas. Before him were a few scattered wood buildings—though not a tree could be seen—and at the base of the cliff at the east side of the valley was the stamp mill, a red brick structure surrounded by a collection of shacks and other buildings. For lack of a better word, this was the town of Bodie.

He led his horse over to the buildings and found one with a sign that read EMPIRE BOARDING HOUSE. It was a two-story structure in need of a whitewashing.

Bodie was a gold camp but had never amounted to much in the ten years or so it had been here. Only two mines operated, and no placer mining was done at all because Rough Creek, the only stream in the valley, had long since been panned out. Besides, placer gold was washed down from outcroppings in the ledges above, and the veins in the hills that were the source of the gold were what everyone was trying to find. That's where the real gold lay hidden.

Gold dug out of the hill was mixed in with quartz. The rock had to be crushed, then leached with quicksilver to get the gold out. This was all done in a stamp mill. Until the stamp mill had been built the ore had to be hauled to the mills at Aurora, seventeen miles back down the road the drifter had just traveled, or crushed in the *arastras*—stone pits into which the ore was tossed and a large rock dragged over it, pulled by a mule or horse.

It took men to operate a mill and to mine for gold, and they needed a place to live. That's what the boarding house was for, but it also took in travelers temporarily.

As the young drifter tied his mount to the porch rail of the house, the front door opened and a large man walked out.

"Whatcha got there, stranger?" the man asked.

The drifter looked up to see a pleasant-faced black man with powerful arms and a winning smile wearing an immense vest over a white shirt, woolen pants, and a pair of Sunday-go-to-meetin' shoes, badly in need of a polishing.

"He's near dead," the drifter replied. "Musta been jumped by robbers."

He went over to the soldier hanging across the saddle and started to pull him off.

"Hold on, son," the black man said. He lumbered off the porch and walked over to help. Together they lifted the injured man off the horse and carried him inside to a room, putting him onto the bed and taking him out of his dirty, blood-stained clothes.

"Thanks," the drifter said.

"Mah pleasure." He extended his massive hand. "William O'Hara. People call me Uncle Billy."

"Pleased to meet you, sir," the drifter said, taking the man's hand. "Matthew Page."

O'Hara took a close look at the soldier's face. "S'cuse me a minute," he said to Page. He walked out of the room and returned a few moments later with a round tin can. He twisted the top off and scooped out a handful of salve, which he gently spread on the man's burned flesh. Page watched in silence.

As he completed dressing the man's face, Uncle Billy spoke quietly. "He a friend a yours?"

"No, can't say that he is. I found him by the side of the road on my way here from Aurora."

"Highwaymen."

"That's what I thought. He didn't have any possessions anywhere in sight."

"You take his boots off?"

"No, they musta took those, too. They pretty much intended for him to die, I guess."

"Judging by the looks of that gash on his head, Ah think they figured he was dead already."

Matt nodded, then noticed two other men sitting apart from each other on the far side of the room. Billy saw Matt looking at them and anticipated his question.

"Yeah, they come in this morning. But they ain't the highwaymen. They ain't together, for one thing. One of 'em is a circuit preacher with questionable background. Th' other a salesman. Bibles, Ah think. They come through every now and then. They undoubtedly saw the poor man, though. That's why Ah was surprised when you come in with him and said you'd come that way."

"They saw him and didn't do anything?" Matt was shocked. That was unheard of where he was from.

"Don't s'prise me none," Billy said. "Nowadays folks like them only care 'bout people as long as their own pockets is bein' filled."

"But, that one's a *preacher*!"

"They ain't all like that. Them are the ones give the rest a bad name."

"That ain't right," Matt said quietly. He reached into his pants and pulled out a handful of coins, counted them out and gave them to Uncle Billy. "I'd appreciate it if you could put him up until he gets back on his feet, feed him, get him some boots. I've got to get on into Bridgeport. If this ain't enough, I'll pay the difference when I come back in a week or so."

O'Hara took the money. "This should be fine," he said. He looked at Matt thoughtfully. "How 'bout a hot meal 'fore you go?"

Matt could tell Uncle Billy wasn't going to take *no* for an answer; besides, it sounded good. He *was* hungry.

"Okay," he said. "Got someplace I can clean up a bit?"

Uncle Billy directed him to a basin and filled it full of water from a pitcher. Matt splashed his dry, parched face, keeping his wet hands up and breathing in the cool moisture, enjoying the relief, then drying himself with a clean towel that had been left. Uncle Billy had thrown a steak onto the stove and the aroma drifted back. Matt took a deep whiff and smiled.

CHAPTER

THREE

M att swung up onto his horse and gave Uncle Billy a wave as he headed out toward Bridgeport.

"I'll be back," Matt told him.

"You do that."

He made a noise with his mouth, and the roan picked up the pace.

The valley Bodie was in was several miles long and a mile wide, higher in elevation at the north end than at the south, and offered a breath-taking view of the mountains about twenty miles away to the south.

Matt rode slow and easy, taking in the sights, sounds, and scents of the area. It was a warm autumn day, but he knew the air was so thin at this elevation that the temperature would drop sharply and quickly as soon as the sun went down.

He wished he had let Uncle Billy treat him to a bed that night; he had forgotten how good one could feel to a tired, aching body. But he felt a pressing need to get to Bridgeport and kindly turned down the offer telling O'Hara he'd take him up on it when he came back. Uncle Billy smiled and gave him a paper-wrapped package containing jerked beef, sourdough bread, and some nuts. They were piñon pine nuts, a staple of the local Paiutes. Billy told him they'd give him energy.

Matt grabbed a handful of the nuts and chewed them while he rode. He figured the pine nuts must have been brought in from somewhere since there were no pine trees nearby, probably by a Paiute who traded them to Billy for a blanket or pair of pants.

He smelled the sweet, thick odor of sage and watched black-tailed rabbits and marmots run through the tall prairie grass that moved like ocean waves in the breeze. A lone red-tailed hawk circled overhead, its wings held still, catching the air currents that propelled him effortlessly through the endless sky. The only trees Matt could see anywhere were small groves of aspens and cotton-woods here and there, below Bodie's valley, their leaves shimmering in the wind.

The sky was a deep blue, and large, white clouds moved rapidly overhead, changing shape and location constantly. They were high and did not bear rain, but when they moved between Matt and the sun he noticed a distinct decrease in the temperature. As the day wore on Matt put on an old rawhide coat and started looking for a place to bed down for the night. He'd be able to get to Bridgeport the next day, before noon he hoped.

He thought about the sense of urgency he felt and wondered what it was all about. There was something inside him, driving him on to Bridgeport. It was more than just the security of his money. No, there was something else compelling him; he just couldn't put a finger on what it was. Although he couldn't explain it, he had been around animals enough to accept the feeling and listen to it, like animals that sense a tornado before it shows itself.

Matt was ten miles or so out of Bodie when the rolling hills gave way to a narrow canyon. The sun had finally disappeared for good behind a hill, and Matt turned the roan off the trail, looking for a protected piece of high ground. While it didn't look like rain, that could change without warning and flash floods could drown a man and his horse in seconds.

As he urged the horse up a rocky embankment he saw a campfire at the top, about two hundred yards away. He could see a man hunched over beside it. The man appeared to be alone. A mule was tethered to a stake nearby.

When Matt was halfway up the rise the man heard the roan's hooves on the rocky ground and looked up with a jerk. Not wanting to frighten him Matt waved an empty hand and called out.

"Ho there, friend. May I warm myself by your fire?"

The man didn't answer or move, and Matt could see he was holding something in his left hand. It was a pistol. Matt kept both his hands in plain view and smiled.

"I said, 'Can I bother you for a bit of your fire?'"

Matt was about twenty yards off now and pulled the roan up. He could see the man but not clearly because the only light came from the fire. He was a grizzled old prospector, with long, snarled hair and beard, and old clothes that had patches and holes in need of patches. His pants were tucked into worn, leather boots, and the suspenders that held them up were red, his flannel shirt a faded blue.

There was a strained silence as Matt waited for the prospector to answer. The man looked him over with one eye closed for a full minute, then spat into the fire and spoke.

"You look okay. Come on, then. Tie yer horse up by Bonehead, give him someone smarter'n him to talk to."

"Thanks." Matt climbed off his horse, led him to the tree where the mule was tied and secured the roan up next to him. He yanked the saddle off and put it on a rock, then walked over to the fire, carrying his saddlebags.

Matt sat down and warmed his hands. The gnarly argonaut stared at him and spit into the fire again.

"I said you could warm yerself, not move in."

Matt was startled. "Oh . . . uh, I'm sorry, I thought you meant . . . uh, well, okay, I'll go. Didn't mean to bother you." He got up and turned to go, then as an afterthought said, "Could you tell me how much of this countryside is yours so I don't trespass any more?"

The prospector spat. "Sit down, son. You can stay. I was jes' testin' you. I don't see people none too much. Got to be careful, there's bad men out here. I could use the company. Coffee?"

He nodded toward the pot, and Matt dug his own tin cup out of his saddlebag and poured it full of the steaming, thick liquid. He put it carefully to his lips and drank. It was bitter but went down warm.

Matt pulled out the parcel Uncle Billy had given him and unwrapped it. He offered some of the bread, nuts, and jerky to the prospector, who accepted it readily. He had long since put the gun away, sure that Matt wasn't a claim jumper or robber, and they enjoyed the food.

"Lookin' for gold?" Matt asked.

The prospector gave him a funny look.

"Noooo . . ." he said slowly. "I jes' look like this and have a mule and carry a pickax and pannin' tins 'cause I want folks to *think* I'm lookin' fer gold. Really throws 'em off when they find out I'm President Grant." He tore a hunk of jerky off in his mouth.

"Okay, I guess it was a stupid question," Matt said. "Just makin' conversation."

The prospector didn't answer. Matt knew he shouldn't have asked the man about gold. It wasn't the kind of question you asked a man. First, they might think you were planning on taking it from them, or force them to reveal where they found it so you could knock them on the head and jump their claim. Second, if they hadn't found any, they'd get all mad and depressed because they'd been out in this harsh country so long looking for it without success. Matt wisely didn't say more about it.

After a short silence Matt asked, "May I bed down here tonight? I'll gather some more firewood for you."

"Suit yerself," the prospector answered. He threw the remainder of a cup of coffee over his shoulder, than lay down in the dirt, pulled an old blanket over himself and closed his eyes. Within five minutes he was asleep.

Matt gathered some dried scrub and brought it to the campfire, then spread out his bedroll and got under the blanket. He lay with his eyes open for a time, looking up at the sky and watching a show of shooting stars, then soon drifted off into a deep sleep.

Matt woke to a light sprinkling of September rain peppering his face. He jumped up, grabbed his bedroll to keep it from getting too wet, and started for his horse but pulled up short. The roan was gone.

Matt wheeled around. The old prospector was gone, too, as was his mule and all his belongings. Matt was left with his bedroll, which he let fall.

"That thievin' old coot!" He said out loud. He went back to the fire, which had gone out, and sat down to put on his boots.

"At least he left me my boots." Suddenly he panicked. "My

saddlebags!" They had been beside him, along with his gun. He looked around feverishly, hoping they were still here, but he knew better.

He dropped his head into his hands and sat there motionless for a moment, then looked up slowly and stared off into the distance, thinking about his predicament. All his money—his life savings, his future—gone, just like that. One stupid mistake.

He was alone, with no horse or anything else, and in a strange place. He exhaled heavily and stood up. He inspected the ground, trying to pick up the prospector's trail but couldn't. Tracking was something he hadn't learned.

Suddenly, he kicked at his bedroll, then bent over and picked up a stone and threw it as hard as he could. He shouted and kicked the ground again, then settled down.

Matt grabbed his bedroll off the ground, realizing his tantrum hadn't fixed anything, and slung it over his shoulder. He took off on foot, picking his way around rocks and brush, back to the bottom of the ravine where the road was. Bridgeport wasn't too far, eight miles or so, and he needed to get there before evening, hoping to pick up a little work to pay for a meal and a room for the night. Then tomorrow he could start looking for a job to earn enough to get him a horse and some gear so he could find that prospector.

The rain increased steadily, and it wasn't long before Matt was soaked. The brim of his hat hung limp, water streaming off the front edge in a stream. The ground was turning muddy.

So much for his trail, he thought. *Doubt if I'll ever see that roan—or my money—again.*

He made his way through a small canyon of dark, red rock. A stream cut a trough next to the road, and its volume had enlarged with the rain. Matt found it hard to enjoy the scenery, considering he was reduced to the clothes on his back, a few soggy blankets, and some coins, and was miles from home in a part of the country he'd never been to before.

Other than that, he was doing okay, so he steeled himself against the pain and uncertainty, still feeling the urge to continue, and trudged through the mud toward Bridgeport.

He had gone five or six arduous miles when the rain stopped, the clouds broke and scattered, and the sun beat down on him once

again. He was hungry, having missed breakfast, and knew lunch
would also pass silently by, but figured he was fit enough to make
it to town with no problem. He hoped his boots were up to the
hike and wouldn't punish his feet too severely. He'd opted for gum
soles when he got them back in Wyoming because the others
looked too uncomfortable with their high heels and pointed toes.
Now he was glad about the choice he had made.

He was just about dry when the canyon walls abruptly fell
away into a wide plain ahead, rising up to the Sierra Nevadas. He
was near the foot of the mountains. Bridgeport was only a few
miles away now. He could see across the road into a ravine where
several man-made piles of crushed rock sat in stony silence next to
a few dilapidated, rotting wood shacks.

A weather-beaten old sign said "DOgtOWn" in uneven letters.
It was hanging from its post by one nail, which itself looked about
to fall out. *This place is deader'n a hammer,* Matt thought. On
another signpost, this one newer, he could read BISHOP with an
arrow pointing south, BODIE with an arrow pointing back up the
road he had just traversed, and BRIDGEPORT with an arrow pointing north. Without hesitation he turned right and headed for
Bridgeport.

If he had looked over his right shoulder he might have seen the
solitary man on the ridge above, watching him.

CHAPTER

FOUR

Matt almost enjoyed the rest of the trip into Bridgeport. The rain had settled the dust and left a sheen on the countryside. The prairie grass was emerald green, the sky a deep blue and the snow on the peaks of the Sierra Nevadas sparkled in the sun.

Had Matt been astride his roan with his saddlebags flopping against the horse's flanks and his Colt in his waistband, he would have been very much on top of the world.

As it was, a sense of foreboding dulled the euphoria generated by the scenery. During the last two miles of the trip Bridgeport was in view. Its wooden buildings gave Matt a little feeling of relief, and hope that, with his arrival back into civilization, he could begin to recover some of what he had lost.

He crossed a wood bridge over a small stream at the edge of town, his gum soles silent on the planks. There was little traffic on the street.

Seeing a water pump in front of a house near the bridge and a young woman in the yard, he walked up to her fence and took off his hat. She looked up at him and smiled cautiously.

"Yes?" she said.

"Uh, I was wondering if I might take a drink from your pump. I just walked in from up the road a piece, and I'm a little thirsty."

She absentmindedly wrapped her hands in her apron. "Of course, help yourself."

Matt went over to the pump and let his bedroll slide off his back. He worked the pump handle several times until the water started to flow, then stuck his head under it. He rinsed his hat off as well, then gave his head a shake.

The woman, who was a few years younger than Matt, watched him from the safety of her yard.

"Where did you walk from?" she asked.

"Pardon me?" Matt looked at her as he swept his hair back with his hand.

"There's not much up the road that's within walking distance."

"I came from Bodie, most recently. Aurora before that. I had a horse until it got stolen last night."

"Oh. Sorry to hear that."

"Yeah, me too. My own fault, really." He didn't elaborate, but shook the excess water out of his hat and put it on. "Well, thanks for the water."

"You're welcome." She paused, then added, "The sheriff's office is up the street on the left."

"I beg your pardon?"

"The sheriff. You want to report your horse being stolen, don't you?"

Matt was puzzled. "I guess so. Does he have jurisdiction way out there?"

"All the way to Bodie and the Nevada state line. He's the county sheriff."

"That's good to know. Thank you." Matt smiled at her and picked up his bedroll. "Well, I'm much obliged Miss . . . ?"

"Sarah. Please call me Sarah."

"Pretty name, Sarah. I'm Matthew Page. People call me Matt."

She returned the smile. "Please to make your acquaintance, Mr. Page." She turned and walked into the house without looking back.

Matt watched her until she disappeared before he headed up the street. He did not see her peek out through the curtains as he strode away.

Bridgeport offered all the necessary services to the populace, Matt noticed as he made his way through town. Feed and grain, general store, saloon, jeweler, assayer, gun shop, tinsmith, saloon, butcher, saloon, dance hall . . . Matt read the signs, noticing the excessive number of liquor establishments. *The reason the West is so wild,* he thought.

He saw the sign he was looking for. MONO COUNTY SHERIFF was painted in gold on the glass part of the door. He couldn't see inside due to the lace curtain. Matt removed his damp hat, turned the knob, and stepped in.

A man in a black suit sat at a small wood desk, reading. He had a long, bushy mustache and eyebrows to match. His hair was close-cropped with no sideburns and was parted on the side and greased. A tall, black hat hung from a rack behind him.

The wall behind the hat rack was littered with wanted posters, and several rifles and shotguns were stacked in a locked cabinet in the corner. The floors were bare wood, well-worn and dusty.

The man at the desk wore a star on his lapel. He looked up at Matt and squinted. "Howdy. What can I do for you?"

"Mornin'," Matt said. "Name's Matt Page. I've just come to town, I was wondering if I could ask you a few questions."

"I'm Sheriff Taylor," the lawman said. He looked Matt up and down. "I didn't hear a horse. You walk here?"

"Yessir," Matt said. "That's part of what I wanted to ask you about."

"Oh?"

"Yeah. I rode in from Aurora, stopped in Bodie, then headed out again. I was carryin' a lot of money."

"Money?"

"Yessir. Sold my farm back home. I wanted to put it in a bank here. Been makin' my way to Bridgeport for several months now. Heard the Sierra Nevadas was the place to be."

"That's true," the sheriff conceded. "Most beautiful place on earth. So what happened?"

"I met an old prospector about halfway here from Bodie. He let me share his campfire for a night. I guess I slept kind of hard. I never heard anything."

"Took your horse, did he?"

"And my saddle, my gun, my saddlebags—"

"Where your money was."

"Yessir."

"Then you walked all the way here in the rain."

"Yessir."

"I hate to tell you this, son, but you've got a problem." The chair creaked as he leaned back.

"I know that. That's why I came here. I was hopin' you'd help."

"Best help I can give you is advice. Don't trust prospectors."

"You're not gonna go find him?"

"You have an idea where he went?"

"No, I couldn't find his tracks."

"No, I suppose not. The problem, Mr. Page, is the hills around here are full of prospectors. They don't stay put long, especially right after they've stolen a horse and saddle, and they could be in another county or even another state in a few hours. Your prospector's long gone, friend."

Matt looked dejected. *Now what?* he thought.

Taylor could see the hopelessness in Matt's face.

"Need work, I take it?" the sheriff said.

"Yessir. I don't have much money."

"Tell you what. You came all this way just to make your home in Bridgeport. It wouldn't be right for Bridgeport to turn you away just because you fell on some bad luck." He got a clean sheet of paper out of the desk drawer and dipped his pen, then scratched out a quick note. He rolled the blotter across the wet ink, folded the note up, and handed it to Matt, who accepted it without question.

"Give that to Harvey Boone at the Emporium, across the street. He can fix you up."

"Much obliged," Matt said. "I appreciate it. Thank you." He walked to the door.

"Good luck," the sheriff said. "Listen, if I do run across your prospector fellow, how will I know him?"

"Truth is, I didn't get much of a look at him. Just a few minutes by fire light. You'll know my saddle, though. Has my name scratched into the bottom. The horse is a roan, good horse but nothing special 'bout his looks."

"Any marks on the saddlebags?"

"No, but the money is sewn into the bottoms."

"You mean he might not know he has it?"

"I suppose not," Matt admitted thoughtfully. "No, maybe he doesn't. Is that good?"

"Doesn't make him easier to find. Just means he won't spend it so soon."

Matt stood at the open door for a second.

"Well, thank you," he said, holding up the letter.

The sheriff nodded and went back to the papers on his desk, and Matt slowly stepped out and shut the door behind him.

He sized up the street in both directions and spotted the Emporium. He inhaled deeply and let it out through an open mouth, then stepped off the boardwalk into the street. He crossed the wide dirt thoroughfare, dodging a freight wagon, and made his way to the store without reading the letter.

Matt opened the door to the Emporium and a little bell hanging above announced his arrival. He stopped just inside and glanced around the room. It was full of everything a man, woman, or child could ever possibly need.

There were kitchen items in one corner; blue tin coffee pots, china plates, cast iron skillets, muffin pans and pie tins, egg beaters, whips for cream, and a butter churn. The clothing section had stacks of blue canvas jeans, bolts of calico cloth and white linen, plus boots and ladies' button-up shoes.

Miner's picks, panning tins, canteens, and other such items on a table in front of him reminded Matt of the old prospector. He quickly turned his head away from those things to a narrow shelf against a wall holding stacks of airtights; canned fruits and vegetables with colorful labels. He laughed to himself when he saw these, remembering the game he learned from a group of cowpunchers in Wyoming called "Know Your Cans." They had to recite from memory every word printed on a certain brand of can called out by another. Failure to do so cost two bits, and after a few rounds the one with the best memory collected the kitty.

Suddenly Matt saw someone in an apron out of the corner of his eye, watching him. He turned his head toward the man, who nodded.

"What can I do for you, son?"

Matt held the letter up. "Sheriff Taylor sent me over here. I'm new in town, had some bad luck. I'm supposed to see Harvey Boone."

CHAPTER

FIVE

The man in the apron walked slowly over to him. He was about thirty-five, maybe forty, Matt figured, average height and weight, with dark hair and eyes. He looked peaceable but was solidly built. His rolled-up sleeves revealed pale arms, probably from spending all his daylight hours in the store.

"I'm Harvey," he said. "This is my place."

He took the letter from Matt and read it.

"Sheriff says to give you a job if I have one." He looked Matt over. "What's the story?"

Matt told him and Harvey listened in silence. When Matt finished the short retelling of his misfortunes, Harvey said, "Hmmm. I think I can help you out a bit. Put your gear in the back, through that door." He pointed. "Then come with me."

Matt thanked him and did as he was instructed, then followed Harvey out back.

"You any good with a hammer and saw?"

"I reckon," Matt said. "Built a barn once."

"Okay," Harvey said. "See that pile of lumber? I need a shed built up against the back of the store here. Make it about ten by fifteen feet with a lean-to roof and a door on the end, here." He pointed as he spoke, then left Matt and went back into the store.

Matt surveyed the scene and for the first time realized he

hadn't eaten all day. His feet were sore and his legs tired, but he couldn't afford to walk off his new job. He rolled up his sleeves, spit on his hands, and went to work.

Starting with some two-by-sixes, he laid out the frame, marked the cut lines with the point of a square nail, and cut all the framing studs with the handsaw he found. He nailed them all in place, whistling and humming as he always did when working.

Matt enjoyed the labor and the feeling of accomplishment it gave him. The sweat on his arms glistened in the sun and dripped from his chin. Harvey came out once to assess his progress, bringing him a glass of water. When Matt downed it in one breath, Harvey went back in and brought out a bucket of water for him.

While Matt drank some more Harvey inspected the work the young drifter had done. It looked as if the framing would be finished by suppertime.

"Not bad, young fella," Harvey said. "You do good work. Wish there were more people like you around."

"Thank you," Matt said. "It's not hard, and I enjoy doin' it." He looked Harvey in the eye. "Truth is, every nail head had that old prospector's face on it."

Harvey laughed. "It's one thing to be angry, Matthew. It's quite another to seek vengeance."

Instantly Matt felt the prick of Harvey's words. It was true, he was wishing vengeance on the man. His shoulders sagged. His mother had always warned him not to go through life getting even.

Harvey changed the subject.

"Look here, Matthew. You got someplace to stay yet?"

Matt looked up. "No, sir."

"Tell you what. I got room at my place. We'll go there when I close up at six. You can clean up, and I'll treat you to dinner at the Argonaut. Sorry about the name, but it has the best food in town. What do you say?"

"You sure I won't be no trouble?"

"No, son, none at all. It'll be good to have the company for a change. Been kind of lonely there since Esther moved on."

"Esther?"

"My wife," Harvey said quietly. "She died a year or so ago. Pneumonia. We have some pretty harsh winters here in Bridgeport. Didn't no one warn you 'bout that?"

"No."

"Oh, it gets *cold*! 'Course, Bodie's worse. They get snow ten, fifteen feet deep up there. Don't know how them people live there."

Just then the front-door bell dingled, and Harvey rushed inside without comment. Matt went back to work and soon finished the framing. He was just putting down the hammer when Harvey came back out, his apron off. He was carrying Matt's bedroll and coat, and a large package wrapped in brown paper, tied with string. He locked the door behind him.

"Quittin' time," he said.

He handed Matt his gear and led him through the rear yard and down an alley to a small, whitewashed frame house on a side street. Matt noticed the flower boxes, lace curtains, and a vegetable garden—all bearing the obvious mark of a woman's touch—but they were now sadly in need of care. Vegetables had died on the vine, and there were no flowers on the scrawny brown stems. The curtains were ragged and weathered.

Matt took it all in silently, feeling like an intruder. He followed Harvey inside. The house was neat, and much of it looked as though it hadn't been disturbed for quite some time.

Harvey led Matt to a bedroom and opened the door. The small room had a bed and a dresser, and Matt wondered who it had originally been intended for. As if reading his thoughts, Harvey spoke softly.

"This was the room we prepared for the child Esther and I never had." That was all he said. He put the brown paper package on the bed, along with a few coins.

"There's a bathhouse across the alley. Get a new one, you're too dirty for a used bath. There's some new clothes for you in the package. I took the liberty of taking it out of your wages." He turned to leave.

"Thanks," Matt said, somewhat overwhelmed. Harvey left the room, and Matt gathered up the package and coins and left the house.

He returned in about a half-hour, clean and shaven, and when he walked in Harvey was in a rocker, waiting. Matt had on a new pair of jeans and a linen shirt.

"Hungry?" Harvey asked.

Matt nodded.

"Okay then, let's go." Harvey got up and they walked out into the cool evening. The sky was a deep blue overhead, fading into an orange sunset. There were broken clouds that reflected the sunset colors on the edges, which contrasted sharply with the blues and grays of shadow on the rest of the cloud surfaces.

They crossed the street, and Harvey stepped into the restaurant ahead of Matt, greeting the woman behind the counter.

"Good evening, Mary. Beautiful sunset tonight."

"Hello, Harvey. It certainly is." She saw Matt. "You got company this evening?"

"Yep. This here's Matthew, he's new in town. Gonna help me out for a spell."

"Welcome to Bridgeport, Matthew," she said.

"Thank you, ma'am," Matthew replied.

"It's 'miss', but you may call me Mary." She turned to Harvey. "Your table's ready."

"I see it, thanks." Harvey weaved his way through the half-filled restaurant to a small square table next to a window. They sat opposite one another and Mary followed them over, setting before each of them a cup of steaming coffee.

"What's your pleasure, boys?"

"How about a couple of your famous T-bones, with mashed potatoes and gravy, corn-on-the-cob, some hot buttermilk biscuits and lots of butter and honey." He turned to Matt. "That sound okay?"

Matt's mouth was open, and he thought he was drooling. "F-fine, just fine." He was starved. He would have eaten just about anything, except perhaps liver and cabbage.

Mary went back to the kitchen then returned shortly with bowls of soup, steam curling off the irregular surface.

"Vegetable," she said. "Fresh and thick."

Matt took a whiff of the soup, smelling the potatoes, carrots, celery, beef broth, tomatoes, and pepper. He bowed his head, something else his mother had taught him, then grabbed his spoon and dug in.

He finished in short order, and Mary brought out the biscuits. This was soon followed by the steaks, and Matt ate without hesitation, almost without taking a breath. He leaned back when finished, wiped his mouth with his napkin and sighed audibly.

Matt sat quietly, full and satisfied, while Harvey finished. When the store owner finally set down his fork Mary came back with two large hunks of apple pie and fresh coffee.

They attacked the pie eagerly, and as Matt ate, he stared absent-mindedly out the window. He was chewing a large piece of sweet apple as Mary refilled his coffee mug when something outside caught his eye.

He stared out the window and down the street, and soon Harvey noticed him.

"What is it?" he asked.

Matt answered without turning his head. "Your bank open at night?"

"No, of course not. Why?"

"Two men walked down the alley next to it, and a light just came on inside."

"That's not right," Harvey said.

"I figured as much," Matt said. He rose and headed toward the door.

"Go get the sheriff," he told Harvey.

"What?"

"The sheriff!" Matt urged. "I'm goin' down the street." He went outside and walked toward the bank, staying in the shadows. Behind him Harvey ran the other way, his napkin still tucked into his collar.

Matt's gum-soled boots were quiet on the dirt. When he got to the corner of the bank he was fairly sure he had not been heard. He stood against the building, pressing an ear to the wall so he could hear inside. There were two voices.

"Hurry up," one of them said, "before someone shows up!"

"Relax, would you?" said the other. "No one's gonna know we're here!"

Matt heard some metallic clicking sounds, then the second man spoke again.

"There, she's open! Let's git the stuff and git out of here!"

Matt looked down the street for some sign of the sheriff, but he wasn't in sight. The light in the bank blinked out, and he could hear the men's footsteps on the plank floor. If he was going to act, it would have to be now. He heard the latch on the back door move and charged into it as fast and hard as he could.

He arrived at the door just as the latch was turned and put his shoulder into it at full speed. He hit it hard, shoving it open, and slid off into the first man, taking him completely by surprise and knocking him back into the other thief. All three of them went down in a heap, Matt on top. The other men didn't know what had hit them, and it took a few seconds for them to react. This was enough time for Matt, and he sat upright on top of them and relieved the closest man's holster of its six-shooter, sticking the business end of it between the eyes of its owner. The second was helpless underneath them.

"Don't move, gentlemen!" Matt ordered, noticing that the force of the blow had knocked the canvas bags loose from their hands, and the contents, other people's hard-earned money, had spilled out onto the floor.

They didn't have time to respond. Sheriff Taylor ran in through the door, holding a double-barreled shotgun at his waist, closely followed by Harvey and a host of other citizens.

The sheriff disarmed the men and put them in handcuffs while the bank president, who arrived wearing a nightgown and shoes with no socks, began picking up the scattered currency.

Taylor turned to Matt as he started to march the desperadoes off to the jail. Matt was grinning sheepishly.

"That was a blame fool stunt you pulled," the sheriff scolded. "You stick to workin' in Harvey's store." He yanked the gun out of Matt's hand and walked abruptly out the door, prodding the two crooks with the barrel of the shotgun.

"Okay, you two. Let's go. You got yourselves caught this time."

Matt's head swirled as he stood next to Harvey and watched the sheriff nudge the men down the street.

What did I do wrong? he wondered.

CHAPTER

SIX

He walked with Harvey back to the shopkeeper's house, wondering what was in store for him. He was confused, thinking he had done something good. Harvey seemed to like it and made a big deal of it all the way home. *What in the world made the sheriff so angry?* he kept wondering.

They went into the house where Harvey made coffee, but Matt begged off saying he was exhausted from his long, hard day. And while that was true, it wasn't the real reason. Fact is, he just didn't feel much like talking.

Matt retired to the bedroom, expecting to have trouble falling asleep, but as soon as his head hit the pillow he realized nothing could keep him awake any longer, and he slept fitfully.

Matt woke at dawn, snapping out of a dream about coffee and bacon. As soon as his head cleared a little he realized his dream had been born out of reality; he could smell not only coffee and bacon, but hotcakes and biscuits, too.

He was beginning to think his life revolved around good food and hard work. Not that he minded either one, but he could have stayed on the farm and gotten that. He came out West for something different; some excitement, the freedom of the open range, the challenge of nature.

Almost reluctantly he got up and slid into his new clothes, then

wandered out into the kitchen where Harvey was cooking breakfast. The store owner looked at him and laughed.

"What?" Matt asked.

Harvey just laughed as Matt looked down at himself.
Everything seemed to be in order.

"Your hair," Harvey explained.

Matt felt it gingerly. It was sticking out in all directions. He felt
silly.

"Just keep your hat on," Harvey suggested. "You'll be okay."

He dished up the food while Matt spit on his hands and tried
to slick his hair down. They ate together, enjoyed some idle chat-
ter, then Matt brought up the night before.

"What do you think the sheriff was so mad about?"

Harvey stirred his coffee with a stick of cinnamon and shook
his head.

"I don't know," he said. "Maybe he's mad because he didn't get
to catch them guys himself."

Matt thought for a second. "Is he that kind of man?"

"Not really. But he's been looking for those guys for a couple
months, and you pop into town and catch them right off. During
dessert, no less."

"Boy, I'm sorry." Matt shook his head. "I sure didn't mean to
do anything wrong. I mean, someone had to stop those guys!" He
furrowed his brow. "Well, I've got a shed to finish. I best be gittin'
to it." He started to get up, then remembered his manners. "Oh,
here, let me do the dishes first." He started to clean off the table.

"That's okay," said Harvey. "I managed for a year, I can do it
one more time. I'll see you at the store."

Matt reluctantly started for the door.

"Matthew."

Matt turned and looked at Harvey, who was smiling and pointing at his head. Matt grinned and picked up his hat, then went out.

The day passed quickly as the shed took shape. Matt nailed up
the siding boards and battens, then shingled the sloping roof, all
by noon. He ate lunch out of a box that Harvey had brought over
from the Argonaut, enjoying fried chicken and a hot yam, washing it down with fresh milk.

He built the door and hung it that afternoon, then spent the rest
of the time putting the finishing touches on the shed and cleaning

up the mess. Harvey took him to the Argonaut for dinner, but this time they sat in the back. Matt couldn't see out the window, and he wondered if this was intentional. He also noted that Harvey seemed to perk up around Mary.

When they left Matt took a deep breath, smelling the smoke from fireplaces around town. He always liked that smell.

"Do you mind if I take a walk around town?" he asked Harvey.

Harvey looked at him funny. "You're not a slave, Matt. Your time is your own, do whatever you want."

"I just wanted to make sure it was okay, that you weren't expecting me to sit around and talk or something."

Harvey looked away and was quiet for a moment, then said, "Does it show that much?"

"Uh . . . well, you do seem kind of lonely."

Harvey sighed. "I am. I miss her very much."

"I can understand that. I feel the same about my mother."

"What happened to her?"

"She passed away one night in her sleep. She wasn't sick; her heart just stopped beating. People say it was broken."

"Goodness me, what caused it?"

"Well, I really can't say. My father was killed in the war. Mom and I kept the farm going as best we could. She never even considered remarrying, said it wouldn't be right, that Pa gave his life for his country and she should honor his memory." Matt wiped an eye with his sleeve. "Then one morning she didn't wake up. I didn't want to run the place any more so I sold it and came out here."

Harvey respected Matt's grief with silence as they continued walking. When they got to the house he stopped. "Matthew, you work for me, and I let you stay in my house because I have the room and enjoy your company. But you don't have to hang around me all the time. I appreciate how you feel, but I'm fine. You need to get to know Bridgeport, and Bridgeport needs to get acquainted with you. Go ahead, have a good time. There ain't much to do here, but what there is, I'm sure you'll find."

"Thanks."

Harvey slapped him on the shoulder and went inside.

Matt took a look around, wondering where to start. This was the first time in several days that he didn't have something to do, somewhere to go, or something to be mad about.

He walked back up the street, his hands stuffed deep into his pockets, and took in the sights and sounds of the Mono county seat. He passed several saloons and could hear the men shouting, swearing, and drinking to the tinkling of out-of-tune pianos and the twanging of banjos. Occasionally a man would burst out through the batwing doors of a saloon and sprawl headfirst into the dirt street, only to stand up, brush himself off, and head down the way to the next saloon, unconcerned about his previous dismissal.

Matt passed quickly by a dance hall, somewhat intrigued with the girls he knew were inside but knowing better than to give in to the temptation to investigate. His mother had taught him about the dangers of loose women, and Matt didn't want to soil her memory by trying to find out if she had exaggerated. And what if she hadn't? He shuddered to think of the consequences.

He continued on down the street toward the bridge that marked the entrance to town. As he passed the house where Sarah allowed him to pump water he thought of the young, attractive woman, her dark hair tied with a pink ribbon, and her fine, soft features.

He looked at her house out of the corner of his eye, his heart pounding, and slowed to a crawl. He hoped she would see him and come out. He thought about marching up to the door and knocking but couldn't work up the nerve or think of a good excuse so as to hide the fact that he just wanted to see her.

Matt pretended to be unconcerned, looking up at the star-filled and cloudless night sky, inspecting the pump for wear, and figuring the distance from his position to the moon.

Finally his strategy worked, yet even so it caught him flat-footed. When he was just about to move on, his heart racing in anticipation and relief, the front door creaked. He flinched a little and looked over at it.

Sarah stuck her head out.

"Who's out there?" she called.

Matt had forgotten how clear her voice was.

"Uh, it's me, Matthew Page. We met yesterday."

She came out, slow and cautious.

"What are you doing?" she asked hesitantly.

Matt suddenly felt defeated. He was acting silly and to make up a lie now would only make it worse.

"Uh . . . just taking a little walk." He knew even as he said it that she could see right through his excuse, and he groaned at himself.

"Oh. Nice night for it." She had let him off the hook, and Matt sighed in relief. This gave him a little shot of courage.

"Yes, it is," *Oh, that was intelligent!* he berated himself. He wished he wasn't here. He was making a mess of it.

She stood silently on the porch. She had him pegged but thought she'd watch him tread water for a while. Matt looked around nervously, desperate for words. Finally Sarah spoke. "You look a little different than you did the other day. A little . . . cleaner."

Matt laughed nervously. "Oh, uh, yeah, I guess that's true. Ha, ha. Got some new clothes, too."

"Sarah?" It was a man's voice, inside the house.

"Out here, Father," she called. She turned back to Matt. "I have to go in."

"Okay. Well maybe I'll see you again sometime." He tried sounding nonchalant, but it came out hopeful.

Sarah gave him a little wave and disappeared into the house. Matt turned and walked back up the street toward Harvey's house. He made up his mind to see her again, next time during daylight and with a bit more boldness.

Inside the house Sarah closed the door behind her. She was excited and her father noticed a little smile on her face.

"Who were you talking to?" he asked.

"Oh, just someone walking by."

"Don't be coy with me, Sarah Taylor. I'm not the county sheriff because I'm stupid! I like to know what's going on in my town, especially when it involves my daughter."

"Oh, Daddy!" she teased. "It was just that new young man." She pretended to think. "What's his name? Mark? Mike?"

"Matt," Sheriff Taylor said, "and you knew good and well what it was. You steer clear of him."

"He seems nice enough."

"Oh, he's nice but not very level-headed."

"You're just mad because he caught the thieves."

Sarah's mother walked in from the kitchen.

"Sarah, don't talk to your father like that."

"How do you know about that?" Taylor asked his daughter.

"The whole town knows!"

"*Great!*" he bellowed. "Just what I need! Some upstart kid gonna breeze into town and take my job!"

"Does he want to be sheriff?" Mrs. Taylor asked.

"He seems level-headed to me," pined Sarah.

" . . . Gits lucky doin' a foolhardy thing and now everyone wants him to run the place!"

"Dear, I don't think anyone wants that at all," suggested Mrs. Taylor.

"Are you afraid of him, Daddy?"

"*Afraid?*"

"I've got an idea, John," said Mrs. Taylor. "Why not put him where you can keep an eye on him?"

"I can't arrest him. He hasn't done anything illegal."

"No!" cried Sarah, surprised.

"I don't mean arrest him," corrected Mrs. Taylor.

"Then what in tarnation *do* you mean?"

"Hire him. Make him a deputy. You're always saying you need another one."

There was silence for about fifteen seconds while the sheriff looked at his wife as if she'd just asked him to wear a dress and do cartwheels in the yard.

"It'll be a cold day in the southern regions before I deputize that fool kid!"

CHAPTER

SEVEN

The wounded ex-soldier brought to the Empire Boarding House by Matt remained unconscious until evening. His eyes opened ever so slightly when Billy turned up the coal oil lamp while checking on him.

This must be terrible for the man, Billy thought. *He's in pain, don't know where he is, how he got here, and the first thing he sees is my face.* He chuckled to himself at the irony of it but didn't reveal that to the soldier.

The man's eyes closed without him saying a word. He didn't move, either. He just groaned and went back to sleep.

Billy left him and went to bed himself. Early the next morning he got up and put on some coffee. While it boiled he listened to the constant pounding of the Empire Mill's stamps, which ran for twenty-four hours a day. It took too long to get the boiler stoked and the steam engine up to speed to shut the mill down, so they operated around the clock.

Billy usually didn't pay attention to the mill, except when things were quiet and he wanted to think. Like most people who lived in a gold or silver town, he only noticed the stamps when they stopped.

Billy went into the soldier's room and the man woke up. He spoke for the first time.

"Who . . . are you?"

Billy stood next to the bed and smiled down at the man.

"Mah name's William O'Hara." He was intentionally brief, not knowing how much information the man could absorb.

"Where—?"

"You're in Bodie, California. You was brought here by a man who found you on the road from Aurora. You'd been robbed and beaten, left for dead."

The soldier mulled this over for a while and took inventory of himself by moving his body around and finding out where it hurt—which was all over.

"Anything broken?" he asked slowly. He found out his lips were burned, as they cracked when he spoke and started bleeding.

"Naw, you'll be okay, Ah think. Your face is burnt from laying unconscious for a day or two in the sun. You got a headache?"

The soldier nodded.

"You got a nasty cut on your noggin'. They knocked you out." Billy could read the question in the soldier's eyes. "No, Ah don't know who. Jes' some robbers. You feel like eatin'?"

He shook his head. "Water."

"All right."

Billy left the room and came back with a glass of water. He helped the soldier drink, then set the glass that was still about half full on the dresser. "Ah'll check on you later," he said, and quietly left the room.

The soldier drifted back into an uncomfortable sleep, and Billy shut the door.

O'Hara puttered around the boarding house for a while, trying to keep busy. There wasn't much to do, what with so few people coming to Bodie these days. There wasn't much work available because only two mines were operating, and they weren't producing much quality ore.

Billy finally sat down in a creaking rocker on the front porch and watched the clouds. One puffy formation reminded him of the riverboat he used to pilot up and down the Mississippi River. He was the captain's steward for almost twenty years and had handled the wheel many times. When word of the strike at Sutter's Mill reached them and gold fever hit, the captain set out for San Francisco. Not knowing what else to do, Billy went with him.

He eventually separated from his employer and made his way to Aurora with the wife he had married in San Francisco. There they ran a successful hotel and restaurant. After she died Billy continued on, until the Empire Mining Company asked him to go to Bodie and run their operations there.

A good vein had been found, but it soon petered out, and the only mining being done now was by a couple of low-budget companies with high hopes and little else.

Billy also had hopes for Bodie. Although it was probably the harshest climate in the world for humans to live in, O'Hara had a feeling that somewhere in the hills behind his boarding house was a motherlode of gold. But he was content to let someone else find it; he was getting on in years and had lived a good, full life.

As Billy rocked, drinking coffee and mulling this over in his mind, he heard something heavy hit the floor inside. It sounded as if it had come from the soldier's room. Billy jumped up and hustled in there, finding the soldier on the floor.

"Here, lemme help you," Billy said to the man, who was struggling to get up.

"Git away!" he snapped. "Ah can do it!"

"Jus' tryin' to help."

"Ah don't need it," he said through clenched teeth. "'Specially from someone like you!"

Billy was not surprised by this. Although it had been six years since the war, any man who still wore his uniform coat surely had not stopped fighting.

"Where's mah clothes!" the soldier demanded. "Ah s'pose you burned 'em! It's just like your kind to do that!"

"No, suh," said Billy softly. "They right in here." He opened a closet door and brought out the uniform coat. "Ah cleaned it for you."

He handed the coat to the soldier, who, after much painful effort, was now sitting on the bed. Although still tattered and worn, the coat was clean and some large tears were mended. He took the gray coat from Billy and held it tenderly, as a mother embraces a child.

"Feel like eatin' somethin'?" Billy asked.

"Ah'm hungry, but you answer me some questions first."

"Well," said Billy slowly, "Ah'll be happy to answer you some questions, but we need to straighten a few things out 'fore Ah do. This here is California; the war is over; the slaves was freed a long time ago, Ah run this place, and you are my guest. That's how things are now. You understan' that?"

The rebel soldier seethed, but he was not in a position to argue. He still wasn't ready to stand up, much less put the Negro in his place and walk out.

"All right," he relented. "Have it your way." He said it as though he was making a concession, then paused while he painfully shifted his position on the bed. "Who brought me here?"

"Like Ah tol' you, a young man from Aurora found you on the side of the road. He patched you up, brought you here, and paid for your room and board for a week. Then he moved on."

"How do you know he weren't the one what dry-gulched me?"

"Whoever clubbed you thought you was dead. Don't make sense for him to try to kill you, then save your life, now, does it?"

The soldier ignored Billy's logic and went on to something else. "Did he say how Ah'm supposed to pay him back?"

"Ah don't believe he expects it. You may find this hard to understan', but there are people in this world who do things for others without expectin' a payback."

"We got a lot of that where Ah come from." He gave Billy a hard look. "Where *we* come from. We call it Southern hospitality."

Billy refused to be baited and ignored the soldier's sarcasm. "Why don't you jus' lay down. Your bed and board's paid for as long as it takes you to get well. When you're ready, you can put on them new boots and walk out." He pointed to the shiny pair of black leather boots on the floor.

"What happened to mine?"

"Same as the rest a your gear. They figgered you wouldn't be needin' 'em." Billy turned and walked toward the door. "Ah'll get you somethin' to eat," he said as he left the room, not waiting for a reply.

Billy returned with a tray, and the soldier accepted it in silence. He ate with relish. It had been a couple of days since he had had anything besides water. When Billy came for the tray the soldier was asleep, clutching his coat tightly.

Mighty opinionated for someone so vulnerable, Billy thought. He left the room quietly, leaving the coat in the soldier's grasp.

Over the next few days the soldier's health improved, and soon he was able to get up and walk around the room. His burned skin blistered and peeled, and his face became pink and sore. His attitude did not improve.

As the lump on his head receded his headache went away, but his surly attitude remained. It wasn't that he wasn't used to being waited on by Negroes, just that they had never before told him off without being whipped for it.

Uncle Billy was never unkind to him. He just put his foot down when it came to being bossed around. He ran the boarding house; it didn't run him. Billy didn't mind caring for the man, but verbal abuse wasn't part of the deal.

And it was no surprise to him a few days later when he found the soldier's bed empty and his few belongings gone.

CHAPTER

EIGHT

The floor of the Emporium had never been so clean. With the completion of the shed, Harvey brought Matt inside and for the past several days he had given his young charge the task of tidying up the store.

Matt wielded the spruce-handled implements, as well as the feather duster and the polish rag, with the same dexterity as he had the hammer and saw. Harvey had never given more than cursory attention to sweeping. When he wasn't helping customers he was doing the books, stocking the shelves . . . and remembering Esther.

Having grown up on a farm, menial labor was not at all offensive to Matt. He handled his broom in as dignified a manner as he handled a pitchfork, his spirits buoyed by his recent good fortune. His broom swept him past the glass case where the guns were kept under lock and key, and he stopped a moment to admire them. He missed his forty-four, the shiny blue metal and smooth walnut grips . . . He sighed, and resumed pushing the broom.

As he moved about the store, pushing and flicking the broom into long-forgotten crevices to remove ages-old dirt and debris, he replayed the events of the last few days. *What a whirlwind I been ridin',* he thought.

He remembered the months he had spent moving from place to place, always headed West, always without trouble, until the goal was virtually in sight. Then, just like *that*—he snapped his fingers to emphasize the point to himself—it turned sour. His savings were taken by that old prospector, not to mention his horse and gear.

He thought about his long walk into Bridgeport, his despair, his luck at getting the job at the Emporium. But most of all he thought of Sarah. Meeting her was a real stroke of luck.

No, this was more than luck, he realized. His mother had raised him to believe in God. He respected that in her, but he had always been too busy to make it personal. He thought being raised by a God-fearing mother was enough to get him into Heaven, if there was such a place.

Now he wondered. Could there be something more to it? Was his future being guided by an unseen hand? Naw. He shook his head. There was good luck and there was bad luck, and he was just getting a little of both. More bad than good, perhaps, but both just the same.

He squatted down under a table loaded with cookware and reached to pick up a belligerent piece of debris. As he tried to pry it loose from the floor with a fingernail, he heard the jangling of the doorbell and the heavy footsteps of several people entering the store.

Matt stopped his work and listened, hearing the clomp of leather-soled boots on the wood floor and the doorbell sounding again as the door closed with a click. The footsteps didn't continue.

They stopped just inside the door, he thought. *That's odd.*

Then he heard the lock being thrown, and he knew trouble was brewing.

Matt stayed under the table, moving away from the aisle. The rear of the table butted up against the back of a display case for the next aisle, so he could only be seen from one place. His mind raced. Could he make it to the back door? Probably not, he'd be seen or heard.

These men most likely had guns. They were here for a reason and were prepared, he figured. He tried to peek between boxes to catch a glimpse of the men. He could see two, but was positive there were more. Harvey confirmed it for him.

"How may I help you three gentlemen?" he said. He couldn't see Matt but hoped his assistant knew what was going on.

"We come for your money and some supplies," said the leader. Matt could see him. He wore baggy, black, woolen pants and coat, an old flat-brim hat like Matt's, was dirty and unshaven, and had long, greasy hair. He also had a revolver stuck in his waistband. He drew it out and pointed it at Harvey, smiling. His teeth were brown and decayed.

"All right," said Harvey compliantly. "Take what you need. I'll not give you any trouble. Just don't hurt us."

Matt cringed.

"Whaddya mean, *us*?" asked the robber slowly.

"N-nothing," said Harvey. "It's just me here. I mean don't hurt nobody in town, you know, us here in Bridgeport."

The leader looked at his partners and jerked his head.

"Check it out."

Matt tried to make himself smaller in his hiding place, without making any noise, as the two accomplices walked through the store searching for him. Then he noticed his broom in the aisle, and his heart skipped.

He reached out carefully, grabbed the end of the handle and started pulling it slowly toward him, an inch at a time. Any faster would have made it scrape along the floor and brought the men down on him.

When it was close enough he gripped the broom stick in the center and picked it up, bringing it all the way underneath the table with him. His heart thumped inside his chest, and he feared they could hear it.

He no sooner had the broom safely with him than a man turned into his aisle and walked slowly down toward the table he cowered under.

The man approached, and Matt realized he had been holding his breath. He let it out slowly and took in another. As he moved slightly to release the pressure on his chest from being doubled over, the top of his head hit the point of an errant nail sticking down from the underside of the tabletop.

"*Ow!*"

He had only breathed it, but it was enough. He had been heard. The man's footsteps stopped suddenly. Matt gripped the broom in both hands and waited for the inevitable.

"Whatzat?" said the crook. He bent over to look under the

table. As soon as he did Matt drove the business end of the broom hard into his face, the sharp, stiff straw poking him in the eyes.

The man recoiled, yowling in pain, and dropped his gun, putting both hands up to his injured eyes. Matt grabbed the gun then kicked the man in the side of the knee. It buckled as the ligaments tore and he fell onto the plank floor screaming, not having enough hands to grab all his injuries.

"Willard, what's goin' on?" shouted the leader, straining to see over boxes and shelves. When Willard didn't answer he called the other man. "Max, go see what happened."

"Okay, Bart."

Max crouch-walked cautiously to the aisle where Willard had fallen. He didn't see anyone and thought Willard might have tripped. He squatted by his moaning comrade, his gun held loose in his hand.

As he checked Willard's injuries he heard two metallic clicks and froze. Moving only his eyes, he looked under the nearby table and saw a young man in an apron pointing a gun at him, his index finger held up to his lips.

The would-be robber handed over his gun without being asked and raised his arms in surrender. Matt motioned with his head for Max to move away, which he did. Matt crawled out from under the table. Willard was still out of the action, writhing on the floor in pain.

"Max! What's goin' on in there? Talk to me!" The leader kept his gun trained on Harvey, who was scanning the area around him for his own means of defense or escape.

"There you are," said Bart as Max appeared around the corner. "Where is—what the—?" He saw Matt following his partner, two guns in his hands. Bart grabbed Harvey by the shirt and yanked him in front of himself.

"Well, we got ourselves a situation here, don't we?" the robber said, exposing his rotten teeth through a crooked, sardonic smile. "You got yerseff ol' Max at gunpoint, and I got me this here fella." He waved the gun at Harvey. "Diff'rence between us is, you probably care if your boss here gits plugged, but I don't care none 'bout Max."

Max's eyes grew wide in disbelief.

"So why don't you jes' drop them guns and let us git on with this here robb'ry?"

Matt quickly considered his options. He had the drop on Max but didn't want Harvey to get shot. He wasn't a good enough shot to try and place one past Harvey into Bart.

"Bart, whaddya mean you don't care if I gits it?" Max protested.

"Shut up, Max!" Bart ordered.

"But I thought—"

A gun boomed, interrupting Max's comment. His body jerked, and with disbelief spreading across the man's face, he slowly looked down at his chest where a red spot was forming, then back up at Bart and his smoking gun. Then he folded and fell.

The shot had come from beside Harvey's head, and he immediately reacted to the pain in his ear, doubling over and putting his hand to his ear. Matt saw his opportunity and instinctively fired both guns at Bart, then dove for cover.

It wasn't necessary to hide. One shot hit Bart in his gun arm and his revolver clattered harmlessly to the floor. The other shot simultaneously plunked him in the left shoulder, spinning him around and knocking him down. Harvey was on the floor next to him, holding his ringing ear, but aware enough to kick the bandit's gun out of his reach.

The shots attracted attention outside and in moments the store was besieged by townfolk who broke through the locked door. A few seconds later Sheriff Taylor waded through them, shotgun at his side.

Matt had dragged Willard out and all three bandits were on the floor inside the door, one of them dead. Harvey stuffed a wad of cotton in his ear and collected the guns, piling them next to his cash register.

"What's all this?" Taylor bellowed.

"These men came in to rob us," explained Harvey, holding a hand over his ear, "but Matt here stopped 'em."

Taylor shot a look at Matt, who shrugged and smiled apologetically.

Now I'm really in trouble, he thought.

Taylor bent down over Bart. Matt could see Bart's ears now—

they had been covered by his long hair when he was standing—and he noticed a notch cut out of the edge.

"What's that?" he asked Taylor.

"The notch?"

"Yeah."

"Mining camp mark. He's a convicted felon."

Taylor checked the dead man. "You do this?" he asked Matt.

"No, actually he did." He pointed to Bart who lay still, alive but unconscious.

Taylor barked out some orders to the bystanders. "Take this man to the undertaker's! Get the other two over to the jail and call the doc. He can look at 'em there!"

He handed his shotgun to a spectator. "Here, Fred, cover 'em with this 'till they're locked up."

"Yes sir, Sheriff!" Fred said, taking the gun. Several men moved in and lifted the injured bandits while two more carted Max off in the other direction.

Taylor glowered at Matt.

"You did this single-handed?"

Matt shrugged. "Not exactly. Harvey helped."

Taylor cast a jaundiced eye toward the recoiling store owner. "Hmm." He turned back to Matt. "You were unarmed?"

The young man nodded again. "At first, anyway."

"You don't have much sense, boy. That's the second time you've taken fists to a gun fight."

"He didn't go lookin' for it, Sheriff," Harvey defended, one hand still pressing the offended ear. "They came in here and announced they was doin' a robbery, and Matt here outskunked 'em and outshot 'em."

"Hmmm," Taylor said again, his thoughtful contemplations growing longer each time. "Page, you be in my office in fifteen minutes!"

The sheriff stormed out, slamming the door behind him.

CHAPTER

NINE

Matt pulled off his apron as Harvey began straightening up the store and wiping the blood off the floor.

"What should I say?" Matt asked.

"I don't think you're gonna need to say anything," Harvey said. "Seems to me Sheriff Taylor plans to do all the talking. If he asks you a question, just tell the truth."

Matt nodded. "Okay." He walked toward the door.

"Good luck," said Harvey.

"Thanks."

Matt stepped out into the street and walked slowly toward the sheriff's office. Several people said hello to him; one even slapped him on the back and said, "Good job." Matt thanked him and smiled, but it faded as soon as the man had passed.

He stopped at the door to Taylor's office and took a deep breath, then turned the knob and stepped in.

Sheriff Taylor wasn't at his desk. Matt looked around the room and saw him leaning casually against the wall, his arms folded. Taylor didn't say anything, so after a short, uncomfortable silence Matt spoke first. "Yessir?"

Taylor squinted and looked at him hard, then said, "Sit down, son."

Matt obeyed, and Taylor walked over to him.

"You know them bank robbers you caught the other day? I've

been hopin' to catch them for several months now. They've hit several banks in Mono County, all of them at night."

He paused. Matt didn't say anything.

"You could have got yourself hurt, you know."

"I realize that," Matt said. "I just wasn't thinkin' of it at the time."

"Apparently not." Taylor walked around the desk to his chair and sat. It creaked loudly as he settled into it. "What made you do it?"

Matt thought. "I can't say. I just saw something that wasn't right, and I did what I thought I ought to."

"And today. . . . What happened in the Emporium?"

"I was sweepin', Harvey was mindin' the customers, although there weren't any when them three guys came in and locked the door behind them. They didn't see me."

"Do you think they would've shot you if they had a chance?"

"Yessir. Bart, the leader, he shot his own man without even blinkin'."

"Weren't you afraid?"

"Yessir, of course. But sometimes you do what you gotta do."

"Hmm." Taylor leaned back in his chair.

Here it comes, Matt thought as Taylor opened his desk drawer.

"You came to Bridgeport to start a new life?"

"Yessir."

"You need a job."

"Well, I'm over at the Emporium—"

"That's temporary. You need a real job, right?"

"Yes."

"And a horse, saddle, and gun?"

"Well, I suppose . . ."

"And you want to catch that prospector?"

"Definitely."

Taylor took something out of the drawer and tossed it onto the desk.

"Put that on, and we can solve most of your problems."

Matt looked at the object in disbelief. It was a star, the badge of a deputy sheriff.

"Wha . . . why? I thought you were mad at me."

"I was the other day. I would be still if I thought you were a foolhardy, hot-headed kid out for glory. But I'm convinced you've got an instinct, a feel for the work." He paused, but Matt didn't say anything. The young man just sat there, looking at the shiny star.

He had heard they were made out of tin. He reached out and picked it up, slowly and carefully, as if it was sacred. Matt was surprised that it was heavier than he expected.

"Silver," said Taylor. "Won't bend or rust."

Matt held it, felt its weight and smooth surface, except where the letters were stamped into it. He looked up at the sheriff.

"What do I do?"

"If you're accepting the job, pin it on."

Matt was overwhelmed again. Things were almost happening too fast. *Maybe my luck is shifting to the good—some,* he said to himself.

He pinned the badge on his shirt.

"Good," said Taylor. He stood up. "Raise your right hand, Page."

Matt stood and raised his hand as ordered.

"Okay, repeat after me," the sheriff said. "I, Matt Page."

"I, Matt Page."

"Do hereby swear to uphold the laws of the State of California, the County of Mono, and the City of Bridgeport."

Matt repeated it.

"So help me, God."

"So help me God."

Taylor extended his hand to his new deputy.

"Welcome aboard, Matt—er, Deputy Page."

"Thanks."

"Ain't you gonna ask me what the pay is?"

"What's the pay?"

"Not much. Any more questions?"

"No. I guess not."

"Good. Let's take a little walk over to the Emporium and set you up with a gun and supplies, then you can pick out a horse and tack at the livery."

"I don't have any money."

"I know. I'll give you an advance. If you're gonna do the work, you gotta have the equipment."

Taylor walked over to the door and held it open. The young man stepped out into the sunshine, dazed.

"What about Harvey?" Matt asked as they walked to the store.

"What about him? He'll get along without you. Someone else will come along."

Taylor opened the door, and the bell tinkled.

"Morning again, Sheriff," greeted Harvey. "You lock up Page for interfering?"

Then Matt came in and he saw the badge on his chest.

"Worse than that," the shopkeeper said, chuckling. "You gave him a job. Thanks for stealing my employee."

"You're welcome," Taylor said. "He needs a setup. Gun, leather, gear, the works."

Matt felt a little foolish getting all this attention. He also felt he was betraying Harvey. After all, Harvey had taken him under his wing and given him a job.

Harvey was thinking some of the same thoughts. He had mixed emotions. He was happy for Matt but felt a little sorry for himself. He had hoped Matt could stay with him for a spell.

He put that aside for the time being, though, and opened the gun case. He pulled out several new shootin' irons.

"This here one is the most popular these days," he said. "It's a Colt's Lightning."

Matt took the chrome six-gun and turned it over in his hand several times. It was small, with ivory grips.

"Kinda funny-lookin'," Matt said.

"It's the latest thing. Pull the trigger."

Matt started to cock it, but Harvey told him, "No, just pull the trigger."

Matt squeezed the trigger slowly, and, as it started to move, the hammer began to move also.

"It's a self-cocker," Harvey explained. "It'll fire as fast as you can pull the trigger. That's why they call it the Lightning."

Matt looked at it carefully but handed it back. "What else you got?"

Harvey put the Lightning back in the cabinet and took out a Navy Dragoon.

Matt took the large handgun from Harvey, gripped it, hefted it and pointed it, and gave it right back. "Too heavy," he said.

"How about this?" Harvey said. He handed Matt a plain little six-shooter, dark blue with wood grips.

It was a Colt Peacemaker, like the one the prospector had stolen.

"Sold," he said. He pulled the hammer back a click and spun the cylinder. It felt nice in his hand. He stuck it down into his waist-band.

"Try this," Harvey suggested, handing him a plain brown leather belt with a holster attached to it. Matt buckled it on and slipped the gun in. When he moved, the new leather groaned. He'd have to oil it.

Sheriff Taylor walked around behind the counter and grabbed a rifle and a box of shells. He handed the Winchester carbine across to Matt. "Here. You'll need this. Get yourself a sheath for it, saddlebags, a rope, and a canteen, all the rest, then meet me down the street at the livery.

"Yessir."

Taylor walked out and Matt turned to Harvey. "Thanks for what you've done for me. The Sheriff says the county'll pay for this stuff."

"I know," said Harvey. "And thank you for helping me out. I'd a never got around to building that shed. Just haven't felt like doing much lately." He fell silent, then said, "Hey, we're talking like a couple of folks that ain't gonna see each other again. You'll stay with me tonight, won't you? And I'll probably see you every couple of weeks when you come into Bridgeport to check in."

"Huh?" Matt said.

"Oh, didn't Sheriff Taylor tell you? He's the sheriff, you're the deputy. He works Bridgeport, you work the rest of the county. I thought you knew that."

"No. I figured I'd be in town here."

"Well, really, Matthew. Why do you think he was having you get all this stuff for traveling, like a canteen and a raincoat?"

"I don't know. It's all happening kind of fast."

"I guess it is, at that." He stopped talking and wrote the order down on a pad.

"Twenty-five dollars. I'll give this to the sheriff."

He loaded Matt's arms with the gear, then pulled the deputy's hat off and stuck another one in its place, a beige one with a silver *concho* band and a flat brim. It felt good.

Harvey pushed Matt out the door.

"Livery's down the street a ways. Just keep walking 'til you smell horses."

Matt staggered down the street, certain he looked foolish, and glad there were only a few people out today. When he got to the stable Sheriff Taylor was already there, shaking hands with the owner. They had obviously struck a deal.

"Pick the one you like," Taylor said. He motioned to several horses lined up along the wall. Matt moved down the row, stopping at a large sorrel. It was a good-looking horse, but he knew from the farm that sorrels could be ornery.

The next horse was a dark brown Morgan. He put his open hand gently on the horse's warm nose. It snorted and jerked its head, but Matt kept his hand there and the Morgan came back to it, sniffed it, then let Matt stroke the soft, velvety hair between his nostrils.

"Takes to you," said Joe Walker, the owner of the livery. "Horses can be fickle, and it's a good sign if he likes you right off."

"I'll take this one," he said. He ran his hand gently down the animal's neck. "He broke?"

"Tame as a kitten," said Walker.

"What's his name?" Matt asked.

Walker chuckled. "We call him Blister. He's rather sprightly, and he'll raise a few on your behind if you ain't careful."

"Blister?" The Morgan responded to his name, and Matt patted his neck. "Okay, Blister, let's see what you can do." He led him away from the other horses.

"Need a saddle?"

Matt looked around, seeing a couple of saddles on wooden stands along the opposite wall.

"That one," he said, picking the plainest one. "I'll need a blanket, too."

"Comes with it," Walker said. "Bridle too. Everything you need."

Matt led the horse into the center of the stable and tossed the blanket over its back. He hoisted the saddle up off the stand and threw it onto the Morgan. The horse didn't move, letting Matt tighten the cinch without trouble. The deputy attached his gear, stepped into the stirrup and swung his right leg over the animal as he pulled himself up by the horn.

"Be back in a while, Sheriff," he said.

Taylor smiled and nodded. *I guess the devil'll be putting on his snowshoes about now,* the lawman thought to himself.

Matt heeled the horse gently and Blister responded, walking smoothly out of the stable. Matt urged him into a lope and disappeared down the street, toward the north end of town.

Once out of Bridgeport Matt galloped the Morgan toward the Sierras. The horse responded to his pull on the reins, the pressure of his rider's legs, and verbal commands. Matt was pleased at how solid and powerful the horse was beneath him. The saddle was comfortable, the stirrups secure.

About a mile from town he slowed and let the horse walk. He took Blister to the small creek by the road, and while the animal drank, Matt sat back against the cantle and took in the scenery.

The Sierras loomed over him like sleeping giants, their tops dusted with year-round snow. The lights and shadows on the rock revealed colors the casual observer missed.

Matt took off his new hat and let the breeze blow through his hair. He felt alive, his spirit renewed. Suddenly he thought of Sarah and decided to go see her.

What would she think? he wondered. *Will she care that I'm a deputy?*

He rode back through town at an easy pace and reined up in front of her house. She was outside, tending a rose bush.

"Mornin'," he said cleverly.

She looked up. "Good morning."

Matt smiled at her.

"Yes? Is there something I can do for you, Deputy?"

Matt was crestfallen. Apparently she didn't care.

"Uh, no, that's okay. I . . . uh, just wanted to say hello."

She put her hand over her eyes and squinted at him. "Do I know you?"

"It's me, Matt Page!" He took off his hat and she gasped a little. She remembered what her father had said a few days ago and figured there must have been a cold day down south since then.

"You're the new deputy?"

"Yep!"

She walked over to the fence. "That's a real . . . surprise. I thought he'd never—" She caught herself.

"Who'd never what?"

"Oh, nothing. You know, Matt, every time I see you, you look different. One day you're a dirty traveler, the next you're in an apron sweeping a store, the next a deputy sheriff. What do you plan on being tomorrow?"

Matt laughed. "Hopefully, this is it for a while."

He smiled at her and she smiled back, then Matt said, "Well, I gotta be gettin' back. The sheriff is expecting me, and he can be pretty ornery sometimes."

"Yes," she said, stifling a chuckle. "I know. Are you going to be working in town?"

"No, I guess not. I'll be leaving today or tomorrow sometime, but I'll be back in a few weeks."

"I'll be here," she said.

"Well, so long."

"Good-bye."

Matt put his hat on and turned the horse up the street, waving to Sarah as he left. It wasn't until he was well up the street that Matt wondered what she meant by *I'll be here.*

Matt was back before lunch, and Taylor told him to go to the Argonaut and eat, he'd be busy for a while. When Matt walked in, Mary was there and remembered him.

"Aren't you that young man who was here the other day with Harvey?"

"Yes, ma'am, that was me."

"Please, I told you to call me Mary. When a deputy calls me 'ma'am' I get to feeling real old." She laughed.

"Okay, Mary."

"And today you're a deputy! My, how things do change in these modern times!"

"Yeah, it did happen rather quick. My head is still spinning."

"Well, from what I hear from Harvey, you deserve it."

Matt blushed. "Harvey's a good man."

"Yes, he is," agreed Mary. She looked dreamily out the window at the Emporium. Matt noticed this and wondered if Harvey knew she liked him. He made a mental note about mentioning it to him.

After a lunch of thick beef and potato stew, Matt walked to the sheriff's office where he found Taylor sitting at his desk.

"Well, Page, you ready to start work?"

"Yessir."

Taylor leaned back in his chair. "Okay, you'll start tomorrow. I want you to get a good night's sleep tonight. You'll be on the road for a spell."

"What will I be doing?"

"Well, there's a couple of things. First, I want you to head up to Bodie. I've got something I want you to deliver to a man there."

He handed Matt a sealed envelope. The name on it read *William O'Hara*.

"Uncle Billy," he said out loud.

"You know him?"

"We met when I passed through Bodie on my way out here."

"I suppose you did, if you stopped at all. Bodie ain't that big. Billy's a good man."

"Seemed so to me."

"After you do that you can ride around the country for a week or two, get the feel of it, meet the people. If you happen to run across that prospector fella, well, just remember, you're a lawman now. Don't do nothin' stupid."

"Yes—I mean no, sir."

Taylor got up. "I'll see you in a week or two." He shook Page's hand.

"Oh, by the way. I got a wire that there was a breakout from the Nevada State Penitentiary in Carson City. Some of the men were headed south. Keep your eyes open."

Taylor left and Matt walked to Harvey's house. He spent the afternoon thinking about his future.

CHAPTER

TEN

The Confederate soldier trudged up the hill east of Bodie, a blanket draped over his shoulder and his pockets full of food stolen from Billy's kitchen. It took about an hour of strenuous but uneventful hiking for him to crest the ridge. When he did he found himself looking down on thousands of square miles of California.

Below him, about fifteen miles walk, was Mono Lake. Blue and serene, this circular body of water with an island near the north shore was several times saltier than the ocean. Devoid of fish, it teemed with insects and brine shrimp and the larvae of small flies that were the staple of the Paiute diet.

To the right of the lake—from the soldier's point of view—were the Sierra Nevadas, tall, dark, and ominous. A bank of clouds butted up against them halfway up, casting a shadow on the ground below and over part of the lake. Opposite the Sierras were the flatlands, the deserts and sagebrush plains of Nevada.

Beyond the lake was a series of what appeared to be several extinct volcanoes. They looked like beige piles of sand, lifeless and foreboding. In the distance beyond these were the White Mountains. On the far side of these, the soldier knew, was Death Valley, which he couldn't see from here.

But the soldier wasn't interested in what was on the far side of

the White Mountains. He was concerned with what was on this side
of them—the town of Bishop. There, he figured, he could get work.

Bishop was a restless town with many job opportunities. He
could get work sweeping floors, chasing cows, or digging for gold
and silver. Or he could get work that required a steady hand,
steady nerves, a six-gun, a horse, and a large chip on the shoulder.
Right now that's what appealed to him the most. He didn't want
to have anything to do with manual labor if he could help it.

He was good at protection and intimidation, as he called it. It
had been his own fault he got dry-gulched. He slipped up, let them
get the drop on him. That cost him a week and all his gear.

Well, no use fretting about that now. He started off again, making his way down the slope toward the lake and Bishop.

He neared the lake shore by evening and set about looking for
a place to sleep. There was enough dry sagebrush around to fuel a
campfire so he concerned himself with locating a protected area,
to keep himself secure from animals and the elements.

He suddenly heard a whinny, carried by the breeze from farther
down the slope, closer to the lake. That's what he needed, a horse.

He followed the direction the sound had come from until he
saw a small, flickering campfire. Next to it was a dirty little
prospector whose horse and mule were nearby, tethered together.

The soldier approached from the prospector's blind side. He
wasn't in the mood to make friends nor to kill the man, he just
needed a horse and a gun.

The soldier figured this prospector must not have any claim
going; this just didn't look like a decent area for that. He must just
be on the move. Probably didn't have anything worth much. Just
that horse and a gun. At least, the soldier hoped the man had a
gun. Everyone did.

Sitting down carefully, he decided to wait until the old man was
asleep. That way he could get his gun and take the horse without
anyone getting hurt.

He watched for an hour. Finally the prospector settled back
down and pulled a blanket over himself. Soon he was snoring. The
soldier stood up and began carefully moving forward.

He was just about on top of the prospector when the argonaut
turned over and stuck his arm out from under the blanket. He was
pointing a gun at the soldier's midsection.

The prospector spat into the fire.

"Whatcha thinkin' there, Johnny?" the old man asked. "Gonna kill you a defenseless ol' prospector tonight? Steal his gold? Well, I ain't got no gold! I ain't *never* found no gold! In eight years of lookin', no gold! Now, why don'tcha jes' git, go bother someone else?"

"Ah don't want your gold, old man," the soldier said, holding both his hands up so the prospector could see he was unarmed.

"What is it then, Reb? Why you been sittin' up the hill fer so long?"

"Truth?"

"I'd like it, though I don't expect to hear it."

"Ah need your horse and your gun."

"You know, I believe you. There's a problem, though."

"What?"

"I need them, too."

"That's not a big problem, Yank."

"No?"

"No. Ah'll just take them from you."

"How you gonna do that?"

"I'll wait. You gotta sleep sometime."

"I kin sleep with you dead. Won't bother me none."

"No, Ah s'pose not."

"It's settled then. You hightail it on outta here or you die here. Take yer choice."

"Ah'm in no position to argue," the soldier said. He started to turn. When he did he kicked a toeful of dirt into the prospector's face.

Before the prospector could recover the soldier ran up and stepped on his wrist, then bent over and took the gun from his hand.

"You gonna kill me now, Reb?" The prospector moved his now-empty gun hand up to wipe the dirt out of his eyes.

"No. Ah ought to. But Ah only kill when Ah need to."

"I'm mighty comforted by that, Johnny," said the prospector sarcastically. "You takin' my mule too?"

"No, you can have that. Like I said, just your horse and this piece of iron."

He stuck the gun in his waistband and untied and mounted the still-saddled animal.

"Good night, Yank. Hope Ah didn't hurt you none. Now, don't you go tryin' to find me. I see you again, you'll be spittin' lead."

He shook the reins and dug in his heels. The roan took off toward the lake. The old man lay still until he couldn't hear the horse, then spoke to his mule.

"Well, it's jes' you and me agin, Bonehead. You and me and them saddlebags full of money."

Matt was up before the sun. Harvey got up with him and fixed breakfast, then gave him a parcel of food—just as Uncle Billy had.

Matt took it. "Thanks, Harvey, for givin' me a chance."

"Matt, you're the kind of person who makes his own chances because you're honest. People respect that and trust you."

"Well, I don't know. I can't see bein' any other way. I hope I do all right."

"You'll do fine. Just remember, you're to uphold the law. Not everybody appreciates that, but I don't know anyone who doesn't like an honest man."

Matt didn't answer. He thought about Harvey's words as he packed his saddlebags and about the task that was set before him.

He couldn't believe the way things had turned around for him. If pressed he would just have to admit to at least some involvement by God. Maybe his mother was right. Maybe there was a God who cared for His "children," as she liked to say. But if that's true, why had she suffered so? If there is a God who cares, how come the really good people have to endure so much pain?

He tossed his bags over his shoulder, grabbed the rest of his gear, and stuck his hat down on his head.

"I'm off."

"Good luck," said Harvey, extending his hand. "You're always welcome to come back to work here. And if you don't come back, send someone like you."

Matt smiled. "Will do, Harvey. Good luck to you." He shook the storekeeper's hand briskly, then left the house.

Deputy Page walked down to the livery and saddled Blister. He pulled himself up onto the Morgan's back and walked it out of the stable and down the street. He took in the little town he now called home and wished he could stay.

Matt reined the horse up in front of Sarah's house, not expect-

ing to see her; he had told her good-bye the day before. He was
surprised when Sheriff Taylor walked out onto the porch.

"Well?" Taylor barked. "You goin' or not?"

"Wh-what are you doing here?" Matt stammered.

"I usually have breakfast here," the sheriff said. "It just kinda
makes sense considerin' I *live here*!"

"Then . . . you're Sarah's—"

"Father, that's right. You're pretty quick, there, Deputy Page."
He paused.

Silence.

"Don't just stand there gawkin', Deputy," the sheriff said, flicking his hand at him. "Go to work! Git!"

"Y-yessir."

Matt smiled, waved, and gave Blister a kick. He rode across the
bridge and out of town, his life ahead of him.

Sarah ventured out onto the porch and watched him with her
father until he disappeared.

"Daddy . . . ?"

"Don't worry, honey," said Taylor, putting his arm around her.
"He'll be back."

A young man wearing ill-fitting, dirty clothes walked by the
side of a narrow road toward a ranch. He walked slow, tired-like,
and kept a nervous eye to his rear.

Hungry, he was enticed by a potato field. Checking first for the
rancher, he slipped through the fence and began digging up spuds,
putting them in his hat.

He heard something and stopped to listen. A horse. He ducked
down behind some sagebrush that grew by the fence as a single
rider went by, headed south. The rider was in a hurry and didn't
see the potato thief.

Moments after the rider disappeared down the road, before the
dust had settled, the potato thief heard two shots. He quickly finished gathering potatoes and stepped back through the rail fence,
then headed down the road the same direction as the rider.

When he had gone about a half-mile he came upon a group of
men and greeted them.

"I got some taters!" He held up his hat. "Hey, what were them
shots?"

"What do you think they were?" said Charlie Jones, a small but wiry man about twenty-two.

J. Bedford Roberts, the potato thief, shrugged. He didn't know. He didn't *want* to know. Then he realized that Jones was wearing civilian clothes, not his prison stripes.

"Where'd you get them duds?" Roberts asked.

"What, these?"

Jones looked at himself as though he wasn't sure what Roberts was talking about.

"Oh, some guy rode by so fast they just blew off'n his back. I couldn't catch him, so I figured I'd just wear 'em."

"You shot that rider!"

"Shut up!" said Leander Morton.

"Why'd you have to kill him?" Roberts asked. "He hadn't done nothin' to us!"

"It was an accident," explained Moses Black, scratching his heavy beard.

"I heard two shots," said Roberts. "Two shots ain't an accident."

"Oh, we shot him on purpose, all right," said Jones. "But it was an accident that it got that far."

"That's right," agreed Morton. "We was waitin' for someone else, man named Dingman, used to be a guard at the prison. We heard he was s'posed to be ridin' by here. Well, when this guy rides up we thought it was him. Guess the joke's on us!"

"Didn't quite happen that way," said John Burke. "They stopped the rider and asked him about Dingman, and when he didn't know, Jones shot off his mouth and said they was lookin' to cook Dingman's goose."

"Then we had to kill him," said Morton. It obviously made sense to him.

"Where is he?" Roberts asked.

Black jerked his thumb over his shoulder. Roberts walked over to a large boulder and looked behind it. A body wearing Jones's prison garb was crumpled in the dirt. The man's head had been burned so badly even his next of kin wouldn't have recognized him.

"They'll think it's one of us!" said Jones gleefully.

Roberts's knees gave out. He knew his life was over. It was just a matter of time. If one of the other escaped convicts, the elements, or the posse didn't kill him, the hangman would.

The young escapee sat down, regretting that he had ever fled from the prison.

Matt was a little surprised at how short the trip seemed to him. When he made it back to the Bodie cutoff at Dogtown the sun was barely full in the sky. What had taken hours on foot was effortless and short on a good horse.

He was just about to head into the canyon at the beginning of the Bodie road when he thought he saw movement on the top of the cliff. He scanned the ledge for several minutes, hoping to see it again, but he didn't and cautiously urged on the Morgan.

About a mile into the shallow red rock gorge it happened again. This time Matt didn't stop but slowed Blister down to a walk and kept his eyes straight ahead, straining to look to the side without giving himself away.

It paid off. Another mile up the road he saw it again, this time without question. Someone was up there following him.

Matt kept going. If they were thinking about dry-gulching him they would have done it by now. The gorge was short, and he was almost out of it. The walls fell away up ahead to rolling hills, and either the man would have to keep a good distance behind him, enough that Matt could outrun him if he had to, or the man would have to show himself.

He chose to show himself. Much to Matt's surprise a solitary rider trotted casually down a rise from Matt's left flank, as though he thought Matt was expecting him. Matt tried to act unconcerned and pulled Blister up slowly, then turned in the saddle, his hand resting nonchalantly on his gun butt.

It was an Indian.

This caught Matt off guard, and he suddenly felt very uneasy. He quickly scanned the countryside, thinking there would be others. Didn't they always hunt in groups?

The Indian came up alongside Matt, his face stoic. He sat tall and erect on a sorrel horse and wore white man's pants and a coat and an old, battered, black hat. His sun-darkened skin was clear, wrinkled around the eyes, and disguised his age.

"Good morning," greeted Matt.

"Yes," said the Paiute.

"Name's Matt Page." He remembered his new job and added, "Deputy Sheriff of Mono County."

"You lawman when horse get stolen?"

Matt almost fell out of his saddle.

"H-how . . . ?" he stammered, at a loss for words.

"How," said the Indian, mocking the white man. He smiled.

Matt laughed in spite of himself. "No, no. I mean, how did you know about that?"

"One day you ride, next day you walk. Horse not die." He shrugged. It was so obvious to him what had happened, how could anyone not know?

"Did you see the man who took it?"

"Not need to *see*," the Indian explained. "He leave message on ground, everywhere he go."

"You're a tracker!"

The Indian shrugged again. Wasn't everybody?

"I wish I could do that," Matt said.

"Learn to see," suggested the Indian.

"Not as easy as it sounds, I'm afraid," Matt lamented. "At least, it seems that way to me. May I ask who you are?"

"White man call me Charlie Jack."

"Glad to meet you, Mr. Jack."

"Not Mr. Jack. Charlie Jack."

"Okay, Charlie Jack it is." Matt extended his hand, not knowing what to expect in return. He got a standard handshake from the Indian.

"So, you saw me walking the other day?" Matt asked.

"Mmm."

"I could've used a ride into Bridgeport."

"I not going to Bridgeport."

Matt couldn't argue with that logic.

Then the Indian added, "And you not ask." He smiled again slightly, and Matt thought the Indian knew he was getting the better of him. He was having fun with the young deputy.

"You go after prisoners?" Charlie Jack asked.

"You mean the escaped convicts from Nevada? Well, I wasn't lookin' for them specifically. They comin' this way?"

The Indian nodded. "I meet posse in Aurora. Help find."

"May I come?"

Charlie shrugged. "You want to find horse?"

"Do you know where that old prospector is?"

"That way, many days." He pointed east.

"Tell you what," Matt said. "He took more than my horse. He got my money, too. If you help me track him—after we find the convicts, of course—I'll give you a reward."

The Indian thought, then nodded once and kicked his horse and took off up the Bodie road.

That was too easy, Matt thought. But he didn't have time to mull it over. He slapped Blister's rump and galloped off after the Indian.

They covered the ten miles into Bodie in an hour-and-a-half and pulled their horses up in front of the Empire Boarding House. Uncle Billy, always attentive and ready for new arrivals, heard them coming. He was standing on the porch, leaning on the rail.

"Good morning, Charlie," he greeted the Indian. "Headed out to look for the escaped prisoners?"

"Yes," Charlie said. "They here?"

O'Hara laughed. "No, Charlie, I'm afraid not. Looks like you'll have to do some work."

The Indian acted disappointed and went inside. O'Hara turned his attention to the other rider, who was tying his horse to the rail.

"Come on in, Deputy, get yourself some—Matthew? Is that you?"

Page smiled broadly and stepped up onto the porch. He took Billy's hand.

"Wait till you hear what happened to me!"

They went inside. Charlie was sitting at a table, eating a handful of pine nuts.

"Help yourself to the pine nuts, Charlie," Billy said.

"Thank you, Billy. I find."

O'Hara and Page sat down with the Paiute.

"Tell me 'bout it," Billy said to Matt.

Matt related the story to Uncle Billy, which Charlie listened to with great interest as well. When he finished, Matt smiled. "So here I am."

"You had yourself quite a week," O'Hara said.

"Yeah, it's been one to remember." He suddenly recalled the Confederate soldier. "How's the man I brought in?"

"Gone. Soon's he could get up he left. Cut stick durin' the night on foot, near's Ah can figure. Best Ah can tell he went up the rise to the top a the ridge. Don't know where he went from there."

"Do I owe you any more?"

"No, Matthew. We're even. You two want somethin' to eat?"

"Not me," said Matt.

"Time go," said Charlie Jack. He got up.

Matthew followed suit and shook O"Hara's hand again, then remembered the letter.

"Oh, I've got something for you. It's from Sheriff Taylor. It's out in my bags."

They went outside. Matt retrieved the letter and handed it to O'Hara, then untied his horse and swung himself into the saddle.

"I'll be back," Deputy Page shouted as he and Charlie Jack rode off to Aurora.

CHAPTER

ELEVEN

The two men loped their horses for the first few miles without conversing, then slowed to a walk. Matt watched a mule deer graze about fifty yards off the road, oblivious to them. As they rode side by side, Matt tried to strike up a conversation.

"I'm kinda new to this part of the country," he said.

"I not notice," said Charlie.

Matt couldn't tell whether the Indian was being sarcastic or not. He never knew Indians had a sense of humor, but he was finding out there was a lot he didn't know.

"Charlie Jack is your white man name?"

The Paiute nodded.

"Where did you get it?"

"Make up."

"How come? Can't you use your Paiute name?"

"Sacred. Not for your ears." His answer was to the point, and Matt figured the subject was closed. He said no more, but a mile down the road Charlie continued.

"Pick name, men I respect."

Matt was intrigued. "Who are they?"

The Indian looked puzzled. "Two men, Charlie and Jack."

Matt laughed at himself. "Okay, it was a dumb question."

Charlie looked at him. "Not dumb. Silly."

He kicked his horse and it ran, and Matt followed suit.

They arrived in Aurora that afternoon and rode straight to the sheriff's office. The posse that had formed was waiting when they walked in.

"Charlie, glad you're here," said a man wearing a badge. He noticed Matt. "Who's this?"

"Deputy Sheriff Matthew Page, Mono County, California," Matt said as he stepped forward and extended his hand.

The other man took it. "Deputy Mack Palmer, Mineral County, Nevada. You come all this way to join us?"

"Yessir, I met Charlie Jack on my way to Bodie, thought I'd see if I could help."

"Good thing you did," said Palmer. "Looks like they're headed down your way."

"How's that?"

"A posse from Carson City trailed them as far as Hot Springs, then went back when their horses gave out. Another group took it up and tracked them this far. They're about six hours ahead of us."

"We should be able to make that up, right?" Matt asked. "We're fresh and have horses."

"It's not as easy as it sounds. The convicts aren't on foot. By their tracks we know they have five horses. There's six of 'em, and three are cold-blooded killers. They're also well armed. They broke into the prison armory on their way out."

"There's more," interjected Ned Barker. "There's a pony rider missing. Billy Poor, Horace's son . . ." He pointed to Horace Poor seated by a window, " . . . was on a run from Sweetwater to Wellington, a twenty-two mile ride. That took him right across the convicts' route."

"He never made it," said Poor. "They captured my boy—or kilt him."

Silence. Most of the men figured Billy Poor for dead. They knew the convicts needed his clothes and his horse, not him. One more murder wouldn't mean much. A man can only hang once.

"Who are these guys?" Matt asked.

Palmer pulled a telegram from his shirt pocket and unfolded it.

"Let's see, this don't give us much. Moses Black, thirty-four, doin' seven years for grand larceny; Leander Morton, mail robbery, consider dangerous; Charlie Jones, twenty-two, murder—I hear he stabbed a man through the heart—those are the real bad ones. The others are Tilton Cockerill, a miner, sent up for train robbery—"

"And lying about how much gold he found," interrupted Barker. The men laughed at Barker's commentary on miners, but it faded quickly.

Palmer continued. "John Burke, manslaughter; and J. Bedford Roberts. He's only eighteen, robbed a stage."

"What weapons did they get from the armory?" Matt asked.

"As best we can tell, three rifles, four double-barreled shot guns, some six-shooters, and two, three thousand rounds of ammo."

Matt whistled. "Wait a minute. Didn't twenty-nine prisoners get out?"

"Yep."

"What happened to the others?"

"Oh, they scattered. Other posses are chasin' 'em. These six are the ones we want the most. They planned it and did all the killin' durin' the breakout. And we can assume they have most of the weapons."

"Time go," said Charlie Jack.

Deputy Palmer got up. "Saddle up, boys. We got us some bad eggs to find."

He led the men outside, and they all untied their mounts from the porch rail and climbed on, leather creaking and horses snorting and kicking up dirt.

Matt suddenly felt self-conscious as he grabbed his saddle and pulled himself up onto the Morgan. For a moment he couldn't believe he was here, representing Mono County as a deputy sheriff and getting ready to join the hunt for some escaped convicts, several of them murderers.

He shuddered and kicked his horse into motion. It seemed as if just last week he was on the farm, worried about the plow horse going lame or whether he would get enough for his crops to make a profit. In comparison to this, that all seemed relatively trivial.

The posse rode east from town for a half hour, Charlie Jack in the lead, until they came to the place where the convicts had last been seen. The Indian reined up the sorrel and slid off, then walked around slowly, looking at the ground. Matt watched with keen interest, but it was like trying to read Chinese—it looks pretty and mysterious, but you don't have a clue what it says.

The Indian found what he was looking for and stared off into the distance, then trotted back to his horse and clambered on in a single, fluid motion, without using the stirrups.

The Paiute turned his mount to the south and rode off, the posse following. Matt paused at the tracks the Indian had interpreted, trying to make heads or tails out of them but couldn't. He shook his head, then hurried to catch up.

They rode for several hours, all the way across the state line into California. The convicts' trail took the posse east around Mono Lake through the pumice sand of the defunct volcanoes, then across the rolling Adobe Hills into the Adobe Valley.

Matt realized that he was now theoretically in charge, the convicts having passed into his jurisdiction. Aurora's Deputy Palmer continued to give orders, however, and Matt was content to let him.

They traveled as far as Adobe Meadows and Charlie Jack halted them. He conferred with Palmer who ordered the men down. It was past sunset and would soon be too dark to see.

"We'll camp here for the night," he said. "Their trail heads off toward Taylor Canyon. Charlie says their horses are tired, they're probably camped nearby. We'll have them in a day or so."

The men dismounted and unsaddled their tired steeds and watered the lathering horses and themselves. They had ridden hard and a few of them looked ill. Matt noticed that Horace Poor, sullen and silent all evening, stayed to himself and looked worried.

Matt passed out some jerked beef and pine nuts and sat down by Charlie Jack.

They ate silently for a moment, then Charlie spoke quietly. "What Matthew want?"

Matt was again amazed at the Indian's insight.

"Uh . . . well, I was wonderin' if you could explain how you know they are tired."

"Horses tired," Charlie Jack corrected.

"Okay, how do you know?"

"Steps close together. When run, steps far apart. More tired, steps closer. If you escape from prison, you run horse or walk?"

"Run, of course. As long as I could."

"They run before, not run now. Horses tired."

Matt nodded. "That makes sense." He happened to notice what the Indian was eating. The Paiute scooped what looked to Matt like rice out of a leather pouch.

"What's that? Matt asked.

Charlie Jack pushed three fingers full of the stuff into his mouth and chewed happily.

"*Koochabee,*" he said, and offered the pouch to Matt.

Matt took it and scooped out a few of the small, dark objects. He held them under his nose and sniffed. Nothing. Charlie put his fingers to his mouth and smiled, urging Matt to try them. Someone else snickered.

Matt looked up and tried to figure out who it was. The men were all suddenly interested in the stars or their fingernails.

"What?" Matt asked to no one in particular.

"Go ahead," said Palmer, smiling. "Eat yourself a handful."

"What is it?" Matt asked.

"*Koochabee*, like Charlie said," Ned Barker informed him. "Good stuff. Very nutritious." J.S. Mooney chuckled on the other side of the circle.

"What's *koochabee*?" Matt asked Charlie.

"Like Ned say, very good."

Matt knew he was getting nowhere with the men. He figured his manhood was being tested, so he put a fingerful of *koochabee* in his mouth and chewed slowly. It was soft and chewy, kind of sweet and yet not. After Matt swallowed, Mooney laughed out loud.

"He actually did it! Charlie, I owe you a dollar!"

"Pay now," said Charlie, holding out his hand. "No credit."

He flipped a gold coin to the Paiute. "It was worth it to see the kid eat fly larvae."

"*What?*" Matt felt his throat constrict.

"Fly larvae," said Palmer. "The Paiutes eat it like we do bread. They scoop 'em up outta Mono Lake. That and pine nuts are mostly what they eat."

"And rabbits," Mooney said, "but only when the critters run into their camp and give themselves up. Paiutes are no plumb good at catchin' 'em."

"*Maggots?* I ate maggots?" Matt grabbed a canteen and drank while the men laughed. Charlie slapped him on the back.

"You live long now, be strong." He stood up and walked a few feet away to a rock and sat down.

"Time sleep," he said.

The men agreed and spread out their bedrolls. Matt followed suit in silence, sure he would throw up any second, and stared up at the stars before finally drifting off.

He woke as the sky was beginning to lighten. As he struggled to stretch out the stiffness he glanced over at the horses and saw that Charlie Jack's was gone. He figured the Indian was scouting out the trail ahead and wished he could have gone with him.

He got up, as did several of the other men. It was a cold morning and someone started a fire and boiled a pot of coffee. The horses were blowing steam, even before they had exerted themselves. By the time Matt and the rest of the men were ready to go, the Paiute had returned.

He approached Palmer on foot, leading his horse.

"Six men, camped five miles up canyon." He pointed southwest toward Taylor Canyon.

"Let's git to it, men," Palmer ordered. They saddled up, Horace Poor looking more haggard than ever. Six men. They were following six convicts. Either a convict had been left, killed, or had split off from the group and Billy Poor was riding with them as hostage, or the pony rider was dead.

Sleep had not improved the condition of the men who had taken ill, but they continued without complaint, determined to see it to the end. An hour from camp several riders approached from the south, their coming announced by a dust cloud. As they drew near Charlie Jack stopped, followed by Palmer and the rest. Matt looked at the approaching riders. He could see the flickering glint of the sun off the badge of the man on the lead horse.

"That should be Hightower," said Palmer. "He's Sheriff Taylor's deputy in Benton."

Deputy George Hightower drew alongside Palmer. He introduced another man as Robert Morrison, a Wells Fargo agent. There were several other men with him and quick nods and hat tipping all around sufficed for introductions. Matt noticed an Indian wearing white man's clothes staying in the background. He seemed to be more of a hired hand than a tracker or member of the posse. Anytime someone got off a horse, he held it for them.

Matt watched as Charlie Jack ride over to the other Paiute and they spoke briefly. The young deputy thought he heard someone call the Indian "Mono Jim."

Matt urged his horse slowly up to Palmer and Hightower.

"You must be Page," Hightower said upon seeing him. "Sheriff Taylor wired me, said I might meet up with you sooner or later. Good to have you aboard."

Matt shook his hand. "You work for Taylor? He didn't mention you."

"Doesn't surprise me. Benton's rather . . . out of the way."

"Well, good to know you. I thought I was alone out here . . ." He looked at the men around him. ". . . deputy-wise, I mean. I thought I was the only Mono County Deputy Sheriff."

"Nope. But it's just me and you." Hightower turned to Palmer. "What's the status?"

"They're a few miles ahead of us. Taylor Canyon." He leaned forward, so Horace Poor couldn't hear. "Looks like Billy Poor's dead. There's only six of 'em. Charlie's positive Billy's not with 'em."

"Charlie Jack?"

"Yep."

"Good enough for me." He scanned Palmer's posse. "Some of your men don't look too good."

"We rode pretty hard last night. One of 'em is Billy's father."

"Send him back with those two." Hightower pointed to Mooney and McCue. "They'll just slow us down."

Palmer turned in his saddle. "John, you and Mooney take Horace home. Horace, thanks for your help, but you need to be with Billy's mother. She needs you."

Horace nodded. Mooney and McCue were more than happy to go home. The three men swung their horses around slowly and retreated up the trail together. Matt saw Horace's head drop as he began to quietly cry, knowing deep inside that his son was dead.

Hightower wheeled around and kicked his horse to follow Charlie, who was already riding off after the convicts.

CHAPTER

TWELVE

S ix tired, hungry men, one still wearing the distinctive striped garb provided for him by the State of Nevada, plodded their nearly spent horses down an old wagon road that followed a small creek.

The road was lined with sagebrush and wild rose bushes, and the men had been kept alive the past few days by eating snow berries and jerky. They did not talk as they pressed toward the Sierra Nevadas that loomed so large before them.

The mountains offered both a promise and a curse: a promise of freedom on the other side and the curse of hardship in the crossing. If prepared, it would not have been an easy task; for ill-equipped men on the run from the law, it would be arduous. The odds were against them, but they did not—they could not—stop.

The creek ended at the Owens River.

Charlie Jones stopped and slid off his horse. He sat down on a rock at the edge of the river, letting go of his mount's reins. The animal ambled slowly to the edge of the flowing water, too tired to do anything else. It's neck was already bent from fatigue, and it drank from the river without putting out much effort.

Jones squinted back up the trail at the others. The largest horse carried the two smallest men, Leander Morton and J. Bedford

Roberts. John Burke followed them closely, with Tilton Cockerill and Moses Black bringing up the rear.

Black was a large, fierce-looking man with a thick neck and arms and a heavy, dark beard. He had a booming deep voice to match and was the only man still in prison stripes. None of their raids had yielded clothes big enough for him.

"Let's cross," he said to Jones.

"Give me a minute," Jones replied testily. "I'm tired."

"You wanna go back?" Morton asked. "We'll hang for sure, killin' that pony rider."

"I ain't goin' back!" Jones concluded. He got up and trudged across the shallow river, leading his horse.

The other men watered their mounts and followed, once again falling silent. On the other side of the river the escapees climbed a basalt bluff, leading their balking horses up the slippery slope.

When they reached the top they faced a thick grove of aspen and pine trees that formed a barrier sufficient enough to force them to skirt around to the east, where there was a clear trail.

They gave little thought any longer to covering their tracks, concerned more with speed than deception. They were intent on reaching the Sierras—and their freedom.

The sun was going down, resting momentarily on top of the peaks as if giving the men a last chance to get to a suitable place to camp.

"There's a lake up ahead a ways," said Roberts. "Monte Diablo. We can camp there and start crossing the Sierras in the morning." His voice was more hopeful than demanding, being the youngest of the party. Even so, he was the most familiar with this area. It was a good idea, and the others saw the wisdom in it.

They rode the final six miles in the shadow of the Sierras while the chill of the evening descended. When they reached the creek that flowed out of Monte Diablo they breathed a sigh of relief.

Just one more night and freedom would be theirs.

Matt rode with the posse in silent anticipation. He wondered what was up ahead. Would they find the convicts? Likely. Would the convicts give up without a fight? Hardly likely. He began to feel a gnawing in the pit of his stomach: not hunger, but fear, fear of the unknown.

He glanced at the other men, wondering if they felt it too. They were all older, more experienced. Used to it? Do you ever get used to living on the edge, where your life is always an eyeflick from eternity?

Eternity. Matt remembered his mother, the talks they used to have about eternity and about God. She always seemed so peaceful, never afraid of death.

Is that what I'm afraid of? he wondered. His mother always used to say that death is not to be feared by the Christian. It just means you are passing from this life of hardship and sorrow into an eternity of peace and happiness with God. *Maybe that's what I need, to get closer to—*

"Hold!"

Charlie Jack interrupted Matt's thoughts by reining up his horse and ordering the men to follow suit. The Paiute dismounted quickly and walked around, looking intently at the ground. He motioned for Matt to join him. Matt got off Blister hesitantly, feeling conspicuous. *What does Charlie Jack want with me?* He walked up to the Indian, who pointed to the dirt in a wide place in the trail, next to a shallow river crossing.

"What you see?"

Matt furrowed his brow and looked hard. At first, it looked like disheveled, overlapping foot prints.

"I . . . I don't know. A lot of shoe prints." He shrugged.

"You see too many. Look small."

Matt looked again. Okay. There was one set of prints. He followed just the one set, noticing that whoever was wearing those shoes seemed to be wandering or pacing.

He found a different set and followed them, then another. Suddenly a pattern emerged and it made sense to him.

"They . . . stopped here for a few minutes . . . probably to rest, but most likely to talk, to . . . formulate a plan, or decide something."

"Good. How you know?"

"Well, this guy here," he pointed to one set of prints, "he paced a lot. That guy sat for a while—see how he shuffled his feet in the dirt?—and this man had probably been some distance behind. As soon as he got here they left. His prints don't look like they stopped at all."

Charlie Jack slapped him on the shoulder. "You right. Where go?"

Matt looked across the river. He could see the road as it skirted the cliff. At first he wanted to guess that the escapees went around. Then he eyed the basalt bluff.

He couldn't believe it. Even from here he could see the disturbance in the loose, dark rock. They had hiked up, leading their horses, zig-zagging back and forth to make the climb easier. Had he not been tracking someone, he would never have noticed.

Matt pointed to the cliff, and Charlie Jack smiled.

"Come!" the Indian told the posse. "They near."

He got back on his horse and eased him into the river, ignoring the water splashing on his legs. Matt trailed closely, and the Morgan followed the sorrel without hesitation. The rest of the men urged their mounts on also.

After fording the river they clambered up the dusty bank, the horses blowing water and breath, then approached the basalt bluff as the convicts had done before them. As they started up the horses slipped in the loose rock and balked, but the posse urged them forward, keeping a firm rein to let them know who was boss. If the convicts made it up, they could too. The climb took an hour, and several times Matt thought Blister would slip and tumble down, so he spent most of the climb holding his breath. But the Morgan held firm and reached the top moments after Charlie Jack's sorrel.

After assembling at the ridge they gave the horses a few minutes to rest, some of the men taking a drink themselves before following the convicts' tracks east around the timber. They broke out of the woods after a short trek and onto a rolling plain that led to the nearby mountains.

As the Sierras towered in front of them Matt felt the uneasiness return. Charlie happened a glance back at him and read it in the young deputy's face. He fell back next to Page and looked him square in the eye.

"It good you fear," he said. "It mean you feel them, know they are near. You are good tracker, learn well."

He pumped his legs and rode back to the front of the posse.

The mountains grew larger over the sagebrush hills the posse crossed and soon Matt was sure he could see a steep canyon, almost a bowl, carved into the high cliffs.

They crested one more hill and a plain several miles wide spread out before them, leading up to the base of the Sierras. They were now in full view and Matt followed the lines of the canyon peaks down as they converged in a lush, tree-filled valley. A crooked line of trees and shrubbery came out of the valley towards them, marking the path of a creek.

Robert Morrison eased himself down from his saddle and took a pair of binoculars out of his saddlebags. The Wells Fargo agent scanned the countryside, stopping as he peered at the creek. Matt could see his lips moving as he counted to himself.

"Six." He let the glasses down slowly. "There they are, gentlemen." He sounded almost reverent.

Charlie Jack walked his horse up alongside Hightower.

"I find," he said. "Deal not include gunfight."

"I know, Charlie. We can handle the rest from here." He pulled a letter from his pocket and gave it to the Indian. "Here's a letter you can give to the authorities in Nevada. They'll pay you what they owe."

Charlie accepted it and rode over to Matt.

"Good-bye, young Matthew. Keep head down."

"Where are you going?" Matt asked.

"I ride to Bishop tonight, tomorrow . . ." He shrugged.

"What about helping me find that prospector? You said you would."

"I did. I show you how to track." The Indian was serious. "But you not owe me if you don't find."

Matt hated it when people left him to his own resources. He felt too inadequate sometimes. He knew it was for his own good, but that didn't make him feel any more comfortable about it. His father had done that to him, left him with a farm to run before he knew how. Now here was Charlie Jack, leaving him to fend for himself again.

"I don't feel like I learned anything."

"You did. You see."

Charlie wheeled his horse around and took off under darkening skies toward Bishop. Matt watched him until he disappeared.

Hightower wheeled his horse around. "It's too late to try a siege tonight. We'll get them in the morning. They'll camp tonight by the lake. Let's get ourselves back down behind this hill."

Matt sat motionless in the saddle, gazing at the creek line in the distance, trying to pick out the invisible convicts. He couldn't see them, but he could feel them.

"This is good enough," proclaimed Morton.

They were by the creek, a few hundred yards below the lake, near a grove of willow trees. They and their horses were spent, and no one argued.

The men climbed down slowly from the animals and tried to revive their numb hindquarters and get the kinks out. Cockerill tied the animals up while Black sat down and leaned against a rock. He shut his eyes and would have drifted off to sleep right then had it not been for the whinny of a horse somewhere up the creek.

The big man jerked his eyes open. The other men froze in their tracks, looking around at each other with questioning expressions. Black motioned for Roberts and Morton to investigate. The two reluctantly moved up along the creek, using the sound of the water to cover their footsteps.

Under a large willow about a hundred yards from their camp a saddled roan was tied and a man in a gray coat sat with his back to them. His head was hanging down, and his breathing was regular and deep.

Morton snuck up behind the man, his gun trained on him from the waist. When Morton's foot crunched a stick the man jerked awake, startled, but saw the gun and quickly put up his hands.

"Don't shoot!" the man said. "Ah don't have much. Just a horse."

Morton studied the man, his tattered old Confederate army coat, his red, scarred face, and general disheveled, dirty appearance.

"There's more than just me," Morton said, "so don't think of tryin' anything. We got a camp down the creek a bit. You got food?"

"A little."

"Bring it."

The soldier grabbed a canvas bag and walked down the creek, passing Roberts in his hiding place, and came into the convicts' camp. Morton was behind him, still holding his gun at the soldier's back.

"What's this?" Black asked.

The soldier saw Black's prison garb and his mind began to race. He thought back to his dry-gulching and feared it was happening again. For a fleeting second he wished he was still being cared for by that insolent Negro, but he shook off the feeling.

"Uh, what now?" he asked.

It was apparent the convicts hadn't thought of that either. Black looked at Jones, who shrugged.

"I guess we might as well kill him and keep his horse."

Morton and the others were opposed, but Jones argued in favor of it.

"What else can we do? He's seen us. He could have the law down on us in a heartbeat."

"No, Ah won't," offered the soldier. "Ah promise."

"I've had enough killin'," said Burke. "If I get caught I don't want to get hung."

"Too late for that," said Black. "We killed two, three men already. If we get caught, we're dead. That's why we don't aim to get caught." He looked at the soldier and shrugged. "Sorry."

"Listen, can Ah say one thing first?"

"I s'pose that can't hurt," Jones conceded.

"Ah'm not goin' to the law. Ah stole that horse. They're probably lookin' for me, too."

"How do we know that's true?" Morton asked.

"Ah guess the word of a Southern gentleman will have to suffice. 'Sides, there is six a you and one a me."

"He's like one of us," Roberts pleaded. "Let him live. We can always kill him later if'n we have to."

Jones thought about it. "All right. Burke, you get his horse and bring it back here."

Burke nodded and hiked up to where the animal was tied. By the time he returned, everyone had found a comfortable spot, including the soldier, and they were beginning to fall asleep. He found a place for himself after tying up the horse and settled down for the night.

He dreamed of freedom.

CHAPTER

THIRTEEN

The convicts woke with first light, hungry. When Black grumbled, Roberts suggested they gather berries for breakfast and Jones went up the canyon toward the lake with a tin cup. Cockerill and Burke joined him.

The rest of the convicts lazed around the camp, trying to renew their strength for the Sierra crossing. They had decided to stay put for a day to give themselves and their mounts a chance to recover, and to gather whatever grub they could find.

Black was uneasy, still in prison stripes. He'd hoped to find a large enough man to steal clothes from by now, but hadn't had any luck. He scratched his beard and stretched his face with a yawn.

Suddenly the pounding of horses' hooves snapped him out of his early morning stupor. The big man jumped up, saw the posse not forty yards from them, and shouted for Morton and Roberts.

The lawmen were shooting even before they were within effective range and the three convicts ran for cover. Roberts had to cross open ground as the posse closed in and took two rounds, one in the shoulder and the other in the foot, sprawling him in the dirt.

Black and Morton headed for a large pine tree on the far side of the stream and immediately returned fire while Roberts began to crawl, posse bullets kicking dirt up around him. He made it to the creek and slid headfirst down the bank into the water.

Temporarily protected, he caught his breath and tried to assess the damage, then crawled up to the tree where Morton and Black were pinned down.

The posse had still been charging when the convicts started shooting back. The lawmen dove off their horses, some of them firing as they did, and hustled for cover, leaving their horses to wander on their own.

Mono Jim had held back and set about trying to catch a couple horses that had been spooked by gunfire. Four horses had been hit by convict bullets and two of them lay dead. Matt's Blister was unscathed so far and didn't shy away when Mono Jim grabbed his reins.

The soldier, hidden from the posse's view by a rock, hunkered down, not really knowing what was happening. He soon realized, however, that this was a posse that had caught up with these men, and he hoped it was just them they were after. It had to be. They were probably all convicts, not just the one in stripes. He crawled away from the action, taking cover in the brush, and tried to keep still.

In the midst of the gunfire Matt heard a cry from his left. He looked over and saw the gun fall from the hand of one of the Benton posse as blood started to flow from a wound in the man's hand. The wounded lawman slid down behind the rock and writhed in the dirt.

Matt was scared as he came face to face with the reality of death and wondered suddenly why he had accepted the badge. He never dreamed he'd get into anything like this. Then Sarah's face popped into his thoughts, and he heard himself muttering a prayer.

"Oh God," he said out loud, pausing long enough to fire two rounds at the convicts' pine tree. "Please help me get through this. I'd really like to see Sarah again."

A man suddenly ran behind Matt and circled wide, trying to flank the convicts. It was Morrison. He reached an open area and dropped down to the ground to crawl.

Across the clearing Morton saw the lawman's actions and told Roberts to crawl back to a stand of willows.

"They're going to surround us here. You'll be shot if you don't move."

Roberts took off, half running, half stumbling, and made it to the willows.

Black watched Morrison inching on his belly toward their flank. He moved away from the tree to take aim. Morrison spotted him and took a bead on the convict from the ground. He squeezed the trigger, but Black was moving and the bullet missed. He aimed again and fired, but this time the hammer fell on a dead chamber.

Black heard the metallic click and smiled wickedly at the prone lawman, then took careful aim and fired. The bullet thumped Morrison in the side. The lawman groaned, raised his head and tried to reload, but couldn't steady the weapon.

The bearded convict noticed that the rest of the posse had remained under cover. Morrison was alone. Black boldly left his cover and walked casually over to him. While Morton fired at the posse to keep them down, Black drew a final bead on the lawman.

Morrison looked up at the convict. He knew it was over but did not plead, knowing it would be to no avail to this desperate man in prison stripes. Morrison just stared at him, helpless and no longer a threat to the escaped convict. Black ignored this and put his gun at the back of Morrison's head and coldly cocked the hammer as Morrison solemnly closed his eyes and waited. He did not ask for mercy, and none was given

Matt jumped out from behind the rock shouting, heedless of Morton's barrage, and raced toward Black and the fatally wounded Morrison. Black's head jerked up when he heard Matt's cry and he retreated, dodging Matt's wild shots.

The posse witnessed the murder in horror, then saw Matt charge, but they retreated, afraid of the convicts, running wildly back the way they had come. Matt slid onto the ground beside Morrison's body, using it for cover, and looked back in horror as the posse ran off. Why hadn't they followed? He didn't know what to do now. He was at the convicts' mercy. He felt he should stay and fight, but without the others he would be outnumbered. And there were still three convicts out there somewhere. He had no choice now but to retreat.

Cautiously he peeked over Morrison's chest. The three convicts were nowhere to be seen. Matt figured they must have taken that opportunity to make their own escape as the posse fled. Even though the lawmen ran, there would be more coming soon enough, especially now that Morrison had been murdered.

Matt dragged Morrison out of the clearing, then backed off and started for his horse, but as he reached for the reins, a bullet from an unseen foe kicked the dirt up near the Morgan's feet and it bolted. Matt chased after it, trying to stay down, and managed to catch hold of the reins. A bullet whizzing past his ear spurred him on. He shook the reins and shouted "Go!" and the animal took off.

Black and Morton had ignored the retreating Matt, going instead after two horses that had been left by the posse, who couldn't reach them during their hasty departure. The convicts mounted and took off up the canyon, picking up the injured Roberts and firing several rounds blindly back toward the clearing just in case.

Mono Jim was holding his and Deputy Hightower's horses. He saw three men riding toward him and called out, thinking they were members of the posse. Too late, he realized his mistake and quickly mounted his horse and attempted to get away.

Without a thought, Black shot him. Mono Jim went down hard but got his gun out of his waistband and, from his side, shot Black's and Morton's horses out from under them.

They spilled out of their saddles, but Morton recovered quickly and walked over to the wounded Paiute. The convict shot him and took his horse.

Black caught Hightower's and they rode off again, Roberts riding double behind Morton.

The shooting over, the soldier peeked out from behind the rock. It looked all clear, so he came out from his hiding place cautiously. He still had his horse and led it down the creek, out of the canyon. He just wanted to get out of there.

Matt was several minutes behind the rest of the posse and hadn't cleared the canyon. He turned in the saddle checking behind him and saw a man in a gray coat mounting a horse. Surprised, Matt realized it was his roan. He pulled the Morgan up sharply and turned it, then took a better look at the man.

"That can't be!" he said out loud. "What's *he* doing here, and on *my horse?*"

The excited Morgan turned in place and when Matt was able

to look again, he realized the soldier was coming toward him. Since the convicts had all but disappeared up the canyon, Matt stood his ground. When the soldier saw Matt he stopped, noticing only the star. Having been unconscious when Matt rescued him, he didn't know who the deputy was.

Matt didn't move.

"Ah'm not one of them," the soldier said.

"You're here with 'em."

"If Ah was one a them, Ah woulda shot you just now."

"Okay. Then how do you come to be with them?"

"Ah was here first. They came upon me last night while Ah was sleepin'."

Matt thought for a second. "You're riding a stolen horse."

Matt realized too late he'd made a mistake tipping his hand without having his iron out. The soldier yanked his gun quickly out of his pants and fired. Matt faded to his left, anticipating the shot, but couldn't evade it completely and the bullet creased his head, knocking him out of the saddle.

The soldier moved forward at a gallop, then jumped off the roan and ran up to the wounded deputy. He pulled Matt's gun out of his holster, keeping his own trained on the fallen man. The wound wasn't serious, but it had been enough to let the soldier take the advantage.

"Ah'm not gonna hang for stealin' an ol' propsector's horse."

"It wasn't his horse," Matt said slowly, grimacing as he held his head.

"What do you mean?"

"He stole it from me."

The soldier laughed. "If Ah wasn't in such a hurry, Ah'd like to hear this little story." He cocked the gun.

"You'll hang for this."

"Naw, Ah don't think so. You were in a shootout with six escaped convicts. No one else knows Ah'm here."

Matt's mind raced. What could he say? He didn't want to die. *Please God!*

"I . . . uh . . ." Matt was grasping for anything. " . . . I see Uncle Billy mended your coat."

The soldier looked puzzled. "What did you say?"

"Uncle Billy. The man in Bodie who took care of you? I see he mended your coat."

"How'd you know about that?"

"I took you there."

"You're the one who found me on the road?"

Matt nodded. The soldier released the hammer slowly and lowered the gun.

"You saved my life. Ah owe you for that. Now we're even."

"Thank you," Matt breathed.

"Don't. Next time Ah'll kill you." He spat in the dirt. "Goodbye Deputy."

Matt didn't answer but strained to look at the roan to see if the saddlebags were there.

They weren't. He breathed a sigh of relief. Maybe the prospector still had them.

"Did you hurt the man you took the horse from?" Matt asked.

"No, Ah didn't. He gave them up real peaceful-like." He looked at the deputy for a minute, considering. Looking around, he spied a horse standing in the willows.

"Tell you what. Ah want to travel about without worryin' about you or some other hotshot lawman ridin' down on me in the night. Besides, you did more than just save my life, and Ah don't like to be beholden to people." He dropped the roan's reins onto Matt. "Here's your horse back." He opened the loading port on Matt's gun and turned the cylinder slowly, letting the bullets drop into the dirt, then tossed Matt the empty weapon without comment.

The rebel walked over to the other animal and led him out of the willows, and without another word got up into the saddle and rode off up the canyon.

Matt got up slowly, wincing in pain at the oozing crease on his head, and mounted the Morgan. He led the roan as he rode slowly down the canyon to join up with the posse.

It had not gone well. Morrison and Mono Jim were dead, their bodies still sprawled in the dirt. Another man was wounded; they lost most of their horses; all six convicts had gotten away, and the remains of the posse was nowhere to be seen.

He was alive, though, and breathed a silent prayer of thanks to his mother's God for that.

But before he got to the *amen* his vision blurred and the ground began spinning. He quickly hugged Blister's neck and brought his right leg back over the saddle behind him to climb off. As his feet hit the ground, he blacked out and crumpled into the dirt.

CHAPTER

FOURTEEN

Cold water hit Matt hard on the face and he woke with a start, his vision blurred and his head on fire. As his eyes cleared he recognized the form of a man hovering over him. He reached for his gun, but a strong hand grasped his wrist.

"Friend," said a familiar voice. Matt relaxed.

"Charlie Jack?"

"Yes. You okay?"

"I dunno. I got it pretty good. I didn't think it was so bad a little bit ago."

"Two days."

"What?"

"You sleep long time."

Matt started to get up. "Ooohhhh." Thunder rumbled in his head. "Was I out the whole time?"

"No. You have fever, say many things. Who Sarah?"

"Sarah?" Matt thought. "Oh, she's a young woman I met in Bridgeport. Sheriff Taylor's daughter."

"Ahh. That explain." Charlie Jack nodded, smiling.

"Explains what?"

"Things you say in fever."

Matt blushed and changed the subject.

"What are you doing?"

He was watching the Paiute crush some sage leaves and sprinkle them into a pan of water that was boiling over a campfire. The pungent odor reached Matt's nostrils, and he recoiled.

"That smells terrible!"

"Yes, but it taste bad, too."

"I ain't drinkin' that stuff."

"That your choice. You the one sick and hurt, not Charlie Jack." The Indian poured the thick liquid into a tin cup.

"Will it help?" Matt asked hesitantly.

"You try." Charlie Jack held it out to Matt. He accepted the cup and looked inside, just in case there was something in there he hadn't counted on, then took a sip. The concoction made his eyes water and his lips pucker, and it was all he could do to keep from spitting it out. Instead he swallowed hard and shook his head.

"You're right. It tastes horrible!"

"Charlie Jack tell truth."

"This makes the castor oil my mother used to force down me taste good by comparison." Matt downed the rest of it, then shuddered involuntarily.

"What about the convicts?" he asked the Paiute, wiping his mouth with a sleeve.

"They separate. Three go east, three go south. One wounded."

"I thought you were finished with this deal."

"They need again. Can't capture men, they scatter, need Charlie Jack to find." He smiled. "More pay for Charlie Jack."

"You're going after them?

"Yes. They go to Round Valley, near Bishop."

"I'll come with you." He started to get up but couldn't.

"No, you rest. Two days. I give food, water. You rest."

Matt tried to look around, but the movement hurt his head.

"Horses there," said the Paiute, pointing. "You find horse?"

"You mean the one the prospector stole? Yeah, another man was riding it. A Confederate soldier. He came from Bodie, stole it from the prospector on the way here. He's not with the convicts, just met them accidentally."

"He shoot you?"

"Yeah, but he wasn't tryin' to kill me. He could have if he wanted."

Charlie looked at the horse thoughtfully. "Popular horse. Many men want. It not know who own it."

Matt laughed, but it hurt, so he turned it into a groan. Charlie Jack stood up.

"What made you come back here to find me?" Matt asked.

Charlie Jack shrugged. "Not know. Feeling."

"I'm glad you did."

"Charlie Jack glad too. Matthew not bad for white man." He mounted his horse. "Where you go when well?"

"I suppose I'll go down to Bishop when I can, before I head out to look for that prospector."

"You have horse," Charlie Jack observed.

"Yeah, but he still has my money."

"Then Matthew need to find."

"I will," Matt said. "I can feel it. But first I'd like to find out about them convicts."

"Don't worry. We catch."

Charlie Jack nodded a good-bye, then wheeled around and rode off in a hurry. Matt lay back down under the blanket lean-to the Indian had put up for him and closed his eyes. The skies had been threatening and now a light rain began to fall, but Matt was unaware of it.

The next morning, an hour after the sun had fully crested the White Mountains, Matt broke camp. He untied and saddled the Morgan, moving slowly because his head still hurt. He knew Charlie Jack had said to wait two days, but he was restless.

The Indian had put some kind of poultice on the wound to keep out infection, and it had worked. It was already beginning to heal. Charlie had left Matt with plenty of food. Pine nuts, jerky, dried apples, rice grass seeds, and *koochabee*.

Despite a strong aversion to the stuff, hunger drove him to eat it, and he found he could tolerate it if he washed it down quickly with a gulp of water. But it would never replace a thick slice of ham.

Matt longed for normality. It seemed he was either eating steak and potatoes and apple pie, or insects and dried leather, or he was starving. It would be good to get a plate of beans and sowbelly, or some campfire biscuits and boiled coffee.

If every week was like this one, he didn't know how long he could keep going.

Once astride Blister, Page took hold of the reins attached to the roan and headed toward Bishop. He rode easy, expecting to make the thirty-mile trip in two days.

For once Matt had an ordinary ride. The road to Bishop was well-traveled, and he met several people going the other way: a few men were on horseback, but most drove freight wagons and stage-coaches.

He was able to supplement his meager diet with a rabbit one day. Fortunately for him it was a white-tailed jackrabbit, which Charlie had told him were much better tasting than the black-tailed variety. The next day he talked a teamster out of a can of beans. The star on his shirt didn't hurt, although Matt didn't inten-tionally push the point; the wagon driver saw it and made the donation of his own accord.

When Matt rode into town he was weary and decided to get a room right away and do his asking around in the morning.

As he headed down the northern road toward Main Street he saw a wagon coming toward him, surrounded by several men on horseback. As they passed Pinchower's General Store a huge crowd of men came out from behind the building and blocked the road. It didn't take much reckoning for Matt to realize something was wrong, but he didn't know just what. He moved off the road to watch.

When the wagon stopped Matt could see three men tied up in the rear. One of them was a large man with a beard, wearing prison stripes.

Black, Morton, and Roberts! Matt said to himself. *They caught 'em!*

A group of men emerged from a cabin at the side of the road. While one of them retrieved some rope from the wagon, the rest began looking around, trying to find something to suspend it from. The guards milled around outside, acting disinterested. Matt rec-ognized a couple of men from the posse that had been at the shootout. Palmer and Hightower were not there. They were prob-ably riding with Charlie Jack after the other convicts, Matt guessed.

Failing to locate a suitable hangin' tree nearby, the men took three slender timbers—trees that had been felled for firewood and delimbed but had not yet been cut into stove-sized logs—then lashed them together near one end.

They stood these upright, the lashed end at the top, about ten feet from the cabin's chimney, then set a large rough-sawn beam across the space, one end on the chimney, the other held up by the timbers.

The men who had emerged from the cabin assembled noisily around the makeshift scaffold, and it finally dawned on Matt what was happening.

"What about him?" Morton said to his executioners while pointing at Roberts. "He's the one did all the killin'!"

"Shut up!" ordered a man, and he gave Morton a kick. The convict lost his balance and sprawled face down in the wagon. As he was helped back up a man shinnied out to the center of the beam and tied two ropes around it.

"Water."

It was Black, barely audible. In a moment he was handed a cup and drank it down.

"Thank you." He handed the cup back.

The leader of the vigilance committee addressed the condemned men.

"Do you have anything to say?"

"No," Black replied simply. He continued to stare straight ahead.

"It isn't right for a man to be hung without some kind of religious ceremony," Morton said. "If there's a minister here, I'd like to have a prayer."

Matt couldn't believe it when one stepped forward. *Is he part of the lynch mob?* the deputy wondered to himself. Then the leader acknowledged the preacher.

"What? Why are you here, Reverend?"

"It is obvious you mean to do this thing. That's why I'm here, so these men, having been deprived of a fair, legal trial, might at least have the benefit of a last chance to make a final plea to God for their souls."

"Come on, then, though I don't know what good it'll do. These men have gone too far."

"It worked for the thief on the cross beside our Lord," the preacher said. "Let's allow God the freedom to decide the fate of the souls of these men."

"Like they let God decide the fate of their victims?" The crowd cheered the leader of the committee, but he held up his hand for silence. "Have at it, Reverend." He stepped back, and the minister climbed up on the wagon.

"I am prepared to meet my God," said Morton. "But I don't know that there is any God."

The minister bowed his head and said a quick prayer. Matt could take it no longer. He couldn't stand there and let this thing happen, This was a land of justice but not mob justice. He moved out from his hiding place as the *amens* were said and began wading through the crowd.

"Wait!" Matt called.

"Who's that?" asked the leader.

"Matthew Page, Mono County Deputy Sheriff. These men are my prisoners. The murders were committed in my jurisdiction!"

Several men laughed, and the leader issued a warning. "You best not interfere with the dishing out of justice here, Deputy. Not if you want to stay healthy."

Matt knew words were useless and started to reach for his gun, but someone grabbed him by the shoulder and swung him around. Off balance, he spun and looked into the grizzled, hairy face of the prospector. Before he could react, the prospector hit him on the head with the barrel of a gun. Matt's knees buckled.

Page wasn't out long and when his head started to clear he stood up slowly. It was over. The dead men were being cut down and placed back into the wagon. Roberts was sitting next to the cabin under guard, watching in terror, the vigilance committee having apparently decided to spare him the noose, in some perverted sense of justice.

The young deputy picked up his damaged hat and rubbed the top of his head. He had a large goose egg, but when he checked his fingers there was no blood.

He scanned the countryside and the road out of town for the prospector but saw nothing and hurried back to where he'd tied his horses.

At least it had been horses. Now it was horse. The roan was gone again.

CHAPTER

FIFTEEN

Uncle Billy forced himself out of the sack and stumbled with eyes closed into the kitchen to put the coffee on. He stoked the potbellied stove that was in the corner of the kitchen and stood next to it, warming himself and trying to wake up.

He thought about his days on the Mississippi, working on the riverboat that carried people and goods up and down the muddy, turbulent waterway. He had enjoyed those days, doin' for the captain, seeing the sights, the cities, the people.

Billy remembered some of the characters he had met. The river people; the charlatans who thrived on the gullibility of the public; the banjo pickers; the card sharps; the runaway slaves he had hid amongst the cargo.

Lessons had been learned and character developed by life on the river. As a free Negro traveling through slave states he had known fear, resentment and hatred, compassion and love.

It was his wife who had finally brought the latter qualities out in him the most. Men were men, she had told him, and you can't expect them to be any more than what they are. If a man hates, it's because he was taught as a child to hate. If a man fears, he was taught to fear. The only way to fight it is to teach men to love, to tolerate, to trust.

Billy smiled fondly as he sipped his coffee and remembered how she used to get all excited and say only Jesus could really teach those things. Man can do it awhile under his own willpower, but sooner or later he'll drift back to his own ways.

Lasting change, she would say, only comes from God. And he knew she was right. He had to admit it was true, and one day Billy finally realized she had been talking about him all those times, not about someone else. So he gave in to God.

He asked Jesus to save him, to change his heart, that summer day. Not long after that she died. Billy knew she had been sick for a long time. He wondered, as he poured another steaming mug of the dark bitter liquid, if God had kept her alive for as long as He did just so she could get through to him.

Before that day, had he come across the soldier that Page had brought him, he would have let the man die, then justify it by pointing to his coat and saying to himself, *He kept my people in slavery and killed others who were trying to free them.*

Now he realized that all men are in bondage in some way. The slave who trusts God is more free than the man who is a slave to his own passion and hatred.

The slaves were freed in body by the war. Those who wanted to be were always free in their mind and their spirit.

Sudden gunfire startled Billy, and he spilled his coffee. Though still in his nightshirt, he raced outside to see what was going on.

These was a crowd of miners milling around outside the entrance to the Queen Anne. The supervisor of the Empire stood with a smoking gun in his upraised arm, and foremen from both companies were just beginning to get up off the ground and dust themselves off.

They were both battered, bruised, and bloody. The onlookers— men from both companies—threw jeers and accusations at each other.

Billy approached the superintendent who fired the warning shot.

"Mr. Butler, what's going on?"

"I don't know, Billy, but I aim to find out." He turned to the combatants. "Thomas, what gives?"

Thomas Wellman was the foreman of the crew working in the Empire mine. That is, the crew that was *supposed* to be working in the Empire mine.

"They're jumping our claim!"

This immediately instigated another round of arguing, name-calling, pushing and shoving. Billy was almost amused at the behavior of the men, except these disputes often had a way of becoming serious. When gold was involved, hot tempers frequently erupted into violence.

It took a few more shots from Butler's pistol to quiet the group again. Billy stepped into the middle of the men. Despite his unique outfit no one laughed; they weren't in the mood, but even if they were, they had a little fear and a lot of respect for him.

"Okay, quiet down, men. We ain't gonna get nothin' figgered out like this. Lemme have the foremen and supers come with me to the boardin' house. The rest of you men go find somethin' to do . . . besides fight, Ah mean."

He marched back to the boarding house, followed closely by the chosen men.

"Git yourselves some coffee whilst Ah put on mah pants," he said when they were all in the kitchen. He ambled off to his room but was back in no time, his nightshirt tucked into baggy, woolen trousers.

"Okay, gents, what's this all about?"

"They're diggin' under our claim," said Wellman.

"No, you got it backwards," said the Queen Anne foreman, Aaron Goodhew. "You're diggin' under ours."

"How do either of you figger this?" Billy asked.

"Yes," echoed Fred Smith, super for the Queen Anne. "How *do* you know this?"

"Easy," said Wellman. "When we went in to muck at the face of the south end crosscut, there was no floor left. A big hole was opened up right into *their* crosscut, comin' from the other direction. They was tunneling into our claim!"

"And we say you was tunnelin' into our claim!" asserted Goodhew. "That's where the dispute is."

"So you two decided to come up to the surface and decide it with fists?" asked Billy.

"Well, not exactly," admitted Wellman. "We was startin' to talk about it and then we got kinda heated up, the men started yellin' and Goodhew questioned my heritage."

"I questioned your heritage?" Goodhew said, his voice getting louder. "What about the names you called me?"

Wellman stood up suddenly and Goodhew followed suit, but both supers dragged them back down.

"Ah can see how gentlemanly the two of you is," Billy said.

"Well," said Butler slowly, "when it comes to gettin' miners to do their work, a hot-tempered foreman is just what the doctor ordered."

"Anyway," interrupted Smith, "we need to get this resolved. I say it's our claim."

"As do I," said Wellman.

"It seems to me," said Billy, "that all we need to do is get a surveyor to work this out."

The supervisor for the Empire had been quiet so far but cleared his throat loudly as he prepared to speak.

"Mr. O'Hara, it's not as easy as that. Anybody who finds a vein has a right to follow it wherever it goes."

"Not onto someone else's legitimate claim!" said Smith.

"We don't know that we done that," defended Wellman.

"All I can say is, we're followin' our vein and don't git in our way!" said Goodhew.

Butler stood up. "I suggest, men, that you take precautions. We will protect our claim." His tone was ominous and unmistakable.

"There ain't no need for bloodshed," Billy said.

"And there won't be any if they git off'n our claim!" said Wellman.

"It ain't your claim!" shouted Goodhew, jumping up.

"You heard our warning!" Butler put on his hat and stormed out, followed by his foreman.

Smith and Goodhew wasted no time hanging around Billy's kitchen. They stomped away, muttering.

Billy didn't like the look of this. Two groups of greedy men squaring off to fight over a vein of gold. The only consolation was that there were no gunmen in town to hook up with one side or the other.

He heard a horse out front and went into the parlor of the boarding house. Hoping it was the new town constable promised by Sheriff Taylor in his letter, he stepped out onto the porch.

His heart sank.

The rebel soldier was back, and he was wearing a gun.

Matt was getting tired of his head hurting and his horse being stolen. If it wasn't for the money, he'd have given up, let the man have the horse, and gone home to Bridgeport and the Emporium.

But he was close to the money, too close to give up now. With only a few minutes head start the prospector ought to be easy to catch.

Matt shouted at his mount and dug in his heels. He rode wildly northbound but hadn't gone far when he realized he was being followed.

Without slowing he turned his head to see who was on his trail. It was Charlie Jack. Matt reined up sharply, and Blister slid to an abrupt stop on his haunches like a cow pony, raising a thick cloud of trail dust.

Blister shook his head and snorted as Matt turned him in place. Charlie Jack slowed his pace, then stopped abreast of Matt.

"Where go in so big hurry?"

"That prospector took my horse again."

Charlie Jack laughed loud and long. Matt was mad at first but soon had to smile and finally let out with a few chuckles.

"We find," said Charlie Jack, slapping Matt on the thigh. "Then we tie reins to Matthew's belt."

"Thanks," Matt said. "You know they hung two of them convicts."

"Yes. I see ropes when I come back."

"Where were you?"

"Looking for other three. Two in Fish Canyon. Other gone, Death Valley."

"You goin' after him?"

Charlie shook his head. "Not Death Valley." Charlie looked carefully at the road. "There, your horse."

"How do you know that?"

Charlie dismounted and knelt down. Matt did so too and Charlie pointed to a horseshoe print.

"See mark? Front hoof, your horse."

"You recognize that, huh? That's really somethin'!"

"Not much."

"Where do you think he's goin'?"

"Back to camp. He ride mule from camp, no bring camp with him, ride horse, lead mule back."

"Can you help me find him?" Matt was almost pleading.

"Half day only. I need go Fandango."

Matt gave him a funny look. "What?"

"Paiute Fandango, Mono Lake. That what white man call it. We go every year. Sing, race horse, eat, chase squaw."

Charlie smiled in anticipation as he got back on the sorrel. He was obviously expecting a great time.

"Sounds like what white men do to have fun," Matt lamented.

Charlie pulled his horse around to the north and started walking it.

"White man not all bad," he said over his shoulder with a grin.

Matt rode after the Paiute, trying to read the tracks the Indian was following; tracks that led, he hoped, to his horse, gear and money. The convicts taken care of, he could now concentrate on his true objective.

The prospector made it back to his camp in about two hours. Figuring the deputy would be on his trail he broke camp quickly, wanting to put as much time between them as possible.

He was mad at himself and mumbled out loud. When he took the horse the first time it was just some green kid who needed to be taught a lesson. Was he a deputy then? The prospector hadn't seen the star until the kid turned around at the hanging, after he had grabbed him.

He had saved the kid's life. Why, you just don't go wading through a bunch of vigilantes to stop a lynching! Anybody that did got strung up themselves, badge or no badge. So he grabbed the fool kid, not even knowing who or what he was, not recognizing him until he turned around. Knocking him on the head was more a reaction than anything else.

When the prospector saw the kid's face he knew he was in for it. He had to get out of the state for sure. His mule wasn't good enough, and then he saw the roan. *Danged if it ain't the same horse!* he thought to himself at the time.

He had taken a chance going to Bishop, but he needed supplies. Now it turned out he had to run for it, but at least he had suitable transportation.

He hustled about his campsite, tossing his stuff into bags and hurriedly folding his little pup tent. He wasn't concerned about the trivial items; with the money he had found in the bottom of the kid's saddlebags, he could stake himself again, once he was clean away.

The prospector tossed his gear over the mule, which objected to the rush it was being put under. The prospector knocked the animal on the side of the head.

"There's more where that come from, Bonehead! Now you hold still!"

He adjusted the load and hastily tied it on, then jumped on the roan and rode off with the pack animal in tow, its lead rope tied around the roan's saddlehorn. Staying off the road, he fled east toward Nevada.

Charlie Jack stopped and slid off his sorrel as Matt rode up alongside.

"What is it?" the young deputy asked.

"He leave road here." Charlie looked out across the rolling terrain to the cliffs in the distance. He walked back to Matt.

"See notch in cliff?"

He pointed east. Matt leaned forward in the saddle and squinted. He could barely see the cliff, much less the notch.

"Okay, yes, I see it," he said finally.

"He head that way, not far."

Matt was concerned. Charlie spoke like he wasn't going any further with him.

"Are you leaving now?"

"Yes. Time go, and time for Matthew Page to do for himself."

Charlie Jack's words stung, even though they were not harsh. It was true, Matt knew. He *had* been relying on others, especially Charlie Jack.

The Paiute grabbed his saddle's horn and cantle and jumped smoothly onto the horse. He held the reins lightly and backed his horse until he was next to Matt. He extended his hand and Matt took it.

"Good-bye, Matthew. You will find him."

"Thanks, Charlie. You taught me a lot. I owe you a great deal."

"I know. Please, *you* remember when you get saddlebag back. Part mine!"

"I won't forget," Matt said.

Charlie Jack grinned and winked, then rode off toward Mono Lake, his horse kicking up dirt and rock.

Matt took a swig from his canteen as a sage grouse skittered through the brush, chased by another one. Matt evaluated the sky.

Broken clouds were beginning to move in, rolling and tumbling across an azure sky like fat circus tumblers.

There was a lot of daylight left, and he knew the prospector would be headed east, out of California, and could probably make it by nightfall. It was today or never.

Taking a deep breath, Matt kicked Blister into life and guided him off the road and across open ground. Forced to track for himself, Matt rode slowly, his eyes fixed on the dirt in front of him.

The trail was easier to follow than he thought, there being two animals, a horse and a mule, leaving distinctively different tracks, yet staying side-by-side. The trail left by the fleeing prospector meandered around rocks and sagebrush but continued basically due east.

He's in a hurry, thought Matt. *He's not gonna try to be cagey or trick me.* He pulled off his hat, wiped the sweat off his brow and took another sip from the canteen. He poured a little water into his hat and gave it to the Morgan.

Oh please, God, help me find him. Matt thought about making God some kind of promise to insure His assistance, but he knew himself well enough to admit he probably wouldn't keep it. And God certainly knew it. So Matt just said *amen* and left it at that.

Just then he crested a small rise and found himself on a sloping bluff overlooking a valley. Desolate and sparsely vegetated, Matt had no trouble picking out a disturbance in the sand about three or four hundred yards below him. He was surprised he could see the tracks leading away from it and disappearing over a distant hill.

He urged Blister down the loose soil of the rise, its rear legs locked in almost a sitting position as it slid downhill in the soft sand. As the ground flattened out the horse regained its footing, snorted its disapproval, and took off at a run without being coaxed.

Matt reined up hard at the area he had seen and came off his mount in an even motion. Holding the reins, he led the horse as he walked up to what had obviously been a campsite.

There were several items strewn about the ground: empty cans, some dirty cookware, a sock with holes.

"He was here, all right, Blister ol' boy," Matt said out loud, patting the horse on the neck.

He started to climb back on the horse when he noticed something else. He walked over to it, curious. The corner of a small piece of paper was visible, the rest covered by sand with a boot print in it.

Matt picked it up carefully. It looked like an old, brown tintype. He carefully blew the sand off. Upside down, it looked like the photograph of a woman.

He turned it around and looked at her, so stunned by what he saw that his legs gave out and he sat down hard in the sand, his eyes wide and his mouth open.

It was a photograph of his mother.

Matt shook his head. *No,* he told himself, *this fell out of my saddlebags.* He hesitatingly reached into his pocket, just to confirm it was empty, but his heart increased its thumping when he felt the stiff piece of paper. Pulling it out somewhat apprehensively, he held it next to the photo he had found in the sand.

They were identical.

CHAPTER

SIXTEEN

Matt was astounded. *This can't be!* He studied the photo again to be sure. No, there she was, sitting in a chair wearing her favorite dress he remembered from when he was little. They had had the same photo on the mantel over their fireplace.

Matt shook his head to clear it. With questions racing through his head, making his mind reel, he stuffed the photos into his shirt pocket, got up and mounted the Morgan.

With an almost overpowering urgency he kicked the horse into motion and raced off to find the prospector. It was now more than a question of his roan and his money. Something more was at stake. *Where did this guy get a picture of my mother?*

Following the trail was easy now that Matt was familiar with it, and he guessed they wouldn't be going very fast, since the mule was now laden.

He rode at top speed, Blister yielding to his master without hesitation. The horse ran with a easy gait, swift, smooth, and sure. It wasn't long before Matt picked out the dark silhouettes of the prospector and the roan, leading the pack animal, about a mile ahead.

As Matt came within a hundred yards, the prospector suddenly jerked around in the saddle and saw the deputy sheriff bearing down on him. He jumped off the horse and ran behind a large rock. He took out his gun, the one the Confederate soldier didn't get.

Matt saw this and rode another fifty yards, then reined up the Morgan and dove just as he heard a shot and the bullet whizzed by his ear.

Matt crawled for cover as two more bullets hit the sand beside him. He pulled his Peacemaker out of the holster and fired once in the direction of the man, trying intentionally to miss by a mile. He didn't want to kill him, whoever it was. He wanted some answers first.

Another shot was fired by the prospector, but Matt couldn't tell where the bullet went.

That's four. Matt fired again, aiming about ten yards off to the man's left.

Again the prospector fired and missed.

Five.

The prospector put his gun between his knees, opened the breech, and extracted the five spent cartridges, replacing them with fresh rounds. This wasn't an easy task with only one arm and it took him a few minutes.

As soon as it was loaded he fired one round. It missed.

Six!

Matt stood up and walked toward the prospector's rock, pointing his gun at it.

"You're dry!" he shouted. "Put your hands up and come on out."

The prospector peeked out but didn't reveal himself. *I'll wait till he's close then take him out.* He hated to do it to the kid, but he had no choice. He wasn't going to prison, and the kid just wouldn't leave him alone.

"Come on!" Matt ordered. "Be easy on yourself and give up!"

"I'm comin'!" the prospector lied.

Matt thought the man was up to something, so he took the photo out of his pocket and held it up, hoping the man would see it when he looked.

The prospector stood cautiously, his left arm down at his side, still holding the gun. From where Matt stood it looked as if the prospector's right hand was in his pocket.

"Drop the gun and get them arms up!"

"Gun's empty, like you said, and I ain't got but one arm. This here sleeve's empty." He noticed the photo. "Whatcha got there, deputy?"

"No arm?"

"Lost it at Vicksburg. *Hey,* that's my picture, boy!"

Both of them were so intrigued with each other that they momentarily forgot they were having a shootout.

"Vicksburg?"

"I said that's my picture."

"But it's *my mother*!" He continued walking slowly forward and pulled out his photo, holding them both up.

Both men were suddenly silent, the prospector now stunned, considering the possibilities.

"Just so you know, deputy, I'm still loaded." He fired a round into the ground to prove it.

Matt stopped.

"What's your name?" the prospector asked. "And where are you from?"

"Matthew Page, from Kankakee, Illinois."

The prospector's shoulders sagged, and his gun dropped harmlessly into the dirt.

The man's reaction forced Matt to think, and reality hit him like a hammer. His gun hand relaxed, and he stopped walking. Both men knew the truth, and both were speechless. Matt was suddenly dizzy. *No, it can't be!*

"Who are you?" Matt demanded.

"Yer pa."

"Not likely. He was killed at Vicksburg."

The prospector hung his head. "No, I just lost this arm," he said quietly.

It was true. Matt knew it. Somehow, his father had survived the war, but had *deserted his wife and child*. Matt was torn between the desire to embrace his long-lost father and the desire to shoot him.

He was so upset by the conflicting emotions that he just stood there, shaking. With a quivering hand, Matt slipped his Colt back into his holster. He was hurt, angry, confused. *Why didn't I recognize him?* he wondered. The war *had* taken a toll on the man, Matt realized, as had the eight or nine years since then, out here tryin' to squeeze a living out of the rock.

Matt couldn't understand why his father would abandon them.

"Ma's dead," he said abruptly.

Jacob Page looked up at his son, his eyes red and moist. "I loved her, Matthew."

"You had a funny way of showin' it."

"I s'pose it looks that way."

"Why? What happened?"

The prospector grabbed his empty right sleeve with his left hand and showed his son.

"A rebel cannonball took my arm. You can't push a plow or hug your wife with one arm, boy."

It must have hurt, losing an arm like that. But why pretend to be dead? What was it? What made you leave? Not losing an arm! Lots of men lose arms. No, it must be something else. Since you say you loved Ma, it must have been me you wanted to get away from! Matt couldn't control his thoughts. He didn't want to believe this, the thoughts just forced their way into his head.

"You didn't try. You could've tried."

"Yer ma and you deserved better than half a man."

"She didn't remarry. She loved you too much."

The prospector was silent for a moment. "I never thought of that," he said quietly.

"She died of a broken heart. We ran things as best we could for as long as we could. She just couldn't take no more."

There was a strained silence before the prospector spoke again.

"It's good to see you, son." The words sounded forced, apologetic. Matt didn't answer.

"I . . . I'm sorry, Matt."

Matt choked down a lump of anger and pain that had formed in his throat. His eyes burned.

"What for? It's a little late for that."

Jacob Page pawed the ground with a foot. He spoke quietly.

"I s'pose it is." He changed the subject. "Whatcha doin' out west, Matt?"

"Makin' a new life, just like you." He paused. "Only I didn't leave a wife and a son." Matt's face was flushed, and he could feel the heat of it. *Now what do I do?* he wondered. This was too much to deal with all of a sudden. Seeing his father after all these years of thinking the man was dead, only to learn he had actually run out on them. The anger welled up in him, but he tried to choke it down.

"Was you a deputy when I took yer horse?" Jacob Page asked his boy.

"Not the first time. I was when you cold-cocked me at the hangin'."

"I was savin' your life then. They'd a strung you up if you'd tried to stop the proceedin's."

"I guess I should say 'thank you.'"

"No need. Where you goin' now?"

"To Bodie, probably. Why?"

"You'll be wantin' your horse and your money." He turned to go to the roan.

Matt thought a second.

"Wait."

The prospector stopped and turned.

Matt looked at his feet, then back up at his father.

"It ain't my money or my horse. It's yours. I sold the farm when Ma died. It's rightfully yours, since you're alive."

"I gave it up," the elder Page said. "You made the farm whatever it was. Wouldn't be right fer me to keep it."

"I'm gonna have to pull rank on you," Matt said. He walked back to Blister and pulled himself up, stuffing the pictures of his mother into his shirt. He sat motionless in the saddle, still not able to believe it, and stared at his father.

Without another word, he turned the horse and rode off to the north. Before he was out of the prospector's sight tears welled up in his eyes. The next few miles passed by unseen.

The prospector watched his son until he disappeared, remorse settling over him like a blanket.

Uncle Billy sat in the kitchen and tried to think of a way to avert a tragedy. Right now a fight was brewing. Both companies were fortifying the entrances to their shafts, and both had posted guards inside the mines at the place where the two crosscuts met. Unbeknownst to their respective supervisors, however, the guards sat together underground, playing cards by the light of two coal lanterns.

Work in both mines had stopped dead. With the claim in question and the crosscuts unstable because of their proximity, Billy feared the dispute would be decided by force. Whichever side had the most men standing their ground while the other side retreated could go on mining.

What was needed was a lawman. What was definitely *not* needed was a man with a gun and a chip on his shoulder, ready to throw both into the defense of whichever side would pay the most.

Even though Billy worked for the Empire Company, he tried to stay objective. The Empire owned the boarding house, but men from both companies stayed in it. He didn't automatically think the Empire had the rights to the ground in question.

This was something to be decided by a surveyor and a court of law. Not by a gun.

But men being what they are, O'Hara was afraid the gun would win out. The men were hot, ready to fight, and there was no one with enough legal authority to stop them.

He didn't have time to personally get word to Sheriff Taylor. He couldn't leave. Someone had to stay there who would accurately report what went on to the law when they did show up so they could react properly. So he sent someone to fetch him.

Billy stood up and looked out the window. He could see the forts both companies had thrown up. They had used whatever planking they could scrape together, nailing it up around the entrances to their shafts, leaving only small slits to shoot through.

They all owned guns, but none of the men were very accomplished with them. These were men who spent their days underground and their nights in the saloon. If they did any shooting, it was usually at close range, two to three feet, and for a good reason—they had been personally insulted. Half the time they fired until their guns were empty, then bought each other a drink, both of them having missed.

Bodie's saloon was across the street from the boarding house, and O'Hara watched as the soldier walked in after tying his horse to the rail out front.

The soldier stepped through the batwings into the nearly deserted establishment. Everyone worked for one or the other of the mines—or the mill—and with the battle heating up they were getting ready, although the soldier was unaware of this.

He looked around at the stragglers and sauntered up to the bar. It was completely out of place for a camp like this. The building itself was thrown up out of planks, but the bar was Spanish mahogany, highly shellacked and long, with a brass footrest.

The bartender was wiping it with a towel, which he did constantly, even when it wasn't wet or dirty.

"What'll you have there, friend?"

"Whiskey."

The bartender set him up a glass and poured it full of rotgut.

"Passin' through?"

"Could be," said the soldier. He downed the drink in one swig and slammed the glass down on the bar.

"Why's this place so quiet?"

"Ev'ryone's gettin' ready fer the big fight!"

"Fight?"

"Yeah. The two minin' comp'nies is arguin' over a claim. Seems their tunnels crossed, they both sez th'other's infringin'."

"What do you think they aim to do?"

"Don't know, but they'll prob'ly call each other a bunch o' names, fire a few rounds in the gen'ral vicinity o' th'other side, jes' to make 'em keep they heads down, then stall until the law comes."

The soldier thought it over. "How long until the law gets here?"

"Oh, not until tomorrow. Unca Billy dispatched a rider to git the sheriff, but he's in Bridgeport."

"Hmmm." The soldier paid for the drink. *That meddlin' Negro again.* "Thanks."

He walked out into the morning sun and made his way to the Queen Anne.

His approach had not gone unnoticed. Before he was within fifty feet a voice called out. All he could see was a gun barrel sticking out between slats of wood.

"That's close enough, stranger!"

He stopped and held up his hands.

"Ah came to talk."

"What about?"

"Ah can help you."

"Don't need no help."

"You're wrong. You need someone who can shoot straight and don't know the man he's firin' at, so he don't hesitate."

"We won't hire a killer. Git outta here!"

The soldier backed off slowly. This was going to be harder than he thought. Sheer force wasn't going to impress these men. Maybe he'd have better luck at the Empire, but he'd have to change his tactics a little.

He made his way over there, taking a cirular route so they wouldn't know where he was going.

His reception at the Empire was different. He made it all the way to the fort unchallenged and knocked on the boards.

"Whaddya want?"

"Ah understand you could use a gun."

"What makes you think that?"

"The Queen Anne. Ah overheard some of them plannin' an attack on you tonight. They're gonna burn you out, kill as many a you as it takes."

"That so?" The soldier was let into the fort.

"I'm Thomas Wellman, the foreman," said the man who opened the door. "This is Mr. Butler. He runs the place."

"Evenin'."

Hats were tipped quickly, introductions not very relevant right now.

"What do you propose?" asked Wellman, getting right down to business. "And how much is it going to cost us?"

"In the first place, Ah ain't got no interest in this fight. Ah'm just lookin' to make a few dollars. Ah don't care who wins—right now, that is. Soon as Ah'm on the payroll that'll change. In the second place Ah don't say no more and Ah don't do nothin' without cash in hand."

"Okay, how much you askin'?" Butler said. "And what will we be gettin' for our . . . investment?"

"Five hundred dollars is the sum." the soldier said.

"Whew!" Wellman exclaimed. "That's an awful lot of money."

"Not compared to what you're gonna get outta that mine. And there's no risk to you. Ah'll do all the dirty work."

"And what dirty work do you propose to do?"

"Why don't you let me worry about that?"

"I don't know . . ."

"What have you got to lose? Ah ain't gonna murder no one.

Just tell me who the head man is at the Queen Anne and Ah'll get together with him. When Ah talk sense to him, he'll listen."

"You think it'll work without gunplay?" Butler asked.

"That's up to them, but Ah think so."

"And if it don't?"

"That's what guns and forts are for, ain't it? Why'd you and them build yourselves forts and hunker down in 'em with guns? Don't look like you was plannin' an arm wrestlin' match to decide this. Thing is, with me you got insurance with no real risk to yourselves. What do you say?"

"Well . . . all right. But we're not gonna give you the whole five hundred now. We ain't stupid! You could ride right on outta here and we'd be just where we are, only poorer. We'll give you half now, the other half when they take down their fort and block off their crosscut so they can't go in it no more."

"Deal," said the soldier.

Wellman went to the safe in the mine office nearby and came back with the money. He counted it out to the soldier who stuffed it into a pocket.

"I'll be back tonight," he said, and left the Empire fort.

"Keep your eyes on him, men," Wellman said. "Make sure he don't try to leave town."

CHAPTER

SEVENTEEN

The soldier strolled back down the middle of the street toward the saloon, knowing they would be watching. He was feelin' his oats, and planning all this treachery made him thirsty. When he walked in the bartender acknowledged him with a nod and set up a whiskey without being asked.

"Thanks," the soldier said. He slugged down the liquid and wiped his mouth with his sleeve. "Tell me, friend. Do you know who's the head man for the Queen Anne? When this little dispute is over, I'd like to get some work."

"That'd be Mr. Smith. You're in luck. That's him over there." He nodded in the direction of a table in the corner which was occupied by a dark man with a short mustache, wearing a bowler. He was sitting with another man.

"Thanks," said the soldier. He put a coin on the bar and picked up the bottle and two glasses. "I'll take this."

He walked over to the table where Fred Smith sat nursing a glass of his own. The other man wasn't drinking.

"Mornin', friend," the soldier said. "Mind if I sit down?"

"Help yourself." Smith said without looking at him.

The soldier poured two whiskeys and pushed them across the table to the men. Smith glanced up at him without saying anything for a moment, then spoke.

"Something we can do for you?"

"More like the other way around, Mr. Smith."

"Look, I'm not much for games. I prefer people to speak their mind. You got something to say, say it."

"Have it your way." The soldier leaned forward. "Ah understand you and the Empire are having . . . shall we say, a little disagreement."

"That isn't news. You don't live here, do you?"

"No, Ah'm just passin' through, but Ah think Ah can be of service to you."

"How's that?"

"Ah overheard someone from the Empire sayin' they was gonna burn you out tonight."

"That so? Who might that have been?"

"Don't rightly know his name. He was a portly little fella, big mustache, slicked down hair, kinda mad lookin'."

"Thomas Wellman," said Aaron Goodhew, who picked up the drink the soldier offered and sipped at it.

"Hmmm." Smith was interested. *So it has come to this, has it?*

"What's your interest in this?" Smith asked. "You want to be paid for your information?"

"No, the information is free. Ah just thought you could use some help. Ah'm sure you'd like to handle this peaceable, but it don't look like that's gonna happen, so you need someone like myself to make sure things don't get outta hand." He paused. "To make sure your interests are protected."

"What do you aim to do?"

"Well, Ah was thinkin' of goin' to them and tellin' them plain out that you know about their plan and if they aim to dish out violence that you'll be more'n happy to counter it. Ah'm sure they'll get the drift." He patted his gun that was stuck in his waistband.

"I don't like the idea of shooting it out, but I'll be hung if I'm gonna let them intimidate us out of our rightful claim!" He looked at the soldier. "Now how much would this . . . *help* cost us?"

"You tell me. What's the claim worth? If Ah can insure the claim for you, would five hundred dollars be too high a price?"

"Sounds fair. What do you think, Aaron?"

"If he can produce."

"Oh, Ah will. But just to give you my guarantee, Ah'll only ask for half down. You hold the rest until the Empire withdraws their claim to the ground."

"That's reasonable. Meet me in my office in half an hour."

Smith and Goodhew got up and left the saloon, leaving the soldier alone to finish the bottle. He leaned back in his chair and put his boots on the table.

"To greed," he said to himself, raising his glass before downing the contents. "And the things it makes people do."

The soldier picked up his down payment from the Queen Anne supervisor and sauntered back up the street. There was no need to take the long way around this time. Both sides knew he was talking to the other, and both sides believed him to be on their payroll, which, of course, he was.

He laughed when he thought about how they each figured to have exclusive rights to him, not knowing there were really *three* sides to this issue: the Empire's, the Queen Anne's, and *his*. The way the soldier figured it, no matter how it turned out, he had five hundred dollars and someone else set up to take the blame.

He knocked at the Empire fort, just in case he was being watched by someone from the Queen Anne, and was let in.

"How'd it go?" Wellman asked.

"Well, Mr. Smith talked a strong hand, but he ain't holdin' one. Ah think they are ready to cut a deal."

"We don't want a deal. We want them off our claim!"

"Calm down, Mr. Wellman. Ah told them you'd be willin' to talk. That's just the first step. If they know you mean business, they'll do whatever you tell them. Mr. Smith, why, he's a reasonable man. He'll see the wisdom. It's that other man Ah'm worried about."

"Goodhew?"

"Yeah, that's him. He don't seem like he wants to give in so easy. He may cause some trouble."

"What do you suggest we do?"

"Well, Ah was thinkin' we could . . . well, remove him from the picture . . . sort of."

"Kill him? I don't cotton to no killin' in cold blood."

"No, no," the soldier hedged. "Ah weren't suggesting that. Ah mean, just take him out away from town until this is settled. You know, maybe coax him out on a false pretense."

"That would be okay, I suppose."

"Good. Don't you worry none. Ah got it all planned out. Now, Mr. Smith says he'll meet you in the morning at the saloon. Ah told him you'd be there."

"Fair enough."

The soldier started to leave.

"Where are you goin'?" Wellman asked.

"To my room at the boardin' house. Ah want to clean up a mite."

"What if they try something tonight?"

"Oh, they'd have to be mighty treacherous to do a thing like that."

Matt loped his horse toward Bodie, anxious to put as many miles as he could between himself and the prospector. He hesitated to call him his father, even in his mind. His eyes burned, and his throat was tight.

Why, God? Why did this happen? How could a man that says he loved his wife just leave her like that, and a son, too?

Matt was hurt and angry at his father—and confused. He couldn't understand the thinking behind a desertion like that, and he didn't know if he ever wanted to understand it.

He just wanted to forget it, to go back to the way things were a couple weeks ago.

But he knew he couldn't go back. Life was here and now, and in the future. The past couldn't be changed and could hardly be forgotten, however much he wished it.

Matt decided to choke down his feelings and get on with things. Maybe he'd have a talk with Uncle Billy when he got to Bodie. He trusted Billy, and the older man seemed like he knew a lot about life and maybe could help.

The conflicting emotions he was experiencing were overwhelming him. The countryside was a blur as he rode. The hate, the hope for the future, the longing to see Sarah, the fear of the last few days, the shock of seeing his father, the exhilaration of his new job . . . Matthew Page was a tornado of feelings, so many that he couldn't really deal with any of them.

Then he thought about something his mother used to tell him: "God is the author of peace. He can bring peace to your life in the midst of turmoil." *I'm certainly in turmoil,* he thought.

The words haunted him. Peace. Inner peace.

But she also warned him that God wasn't a magician. He didn't just grant your wish, then let you live like the dickens from then on. He only respected a real commitment.

Matt pulled Blister up sharply and pulled the picture of his mother out of his shirt. As he looked at her, more of her words came rushing into his head.

"One of these days, Matthew, you'll have to make a decision. I don't know when it will be, but you'll know. You'll feel something inside of you, a voice asking 'Do you want peace?' What will you say, Matt? What will you tell God?"

They were her last words to him. The next morning she was dead.

Matt steeled himself against the tears that were forming. This was no time to blubber like a woman. He had too much to think about. The man who used to be his father, who had abandoned him and his mother and let them think he was dead, was alive after all and had been living in California all this time. A wave of bitterness rose up in Matt, and he swallowed back his mother's words.

Stuffing the photograph back in his shirt, he heeled the Morgan into a trot.

It was dusk when Matt crested the hill east of Bodie. As the setting sun ignited the horizon in a line of fire, dusting the the rim rock with color like campfire embers, he could barely see the wooden buildings of the sleepy town.

About all he could make out was the yellow glow of the coal oil lamps through the windows. He urged his mount on down the slope, and by the time he reached the edge of town, it was completely dark. The stars were popping out in a cloudless sky, as plentiful as mosquitoes in July, and the moon was coming up full, casting enough light to read a newspaper. Of course, that didn't much matter here in Bodie since most of the men couldn't read.

As Matt was tying his horse to the rail the door opened and a shaft of light spread out onto the porch, then was mostly blocked by the large man who moved into the doorway.

"Matthew? You back?"

"Yessir, Uncle Billy." Page stepped onto the porch and took a seat in one of the rockers.

"How'd it go? You catch them convicts?"

The deputy sat without rocking and stared blankly across the street at nothing in particular.

"Ah say, Matthew," Billy repeated, "did you catch them convicts?"

"Huh?" Matt turned to focus on the big innkeeper. "Oh, yeah. The convicts. They mostly got away, at least for a time. One was seen on his way to Death Valley, they think. Three are caught and being sent back."

"And the other two?"

"They were hung in Bishop by a vigilance committee."

"Oh, mah," Billy said. "Why'd they do that?"

"The convicts killed a pony rider a few days before we caught up to them at Monte Diablo, then one of 'em shot a member of the posse in the head as he lie injured on the ground. In cold blood, Billy."

"You didn't . . ." Billy started slowly.

Matt flashed him a brow-furrowed glance. "Of course not. I meant to stop it, but . . ."

"But what, Matthew?"

The deputy paused for a moment, then said, "I met that old prospector again. He cold-cocked me to keep from stopping the hanging."

"The one who stole your horse?"

Matt nodded.

"Well, you was hopin' to meet him. That's good, ain't it?"

"Maybe, maybe not."

"What do you mean?"

Matt took a deep breath. "He's my father."

"Your *what*?" Billy sat down, transfixed. "But your pa's dead."

"I thought so, too. But he ain't."

Billy thought for a second. "Well, that's wonderful!"

Matt looked down at the floor.

"Ain't it?" Billy asked.

"I don't know," admitted Matt.

"Ah guess that would be quite a shock. But, hey, he's your pa! You only get one."

"He deserted us during the war. Made us think he was dead."

Billy was silent.

"How do I deal with it? I want to hate him—I do hate him—but I know that ain't right."

"That ain't what God wants," Billy cautioned.

Matt was silent, his head hanging as he inspected his dirty fingernails.

"Well," Billy said slowly. "While you're thinkin' on that, Ah got something to show you." He fished in his shirt pocket for something, then handed Matt the letter from Sheriff Taylor, the one Matt had delivered on his way to join the posse.

"Go 'head, Matthew, read it."

Matt opened the letter, puzzled, and read out loud. "Billy. I hired a deputy and I'm going to put him in Bodie. He's going to ride around for a few days to get the feel of the countryside, I expect he'll get himself right into the thick of things." Matt grinned sheepishly and kept reading. "If he makes it through and comes back to Bodie with a star still pinned to his shirt, tell him for me that he's the new town constable in Bodie. It's a fixed post, no roaming around. Sincerely, Sheriff Taylor."

Matt looked up at Billy, who was beaming.

"Congratulations, Constable." Billy extended his hand and Matt, somewhat overwhelmed, reached up slowly to take it.

"I . . . I . . . What does this mean?"

"Well, you're still a deputy sheriff, assigned to Bodie as constable. It's not a promotion, actually, it's just an assignment."

"Should I take it?"

"Ah hope you do. We need someone like you here."

"Thanks," Matt said quietly, then fell silent again before saying, "Billy, what should I do about my father?"

"Nothin'."

"Huh?"

"You need to do somethin' 'bout *you*, Matthew."

"Me? I don't get it."

"Are you a Christian, Matthew?"

"My mama raised me one. I suppose so."

"It don't work that way, Matthew. You can't slip into Heaven on your mama's apron string. You're a good man, Matthew, no question 'bout that. Your mama raised you to be honest, dependable, generous; but that don't save you. Lots of honest people are goin' to hell in a handbasket. You gotta be forgiven of your sins, like the Good Book says, and you gotta forgive those who sinned against you."

"It's hard to forgive *him*," Matt protested. "He deserted us."

"No question 'bout it, your pa don't deserve to be forgiven. But neither do you."

Matt looked at him funny.

"It's true," Billy continued. "You don't earn salvation by bein' good. God don't save you because you help folks, or don't cheat at cards, or 'cause your mama's saved. It's a gift because of what Christ did on the cross, dyin' an all."

"Boy, this is all so difficult to understand."

Billy nodded. "Read the Holy Scriptures, Matthew. It'll come to you. I think God's callin' you, son. When you hear Him, answer. In the meantime, we got us a situation here. As our new constable, you're gonna have to do something about it."

Matt gave his head a shake. Billy was sure jumping around, topic-wise. "What's going on?"

"The two minin' companies, the Empire and the Queen Anne, are fightin' over a claim. They were both dug down about a hundred feet and started crosscuts, more or less towards each other, both of 'em followin' a vein, so they say."

"Uh oh. Didn't they know they were headed toward each other?"

"Miners ain't in the habit of tellin' the competition where the gold is. The trouble started when a blast in the face of the Empire's south end crosscut opened a hole in the floor of the Queen Anne's east crosscut, which was goin' right over it."

"What did they do?"

"What all peace-lovin', sensible men do. They assembled outside and started yellin', cussin', and callin' each other names and fightin'. We broke it up and Ah tried to get the men in charge to come to some sort of solution, but they wouldn't have it. They built themselves forts around the mouth of their shafts, and Ah think they aim to shoot it out."

"I'll have to have a talk with them."

"Ah tried that. Besides, there's more."

"What?"

"The soldier's back in town. Come in today. Ah got a bad feelin' about this. Ah think he's gonna stir up some—"

Billy was cut off by an explosion.

Matt and Uncle Billy tore outside. Men were shouting and running up the street. A column of dark smoke was rising up from the Empire's office, and the fort was a shambles. Men were staggering away from the rubble, their clothes tattered and covered with soot.

It looked like the office took the brunt of the blast. The fort was knocked down by the concussion. Some of the men had obvious injuries, others appeared to just be stunned.

Billy went to work patching them up while Matt found a man who wasn't badly injured to question. He kneeled down beside the miner, who had found a piece of comfortable-looking ground to stretch out on.

"What happened?" Matt asked.

"We got blowed up."

"Did you see anything?"

"We was sittin' around talkin' when suddenly *kerblooey* there's a big explosion and our fort gets knocked over and we go runnin' and fallin'. It's a wonder we wasn't kilt!"

"Did you see who caused the explosion?"

"No, can't say that I did. But I know who it was."

"Oh? And who might that be?"

"Someone from the Queen Anne, that's who. They's tryin' to scare us off'n the claim!"

Matt stood up and looked around at all the men that had gathered to help. It looked as if everyone in Bodie was there.

Everyone except the soldier.

Matt grabbed the arm of the first man to walk past.

"Who's in charge of the Queen Anne?"

"That'll be Fred Smith." The man looked around. "That's him over there." He pointed to a man standing some distance away with a group of men.

"Thank you." Matt let go of him and walked over to the miners. "I'm Matt Page, Mono County Deputy Sheriff."

"So?" one of the men asked.

"Shut up, John," said Smith. "What can we do for you, Deputy?"

"I've been assigned as constable to Bodie and this whole area. If you want to question that, you can consult Mr. O'Hara. He's got the letter."

"I believe you. What do you want?"

"I'd like to find out what happened here tonight."

"The Empire office blew up," said the man that Smith had called John. Another man snickered.

"I may be young, Mr. Smith, but I ain't stupid and neither are you. You know what I'm talking about."

"If you mean you aim to find out who planted the charge, then go ahead. We didn't do it."

"There's them say you did. You certainly had a motive to disrupt the Empire."

"There's no question the Queen Anne is in a dispute with the Empire, but we have no desire to hurt anyone. We just want them off our claim."

"That's why you built a fort, so you could negotiate?" Matt hooked his thumbs in his gunbelt.

"A fort is defensive, Constable, not offensive."

Matt thought it time to ask a more to-the-point question.

"Then why did you hire a gunman?"

Smith held his composure, but Matt was sure the man's eyes flicked slightly when he heard the question.

"Who says we did?" Smith hoped Matt was fishing. He wasn't going to give anything away to the young law officer. Besides, as far as he knew, no one associated with the Queen Anne *did* do anything. The soldier said he was going to talk to the men from the Empire to keep *them* from trying something. Maybe they did it themselves to make the Queen Anne look guilty.

Matt didn't answer the question. Instead, he said, "If you and your people are innocent, you've got nothin' to worry about. But I suggest you keep yourselves clean."

"Thank you for your concern, Constable." Smith said with a hint of sarcasm. He turned and walked back to the Queen Anne's office with his men.

Matt watched them recede into the darkness. Things were not shaping up well. The Empire obviously thought the men from the Queen Anne were responsible and would now feel justified about retaliating.

Matt wasn't convinced they did it. But if not them, who? Smith wasn't being completely honest about the gunman. He hadn't actually denied hiring one, but his evasive response told Matt he probably had.

Who was it? Matt figured the Confederate soldier had to be behind this somehow. Why hadn't he gone to Bishop from Monte Diablo? Probably because of the convicts. They had made things kind of hot for people with less than honorable intentions. The soldier knew about Bodie. Maybe he came back here to get work of some kind and lucked into the kind of job he could do well: treachery and killing.

If Matt's guess was correct, he'd have to head off retaliation by the Empire. He didn't want this to escalate into a full-scale war.

He turned and walked back to the scene of the explosion, looking for the head man of the Empire.

The scene was still chaotic, but as men got their minor wounds patched up they drifted back to the Empire office to survey the damage. Matt walked over to it and poked around. He could tell the blast was centered near what had been a window by the way the debris was spread out.

Other men were milling around. Casually, Matt struck up a conversation.

"So, what do you think? Dynamite?"

"No question," a miner with his arm in a sling answered. "No tellin' where he got it, but it wasn't an accident. We don't keep explosives in the office."

"You think it was tossed in through the window?"

"Yep."

"Who do you think did it?"

The man looked at Matt suspiciously. "Why you askin' so many—" Matt turned just at that time and the man saw his star. "Oh, you must be the new constable we been hearin' 'bout. If you're gonna figger out who done this, you might as well start at the Queen Anne."

"I've already talked to them."

"And they denied it."

"What do you think?"

"Course. I would too."

"May I ask who you are?" Matt said it without an authoritative tone.

"Certainly. I'm Thomas Wellman, foreman of the Empire's diggin's." Matt didn't offer to shake the man's hand because it was injured. "We heard the men from the Queen Anne was goin' to come over in the morning and try to offer some deal. We was waitin' for that. It's just like them to try treachery."

"You say you 'heard' they were gonna try and deal. Who told you that?"

"We got a go-between."

"One of your men?"

"Yep."

Matt smelled something fishy. "Okay, Mr. Wellman. Thank you. If you hear something, let me know. I intend to get to the bottom of this."

Good luck, greenhorn, thought Wellman. *You'll probably just get your tail feathers shot off.* He nodded to the deputy and walked off.

Matt looked at the debris for a few more minutes then wandered up the street. He ducked into some shadows between buildings and cut through, then circled around and went a little ways up the hill until he had a good view of the Empire's area. He settled down to wait and watch.

He wasn't sure what he was watching for. He figured the Empire's go-between wasn't one of the miners but a hired gunman. It only made sense that both companies would want a shootist on their side. Since the soldier was likely on the side of the Queen Anne, the Empire must have found someone else.

Matt's diligence was not long in being rewarded. The men from the Empire slowly started drifting together, and soon a man who was definitely not a miner stepped out of the shadows and walked up to Wellman.

For a second Matt was startled. Could it be? The coat was unmistakable. Wellman was conferring with the soldier.

CHAPTER

EIGHTEEN

We're payin' you to protect us," Thomas Wellman complained. "We got blowed up whilst you was off doin' whatever you was doin'!"

"Protection, as you put it, is only a small part of what you're payin' me for," said the soldier. "Ah'm here to make sure you have full rights to the claim. Ah must admit, Ah didn't expect that kind of treachery from the Queen Anne's men."

"Well, it's just plain luck no one was hurt bad."

"Oh, Ah don't think it was luck. Whoever tossed that dynamite was just sendin' a warnin'."

"They weren't tryin' to kill us?"

"Not this time. But they mean to do so next time, unless we get them first."

Wellman stroked his chin as he thought about it. "What do you recommend we do?"

"Send it right back."

"Blow up their office?"

"Why not? That'll even it up."

"They'll be expecting that, won't they?"

"Probably. What do *you* suggest? You want to go ahead and start a shootin' war?"

"No, no, I don't want to do that yet." Wellman suddenly

remembered something. "Say, I thought you said they was comin' over in the mornin' to cave in."

"That's what they said," shrugged the soldier. "I thought they meant it. Apparently they were just tryin' to snake us."

"I say we retaliate," offered one of the men.

All the men within earshot offered a chorus of approval.

The soldier shrugged. "There you have it," he said to Wellman.

"Listen, I don't want no dead bodies muckin' up this issue—yet. Besides, the new constable is in town. The law is here, and although he's young and green, who knows what he's capable of."

"A young lawman?" The soldier asked. "About so high, mustache, sandy hair, rides a nice Morgan?"

"I didn't see his horse," Wellman said, "but everything else matches."

The soldier hooted. "Ah already met him a few days ago. He's a candy—"

"That's not what I hear," interrupted a miner. "I just come from Bridgeport this mornin', and the talk there is he single-handedly catched three gun-totin' robbers, killin' one, woundin' the others . . . and he was armed only with a broom!"

There was a buzz in the room as the men spoke amongst themselves about this report. The soldier wasn't impressed.

"Ah encountered him face-to-face. He's a beginner. He won't cause no difficulty."

"You believe what you want," said Wellman. "Just remember, you promised, no risk to us. We'll defend ourselves. We won't start it."

"No problem," assured the soldier. He turned and disappeared into the darkness.

Matt watched as the soldier left Wellman, Butler and their men and went back up the street. Although the soldier kept mostly in the shadows, Matt was able to follow his progress because of the full moon and the cloudless sky. The weather here changed so quickly, he was grateful it had remained clear for so long.

When he saw the soldier walk into the Queen Anne office without knocking first, everything suddenly made sense to him. He began laying out a plan in his mind while he hurried down to the boarding house to talk to Billy.

"What's going on?" Smith demanded of the soldier. "You brought the law down on us, blowing up the Empire like that!"

"In the first place, who says Ah did it?"

"If not you, who?"

The soldier ignored the question. "In the second place, what difference does it make? Ah thought you wanted the Empire eliminated."

"We want them to withdraw from our claim so we can follow the vein," Goodhew corrected.

"But we want it done without bloodshed, if possible," said Smith. "Oh, I'll defend our rights, but I don't want to be accused of starting the bloodshed."

"Do you expect them to retaliate?" Goodhew asked.

"Don't know," said the soldier, "but you should plan for it. Clear this place out. Take everything out of here."

"No, I don't want everything disrupted," said Smith. "We'll post guards. You're one of 'em. Pick someone else to help you."

"You ain't payin' me for that!" the soldier protested.

"The point is, I'm paying you," Smith said. "That means you'll do what I ask. I hired you to protect the Queen Anne. Sitting in this office tonight and intimidating the Empire fellas is the best way you can do that."

"Ah prefer to keep a low profile."

"And I prefer keeping this building intact."

"Look, Ah haven't slept in two days. Ah won't be much good fallin' asleep in a chair here."

Smith looked irritated but said nothing.

"You're payin' me to make sure the Empire gives in," the soldier continued. "They will, and when they do, you'll be free to dig out that vein. Until then, let me handle things my way."

The soldier walked out the door, leaving Smith sorry he'd gotten involved with the man.

"We're out two hundred and fifty dollars," Goodhew observed. "Might as well let him do what he says."

Smith didn't like it, but he said nothing.

Matt entered the boarding house and found Billy in the kitchen.

"What's doin', Matthew . . . Ah mean, Constable?"

"Please, Billy, call me Matt."

"Whatever you say, Matthew," Billy said with a grin.

"The soldier's behind it all."

"Ah figgered so. Who's he workin' for, the Queen Anne?"

"And the Empire."

"*Both?* How's he doin' that?"

"I'm not sure, but I saw him sneakin' into both places to have meetings tonight."

"He's playin' 'em against each other, escalatin' this quicker and higher than it should go."

"He's probably on both their payrolls, and he don't care who wins."

"Whatcha gonna do?"

"I don't think either Smith or Butler will listen to us. We're gonna have to prove it to them."

Matt laid out his plan to O'Hara.

"Ah don't think they'll come voluntarily," Billy said.

"Who said anything about voluntarily?" Matt asked, smiling.

Uncle Billy knocked on the door to the Queen Anne. It was opened cautiously, and all he could see was an eyeball and a gun barrel. Then the doorman recognized him and opened the door wide.

"Sorry, Uncle Billy," he said, lowering the gun. "Can't be too careful."

O'Hara gave him a cold stare. "Ain't s'posed to be this way."

Smith and Goodhew walked over to him.

"What can we do for you, Mr. O'Hara? You here to try and talk some sense into us?" His tone was sarcastic.

"No, sir, Ah already know that ain't likely to work. Ah'm here to ask you to come with me. Constable Page has somethin' he wants you to see."

"Why didn't *he* come for us?"

"He's busy." Billy reached into his coat pocket. "Please, Mr. Smith and Mr. Goodhew, come with me. Ah'm heeled." He pulled a small revolver from the pocket. "Ah don't want to do this, but it's important. Ah insist you come."

"Put that away, Billy. We'll come. We're law-abiding citizens."

Smith turned to his men. "Keep a sharp eye out. We don't want the Empire to try anything tonight.

He walked out the door, followed by Goodhew and O'Hara.

"Where are we going that's so all-fired important?" Smith asked Billy as they strolled up the street.

"Ah believe we're gonna catch us a dynamiter."

Matt approached the Empire's area unopposed and found Butler and Wellman standing with their men.

"Good evening, gentlemen," Page said, touching his hat.

"Evening," said Butler. Wellman just looked at Page.

"I wanted to come by before I bed down for the night and tell you—"

"Tell us not to retaliate against the Queen Anne?" finished Wellman. "Don't waste our time. We're gonna be right here, puttin' our fort back up. Then we'll see what happens."

"Fine," Matt said. "Mr. Butler, could you come with me to the boardin' house? There's somethin' I'd like to talk to you about."

"Talk away."

"Not here. At the boarding house."

"I'm not going anywhere."

"I'm afraid I have to insist."

"You can't force me to go."

"You're right," Matt consented. In one quick motion he drew his gun and held it at Wellman's midsection. The injured man couldn't react. "You're under arrest," Matt declared.

"What's this all about?" Butler asked.

"Suspicion of blowin' up the Empire office."

"Ridiculous!" said Butler.

"I was injured!" protested Wellman.

"A clever ploy," said Matt, "to throw us off the track."

"You can't do this!" asserted Butler.

"Sure I can," said Matt. "You're goin' with me to the boarding house, or Wellman will be arrested and taken to Bridgeport. It's your pick."

"I didn't do it!" Wellman said to Butler. "Go with him!"

"All right, constable," Butler said. "But this better be good, or I'll have you for breakfast."

Matt put away his gun and followed Butler and Wellman out

the door. They walked silently to the boarding house, Page keeping them in the shadows, and went in the back door.

Billy was sitting in the kitchen with Smith and Goodhew. When Butler and Wellman walked in, Goodhew jumped up.

"What's he doin' here?" he shouted, pointing at Wellman.

"What *is* this, Constable?" Butler asked. "Some little trick to get us to negotiate?"

"Sit down, all of you," Matt ordered. No one moved, so Billy put a hand on Goodhew's shoulder and pushed him down. Butler and Wellman took the hint and sat down on their own.

"I don't want you men to talk. Not yet, anyway," Matt said. "I'm tryin' to stop the violence before it gets any worse. No, I know, you all deny everything. Fine. Technically, I suppose, you're correct. You haven't done anything . . . other than prepare yourselves for a shootin' match."

He poured himself a cup of coffee. "Anyone else?" he asked, holding the pot aloft. No one answered. "You're gonna be here awhile, you might as well have some." They still didn't respond. "Have it your way." He put the pot back down.

"No, you haven't done anything," Matt continued. He looked at Smith and Butler. "But I'm positive you've both hired a gunman to protect your interests. The result is gonna be death and destruction. All for some gold."

"There's a lot of gold down there, and we have a right to it. We're following a vein," said Butler.

"So are we," said Smith, "and we have just as much right to follow it as you do."

"And so," Matt concluded, "since you both claim a right to it and only one can have it, you're gonna fight for the rights."

"They *could* back off," said Butler. "We were here first."

"It's our claim!" said Smith.

Matt held his hands up. "I didn't bring you here for this. As I was sayin', you both hired a shootist. And since none of you will admit it, I've arranged a little showdown. I thought it'd be better to let the two of them have it out to decide this issue, rather than jeopardizin' all the good folk in town."

"This is all very interesting," said Smith, "but how are you going to arrange this little demonstration?"

"I've had a message sent to both of your gunmen. They'll think they are meetin' you. It'll be interestin' to see what happens when they find they are facin' each other."

Silence.

"Oh, they'll come," Matt went on, reading their thoughts. "I don't go fishin' without baitin' the hook. I offered—or rather, *you* offered—to pay more money for a special job."

Suddenly, the miners looked worried.

The soldier peeked over the batwings of the saloon. He was going to dynamite the Queen Anne in an hour or two to set the final part of his plan into motion, and he had time for a few drinks.

The saloon was clear of lawmen and miners, so he went in.

"How 'bout a whiskey?" he said to the bartender.

"No thanks," the bartender said. "I don't drink whilst I'm workin'."

"Not for you, you idiot! For me!"

The bartender's smile faded. "No sense a humor, huh?" He filled a glass and passed it to the soldier. "Oh, say, I got a message fer you."

"Oh? Who from?"

"I don't rightly know. Unca Billy brought it over. It's sealed, has yer name on it. Well, not yer name. Less'n yer name's Johnny Reb. But he figgered it's fer you. Said he foun' it on a table in the boardin' house. No one was aroun' so he brung it here, figgered I'd see you afore he did. You know, I doan think he likes you much—"

"Shut up!" said the soldier, snatching the envelope out of the bartender's hand. "You talk too much."

"Y-yessir." He moved down the bar and began wiping it.

The soldier retired to a table in the corner with the envelope and his glass. He settled into a chair and opened the letter. Inside was a folded piece of paper. He removed the crisp sheet from the envelope and unfolded it, then read the hastily scrawled note.

We can end this tonight. I have an idea. It means more money. Cash in advance. Meet me at the livery—in the back. Midnight.

It was unsigned.

The soldier refolded the letter and slid it back into the envelope. He held it over the coal oil lamp in the center of the table until it caught fire. He dropped it on the floor and watched it as it burned.

Who had sent the note? Smith? Butler? Wellman? Goodhew? He wondered, trying to figure it out. Could it be someone else? Hardly likely. No one else knew about him except that Negro. Naw, couldn't be him. He's just a gopher. *What a mistake, givin' them people freedom.*

The soldier couldn't decide who wrote it. Any one of 'em were capable of it. They all talked peace but were more than happy to build themselves forts and hire a shootist. But then, after all, it didn't really matter who sent it. He'd just go meet them and find out about this *mission*.

"What's the time?" he yelled over to the bartender.

The man stopped toweling and pulled a pocket watch out of his vest.

"Ten afore midnight."

The soldier didn't thank him, just got up and stepped out into the street. He trudged up the road to the livery, stopping to light a cigar before ducking around to the rear.

The door was ajar, and he peeked in. It was dark. He could hear the breathing and shifting of the horses. A cat meowed and skittered by. The soldier pushed the door open slowly. It creaked on its hinges.

He stepped in.

"I'm glad you came," said a voice.

"Who's there?" said the soldier. He was uncomfortable and put his hand on the butt of his gun.

Across the livery two men stepped into the open, allowing a shaft of moonlight that slipped into the livery through a hole in the roof to illuminate them.

"Oh, Mr. Smith, Mr. Goodhew," said the soldier, taking the cigar from his mouth.

Just then two more men appeared from another corner. The soldier was confused.

"Butler, Wellman?"

Snap! The trap was sprung, and the soldier realized he had just tipped his hand. He yanked the gun out of his belt, but as he did a shot exploded out of the darkness beside Butler. The muzzle flash was the only thing the soldier could see. He hit the ground.

As he fired, Matt stepped out into the light. Billy appeared behind Smith. The soldier lay with his back to the men, and none of them knew Matt's shot had missed, that the man hadn't been dropped but went down of his own accord. It was a ruse, a way to buy time, to lure them all closer. His back to them, the soldier reached inside his coat and pulled out a stick of dynamite, which he quickly lit with the cigar he still held.

As the fuse started to sparkle and hiss, he rolled over and sat up quickly, holding the explosive aloft.

"Watch it! He's got dynamite!" someone shouted.

Everyone but Matt dove for cover or fled out the front doors. Matt didn't move, keeping his Peacemaker trained on the soldier. If he dropped him, the dynamite would blow them into oblivion. The seconds continued to tick away.

Both men were frozen in place, a standoff.

Suddenly a shot from behind Matt hit the soldier in his leg, and he collapsed. Out of the corner of his eye Matt saw Butler, his arm outstretched, his hand holding a smoking gun.

As the soldier fell he cried out and tossed the stick of dynamite toward Matt, then crawled for the back door.

Matt saw it coming, dropped his gun, and dove for it, grabbing it just as it hit the ground. He rolled, and in the same motion, flipped the dynamite toward the open back door, then sprang up and tackled Butler, knocking him into a pile of hay as the rear of the stable exploded with a flash of orange light and a deafening roar.

CHAPTER

NINETEEN

As splinters large and small were propelled toward them, Butler and Page hunkered in the hay, protecting their faces. They both felt the sting of the sharp projectiles, but as the noise dissipated and the smoke and dust wafted over them, they knew they were all right and slowly picked themselves up.

"It's all right," Uncle Billy said, coming in the front, followed by the other men.

"Thanks, Constable," said Butler, dusting himself off and plucking a few large splinters out of his clothing. "We owe you."

"Call off your men, all of you," Matt ordered him. "When that troublemaker's behind bars we'll talk this out. No more violence."

They nodded agreement.

"I've got to catch me a soldier," Matt said. He snatched up his Colt's Lightning from the stable floor, hustled out the door and ran to the boarding house, where Blister was still tied to the porch rail. He released the reins and climbed on, and the Morgan took off.

Matt swung him around behind the livery and picked up the soldier's trail. Besides the footprints, one of them dragging, Matt saw some blood. It was not a difficult trail to follow.

He won't get far, Matt thought.

The man's footprints and blood drops led to some horseshoe tracks behind the saloon. A small puddle of blood told Matt the soldier had stopped momentarily to untie and mount the horse. The animal then ran off to the north, toward the Bodie-Aurora road.

Matt followed the tracks that the full moon made easy to see. The soldier had about a five minute head start, but his injury was certain to slow him down. Matt hadn't gone far when clouds began rolling in and soon covered the moon. He had to get down off the horse and walk so he could see the ground.

He was only a mile or so out of town when a shot exploded to his right and the bullet whistled past his face, close enough that he felt the heat of it. He slapped Blister on the rump then dove for the gulley by the side of the road that was opposite where the shot had come from.

Matt belly-crawled to a low rock and stretched out behind it on his left side. He pulled his Peacemaker out of his holster and held it ready while he scanned the area. He was only able to see a few feet. He didn't want to fire blind. It would waste a round, and the muzzle flash would give away his position.

Matt listened. He could hear Blister nearby, moving slowly through the sage. He tried to pick out the sounds of another horse but couldn't. The shot had come from close by. If he didn't hear the animal, then whoever had fired the shot, and he presumed it to be the soldier, was still hunkered down. If he tried to ride away, Matt would know.

He tried to think this through. Why had the soldier stopped riding? Was he bleeding too bad to go on? Did something happen to his horse? Whatever it was, Matt felt the soldier was stuck and had decided to take his chances on shooting it out. He remembered the soldier's words at Monte Diablo.

Next time, I'll kill you.

No, this was going to be a fight to the end. Matt knew he had the advantage. He was uninjured, and the soldier was not only hurt, but desperate. Matt listened again, trying to think of something to do. He couldn't lay here all night.

Please, God! Help me!

He heard a rustling noise about thirty yards off, across the road and slightly south. He strained to hear. Was it the horse or the soldier? Subtle sounds from all quarters suddenly assaulted his ears as he struggled to isolate the soldier. An owl flew up from the sage. Blister pawed the ground.

A gun was cocked.

A split-second later another shot rang out, and the bullet ricocheted off Matt's rock. He returned a quick volley of two rounds and reloaded the three spent chambers.

"Give it up!" he yelled. "You don't have a chance!"

The soldier's answer was another shot.

Matt moved to the other end of the rock. If he could somehow get behind the soldier, who probably wasn't as mobile as Matt, he could get a bead on the criminal. Matt tossed a rock out to draw another shot, then jumped up and fired several shots as he ran for additional cover off to the soldier's flank.

Matt ran a jagged path, bobbing and weaving, then dove for cover just as the soldier fired again. Again he missed. Matt hit the ground, rolled, and came up firing. His third shot must have hit the mark because the soldier let out a yell.

Suddenly the soldier got up and ran, hobbling noticeably, but did not head for cover. He charged straight for Matt, firing on the run. Matt was stunned. He didn't expect a suicide charge. Matt had three bullets left and no time to reload.

He tried to aim at the invading Confederate, but his hand shook. The soldier gave a rebel yell, and Matt sensed that the man thought he was back in the war—a private war, but a war just the same.

Matt squeezed off all three rounds. All three missed the moving target.

The soldier was all but on top of him with a bullet or two left. Matt prepared himself for the onslaught, and the soldier slowed and took a bead on the deputy to finish him off. The moon broke through the clouds and Matt could see the rage in the soldier's face, and the hate, and for a second Matt could see his own face, and the hate he harbored for his father. Then he saw something else.

Off to his left, the silhouette of a one-armed man, a gun in his only hand, pointed at the soldier. It fired, the muzzle flash momentarily painting that side of the soldier's face with a red and orange glow. Before the soldier could turn his head toward the sound, the bullet thumped him in the side and he dropped hard, rolling twice in the dirt and not moving again.

Matt stood motionless, gazing at the one-armed man. There was no doubt in his mind who it was, but he didn't know what to do. How do you hate the man who just saved your life?

"Son, you okay?"

He began to move closer, but Matt stood rock-still, looking from his father to the soldier and back again.

"Yeah, Pa, I'm fine." Matt's voice was tense. "I guess I should thank you." Matt looked down at the body of the soldier. "How did you end up out here?" he asked, a little suspicious. "I thought you'd be in Nevada by now."

"I rode into town a little bit after you hightailed out after this guy. I came to see if you'd give me another chance. That couldn't happen if you was dead. A big black man told me where you went."

Matt looked away, tears welling up in his steel-gray eyes. "I'm glad you showed up when you did," he said quietly.

"I gotta tell you, if I'da had to ride Bonehead, I'd still be on th'other side of Bodie. That roan's a good piece of horseflesh."

"You taught me how to pick 'em," Matt admitted softly. He reached into his shirt, pulled out the picture of his mother he had found in the dirt, and handed it to his father. "Here, I think you lost this."

Jacob Page took the photo reverently and looked at his son. "Thank you." He admired the image of his wife, his eyes filling with the tears of regret. "You know, you look a lot like her. 'Cept that mustache makes you look old."

"Look who's talkin'," Matt said, the hint of a grin tugging at the corners of his mouth.

Jacob Page rubbed his chin whiskers. "Mebbe we should both shave."

"I'll think on it," Matt said. "C'mon, let's get this guy back to Bodie. We still got some trouble in town."

"What kinda trouble?"

"I'll tell you on the way back."

Matt and his father made the edge of town just as the sky was beginning to lighten. The soldier was draped across his saddle, his horse being led by Matt. Billy came out onto the porch to greet them.

"Ah knew you'd do it," he said. "Ah see your pa found you."

"Yeah, he found me," Matt said as he dismounted and tied Blister to the rail. "He got there just in time to save me."

Matt started to pull the soldier off the saddle, and Billy stepped over to help, then chuckled.

"Ain't this how we met?" he asked.

They took the man inside and laid him on the floor, covering him with a blanket. Matt slumped down in a chair as his father walked in. The elder Page sat next to him, but Matt didn't look his way.

"Ah got everything arranged, just like you told me," Billy said to Matt. "If the man Ah sent doesn't dilly-dally, Sheriff Taylor should be here by supper with the papers."

"Good. Did you tell the miners to hold off doing anything until then?"

"By the order of the sheriff, under penalty of incarceration. Course, they wanted to know what was goin' on, but Ah told them to cool their heels until tonight. You want some breakfast?"

"You're an angel of mercy, Uncle Billy."

"Don't know about that, Matthew. Don't take no angel to recognize tired and hungry men when he sees 'em."

They ate a breakfast of sourdough biscuits and ham, and Matthew realized it had been a couple days since he had had anything to eat. Feast or famine. Looked like that was to be his lot, so he might as well get used to it. They spent the day relaxing and telling stories, but Matt kept his distance from his father, being cordial but not letting himself make an emotional commitment. It had been too many years and the hurt was too deep; besides, the man might just get up and go away again.

As Billy was finishing regaling them with a tale of life on the Mississippi, the door to the boarding house opened and the four head miners filed in.

"I guess we owe you an apology, Constable," Butler said. "We shouldn't have hired that gunman."

"He played you all for the fool," Billy said. "You deserve whatever you got comin' to you."

"I think we can dispense with that," said Matt, "as long as you all can come to an agreement about the mines."

"Just because the Reb is outta the way don't change nothin'," said Wellman. "We still have the right to pursue that vein."

"No, *we* do," said Goodhew. They started to argue, and Matt banged on the table.

"Enough!" he shouted. "You're both wrong! Billy checked out the situation. Tell 'em, Billy."

O'Hara got out a map of the district and spread it on the table. The men gathered around, except Jacob Page, who retreated to a table a few feet away since this didn't concern him.

"Here's the Empire's shaft right here," Billy said, pointing. "And here's the Queen Anne. Now, your crosscut, Mr. Smith, goes like this, about so far." He drew a line. "Is that correct?"

"Close enough."

"And, Mr. Butler, yours goes to here, where the two meet."

"That's about the size of it, Billy."

"Well, unless Ah'm completely blind, your two crosscuts meet in an area between your claims. Neither one a you have any more claim than the other."

"Then it's all a matter of who gets to the claims office first, is that right?" Matt asked.

"That just about sums it up," agreed Smith, studying the map to double-check Billy's assessment.

Wellman was inching toward the door.

"Don't bother, Mr. Wellman," said Billy. "You're already too late."

"What?" said Mr. Butler.

"That's right," said Billy. He drew a line around the area between the claims of the Empire and the Queen Anne. "A claim has already been filed on this area, and you two is both encroachin' upon it."

"Who filed the claim?" Butler asked, glaring around the room at all the men, not knowing whom to suspect.

Billy grinned his biggest.

"*You?*" Several men said it at once.

"Yep," said Billy. "Sheriff Taylor's bringin' the papers any time now."

A storm of protest erupted in the room, and Matt finally had to fire a round into the floor to restore order.

"Gentlemen," he said, "if you would listen for a moment before you go off half-cocked, it will probably go a lot better for you." The room quieted. "Go ahead, Billy."

"Thank you, Matthew. Now, Ah don't have any interest in runnin' a mine operation. Ah got plenty to do already. So this new operation, the Bodie Unified Mine, is going to be a joint venture. The profits are going to be split four ways, all parties agreein'. Me, the Empire, the Queen Anne, and the Bodie Consolidated supervisor. In return for your shares, you gents will furnish the men and equipment to do the minin'."

"You're the owner, we do the work . . ." Butler mused. "But who's this supervisor gonna be, if it ain't you?"

"Someone of my choosing who will oversee all operations and protect my interests." He paused for effect and pointed across the room. Everyone turned and looked at the newest arrival in town, a one-armed prospector sitting quietly a few tables away. No one was more surprised than Matt.

Suddenly aware that all eyes were on him, Jacob Page sat upright.

"Huh?"

After the details had been worked out and the miners departed, Matt strolled out onto Main Street, deep in thought. His father and Uncle Billy had taken a shine to each other and were mired in conversation in the kitchen, planning their new venture.

The deputy took in a lungful of crisp, mountain air and reflected on his busy week: the fights, the chases, the violence he was ill-prepared to participate in . . . he was grateful God had let him live through it. He realized how tired he was and how overwhelmed. He had come to California to start his life over but hadn't expected anything like what he'd gotten himself into.

"I hope I can get some peace for a while," he said out loud to himself.

His words had no sooner left his lips than they turned in the wind and drove themselves deep into his heart. Peace. The peace his mother had told him about, that Matt knew he had never had. God's peace.

It hit him like a lightning bolt. He didn't hear a voice, the words just came to his mind and he knew what he had to do. He dropped to his knees in the middle of the street.

"Lord Jesus, this is Matt. Matthew Page, originally from Illinois. I . . . I know I'm a sinner and don't deserve anything. But I can't go through life hating my pa. Please forgive me, Lord. Please." He trailed off as his eyes filled, and he wiped his sleeve across them.

He looked up and scanned the town. He was alone, and yet he wasn't. There hadn't been a bolt of lightning, or a voice from Heaven, but he could tell something was different. A weight had been lifted from his shoulders. His circumstances hadn't changed; he didn't look any different; he was still a deputy sheriff and still had all the same problems to deal with, but somehow he just knew his life had been changed. The cares that had almost consumed him just a short while ago were still there, but he now viewed them as a challenge. He would ride this bucking bronc of a life, he thought. Ride it to the end.

Because he knew that he didn't have to do it alone any longer.

He was startled by a hand on his shoulder, and he jumped up and turned around. His pa was standing there, and Matt could see his face in the moonlight, smiling down at him. "You okay, son?"

Matt sniffed. "I'm fine . . . Pa."

"I been meanin' to ask you, . . . could you find it within yerself to forgive me, Matt?"

Matt couldn't hold it in any longer. He stood up and flung his arms around his surprised father and cried.

Jacob Page wrapped his arm around his son and held on, tears making tracks down his cheeks, too. "I'm pleased you changed yer mind about me."

"It wasn't me," Matt said. "God changed my mind."

"Your mama spoke about God to me."

"Yeah, she did a lot of that. I just realized she was right. We do need God." Matt looked his father directly in the eye. "I need you to forgive me, too, Pa," he said. "I really hated you for what you did."

"It's okay, son. I took the coward's way out. You'll never know how much I regret it now, all those years I missed, and yer ma . . ." He trailed off, and after a minute said, "We both got a lot of forgivin' to do. Come on, let's git back. Billy's sliced up a fresh apple pie."

The dawn broke clear and cool. Matt untied Blister's reins from the porch rail and mounted the Morgan while the men watched from the porch. Matt rubbed his smooth upper lip.

"I'll be back in a few days," he told Sheriff Taylor, who had arrived the day before with the claim papers.

"See that you mind your manners," Taylor said.

"Yessir," he said. He turned to the innkeeper. "Good luck, Billy."

"Good luck, Matthew. We'll take care of your pa for you."

He nodded and turned his horse to ride off just as a man on horseback rode into town and reined up in front of the boarding house.

"Charlie Jack!" Matt shouted.

Charlie surveyed the crowd and noticed the prospector he helped Matt track. "Prisoner?" he asked, pointing.

Matt laughed. "No, that's my father."

"This is father?" Charlie Jack was perplexed as he looked at Jacob Page. "Why you steal horse of son?"

"It's a long story," Matt said. "He'll tell you all about it."

Matt turned Blister away from the rail.

"Where you go?" Charlie Jack asked.

"I've got some unfinished business in Bridgeport." He kicked Blister in the flanks and rode south.

Charlie Jack smiled as he turned to the men on the porch and spoke knowingly.

"Business named Sarah."

Sheriff Taylor looked at the Indian with his bushy eyebrows raised, then cleared his throat. "Well, that's enough lollygaggin' around here. I best get on back to Bridgeport before the town goes to pot. See you gents later. Billy, you take care of yourself." He nodded and shook a few hands, then pulled himself onto his horse with a grunt and wheeled it around, galloping to catch up to his deputy.

PART

TWO

CHAPTER

ONE

OCTOBER, 1871

A half moon and a blanket of stars peeked intermittently through broken clouds that moved swiftly over the gold camp. The air was cool, and the wind that blew the clouds overhead was just a light breeze at ground level, waving the prairie grass gently without stirring any dust. Deep inside Bodie Bluff, where it was always still, dark, and dusty, the miners toiled, unaware of the tranquil scene on the surface.

Mining was a twenty-four hour concern here. The mill that crushed the rock operated around the clock, and ore had to be taken out of the hillside at all hours to feed the incessant hunger of the noisy stamps.

The night shift had been working at the four-hundred-foot level for about three hours, shoveling blasted rock off the steel muck plate that was placed on the floor to catch the ore shaken loose by the dynamite.

The muckers toiled in the sweltering heat with little air circulation, bending their backs to load rock into the ore cars, which were then hauled by donkey to the hoist and taken up to the surface for crushing. The only light they had came from a few scattered candles and coal oil lamps.

When the muck was clean one of the men stood and stretched,

wiping the sweat from his dirty forehead with the back of his hand. He leaned on his shovel.

"Boys, I think it's time we ate a little."

The other two men nodded agreement and walked down the drift to another short crosscut nearby. This second bore was only thirty feet long and had been abandoned when the small vein it followed ran out. The men used it now for a lunchroom.

The timber framing had been removed from this crosscut for use elsewhere, but it was not considered particularly unstable because the Cornish miners who cut the tunnel left several rock pillars. These columns of rock down the center of the cut were left in place to provide stability to the ceiling. Several feet in diameter, they supported the rock overhead and prevented cave-ins.

Robbing the pillar was not tolerated. Miners who were caught chipping small pieces of gold-bearing ore from a pillar were immediately discharged. It wasn't the value of the gold—the miners were always highgrading small amounts of ore out of the mines in long pockets sewn into their trouser legs or under false bottoms in their lunch buckets.

It was the weakening of the pillar and the potential for cave-in that got them canned.

The three muckers plodded into the crosscut with their tin lunch buckets and settled down at the far end. They did so in silence, too tired to talk.

Beef sandwiches and boiled eggs were the fare for the day, and they ate several of each, leaving the egg shells on the ground. One of the men glanced casually up at the pillar as he chewed, then something caught his eye. He studied the pillar for a moment.

"Looks like someone been robbin' that there pillar," he said finally.

The others turned to look at it.

"Hmmm, I think you're right, Clyde," agreed John.

The third man, Ed, held his candle up to look, then slowly got up and inspected the pillar. He ran his fingers down a large crack in the rock.

"It's shifted some. Too much rock's been removed. It won't hold the weight much longer."

"Our last blast must have loosened it," Clyde said. "There's gonna be hell for someone to pay. Mr. Butler don't cotton to thievery."

"We're gonna have to tell the framers to put some timbers back up in here," said the man standing next to the weakened pillar.

As he inspected it again there was a rumbling from a distant blast inside the hill, in an adjacent mine. At first they felt nothing, then the floor where they sat shook slightly. It wasn't a hard jolt or a long one, but small pieces of rock began crumbling off the pillar.

"Get out!" Clyde shouted.

Ed bolted, but a rock fell and struck him on the head, and he crumpled to the floor. The ceiling then gave way and in seconds he was buried. The other two men never had time to move.

When the rock stopped falling and the dust that swirled around in the sweltering air began to settle, Clyde moaned. He was alive, but he couldn't move. His legs were pinned and in pain.

"John?" Barely audible, Clyde's voice cracked.

There was no answer.

Clyde forced air out of his lungs as he tried again, louder. "John!"

Still there was silence. Clyde closed his eyes, winced at his pain, then heard a faint groan. The candles had been put out by the rushing air and Clyde couldn't see the other miner. They had apparently been partially protected by the overhang of the wall they sat against, and somehow they were both alive.

But they would not be missed for another eight hours.

CHAPTER

TWO

Deputy Sheriff Matthew Page stepped casually out of the wooden shack he called his office and inhaled deeply. The crisp, cool morning air in Bodie expanded his lungs and he exhaled, steam hovering momentarily in front of his face.

The clean-shaven young lawman set his hat on his sandy-haired head and looked up and down the dirt street. The sun had not yet crested the bluff, and the town was still in shadow. The steam engine that powered the Empire Mill was clanking and hissing, and the stamps were pounding the ore. He could hear the shouts and talk coming from the saloon, which was open twenty-four hours a day to accommodate the miners.

Matt started to cross the deserted street to the Empire Boarding House, lured by the smell of breakfast, his gumsoled boots crunching quietly on the dirt. Just as he was about to step up onto the porch the sound of breaking glass made him turn, but even before he looked he knew what was happening and who was involved.

Red McDougal, a small Scotsman with a big mouth, was squaring off against another miner from a different company, James Nixon. The lawman had been in the saloon twice the day before, separating the two miners. But they wouldn't leave it alone and had returned to settle unfinished business.

Matt trotted to the bar, irritated, stopping at the batwing doors to access the situation and size up the crowd. His shoes crunched on broken glass, and he saw the heavy beer mug on the boardwalk below what used to be a large pane glass window.

Both combatants had spent the night liquoring up and trading brags and insults, and everyone had been having a good time. But as the crowd began to thin out in the early morning, the talk grew more serious until Nixon punctuated his derision with a racial epithet.

Even the men who had been asleep in chairs or on the floor at the back of the saloon woke up and joined the circle of onlookers. The men quickly took sides and placed bets as the combatants prepared for a brawl. It had been too long a time since the last fight.

McDougal, a feisty scrapper, threw the first blows, pummeling the larger Nixon in a show of bravado that brought a rousing cheer from all spectators. Nixon, whose long black hair flailed as he was struck, managed to block several of the blows, then retaliated with his own sweeping right to the side of the Scotsman's head. This sent the little man spinning, but he was caught by several men, steadied, then shoved back into the fray.

McDougal went in with his head down and butted Nixon in the stomach. Both men crashed into the bar and were wrestling on the ground when Matt had seen enough and charged through the batwings, sending a man standing just inside the door sprawling. The rest of the spectators, interested in the battle, didn't notice the deputy. Matt had to shove them aside to get into the center to see what was going on.

Just as he did there was a muffled shot, instantly quieting the crowd. McDougal, who was on top, stiffened, then rolled off, clutching his belly. Nixon held a smoking derringer in his hand and had a look of wide-eyed disbelief on his face.

McDougal was bleeding, but the wound was a graze and did not appear serious. He swore at Nixon. Matt drew his Peacemaker.

"Put it down, Nixon!"

Nixon let the derringer fall out of his limp hand.

"I . . . I . . ."

"Save it for the judge," Matt ordered. "Get up and come here. Easy now. Keep your hands up."

Nixon obeyed. Several men stepped in to help McDougal. They picked him up and carried him to his shack up the road past the mill while one of them ran for Mrs. Wellman, the closet thing to a doctor in Bodie. Matt took the now compliant Nixon to the jail and slammed the cell door behind him.

"I been tellin' you, Jim," Matt scolded, "one day you and Red would try to kill each other."

"We was fine all night. He just had one too many."

"This was your third fight that I know about."

"Them others was friendly. I don't know what happened, but ol' Red decided to get serious."

"Well, I'm gonna have to take you to Bridgeport. It's either that or wait 'til the justice of the peace makes his rounds. That could be several weeks."

"Naw, let's git it over with," Nixon relented with a wave of his hand.

"Have it your way." Matt hung the key up, well out of his prisoner's reach. "I'm gonna have some breakfast first. Want anything?"

"Maybe some eggs," Nixon said. "When you're done."

"Okay." Matt left the jail and headed across to the boarding house for the second time. When he opened the creaking door several men inside turned to look at him.

Uncle Billy smiled broadly at the deputy, pushed his chair back and stood up. He and the others had been enjoying a hot cup of coffee to kick off their day, along with some good, irrelevant conversation.

"Mornin', Matthew." He motioned for the deputy to sit in the vacated seat. "Ah'll get y'all a cup."

"Thanks, Uncle Billy," Matt responded. He took off his hat and eased himself into the wooden chair. "Do I smell your famous ham and eggs?"

"Ah think mebbe you do. Ah take it you want some?"

"Yessir, if you please."

"What was all that ruckus down the street?"

"A couple of miners got into a fuss. James Nixon and Red McDougal."

"No big s'prise," said Jacob Page, still seated at the table. As superintendent of one of the mines, he was James Nixon's boss. "They been buildin' t'ords it fer weeks."

"True enough," Billy agreed. "I heared from some a the men

that stay here there was bad blood between them. So what happened?"

"They duked it out for a while, took to wrestlin', then Red shot McDougal in the gut with a derringer. McDougal'll be okay, and Red's coolin' his heels at my place."

"Seems a shame," Billy muttered, shaking his head. "I'll get your breakfast."

Billy O'Hara lumbered off to the kitchen.

"What're you gonna do with Nixon?" Jacob Page asked his son.

"Take him to Bridgeport for a hearin'," Matt said. Billy returned with a plate of breakfast and set it in front of him. Matt cut off a piece of ham and stuffed it into his mouth. "I needed to take a ride down the road a piece anyway, see what shape it's in." He took another bite. "How's our mine doin'?"

"Jes' fine, son." Jacob Page continued eating.

"That vein's holdin' out so far," Billy interjected. "But it's a small one. It ain't likely to trigger a boom. Ain't that right, Jacob?"

"Right as rain, unfortunately," the elder Page assented. "Too bad, too. Be nice to see more people comin' in, buildings'll start poppin' up like mushrooms."

"More mouths to feed," O'Hara said.

"And more need for merchants and barbers and livery stables..." said Jacob.

"Jails, undertakers, grave diggers," said Billy.

"And churches," said Matt.

The third man at the table, who thus far had remained silent, gave Matt a puzzled look.

"What for church?" he asked.

The men laughed. "Charlie Jack, you kill me!" Matt said to the Indian tracker.

"No, Charlie not kill you," the confused Paiute corrected.

"Churches are where we worship God," Billy explained to him. "Course we'll need churches. And ministers. Someone has to do the weddings and funerals, and preach about the evils of loose women, gambling, and liquor. Not that anyone'll listen."

"Why church for that? You do."

"Good point, Charlie Jack," Matt said. "Good point. Billy can preach." Matt finished his breakfast and got up to get another cup of coffee. "What are you doin' here, anyway?" he asked the Indian.

"Pass through. Stop, get pine nut."

"Well, it's good to see you again."

"Good see you, Matt. Charlie Jack hear you good tracker now."

"You taught me everything."

The Indian shook his head. "No, Great Father teach more than Charlie Jack." He rolled his eyes heavenward when he spoke. Matt nodded, amazed at the Paiute's insight, and walked toward the kitchen.

While Billy chatted about Bodie's future, Jacob Page was silent, staring into his empty mug.

"Billy, I been wonderin' 'bout somethin'," he said finally. "Now, 'tain't none of my business, you un'erstan'. You don't have to answer if'n you don't want to. But I was wonderin' why you give up yer interest in you and Matt's mine. It looks like it might turn out to be a . . . well, a real good thing."

"Well . . ." Billy started slowly, "Ah guess Ah jus' warn't made to be a minin' person. Ah'm satisfied runnin' this here boardin' house, cookin' for the men, talkin' like this in the mornin' and evenin'. Mah life is rich enough."

When Matt and Billy had filed their claim to solve a mine dispute between the Empire and the Queen Anne companies they had set up Matt's father as superintendent. But a few weeks later Billy turned his share over to the elder Page—no strings attached—without any explanation. No one was surprised; Billy had always been generous that way. But they were curious.

O'Hara slapped Jacob Page on the shoulder. "Jacob, you worked real hard for the last seven years tryin' to make a livin' outta these hills." He swept his arm in an arc as he spoke. "It was the least Ah could do."

"You don't owe me nuthin'," Page said.

"Oh, but Ah do," Billy assured. "You raised a son that came to town and saved Bodie from destroyin' itself, then kept him alive so he could stay on and represent law and order here."

"I didn't raise him. His mother did." Page was uncomfortable. "An' it was dumb luck that I got there in time to shoot that bloody Reb."

"You raised me until I was eleven." The voice was Matt's, back from the kitchen carrying the coffee pot. He walked to the table and poured fresh brew into his father's mug. "Whatever I am, I'd already become by then. You taught me how to work hard and how to respect other people. That stuck with me. And as for gettin' there in time to plug that Reb, you think that was luck?"

"What would you call it?" Jacob asked.

"Ah call it God sendin' you there, whether you care to admit it or not," Billy said. "He was the one told you to foller Matt to Bodie."

"That were jes' a feelin'."

"Where feeling come from?" Charlie Jack asked.

Page couldn't answer. "Lemme think about it," he shrugged.

The men let it go at that. At least the seed had been planted. There was silence for a moment before Matt spoke.

"Say, Pa, are you growin' your beard back?"

"Huh?" Jacob was caught off guard by Matt's sudden change of direction.

"I thought we agreed to keep our faces clean." Matt reminded his pa of their pledge a month or so back. Matt had removed a shaggy mustache.

"Well—" Jacob rubbed the several-day-old stubble on his chin. "I got so used to that mess a hair down there that I kinda missed it. I hope you don't mind."

"It's your face," Matt allowed. "In fact, I kinda miss my mustache, too." He fingered his upper lip. "But I think Sarah likes me better without it."

"Did she say so?"

"Well, not exactly. It's just the way she reacted when she saw me up close. She . . . I could tell she was looking at my lip. She kinda considered it for a second, then wrinkled her nose, just a little."

"Sounds to me like she likes you, son. Now, don't go forcin' it or nuthin'. If'n there's anythin' to it, you gotta let the feelin's grow. Get to know her first."

"I'd like to," Matt complained, "but no sooner do I start to talk to her than her father . . . uh, Sheriff Taylor . . . finds something for me to go do."

"He's jes' bein' careful. Sarah's his daughter and he's not gonna let her git involved with jes' anybody."

"Yeah, but we're both old enough—"

"That's not the point, Matt. She's his daughter no matter how old she is, an' he's gonna protect her. Look, don't go gittin' anxious.

Bes' way I know of to kill a relationship is to git anxious. Relax. If she's gonna warm up to you, it'll happen. You cain't force it."

"I'd at least like to talk to her for a while . . . you know, uninterrupted."

Jacob looked his son directly in the eye. "Then go to the sheriff and ask him. Tell him how you feel and git him to say yea er nay!"

"You think I should do that? What if he says no?"

The one-armed miner leaned back in his chair. "Son, Sheriff Taylor ain't known you all that long. He's still learnin' what yer like. Why, shoot! I ain't known you more'n a few weeks myself. As an adult, that is. But I know 'nough 'bout yer character to know yer honest, hard-workin', you finish whatcha start and kin be trusted."

"Sheriff Taylor knows it, too," Billy said, "or he wouldn't've given y'all this responsibility."

"That's right," said Jacob. "An' let me tell you, his daughter is dearer to him than this whole county, so he's bein' extry careful."

Matt thought about this without saying anything, then Billy said gently, "He's seein' how patient y'all can be. It's one a the greatest traits a man can have. If'n y'ain't patient, the other good things y'are won't be noticed 'cause you'll be gettin' into one mess after 'nother outta haste. Y'all need to ask God to give you patience."

"I'd like to have patience, but I don't think I want to ask God for it."

"Why not?" Billy asked.

Jacob Page roared with laughter. "'Cause if'n God gives it to him, he figgers he'll be waitin' forever!"

They laughed together over this, except the stoic Charlie Jack, then the elder Page stood. "Well, I gotta go to work." He pressed his limp old hat onto his head and winked at his son. "When yer in Bridgeport why don'tcha take a ride on over to Sarah's house?"

Matt thought about it, then turned to Billy. "What do you think?"

Billy grinned. "Ah'll pack y'all a lunch."

Deputy Page rode easily toward Bridgeport on Blister, his powerful Morgan, his leather saddle creaking in cadence with the pounding of the hooves on the rocky trail. Blister snorted the dust out of his nostrils without slackening his pace. The rope tied around Matt's saddle horn led the horse James Nixon sat on. He was handcuffed in front so he could ride.

The young lawman was anxious to see the sheriff's daughter. He had met other girls in the towns he had been through, but there was something about Sarah that set her apart. He felt it instantly. He wasn't sure if it was her demeanor or her appearance. But the day he first walked into town and saw her in the yard was a day he would long remember. He knew she was different.

His new responsibilities in Bodie were not as thrilling as his first week had been, but Sheriff Taylor kept him busy nonetheless, filing reports and running errands. Matt had only been to Bridgeport twice—once when he had concluded the mine war business and once a few weeks later with a prisoner—and he had spoken to Sarah just a few times, in passing conversation on the street and once in Taylor's house while Matt waited for the sheriff to finish his lunch. Since then he'd been back in Bodie, pining away. Nixon was his first arrest since he settled into the routine.

This trip was much easier than his first. The road was clear, the sky filled with white, billowing clouds that tumbled overhead, and there were no obstacles—like thieving prospectors—in his path. As Matt moved from sunlight to shade and back he wondered how soon the rains would come.

The air was clean and sweet and the prairie grass had turned golden. Matt was always awed by the majesty of the nearby Sierra Nevadas that rose abruptly from the plain without the transition of foothills. There was little snow on the peaks, but that would change soon enough. Winters here were harsh, Matt had heard, with snow several feet deep everywhere, and upwards of ten to twelve feet in Bodie, due to its higher elevation.

Around a bend and over a rise, and there it was: the whitewashed buildings of Bridgeport came into view. Matt reined his horse back and Nixon's stopped on its own. The deputy took a swig from his canteen and poured a little into his hand, wiping his face to remove road dust. He dried off with his neckerchief, then handed the canteen to Nixon.

"Beautiful day," Matt said.

"Depends on your point of view, I suppose," Nixon replied dryly.

"Yeah, I suppose so."

Matt kicked Blister back to life and they rode the final miles into town without stopping. The closer he drew, however, the more nervous he became. The possibility of seeing Sarah, of talking to her, of being rejected by her, slowed him down as he crossed the bridge into town.

There was the house, with its white picket fence, colorful flower and vegetable garden, the red water pump just outside the gate where he stood the first time he saw her. He passed by the house slowly, looking at it the entire time.

At the sheriff's office he got off the Morgan and marched Nixon inside. Taylor wasn't there, so Matt locked his prisoner up and quickly filled out the report, leaving it on the desk. He promised Nixon he'd see to it he got some food, then climbed back onto his horse and returned to Taylor's house.

Matt stopped just shy of the property. *Now what?* he wondered to himself. *Should I walk on in and knock on the door? Maybe I should stay outside the fence and let Blister make some noise to attract their attention. Or I could draw some water.*

No, none of those would work, he decided. Then he remembered what Billy and his father told him: talk to Sheriff Taylor himself about it.

"That's what I'll do," he said out loud. He urged Blister forward. "I'll talk to him man to man, tell him how I feel. He'll understand."

"Who will understand what?"

The female voiced surprised Matt, and he jerked around in the saddle so abruptly he almost fell off.

There she was, standing by the gate smiling up at him.

CHAPTER

THREE

O h . . . uh, hello, Sarah," Matt stammered, his voice cracking. Sarah smiled politely at the young man with the star on his shirt. She admired his grace as he climbed off the Morgan, the saddle groaning with the shifting of his weight. The horse snorted and pawed the ground.

Matt removed his hat and walked over to the fence, leading his mount. Sarah was wearing a plain, calico print dress with white collar and cuffs. Her hair, light brown with a hint of red, hung past her shoulders and her large green eyes were fixed on his.

He was certain she could hear his heart pounding.

Sarah thought he had been good-looking when he had a mustache, but now! What a difference! His clothes were loose-fitting, but she could tell he was solidly built from all that hard work on the farm growing up.

She was certain he could hear her heart pounding.

"Good mornin', Sarah." He smiled.

"Matt." She said it sweetly, nodding her response.

"How are you today?"

"Oh, fine, just fine," she said. "I saw you riding in with another man. Do you have business with my father? He didn't mention that you were coming."

"Well, he didn't exactly know. We had a little problem in Bodie this mornin'. That was a prisoner. Otherwise, I had no reason to come to Bridgeport."

"Oh, I see." She sounded disappointed. He suddenly realized his mistake.

"Officially, I mean," he added quickly. "I really came to see you." There it was. He had blurted it out, surprising both of them. Sarah's eyes brightened while Matt inspected the toes of his boots.

"Me? Why, whatever for?"

"I thought maybe we could talk, spend a little time together. You know, get to know each other better." He paused, then added, "If that's okay with you."

"I think that would be nice," Sarah said.

"When do you think we could . . . do that?"

"I don't know. I'll have to ask Father."

"I was just coming over to talk to him," Matt said. "I'll ask him."

"All right. But he's not here right now."

"Sarah!" It was her mother, calling from inside the house.

Sarah turned. "Coming!" She turned back to Matt. "Goodbye. Nice to see you again. I'll be anxious to hear what Father says." She twirled around and ran to the door but stopped before she went in and gave Matt a smile and a wave. He waved back, and she was gone.

Matt stood there for a few moments, then put his hat on backwards and mounted his horse. As Blister walked up the street, Matt's gaze remained fixed on the front door of Sheriff Taylor's house. He could not see Sarah and her mother watching him through the lace curtains.

Matt went back to the office to wait for the sheriff. When he stepped in he was surprised to see Taylor sitting at the desk, reading his report on Nixon. Taylor looked up.

"Deputy Page! I see you've been busy."

"Yessir. Quite a little battle."

"Good work. I'll have Nixon go before the judge tomorrow so he can plead. If he pleads innocent, self-defense—and they always do—we'll have a trial and the witnesses will all have to come down here. When do you think McDougal will be ready to make the trip?"

"Couple, three days maybe."

"Okay, that's fine—Deputy, why is your hat on backwards?"

"Huh?" Matt took it off, looked at it sheepishly, and shrugged.

"Is there anything else you wanted to talk about?" the sheriff asked. "If not, I've got a job for you, since you're here."

"Well, sir . . . actually, I'd like to talk to you about . . . your daughter. You know, Sarah."

Taylor's eyes moved up to the ceiling, then back down again. "Yeah, I've met her once or twice."

Matt grinned. "Oh, yeah."

"What about her?"

"Well, sir, I . . . uh . . . I've taken a fan—that is, I'm attrac—I'd like to spend some time with Sarah, get to know her."

"What are your intentions, Deputy?"

"Purely honorable, sir. I like her, and I think she likes me—I *hope* she does—and I want your permission to spend a little time with her."

The sheriff opened his desk drawer and pulled out a piece of paper. It looked to Matt like a telegram. The sheriff read it before speaking.

"What day is it?"

"Today?" Matt asked.

"No, some vague day in the future. Of course today."

Matt flushed. "Today's Wednesday, sir."

"Okay. I'll tell you what. Sunday me and the missus'll have you over for supper, right after church. In the meantime, since you're here with nothin' to do, I've got a little job for you. I was going to do it myself, but that's what deputies are for, ain't they?" He smiled. "You sure Bodie's under control?"

"Nixon and McDougal are the only real problem we have. Besides, Uncle Billy's watchin' it for me."

"Good enough." He pushed the telegram across the desk to Matt, who picked it up and read *Fred DeCamp*.

"Judge Wadell issued a warrant for him just now. That's where I was when you came in with your prisoner." He handed the warrant to Page. "I don't think he'll present a problem. He's a family man, they tell me, but he got a burr under his saddle and destroyed a loan office up in Coleville after they foreclosed on his property, then hightailed it out with his family this mornin'. He's got a little head start on you, but the woman and children'll slow him down."

"You want me to leave now?"

"Naw, it's near dark. Get some sleep and you can get an extra early start in the mornin'. You'll catch up with him in no time with that horse you got."

"Bring him back here?"

"Yeah. We had an office in Coleville but closed it a year ago. Listen, try not to hurt him. I got a feelin' a jury would side with him anyway. Nobody likes to get foreclosed on."

"What should I do with his family?"

"Have them follow you back, if they want. Or wait in Coleville. It's up to them." Taylor got up. "I'm lockin' up now, Matt. Why don't you go over to the Argonaut and get yourself a bite? You can sleep here tonight, if you want, save the hotel bill. The key's above the door frame."

Matt stood when the sheriff did and put on his hat. He unconsciously checked it to make sure it wasn't backward.

"Thank you, sir," he said. "I'll see you back here in a couple days with the prisoner, and I'll be lookin' forward to Sunday."

He turned and stepped out, then led Blister down the street to the livery as Sheriff Taylor plodded back up the street to his house.

Lucky guy, Matt thought to himself. *He can go talk to her anytime he wants—and probably doesn't bother most of the time.*

Matt put Blister into a stall and gave him some oats and a rubdown. He flipped the stableboy a coin and told him to take real good care of the Morgan, then strolled back up the street toward the Argonaut.

When he walked in the proprietress looked up and her face brightened considerably.

"Matthew Page? Is that you?" She walked over to him, wiping her hands on her apron.

"Oh, hello, Mary," Matt said, removing his hat. "Good to see you again."

She surprised him with a big hug, crushing his hat between them.

"Goodness me, something's different!" she declared. "Let's take a look at you." She held him at arm's length with her hands on both his shoulders and studied him, then looked again at his face. "Why, you've gone and shaved your mustache off! Looks real nice! You here for supper? C'mon back here, I got a table all ready for you." She put her arm around his shoulder and led him back through the restaurant to a table set for two.

"Thank you, ma'am. Are you expecting someone else?"

She looked surprised. "Harvey, of course. Aren't you here to meet him?"

Matt remembered how Mary seemed sweet on the owner of the Emporium, but poor Harvey Boone hadn't noticed. He was still too upset over his wife's death the year before. This was the night Harvey set aside every week to eat at the Argonaut.

"When's he due in?"

"Any time now." Suddenly she looked worried. "Oh dear, if you're not here to meet Harvey . . ." She trailed off.

"What?" Matt asked.

"Well, Harvey told me earlier to set a table for two. When you came in I figured it was for you. I—"

"No problem," Matt assured, standing up. "I'll just go to that table over yonder. It's okay."

Just then Harvey walked in. He saw Mary and Matt and broke into a huge grin.

"I knew you'd show up here," he said, grabbing Matt by the hand and shaking it. He turned to Mary. "I saw him ride into town, figgered he'd come by here for a bite. Everyone always comes back." He winked.

Mary blushed and excused herself while the men sat down.

"So what brings you to town?" Harvey asked. Matt told him the story of Nixon and McDougal.

"Oh," Harvey said, sounding disappointed.

"What do you mean, 'oh'?"

"I was hopin' you came here to see Sarah."

"Wellll . . ."

"I thought so!" Harvey shouted. He leaned forward. "It's all over town that she's . . . sweet on you. Ever since you showed up she's been actin' kinda strange. You know, dreamy-like."

Mary came back with coffee and biscuits and a slab of pale butter. She set it all down in silence and returned to the kitchen.

"Do you think so?" asked Matt hopefully when she was gone.

"Don't think. I *know*!"

Matt sat back in his chair, his heart thumping. He thought again of the girl—the young woman—who was so delightful. He suddenly couldn't wait to go capture the wanted man and get back for Sunday supper. He was staring down at the table without realizing it, and smiling. *Thank you Lord!* he prayed silently.

Harvey grinned as he sipped his coffee. "C'mon, Matt. Tell me about your adventures while we eat. I've heard some tales, but you know how stories change as they get passed around."

Matt shook off the daydream and buttered his biscuit. He took a drink of the hot, black coffee and exhaled in admiration.

"Mary sure is a great cook!" he said. He looked at Harvey, who was devouring a mouthful of strawberry preserve-covered biscuit. Harvey saw the deputy staring at him.

"What?" he said between chews.

"Don't you know?" Matt asked.

"Know what?"

"Mary. She . . . uh, admires you. Why do you think she treats you like a king here?"

"I never thought about it."

"How long have you known her?"

"Two years or so."

"And she and your wife Esther were good friends. Does Mary have a . . . beau?"

"Now that you mention it, no, she doesn't."

"She ever see anyone casual-like?"

"Not that I noticed."

"There you are . . . It's you! She's waitin' for you to notice her."

"I . . . uh—"

"*Shhh!*" Matt stuffed a bite of biscuit into his mouth as Mary brought two steaming bowls of soup. As she set the bowls in front of the men, she gave Harvey an adoring smile. The store owner caught it out of the corner of his eye. She retreated into the kitchen.

Matt smiled smugly as Harvey looked at him, unbelieving. "See?" Matt folded his arms triumphantly.

"You sure?"

"Harvey, this sounds like a conversation we just had."

Harvey shook his head. "I just never thought about it."

"Well, maybe you should. Mary's a good woman. She'll make a fine wife."

"Oh, look who's the authority now!" Harvey laughed. "You couldn't even tell Sarah had her eye on you."

"I guess we both need a double shot of smarts."

They laughed heartily and plowed into dinner.

Later that evening, after both men were stuffed and Mary's fried chicken and rhubarb pie were just pleasant memories, they parted company. Harvey had asked Matt if he wanted to stay at his place, but Matt declined.

Matt sat in the sheriff's chair and inspected the room. He gazed at the walnut bookcase and the Winchester repeaters behind the glass. A Sharp's long rifle stood menacingly in the midst of the others.

Matt peered at several framed sheets of paper, citations awarded to Taylor for his heroism and bravery during the War of the Rebellion. They were signed by General Ulysses S. Grant. Matt whistled low.

He swung the chair around and faced the desk. Sunday was a long way off. He hoped this guy up in Coleville didn't give him any trouble. He remembered the swish of Sarah's dress as she ran off into the house, and he could still smell her lilac water. Try as he might he couldn't get Sarah out of his mind. He couldn't wait. He had to see her. Resolutely he pushed away from the desk and stood, then walked outside and stepped into the street.

It was sunset, and the overcast sky reflected the pink-orange rays of a dying sun. Mostly deserted, the street was beginning to benefit from the coal oil lamps the town council had recently hung every twenty feet or so along the boardwalk.

Matt strode tentatively to Sarah's house, not knowing quite what he'd find. When he arrived at the picket fence he could make out silhouettes on the curtains. There were two, but neither of them were Sarah's. Matt thought for a minute, then walked around to the back of the property. He didn't have a plan. He hoped he would think of one by the time he got there. From a viewpoint behind the rear fence, he could see the back of the house. He was hidden by some sheets drying in the gentle breeze.

He suddenly began to laugh quietly. *Look at me. Here I am, a deputy sheriff, I chase criminals all over the county, get into shootouts and fights, maintain law and order over hundreds of square miles, and I'm skulkin' around in an alley, scared stiff, just so I can talk to a—*

His thoughts were interrupted by the creaking of the screen door as she glided out into the yard.

CHAPTER

FOUR

Even as Matt was criticizing himself for acting foolishly, he ducked down to avoid being seen by the girl, as if she would summon the law at first sight of him. She carried a laundry basket and headed for the clothesline, intent on bringing in the sheets so they wouldn't be ruined by the night air and morning dew.

As she pulled the clothespins off the top of the sheets and gathered them to her, she hummed. Matt recognized the song as one his mother used to sing. What was it? Amazing something. *"Amazing Grace."* That's it!

Sarah's a Christian!

Matt was even more delighted now. He wanted to stand up and let her know he was there, but he didn't want to startle her. She might cry out and Sheriff Taylor would come outside and catch him and he'd be in trouble.

Matt didn't notice that Sarah kept glancing over to where he was squatting.

"What's that?" she said suddenly. "Is someone there?" Matt was puzzled. He was certain he hadn't made any noise. He stood slowly.

"Uh . . . good evening, miss. It's just me." He grinned sheepishly and took off his hat.

"What are you doing out there at this time of night?"

"Hiding." If Matt had a fault, it was his honesty.

"Are you sure you weren't looking for something you lost earlier, or maybe you were providing special protection for Fa—that is, for the sheriff because someone he arrested got out of prison and vowed to get revenge?"

Matt thought for a moment, perplexed. "No, I was just hiding. I wanted to talk to you, but when the door opened I was afraid it was your pa, and I didn't want him to see me."

"When you saw it was me, why didn't you let me know you were here?"

Matt blushed and shrugged. He shifted nervously.

"Oh, well, no matter," Sarah cooed. "Now that we're together, what did you want to talk about?"

"I . . . uh . . . just wanted to hear your voice. I'm goin' away for a few days, and I wanted to have it fresh on my mind."

It was Sarah's turn to blush. Her head dropped a little, and she looked up at Matt. "That's sweet. I hear you're coming over for dinner on Sunday." She moved closer to the fence.

"Yep. Your pa—uh, the sheriff—wants me to go up Coleville-way and bring back a wanted man first."

"Will it be dangerous?"

Not as dangerous as what I'm doing right now! "Oh, no, it'll be peaceable enough." *I hope.*

"You be careful. I'm anxious to hear you tell all about your adventure and about how you found your father."

"Nothing could keep me away," Matt assured.

"Sarah!" It was her mother inside the house.

"Out here, Ma! I'm coming!"

"All right, dear. Don't dilly-dally!"

Sarah turned back to Matt. "It was nice while it lasted. See you Sunday."

"Okay." Matt put his hat on. The moon had come out and was bathing Sarah's face in its yellow glow. As he gazed at her beauty he almost couldn't stand it, but he had to leave.

"Good night," he said abruptly. "See you on Sunday." He turned quickly and beat a hasty, although reluctant, retreat, his heart pounding. Sarah watched him disappear into the darkness.

Inside the house Mrs. Taylor smiled as she moved away from the window in the darkened kitchen.

The next morning Sarah threw herself into her chores. After straightening the quilt on her bed, she washed and dressed, then sat down in front of a small mirror to comb her hair. She looked at herself in the glass, imagining how Matt would like seeing her in the morning. She played with different arrangements of her thick locks. Never satisfied, she eventually gave up and set the brush down.

Sarah glided down the stairs, singing lightly, and went to the kitchen. Her mother had not yet risen, so Sarah set about making breakfast. She sifted a bowl of flour and started dough for biscuits. While it rose she lit the stove, then sliced off several slabs of ham and tossed them into the cast-iron skillet she had already put onto the stove. The meat sizzled and popped as it hit the pan.

Sarah whistled as she threw the dough down on a piece of marble and rolled it out. She cut a dozen biscuits, put them on a sheet, and slid them into the oven.

Like a finely-tuned machine, Sarah put on the coffee, turned the ham, and ran outside. She collected an apronful of eggs from the chicken coop and hurried inside in time to take the ham off the griddle and the biscuits out of the oven.

Sarah fried the eggs, poured the coffee, and set the table as her parents staggered into the kitchen.

"I'll just have coffee," the sheriff said.

Sarah didn't flinch. He was going to eat whether he liked it or not. She pushed him down gently into a chair and tied a napkin around his neck.

"Thank you, Sarah," her mother said, surveying the scene.

"You two were sleeping so soundly, I didn't want to bother you. You must have stayed up late."

"I suppose we did," Irene Taylor admitted. "The fire was nice, and we had a lot to talk about."

"Like what?" Sarah asked innocently.

"Never you mind," said her father. "Where's this breakfast you're gonna make me eat?"

"Coming up!"

She set the plate in front of him. The sheriff leaned down and took a huge whiff of the food.

"Smells fair-to-middlin'," he said. Sarah glared at him until he cracked a grin. Then he quickly cleared his throat, picked up his fork and dug in.

After clearing the breakfast mess, Sarah prepared herself for another day. She planned on cultivating the garden and gathering whatever was ripe. She hoped her potatoes were ready. She was counting on tossing them in with her carrots and onions and a large cut of beef from the butcher for supper.

Her mother usually let her do the cooking, but Sarah didn't mind. She didn't take to knitting and quilting as much as her mother, although she could do both well, but she enjoyed creating in the kitchen. After all, men appreciated good cooking more than they did good knitting.

As Sarah dug in the garden on her hands and knees, she thought about Sunday and what she could cook for Matt that would really impress him. She hadn't thought to ask anyone what he liked. Maybe when she went shopping later she could drop in on Mary at the Argonaut. She knew Mary had served Matt several times; the restaurant owner had mentioned it to her in church.

Come to think of it, Sarah realized, Matt had been the principal topic of conversation in church for the past several weeks, especially during the Tuesday night social when the younger women sat around and gossiped.

There were a few single women Sarah's age in Bridgeport and, as she pulled up spuds, she remembered how interested they had been when Mary told about the first night Matt had come into the restaurant with Harvey Boone, then ran out after pie and caught the men who broke into the bank.

Sarah wasn't worried about Mary; she knew Mary was keen on Harvey. Besides, she was older than Matt by a decade. It was the other girls Sarah objected to. She suddenly found herself digging large, angry holes in the ground, and had to stop and laugh at how silly she was being. Hadn't Matt come to see *her* last night and not the others? As far as she knew, Matt hadn't even met any of them.

Still, it wouldn't hurt to be careful, lest one of them tried to weasel in on her territory.

Sarah struggled to carry her harvest inside, cleaned up, then walked to the butcher shop. She picked out a nice roast for dinner and signed the ledger, billing it to her father's account, then left the shop and made her way to the Argonaut.

Mary was busy with lunch customers but greeted Sarah as she bustled past her on the way to the kitchen.

"Good morning, Sarah! Or is it afternoon? I've lost track."

"Just after twelve o'clock."

"Oh, my." Mary disappeared into the kitchen, then reappeared moments later with two plates. She took the food to two local businessmen seated by a window, then came back to Sarah.

"Don't know what it is. Where'd these folks come from? I'm not usually this busy at lunch time. My help doesn't come in till four."

"Can I give you a hand?" Sarah offered. "I wanted to talk to you anyway."

"Put on an apron and go take their order." Mary nodded toward a table in the corner. Three ranch hands from the Double Bar were anxious for a woman-cooked meal after eating chuck wagon victuals for a week.

Sarah took off her shawl and tied on one of Mary's yellow aprons. She found out what the men were hankerin' for and wrote it down on a little piece of paper. Her memory wasn't as good as Mary's, who never needed to write down orders no matter how busy she was.

Sarah went to the kitchen and handed the order to Mary.

"My daddy's having Matt Page over for Sunday supper." Sarah figured that by telling Mary soon everyone would know. That would establish her claim.

"Lucky you!" Mary threw a steak on the griddle and spooned out a large ladle of chili into a bowl. She sliced a hunk of corn bread. "He's a nice young man."

Sarah smiled. "Can you help me? I want to make a meal he'll never forget. What do you think he'd like to have?"

Mary stopped what she was doing and looked at the young woman. "Lemme tell you something, sweetheart. Matt is young and strong and cleans his plate every time he comes in here. He spends days at a time in the saddle eating sourdough, beans, and jerky. He'll be happy no matter what you serve him." She flipped the steak and checked the progress of an apple pie. "I heard that he's even eaten Paiute *koochabee*."

"What's that?"

"Honey, you don't want to know. But it's rumored to be pretty offensive."

Mary dumped some potato slices into a skillet and tossed in a handful of cut-up green peppers. "Listen, Sarah. The way Matt's taken with you, you could serve him corn husks and old shoes and he'd think it was great."

"I hope you're right." Sarah sighed, then smiled coyly. "I heard Harvey's the same way with you."

"Have you now? He's a good man. Here, grab that plate for me." Sarah picked up the blue china and held it so Mary could fill it with the T-bone and a large portion of potatoes.

"Take that to the man in the gray coat near the door."

Sarah started to move, but Mary put her hand on the young woman's arm and smiled.

"Juicy meat, corn on the cob, mashed potatoes with a flood of thick gravy and hot apple pie. Never fails." She winked.

Sarah smiled broadly and left the kitchen.

Sheriff Taylor sat at his desk, chewing on a piece of caramel, when Sarah peeked around the door.

"Hello, Daddy."

Taylor stopped chewing and smiled with his lips tightly closed. Sarah was carrying a basket, which she set on the desk and opened. She took out her father's lunch and without any comment spread it out before him. Taylor winced as he swallowed the forbidden caramel whole.

"I trust that candy won't spoil your supper," Sarah said.

"What candy?"

Sarah gave him a disparaging look. "The candy Mama doesn't want you eating because it's bad for your teeth but you sneak it in here and eat it anyway, that's what candy."

"Uh . . . I—"

The sheriff was saved by shouting outside. A galloping horse slid to a stop in front of his office and the rider jumped off, flew up the steps and through the door before Taylor could stand.

"Need help!" said a tired Paiute.

"Charlie Jack, isn't it?" asked Taylor. The Indian nodded. "What's the problem, friend?"

"Uncle Billy send. Bad cave-in, Bodie. Need medicine . . ." He circled a hand around the other arm.

"Bandages?" Sarah asked.

The Indian tracker nodded. "And doctor man."

"Okay," Taylor said. He thought out loud. "Who can I send? Doc Smithson's out at the Hendricks' place, deliverin' her baby. Number three," he added, looking at Sarah.

"I'll go," she said.

"Huh?"

"I can nurse, fix food, whatever is needed until Doc Smithson can get out there."

"No, too dangerous a trip."

"I protect," offered Charlie Jack.

Taylor was well acquainted with the Indian's abilities and trusted him, but he wasn't sure about sending his daughter to a mining camp.

"I don't know . . ."

"I'll be fine, Daddy," Sarah pressed. "It'll just be for a few days, and your friend Uncle Billy and Matt's father will be there."

"All right," Taylor relented. "Go over to Harvey's and get all the supplies you'll need. Some bandages, tins of food, medicine, whatever he has. Have him put it on the county account, I'll get it back from whatever minin' company it is. Me and Charlie'll get the buckboard ready."

Sarah and Charlie Jack ran out and Taylor followed, but he stopped short of the door, went back and grabbed a piece of Sarah's fried chicken before heading up the street.

CHAPTER

FIVE

Sheriff Taylor pulled the wagon up in front of Harvey Boone's general store as Harvey, Sarah, and Charlie Jack came out, arms laden with supplies. They dropped them in the back of the buckboard and Taylor helped his daughter up into the seat. He followed her into the wagon and the seat springs creaked and groaned under his weight.

"Thanks, Harvey. 'Preciate it."

"No problem, Sheriff. Sarah, you be careful."

"Thanks, Mr. Boone, I will. Say good-bye to Mary for me, will you?"

"*Hup!*" Taylor shouted at the horses as he shook the reins and the animals strained at the harnesses. The wagon lurched forward. Charlie Jack followed on his sorrel.

In front of his house, Taylor climbed off the buckboard. "Go get some clothes for yourself and something to take with you to eat," he told Sarah as he helped her down. "Charlie, stay here with the wagon. I'll be right back."

Charlie nodded as Taylor ran to his office and Sarah hurried inside the house. She came back out moments later carrying a satchel with a heavy shawl draped around her shoulders. Her mother followed, a worried look on her face, carrying a food basket.

"You sure you want to do this?" Mrs. Taylor asked.

"Yes, Ma," Sarah said. "I'll be okay. I've been driving a team since I was ten and cooking since I was six. I learned bandaging and nursing last summer at the Petersens' barn fire, remember?" She opened the gate and glided confidently through.

Sarah heaved her bag up into the back of the buckboard behind the seat, then climbed up. Her mother handed her the food basket, which the young woman placed on the seat beside her. She adjusted her skirt.

"You be careful, now, Sarah," her mother cautioned. "Remember Sunday." She smiled at her daughter.

"Don't worry, Ma. Wild horses couldn't keep me from being back for that."

"All the same, don't dawdle. The sky is beginning to look a little threatening."

Sarah looked up and noticed a dark, gray mass hovering over the peaks of the Sierra Nevadas behind her.

"I'll beat them there," she said. "Besides, Charlie Jack's gonna be with me."

"Okay, darling." Mrs. Taylor patted her daughter's hand then glanced around. "Where's your pa?"

"He ran that way—Oh, here he comes now."

Sheriff Taylor trotted back to the wagon, huffing and wheezing. He carried a Winchester rifle, which he set under Sarah's seat.

"Just in case," he explained.

"Now, John . . ." started Mrs. Taylor.

He held up a hand. "Don't start on me, Irene. I taught her how to use it two summers ago. You never know what she'll run into."

"What about Charlie?"

"Charlie Jack no shoot," the Paiute explained. He lifted both hands and Mrs. Taylor could see he didn't carry a firearm. "Charlie Jack use this." He pointed to his head and smiled.

"Better git goin'," Taylor said. "You can make it by dark if you don't stop. Be good."

"I will, Pa. Thanks."

"Take care of my daughter," the sheriff told the Paiute.

The Indian nodded and turned his horse into the road. Sarah gave the reins a shake and the team started out, the buckboard moving over the dirt street following the Indian's sorrel.

The Taylors stood out front and watched until the buckboard

rumbled over the bridge at the edge of town and disappeared around a bend.

"She'll be fine," the sheriff said, putting his arm around his wife's shoulder and giving her a squeeze. "She's got some pretty strong incentive for gittin' back here in one piece."

The trip for Sarah and Charlie Jack was largely uneventful. The going was slow because of the buckboard, but the weather held. It was a bumpy trip, and Sarah was jostled. The seat springs were relentless and several times Sarah reined up the team just so she could catch her breath and let her backside regain some feeling. When they reached the Bodie road turnoff Charlie Jack rode ahead. For the first few miles the road wound through a red rock canyon before rising to the top of the plateau. Gaining a thousand feet in elevation in about thirteen miles, the thinning air, constant incline, and the heavy wagon tired the animals.

As they cleared the canyon, Charlie Jack dropped back and rode next to Sarah.

"This where I meet Deputy Matthew," he said.

"Really?" Sarah asked. "Tell me about it."

"He ride to Bodie, new badge, big smile."

Charlie Jack put his right fist over his left breast and showed his teeth. "He proud."

"I wish I could have seen it," Sarah sighed. "What happened?"

"I go to Aurora to track escape prisoner. Matt say he go too. We chase, we track, we find." Sarah listened intently. "Matt learn many things: how track, courage, who is father . . ."

"That was some coincidence."

The Indian looked at her, perplexed.

"Uh . . . strange happening, but good. Lucky," Sarah explained.

"No, Charlie Jack think it meant to happen."

Sarah blushed. "I do too, really. Sometimes white people use the wrong words to describe how we feel."

"I notice. Make talk hard."

"It sure does. I think God was directing Matt's path."

"Charlie Jack did that." He looked a little hurt.

"Sorry, I'm still using the wrong words. What I mean is, God— do you know what I mean by 'God'?"

"Paiute have many gods. White people only one. Matt say your god make earth, then come like man, get killed, but not dead now."

Sarah laughed. "That's true, although it's a little more complicated than that. What I was saying was that God helps us by giving us opportunities, using people to teach us, and . . . kind of . . . well . . . makes it possible for us to be in certain places at certain times by controlling what happens to us . . . kind of."

"Hmmm," mused Charlie Jack. "I curious. You explain again how your God die and not be dead, and how He help you."

For Sarah, the rest of the trip into Bodie went by quickly as she shared her faith with the Indian tracker.

By the time Sarah rolled into Bodie the sky was dark but not from the setting of the sun.

The clouds that had been threatening when she left Bridgeport had followed her to Bodie and closed in, driven by a cold wind. Sarah had brought her greatcoat, a heavy, gray wollen piece with a hood. She had been forced to put it on several miles out.

As they were within sight of town, Charlie Jack rode on ahead again. Sarah reined the buckboard up in front of the boarding house where Charlie Jack's horse was standing, untied, but no one came out to help her. She started to climb off the wagon when she heard a shout up the street.

She peered into the darkness and saw the Indian waving for her. She jumped down and ran up to him as men passed her going the other way. They stopped at the wagon and started unloading it, taking everything into the boarding house.

A gigantic black man hurried toward her. The sight of him moving so rapidly was a little unnerving at first, but she quickly realized who he was and relaxed.

"Thank you for comin', missy," he said, losing her hand in both of his. "Ah'm Billy O'Hara but everyone calls me Uncle Billy or Ah don't answer. Charlie Jack tells me you're Sheriff Taylor's little girl." His smile was as big as the rest of him.

"Yes, sir." She flinched at the term "little girl," but figured it was just Billy's way of being friendly. "Sarah."

"Ah'm pleased to meet you, Sarah, although Ah must say Ah was hopin' for a doctor. We got three men trapped inside." He motioned toward the mine entrance.

"They're still in there?" She was surprised, thinking that by now they'd have been freed.

"Yes'm. It's real touchy, you see. They're behind ten, fifteen feet of rock. We have to move it by hand and that takes awhile. We can't blast with them in there. And we have to build a support frame as we go so it don't cave in any more'n it already done."

"How do you know they're still alive?" She pulled her coat tightly around her.

"We done some shoutin', and they tapped on the stones. That was a few hours ago we last heard 'em. They must have some air, so we're hopin' they got enough to last a mite longer."

"What can I do?" Sarah asked.

"Can you cook, Miss Sarah?"

"Absolutely. And nurse, too. Doctor Smithson will be delayed. That's why I came."

"That's good news. Go on over to the boardin' house yonder and start fixin' some grub, if you please. We got a lotta hungry men. When we git someone out we may need yer nursin'." Sarah turned to go. "And thank you, Miss Sarah. We surely do 'preciate it."

"You're welcome," she said over her shoulder as she picked up her skirt and hurried off to the boarding house.

Billy ambled back to the mine to check on the progress. The buried men were deep. The main vertical shaft was clear, so the hoist could still be operated. As many men as could fit in the caved-in crosscut—two or three at the most—loaded rocks into the ore car as quickly as they could. They then retreated as the car was taken to the hoist and the ore was hauled to the surface while a timber crew moved in to raise ceiling supports. The work was slow, tedious, and taxing. As men became exhausted, they would ride up in the hoist bucket and be replaced by fresh men.

Not one to miss an opportunity for profit, Hiram Butler, the superintendent of the Empire Mine and Mill, was quietly having the ore taken to the mill to be crushed later, just in case there was something of value in it.

Jacob Page was trying to stay out of the way. With only one arm, he felt he could be more help topside directing traffic and running errands. Billy was so large he was uncomfortably crowded in the small mine and couldn't work for long.

The heat and the dust in the mountain were taking their toll, and because of the urgency of the situation, most of the men were overdoing it. By the time Sarah came back with a tray of food, many men were too exhausted to continue and two of them were in dire need of medical care.

Billy had some cots put up in the main room of the boarding house, and Sarah started her angel of mercy activities. She treated a few minor wounds, many blisters, dabbed hot faces with cold rags and spoon fed the fatigued. Most of the injuries were minor, so far. There was some heat stroke, skinned fingers, and pulled muscles, and one poor miner had his foot crushed when he dropped a stone that was too heavy for him. There was little she could do with him but sympathize and wrap it tightly.

Charlie Jack, Jacob Page, and Billy were helping a crew disembark from the hoist when they learned some bad news.

"How's it goin', Mickey?" O'Hara asked one of the returning men. The miner stepped out of the bucket and collapsed into a sitting position. His clothes were saturated with sweat, a dangerous situation on a cold night. Charlie Jack wrapped a blanket around his shoulders.

The man looked up at Billy and took several deep breaths.

"Not too good. They ain't poundin' on the rocks when we call no more. They may be done for."

"How far do we have to go?" Page asked.

"Couple, three feet maybe." He inhaled and exhaled, then coughed a few times. "But we're slowin' down."

Billy looked around. Too many men were at the boarding house recuperating, and those still at the mine were too tired to go back down right now.

"It's up to us," he said bluntly to Charlie Jack and Page. He turned on his heel and got into the hoist bucket. "You comin'?" The two followed immediately.

They descended slowly, their only light coming from a coal oil lantern hanging above them. None of the men spoke, thinking of the grim task ahead. Charlie Jack was nervous. He had gotten into the bucket without thinking but knowing he needed to go. Although generally courageous, he had never been down in a mine before. He was much more comfortable climbing around on the outside of the mountain than being lowered into it, held only by a thin cable he didn't understand. The tension on his face was evident to the other two men even in the dim, flickering, yellow light of the lantern.

"Jes' close yer eyes and preten' yer riding a horse at midnight with no moon," suggested Page.

The Indian shut his eyes for about two seconds. "Not same."

The one-armed man shrugged his right shoulder. "Jes' tryin' to help."

"Much grateful. Charlie Jack fine."

O'Hara would have laughed any other time. Things were too grim right now to enjoy the Paiute's discomfort.

Just then the bucket jerked, and Charlie Jack grabbed the side rail.

"Don't worry," comforted Billy. "They do that."

"So do horse, but Charlie Jack still worry."

The bucket slowed finally and came to rest. Carefully the men crawled out and made their way down the dim tunnel, following the ore car tracks. They soon came to the end of the tracks and could see where the old ones had been pulled up when the tunnel was abandoned. A few more feet back and there it was. Billy held up the lantern he carried.

Beyond some new timber bracing was a pile of jagged rock, floor to ceiling. Driven by the necessity of rescue, Billy ignored the ominous nature of the task and climbed across the near slope of the rock as far as he could. He motioned for the men to be quiet so he could listen.

Nothing.

"Hello!" he called. As his echo subsided he turned his head and cupped a hand behind his ear.

Tap . . . tap.

It was so quiet he wasn't sure he heard it. He pressed his head into the rock.

Tap . . . tap

It was weak, but he definitely heard it.

"Someone's still alive!" he shouted. He quickly began tearing at the rock, tossing boulders away from the blockage. Charlie Jack hefted them into the nearest ore car with a grunt while Jacob Page held the lantern aloft. With sharp eyes Page scanned the rock, looking for the shortest and easiest way in.

O'Hara toiled without let up for a half hour. The only sounds in the tunnel were the clicking of the rocks, the distant creak of the bucket as the rock was hauled up, the squeal of the ore car as Charlie Jack pushed it along the track, and their own heavy breathing.

Suddenly Billy let out a yelp and jumped back, startled.

"C'mere with that light!" he said.

Page moved forward, his arm outstretched. As the light passed O'Hara's body, it illuminated a long, pale object.

A man's arm.

Billy grabbed the wrist, then shook his head slowly.

"This one's dead," he said quietly.

"There's two more, ain't there?" Page asked.

"Yeah." Billy leaned forward. "You still there?" he shouted.

Tap.

With renewed fervor Billy continued and soon the dead man was nearly exposed. Charlie Jack grabbed him by both arms to pull him out, but Billy stopped him.

"You pull him out now, these rocks may break free. If that happens them other two could be crushed, mebbe even us." He continued to pick the rocks off one by one.

When the dead miner was fully exposed Billy turned to Page. "Check it out. Think it'll hold or should we frame it?"

Page held the light up. "Don't look too good, Billy, but I don't think we kin take the time. Their taps is gittin' weaker."

O'Hara took a deep breath. "Lord, help us," he said quietly.

Page looked at him. "I ain't religious—like you an' my son—but do you think it would help if I said a prayer?"

"Might be a good time to say one for yerself, Jacob. You might not have a 'later.'"

"Sarah tell Charlie Jack about God who die but not dead."

"Good for you," Billy said, irritated. "If we get outta here, we can all three sit down and have a nice, long talk. But for right now, Ah already done prayed. God can't help us if we don't get to work!"

Billy turned back to his task, passing the rocks back to Charlie while Page kept watch on the walls and ceiling. They worked steady for an hour when Page suddenly shouted, "Get back!"

Instinctively and without question Billy jumped back, so

quickly that he collided with Charlie Jack. The men scrambled clear as several large boulders tumbled down. They rolled up to the men and stopped.

They stood motionless. Would more follow? Would the whole thing give way? For a full minute there was silence. Finally Billy moved forward.

"Whaddya say, Jacob. We okay?"

"Yeah, I think so. It was jus' a few rocks shaken loose by us."

Billy went back to work one more time. He grabbed a rather large rock and hoisted it with a grimace. The Indian shouted as Billy picked it up and pointed. Page moved the lantern.

Behind the rock was a black hole. They were through.

CHAPTER

SIX

Jacob Page bent down with the lantern and peered into the darkness. He was staring into the face of a miner.

Page almost didn't see it. The face was dirty and swollen, and caked with blood. The eyes were closed. Page couldn't see the rest of the man, partly because of the limited light and partly because of the rocks he was covered with. At first, the man didn't move.

But the rush of air through the hole hit the miner and his mouth suddenly opened. He gasped and took in air in great swallows. Slowly his breathing normalized, and his black eyes opened slightly. All he could see through the slits was the light.

"Is this . . . Heaven?" His voice was weak.

"No, son, 'fraid not," Page said. "Yer still here on this earth, and we're here to git you out. Kin you move?"

"No."

"Okay, we'll take care of it. How 'bout yer partner?"

"I had two."

"Well, friend, one of them, I'm afraid he didn't make it. Do you know about th'other."

"No."

"Okay. Well, chin up. We'll be there in a bit. Don't you go nowheres."

Billy took the lantern and looked in. "That you Clyde?"

The buried man looked quizzically back. "Billy?"

"That's right," O'Hara said. "Ah'm gonna get you out, Clyde, don't worry none. You owe me a month's room and board."

The corners of the man's mouth turned up slightly, then he closed his eyes.

"Let's move!" Billy said as he handed the lantern back to Page. The big man, more slowly and cautiously now, resumed moving rocks aside. In a few minutes, the hole was large enough for a slender man.

"Ah can't reach," Billy said.

"Charlie Jack try," the Paiute offered. Billy moved aside. Charlie squeezed through until just his feet stuck out. Page and O'Hara could hear Charlie talking to the man and the clicking of rocks as Charlie moved them from on top of the miner.

The Indian was blocking the light and had to work in the dark. He spoke gently to the injured man.

"Where hurt?"

"Everywhere," the man whispered.

"Mmmm." He called back to the others. "Make hole big. Hurt bad. We carry."

"Okay." It was Page that answered. Billy carefully removed the rocks from around Charlie Jack's feet, then moved the lantern and peered in. Charlie Jack had the man completely uncovered. It was obvious he had some broken bones.

O'Hara pushed the lantern into the airspace and looked up. There was a rock overhang above them, and it appeared to be solid. *That's what saved 'em,* he realized. *Thank you, Lord, for that.* He looked past the Indian and the badly injured miner and was startled.

"There he is!" Billy could see the other man. He was only partially covered by rocks but was unconscious. "He's still breathin'!"

"I get him out now," Charlie Jack said pointing to the first man, "then go back."

"Okay."

Charlie Jack faced the miner. "This hurt much, but you die if we not do. Okay?"

"I . . . understand."

The Paiute removed the bandanna that he kept tied around his arm, wadded it up, and stuck it in the man's mouth. "You scream, it okay."

The Indian moved in the confined space until he was crouched down beside the man. He carefully slid his arms under the miner's back and thighs, peeling skin from his arms on the jagged ground beneath.

"*Ahhh!*"

"Is he okay?" Billy asked.

"That me!" complained the Paiute.

"Oh," said Billy. "Okay, I got his feet."

"Pull now!" Charlie Jack said, and hefted the man. Billy pulled gently, and they eased him feet first through the hole, his screams muffled. As soon as he had room, Charlie moved around to the injured man's shoulders and lifted as Billy pulled. When Clyde was all the way through the ragged hole, Billy picked him up while Page steadied the man's legs. Clyde had passed out from the pain. They carried him down the tunnel to the hoist bucket and laid him carefully inside.

Charlie went back to the other man and began moving rocks off him. He had a large knot on his forehead, and his breathing was shallow. Charlie grabbed the man under the arms and pulled him toward safety, oblivious to the pain in his own arms.

The Indian crawled through the opening, then reached back in to pull the man through. He was tired and his leverage poor, however, and the man wouldn't budge. He stopped straining for a moment and caught his breath.

O'Hara and Page picked that moment to return.

"Move away, Charlie, Ah'll git'm," O'Hara said. He helped Charlie up, then stretched himself out, reached in and grabbed the man, and dragged him out of his prison. He and Page carried the still unconscious man to the hoist bucket, with the Indian following behind. They eased the injured man into the bucket, and O'Hara rang the bell to signal the hoist operator. In a few seconds the cable went taut, and the bucket slowly rose.

There was only room for the two rescued men proned out in the bucket, so the three rescuers sat down to rest and await its return. After a few moments Page stood up.

"I left the lantern in there when I helped Clyde out," he explained, and walked back down the caved-in tunnel.

"Forget it," Billy said, but Page didn't stop. They couldn't see him with the small amount of light they had coming from a lamp hanging above the bell. No sooner had Page disappeared than they heard the rumble from inside the crosscut as it collapsed.

Billy and Charlie Jack jumped up and ran toward the tunnel. They couldn't see him at first, but he heard them coming.

"I'm okay!" he shouted. "I'm down here. I think my leg's broke."

"What happened?" Billy asked. He reached his friend and knelt down beside him. Page's legs were under the rocks, which Billy carefully removed. Page winced as the weight was taken off.

"I slipped and loosened some rocks. It was my own fault."

"Don't look too bad," Billy said quietly. "Ah'm gonna need something to splint it with—"

"How come, if it ain't too bad?" Page asked. "You didn't splint them other fellahs."

"Uh . . . they was unconscious, it didn't matter. You'll feel it. Charlie, go on up . . . take the dead man with you . . . and send down some splints and wrappin's. Ah'll help you load the body." He pushed himself up. "You stay here," he told Page.

Page gave O'Hara a perturbed look.

As Charlie ascended with the dead man, he inspected the bruises and deep cuts on his forearms, then focused on the miner. The man had been horribly crushed, something Charlie Jack hadn't noticed before. Then he suddenly realized how alone he was in this cast-iron contraption, suspended hundreds of feet above the shaft floor, supported only by a steel cable, while the man on the floor stared at him mercilessly. He reached over and closed the man's eyelids.

With the arrival of the bucket at the top, the men waiting had to lift the miner out, while Charlie Jack struggled through his nausea to relay Billy's request.

A couple of planks were dropped into the bucket and the dead man was carted off. They took him to the boarding house—for lack of a better place—where the injured miners were being tended to by Sarah. The engineer rang his bell and lowered the bucket one more time.

Charlie Jack made his way to the boarding house unassisted.

He walked slowly up the steps and went in, found an empty cot in the corner, and eased himself into it. He was asleep in seconds.

Sarah had busied herself with the exhausted rescuers, treating their aches and pains, bruises and cuts, but mostly she fed and encouraged them. Some of them felt good enough to leave after eating her stew. Others, especially those who had been in the seclusion of Bodie for a long time, were smitten by the attention of such an attractive young woman and hung around the boarding house longer than necessary.

Sarah had graciously declined one offer of marriage, and overheard one miner tell another not to even think what he was thinking, that she's the deputy's gal. She smiled to herself and didn't let on that she heard.

Weary from her efforts, Sarah sank into a chair, her hair hanging limp. Sweat dripped from her forehead. The stove in here worked too well and she was broiling, regardless of the temperature outside.

As she was considering changing into something lighter, a shout rose up outside. She ran to the door and saw two men being carefully lifted from the hoist bucket.

They're alive! Sarah was suddenly nervous. They didn't look to be in too great a shape from where she stood. Had she taken on too big a burden? It was up to her, she felt, to make sure the men pulled through. She swooned a little at the thought but steadied herself on the doorpost.

As they approached, Sarah glanced back inside the room and saw a man who looked perfectly healthy sitting on a cot.

"Sir, can you help me?"

He looked up. "Me?"

"Yes. Could you go out to the kitchen and find me a big pot and boil some water?"

"Y-yes'm," the man said. "Be delighted." He grinned, showing Sarah a remarkable absence of teeth, and ambled off to the kitchen.

Good thing I didn't cook steaks, she thought, smiling.

The crunching of feet on the rock turned to echoing clumps as they stepped onto the porch and tramped into the boarding house with the two men. The injured were set down carefully on the cots, and the men backed off and stood idly by, their task completed. It was the young woman's turn.

Sarah took a deep breath and wiped her brow. She moved forward and bent down over Clyde, who was coming around again.

He looked up at her, and she smiled. His lips began to quiver.

"An angel . . . Now I . . . know I'm . . . dead."

"No, you're not," Sarah assured. "And I aim to keep it that way." She smiled reassuringly. "What's your name?"

"Clyde."

"Okay, Clyde. Where does it hurt?"

"Mostly . . . all over . . . I know . . . my leg's broke . . . maybe both of 'em."

"Okay." She moved down and cut his pants legs off. The right leg was bruised and cut but appeared otherwise intact. The left, however, was severely swollen from the knee down. It had been a day and a half since the accident and infection had already set in. Sarah knew enough to realize she'd probably have to take it off.

She hoped Dr. Smithson wasn't delayed getting out here. If the leg wasn't removed, the man would die. She tried not to let her despair show.

She patted Clyde's arm. "You'll be okay for a bit longer, Clyde. Let me check your friend, okay?" She gave him a reassuring smile, covered him with a blanket and turned away.

The other man was breathing, but it was labored. She opened his shirt. Deep bruises covered his chest. His left arm was broken and had an open, dirty wound. It wasn't bleeding, but there was an abundance of dried blood stuck to him. The knot on his head was purple and red, very angry-looking.

"Someone take off his trousers, please." She turned to the men. "And the rest of you, if you're hungry, please go in the kitchen, there's stew and bread. Help yourself, don't make a mess, then clear out. I've got work to do."

Two men shuffled forward to help her while the rest wandered toward the front door or into the kitchen.

The second man, whom someone had called John, was now just wearing his long underwear. Sarah cut off the legs and torso of the garment, cleaned and dressed his cuts and bruises, then examined his chest closely. She listened to his breathing. Although some ribs appeared broken she couldn't hear any gurgling as he breathed, so she knew his lungs weren't damaged; at least, not badly.

"Not much I can do for you, John," she said softly. "But I'll do my best." She placed a cold compress on his forehead.

"Okay, I'm gonna need some help for this," she told the toothless man, who had just come back with the water. "I've got to set this arm. You're gonna have to hold him still, but be careful, don't aggravate his injuries. Hold him there," she pointed, "and you, could you hold his shoulders?" She spoke to a man standing near the door, watching. He moved over slowly and took his position.

The broken end of the bone had pierced the skin, but it hadn't started to heal incorrectly because the ends weren't touching.

Taking a deep breath and saying a silent prayer, Sarah gripped John's arm by the wrist and elbow and pulled. The man at John's shoulder held fast. Sarah kept pressure on the arm as she pulled and held her breath. She felt the muscles stretch and the broken bone disappeared back into the man's arm and slipped into place. As she eased off the pressure, the injured man whined in pain momentarily but did not regain consciousness.

Sarah stitched the wound closed with waxed thread and splinted the arm, then suddenly felt woozy. She backed up to a chair and plopped down, her head spinning. She shut her eyes, then felt a hand on her shoulder.

"You okay, miss?"

She looked up into the face of the toothless man. "Yes, I'm fine. Just tired."

"Can I git you somethin'?"

"Some water, please." He patted her and walked off to the kitchen, returning with a glass. Sarah accepted it gratefully and drank it all.

"You've been a real help," Sarah said. "Thank you." She looked around for the other man, but he was gone.

"Shoot," the toothless man said. "I didn't do nuthin'."

"What's your name?"

"Luke."

"Nice to meet you, Luke. I'm Sarah Taylor."

"I know. You're Sheriff Taylor's daughter, ain't you?"

She nodded.

"He's a good man. Treated me well last time he threw me in the calaboose." He had a thoughtful look on his face, remembering whatever it was he had done. Sarah didn't ask.

"Well, I need to get back to my patients," she said. "I could use some help. You up to it?"

"Be more'n happy to."

Sarah pushed herself out of the chair and walked over to Clyde. He had fallen asleep. She pulled back the blanket from his legs and looked at the damage again. There appeared to be many breaks, but it was hard to tell. The swelling was extensive, the skin torn and oozing. She gently touched his left leg. It was hot and had turned purple and red. His toes were black.

"Gangrene," she said.

Luke came over and stared. He whistled low. "Looks bad, miss. I saw this during the war. You know watcha have to do, don't you?"

She nodded and sighed. "I'll have to take it off." She checked his thigh. The infection extended well above the knee. "Better do it now." She glanced up at Luke. "Can you get me a saw? One that'll go through bone? And a sharp knife from the kitchen to cut through muscle."

Luke swallowed hard. "I'll see." He ran quickly out the door.

Sarah stroked Clyde on the forehead, hoping to wake him up easy. His eyes flickered open, his face winced and he groaned as the pain resumed, but he slowly regained his composure and stared up at the attractive, young woman. He didn't notice her sweat, the dirt, and her worried brow.

"Ah, there's my angel," he whispered.

"Clyde, do you remember what happened?"

"Not real clear. I was in a cave-in."

"That's right. Your left leg was crushed by the rocks."

"That explains the pain," he said. "Is it bad?"

"I'm afraid so." A tear welled up in her eye. "You've got . . . gangrene and I—"

"Got to take it off, right?"

There was a pause before Sarah answered. "Yes."

"You sure?" Clyde didn't doubt the woman. He couldn't help asking, just in case he hadn't heard her correctly. Anything to delay it a second or two.

Sarah nodded.

"When?" he asked.

"As soon as possible."

Clyde closed his eyes for a moment, then looked up at the ceiling. Sarah's tears rolled down her cheek and when Clyde opened his eyes again and saw them, he gently reached up and wiped them away with his callused thumb.

"Don't cry now, miss. You got no choice. Do your best, y'hear?"

She nodded.

"Can you get me some whiskey?"

"I'm not big on drinking," she said hesitantly.

"Drinkin's for pleasure," Clyde explained. "This is for pain."

Luke returned with the tools, and Clyde watched as he put them on a table nearby.

"Anything else?" Luke asked.

"Yes," she said. Clyde watched her as she moved away from him. "I'm gonna need some gunpowder, some strips of cloth, and a stick about so big." She showed him the dimensions with her hands, then looked at Clyde. "And some whiskey."

Luke left again while Sarah got ready. She had brought a bottle of drugstore alcohol with her and soaked a clean cloth. She wiped the saw repeatedly, removing all visible traces of foreign matter, wiped the knife, then wet another cloth and wiped Clyde's thigh.

"That . . . high?" he asked, grimacing at the pain.

Sarah nodded. "Sorry." Clyde didn't answer.

Luke returned shortly with the items she asked for. "Hardest part was the stick," he said. "There ain't no trees up here. Had to cut it off someone's broom. Whiskey was easy. Had it in my pocket!" He grinned and helped Clyde take a swig.

Luke saw the concern in Sarah's face. "Don't worry none, little lady," he assured. "Soon's you start cuttin', he'll pass out."

Sarah shivered and went to work. She tore strips from the sheet and wrapped them around Clyde's thigh tightly, tying a knot on top. She put the stick on it and tied another, then twisted the stick several times, cutting off blood to the leg. Tying the ends of the stick in place, she was ready.

The young woman put her head down. *Father, please guide my hands as I—*

"Say one for me, too." It was Clyde. He had been watching her. "Then do it real fast, okay?" She nodded, and closed her eyes again, this time praying out loud.

"Father, I pray that you will guide my hands and be with Clyde, protect him, and heal him. In the name of Jesus, amen."

She took a deep breath and picked up the knife.

CHAPTER

SEVEN

W ith a clank and a groan, the hoist bucket reached the surface. Billy helped the men lift Page, then dragged himself out after him. Page was carried to the boarding house as several miners supported the exhausted Billy as he walked under his own power.

When Page was hauled in he saw Sarah sitting beside Clyde, her face in her hands. Her shoulders shook. He could smell burnt gunpowder.

Then he saw Clyde's leg on the floor.

Luke was consoling her. "You done good, Sarah," he said, patting her shoulder. He looked at the men who had just come in. "Uh oh, you got another customer."

Sarah lifted her head and wiped her eyes so she could see. She watched a man with one arm—could it be Matt's father?—being laid on a cot, his leg in a splint. She got up and hurried over to the man she had heard about but never met.

"What happened?" she asked.

He turned his head to the side and gazed at her. "Oh, you're a pretty thing!"

"Th-thank you." Sarah wasn't prepared for this, and it flustered her. She could see her reflection in the window. She had dirt and dried blood on her face, her hair hung limp and wet, and her dress was wrinkled and stained. "Are you Matt's father?"

"Yep, young lady, an' proud of it!"

"Pleased to meet you, sir. I'm Sarah Taylor.

"Sarah Taylor!" he repeated. "Why, I've heard a great deal about you. In fact, I ain't stopped hearin' 'bout you fer the last month. You look a mite under the weather. Oh, I guess you been busy, tendin' t'us dumb ol' miners what cain't stay outta their own way. Listen . . ." He pointed to Clyde's leg as Luke took it away, " . . . you ain't a plannin' on doin' that to me now, are you?"

She looked heartsick and horrified all at once. "Oh, no, sir, I—" She suddenly realized she was neglecting his injuries. "Oh, I'm sorry. Let me take a look at that leg." She started to cut away his pants but he protested.

"Whoa, little lady, them's the only pair of Levi's I got!"

"How do you expect me to look at your leg?"

"Well, if ya'll turn away a minute, mebbe the men here can ease 'em off natural-like so I'll be able to wear 'em again another day."

"Ah'm afraid that'd hurt quite a bit," warned O'Hara who was sitting nearby.

"So? Y'all've heard me yell before. I ain't gonna have my pants cut!"

Sarah shrugged and turned while the men helped Page off with his jeans. It was then Sarah noticed Charlie Jack in the corner, and, at the same time, Page's shouting woke the Indian.

He sat up and looked around the room, dazed. The crisis all but over, men were milling around, discussing the rescue, trying to figure out how it happened, or just resting. Sarah noticed Charlie Jack's arms and went over to him.

"Mr. Jack, may I bandage your arms for you?"

"Charlie Jack fine. Have medicine. How Matthew father?"

"I was just about to check his leg, but I think he'll be fine. He's being real ornery right now."

"He fine," Charlie Jack concluded. "And other men?"

"They both should pull through. One man lost his leg."

"No worry, Charlie Jack good tracker. I find."

Sarah laughed in spite of herself. "What I mean is, I had to cut it off." She shocked herself with her matter-of-fact attitude and began immediately to feel the emotion welling up. "Excuse me," she said, and went back to Page's side, biting her lip, and moving a lock of wet hair off her forehead.

"All right," she said to her patient. "Let's see how we're doing."

"I hurt and you could use a clean-up, that's how we're doing," the elder Page assessed. "Other'n that, my leg's broke. Let's git it set so's I kin git some sleep."

"Okay," Sarah agreed. "Can I get some help?"

"Ah'll do it," volunteered Billy. "Ah been with him this far, Ah may as well git a little pleasure outta it. Whaddya want me to do?"

"Grab his arms—I mean—his shoulders." She blushed at her mistake. Page didn't react. "Hold him from moving." Luke walked in just then and Sarah called to him.

"Luke, come grab his foot and pull, I'll make sure the bones line up." He got in position. "Okay," Sarah said. "Now."

Luke pulled slowly, Sarah manipulated, Billy held on, and Page yelled. "Okay, they're in," Sarah said. Luke eased up and finally released his grip. Page was taking deep, quick breaths. Billy let go.

Sarah replaced the splint and covered Page with a blanket. He said no more, sweated profusely, and finally drifted off to sleep.

Billy walked over and surprised Sarah with a big, grimy hug. "Matt'll be so proud of you," he whispered. Exhausted, she just smiled weakly.

Finally alone, except for her sleeping patients and her new friend Luke, Sarah sat in a chair near the stove drinking a cup of hot cocoa.

"I'd give anything for a bath," she muttered, not knowing Luke was within earshot.

"Go ahead and clean up," he said. "I can watch 'em for awhile. Get some sleep, too. Lord knows, you need it and deserve it."

"That sounds so good."

"Go on, then."

"You sure you're okay?"

"Yes'm, jus' fine. Shut the kitchen door. I'll keep people out if someone comes."

"Thank you, Luke."

"Aw, don't mention it."

Sarah walked slowly into the kitchen with her bag. She took off her heavy dress, soaked a rag in warm water, and wiped her face, neck, and arms. She found her brush and ran it through her long, matted hair. It felt good.

The young woman changed into clean clothes, putting on a printed-cotton calico dress, then went back out with the injured. Luke was asleep in a chair. Sarah sat down nearby and before long had dozed off herself.

Deputy Page urged the Morgan along at an even pace, trying to put as many miles behind him as possible. His first day had been uneventful and his first night cold. He hoped to make Coleville early in the second day, find the man he was looking for, and return by Saturday morning.

The day broke with scattered clouds, the rising sun bathing the bottoms of them in pinks and oranges. But before it was fully up over the horizon, the cloud cover was complete and sinister. As they thickened, they also darkened, until Matt was sure he'd see rain before nightfall.

The air was biting cold, and the deputy buttoned his leather coat, turning the sheepskin collar up to protect his neck. He and Blister exhaled clouds of fog.

This was his first trip up here, and he marveled at the spectacular scenery. There were canyons with streams and a high waterfall, round grass meadows surrounded by purple cliffs, a smooth lake shining silver-blue in the morning, giving off a low-hanging mist, the surface disturbed here and there by jumping rainbow trout or swimming ducks.

"Look at that," he said to Blister. "A right pretty sight. Maybe we can bring Sarah up here someday. I bet she'd enjoy this." He patted the Morgan on the neck. "What do you think, huh?" Blister snorted and shook his head.

Sarah. The thought of her made him wistful and lonesome. How he longed to be with her! When he came out West he never imagined meeting anyone like her. He tried to put his finger on exactly what was so special about her, but he couldn't. Everything about her was special.

So much so, in fact, that he had trouble believing she felt anything for him. She could have any man she wanted.

"I don't get it, God," he said softly as he rode slowly through a meadow. "How can this be? It's—it's just too good to be true. I don't deserve anything like this."

His comments jarred his memory. Hadn't his mother always told him that no one deserves for God to save them, that we can't earn it? Why does He do it then? He has a purpose for everyone, she told him. And if you let Him, He'll direct your life.

But Matt didn't understand and had always figured that a man had to forge his own destiny, make his own way, create his own opportunities. That's why he went West, wasn't it?

He shook his head in amazement, realizing that God sent him West to reunite him with his father. What was that verse? He had run across it a week ago while reading an old Bible Billy had given him. *A man's heart deviseth his way, but the Lord . . . the Lord directeth his steps.* Something like that.

"Is that what's happening, Lord? Is Sarah part of my future? What do *you* think, Blister ol' boy? Is Sarah the one God has for me?"

Excited by the thought, Matt kicked the horse gently and the Morgan took off, carrying his excited rider closer to his destiny.

CHAPTER

EIGHT

Coleville was a small town at the northern tip of Mono County, just miles from the Nevada border. Travelers headed to or from Carson City and Lake Tahoe passed through it, but not many stayed. Just a collection of small wooden buildings, most of them on the main street, Coleville had little to offer other than trees and sky and wind.

Matt allowed Blister to saunter up the street while he looked for the land office or city hall. He wanted to find out what he could about the man he was looking for; might make it easier to find him.

The deputy saw the stores, saloons, a stable and livery, a bank, and a burned-down loan office. Seeing the nature of the buildings, their highly flammable siding and shingles, Matt could well understand why people here would be upset by an intentionally set fire: the whole town could go up in a very short time.

There it was—the land office. As Matt rode up to the boardwalk, climbed off the Morgan and looped the reins over the rail, he was surprised to see a door nearby marked SHERIFF. He changed direction and walked over to it. The door was locked. He peered through the dirty window. It hadn't been used in quite some time.

Matt strode back to the land office, ignored by the few people who were out on the street. A mongrel lying on his side picked its head up and growled at Matt, then put it back down and closed his eyes, having done his job.

Matt opened the door to the land office and stepped in, closing it behind him. The glass rattled in its frame. A man sat at a desk behind a high counter. All Matt could see was his head. The man turned to look at the new arrival into his domain. His black hair was heavily greased and slicked straight back. He had long, mutton-chop sideburns tinted with gray, a thin, well-trimmed mustache, and round spectacles. He stood and approached the counter.

"Yes?"

"Mornin'," Matt said. "I'm lookin' for someone, a Mr. Frederick DeCamp. Could you tell me where his place is?"

"He ain't there, most likely," the agent answered with a surly tone. "Why do you want him?"

Matt unbuttoned his coat and pulled it aside to retrieve the warrant in his shirt pocket, and when he did, his silver star was revealed. He handed the warrant to the agent.

"I'm Matt Page, Deputy Sheriff, Mono County. I'm here to serve this on DeCamp for burnin' down the loan office. And you are . . . ?"

"Huh?" The agent looked up from the warrant. "Oh. George Benning. I'm the land agent here. That was a terrible thing he did! Could've burned down the whole dang town! If we hadn't been so busy trying to put it out, why, some people were mad enough to go after him and hang him right there!"

"Why'd he do it?"

"He got foreclosed on. Wasn't making his payments."

"Tough times, eh?"

"Oh, yeah, tough times." Benning was being sarcastic. "But his problem is, he's just a shirker. Didn't work his land. He wanted to find gold, strike it rich. Spent all his time running around the hills. Ran up large accounts at the general store, wife and children went hungry all the time."

"Maybe he really believed he could find gold."

"Fool! That's what he is. And a liar! Told the store owner he had found some yellow. That's how he got credit."

"You sure he was lyin'?"

"Humph! Catching a prospector lying is like catching a termite eating wood."

"So he was a prospector?"

"Not really. You know any prospectors that drag the family all over the place?"

No, most of 'em leave the family behind when they take off, Matt thought.

Benning went on, "No, sir, he was a drifter. That's all. A shiftless drifter."

"Well, Mr. Benning, do you know what happened to him?"

"Hightailed it outta town. A group of . . . citizens, shall we say, went over to his house as soon as the fire was out. He was already gone, family too. They left just about everything they owned."

"Which way'd they go?" Matt asked.

"Don't know."

Matt was hoping it would be easier than this. "Did DeCamp have any friends in town?"

"Not really. Dave Barrow at the store yonder knew him, of course. So did Sally at the cafe. Nobody really knew much about him, though, as far as I know. He didn't come to town much. Family never came at all. Oh, to a church social when they first came to this area. But that's all."

"Hmmm." Matt was trying to formulate a plan when he suddenly remembered the empty sheriff's office. "Say, maybe you could tell me something. How come your sheriff's office is all locked up? Don't you have a sheriff?"

"Naw. If we did, would they have sent you? This place just don't need one much anymore. Every couple weeks Taylor rides up from Bridgeport when he ain't busy. Here, I got the key." He opened the drawer and handed an old brass key to Matt. "Feel free. You're a deputy."

Matt looked at the key and turned it over in his hand. It was heavy. "Thanks," he said. "Oh, by the way. Can you describe DeCamp to me?"

"Sure. He's a swarthy little man, red-faced, dark hair, mustache, well-built—but not from honest work. He's a braggart and a boor."

Matt peered at Benning. "I'm not sure I'll be able to detect those last two from a moving horse but thanks anyway. Where's their place?"

Benning gave the deputy directions and wished him luck, then went back to his desk as Matt retreated slowly outside. The dog, having already proven its dominance over the stranger, didn't stir. Matt passed his horse and headed for the vacant sheriff's office.

The lock was rusty and the key hard to turn, but he got it to work, and the lock fell open with a dull click. He pushed on the door. It was stuck. He put his shoulder into it and the corroded hinges slowly gave way with a groan.

Inside, the office was musty. A thick coating of dust and dirt covered everything. Matt looked around at the walls. Things were just as they had been left, except the gun case was empty. In the desk drawers were old papers and pencils and assorted junk.

Moving through a door Matt saw the jail cell. The front wall of the cell was all bars, and the door was open. Matt wandered inside, curious. An unpadded iron cot sat unceremoniously in the corner. The dust floating in the air added sparkle to a shaft of sunlight that was angling through the small, barred window, lighting an oddly shaped rectangle on the bare floor.

"Kind of eerie," Matt said out loud. "I wonder who—"
Clank!
Matt whirled at the sound. The cell door had slammed shut.

"Ohhhh!" Matt closed his eyes and dropped his head down, running his hand over his face. "Great! Now what?" He gazed around, trying to think of something. This didn't just mean a possible delay, it was also embarrassingly stupid. He stepped over to the cell door and shook it. Locked tighter than a tick on a new dog.

"Shoot!" he sputtered. *What a dumb mistake.* He leaned against the bars with the top of his head.

"How am I going to get out of here without anybody knowing?"

"Go out the door."

"Oh, sure, just go right—huh?" The voice came from behind him, and he whirled. There was a young boy's face in the window.

"Hi," Matt said, strolling toward the window. "Can you help me?"

"I dunno."

"Sure you can. Come around and get the key for me."

"I can't let you out. You're a bad man."

"No, I'm the sheriff, see?" Matt showed the boy his badge.

"That's a deputy badge. I can read."

"You're right, but I work for the sheriff."

"Maybe you stole it."

"That's true. Very good, son. You'd make a good deputy."

"I'd never lock myself in the jail."

"Probably not. What's your name?"

"Samuel."

"Glad to meet you, Samuel. My name's Matt. Deputy Sheriff Matt Page. I'd like you—" The boy disappeared. "Hey, Samuel, wait!" Matt jumped and grabbed the bars, straining to see outside, and called the boy. "Samuel?!"

"What, Deputy?"

Matt let go of the bars and dropped hard to the floor, turning to face the cell door. Samuel stood just outside the cell.

"I wish you'd quit sneakin' up on me," Matt complained.

"Can I ride your horse?"

"Huh?"

"Can I ride your horse?"

"No!"

"With you locked up in there, I can ride it anyway."

"Tell you what. You let me out of here and you can ride on him with me. He won't let you get on him if I ain't there."

Samuel turned and walked out.

"Hey, wait!" Matt called, running toward the cell door. He grabbed the bars to stop himself, but the door sprang open and Matt fell headlong onto the floor. He jumped up and ran outside while dusting himself off, then stopped dead in his tracks on the boardwalk.

Samuel was in front of the jail, sitting in Blister's saddle.

"What's the deal?" Matt asked.

"I just got on him and—"

"I mean with the cell door."

"It wasn't locked. Lock broke a long time ago. It's just rusted. You shoulda pushed harder."

Matt's hands were on his hips. "How'd you know that?"

"Sometimes I play in there."

"The front door is locked."

"Didn't useta be."

"Okay, smart guy. Listen, I need my horse. I said I'd give you a ride." He started to move casually toward the Morgan. "I meant it when—"

Matt suddenly lunged and grabbed the horse's reins just below the bit. Blister responded to his master, and Matt snatched the boy off the saddle.

"Where do you live, Samuel?"

"Nowhere."

"I mean it, Samuel! Don't lie!"

"I'm an orphan."

Matt set him down and squatted beside him. "Sorry, buddy, I don't believe that."

"It's true. When a kid doesn't have parents they're an orphan, right?"

"Sometimes. What happened to your parents?"

"They left without me. Ruth—that's my sister—went with them, but I didn't. I was playing here when they left. I was hiding. They couldn't find me, and they left. I guess they don't want me, so I must be an orphan, now, right?"

"When was this, Samuel?"

"Couple days ago."

"Samuel . . . what's your last name?"

"DeCamp."

CHAPTER

NINE

Noontime in Coleville found Deputy Sheriff Matt Page con-
fronting something new: a child, abandoned by his parents
and alone, his father a wanted criminal. Matt hung his
head for a moment, taking it all in and holding the sobbing six-
year-old.

"You hungry?" he asked the boy. Samuel nodded. "Whatcha
been eatin' the past few days?"

Samuel shook his head. "You'll arrest me."

"No, I promise I won't. You steal some food?"

"Apples from the store."

"Tell you what. I'm hungry myself. How 'bout me and you
goin' over to the cafe for some grub, okay?"

Samuel nodded. Matt took him by the hand, and he let out a
little yelp.

"What's the matter?" He checked the boy's hand and saw blisters on the tips of his fingers. "Been playin' a little too hard, I see."
Samuel nodded. "We'll get those fixed up, they'll be fine."

Matt led the boy and the horse across the street. He tied Blister
outside and went in with Samuel. The place was deserted, and
Matt found a table near the window. In a moment, a woman bustled out from the kitchen. She was middle-aged and plump, with
bright eyes.

"Good day!" she greeted cheerfully. "What can I get for—say, isn't that the DeCamp kid?"

"Yes, ma'am," Matt answered.

"My goodness, what's he doin' here? And what are you doin' here with him? Who *are* you?"

"I'm Matt Page," he told her, pulling his jacket back to reveal the star. "That's about all I'm at liberty to say right now, but I do appreciate your concern." Her face flushed.

"W-what can I get for you two?" she stammered, forcing a smile.

"Whatever would be the least trouble for you, ma'am. We'll eat anything."

"I have some ham and eggs. And bread, made this morning."

"Sounds fine," Matt said, smiling. "Why don'tcha scramble them eggs up. We don't like 'em runny, do we, Samuel?"

"Yes."

"Like I said," Matt went on, "over easy and don't break the yolk, we like 'em runny."

"Certainly, sir," the woman said. "Be right back." She turned to leave.

"And two milks."

She nodded and disappeared into the kitchen. Matt sat quietly for a moment, then smiled at Samuel.

"So where do you think your parents went?"

Samuel shrugged.

"Did your pa ever talk about another town, someplace else he wanted to see?"

The boy thought. "Ruthie said something about an organ."

"Organ? Like in a church?"

"No, it's a place, I think. She said Pa talked about goin' there."

"*Oregon,*" Matt said. "It's another state, north of California. Very pretty country, I hear."

Samuel nodded. "That's what Ruthie said Pa always said. He said there weren't as many people there. Are you going to find my pa and take him to jail?"

Matt was caught off guard by the question. "Uh . . . I—"

"Here's your breakfast, men," the woman said, arriving with the plates. She set them down while Matt sighed, grateful for the momentary reprieve.

"Thank you," he said. "Looks good."

Samuel was already eating.

"Whoa, son, wait up." Matt put a hand on the boy's arm. "We haven't thanked the Lord yet."

"For what?"

"The food." Matt bowed his head. "Thanks, Lord, for Your provision and help us find Samuel's family. Amen."

When Matt looked up, Samuel was staring at him.

"What?" Matt asked.

"I never seen a deputy pray before. Only women pray."

"Not true, Samuel. Remind me to tell you about Samson later. Right now, eat your food."

They both dug in, not setting down their forks until after the peach cobbler. Samuel looked tired.

"Why did your parents leave town, Samuel? They must've been in quite a hurry to get away to leave you behind."

"They were afraid—and ashamed of me."

"Ashamed of you? I doubt that. What do you think they were afraid of?"

"Getting lynched, no doubt." It was the cafe owner. "DeCamp burnt down the loan office, and they skedaddled."

"No, he didn't!" protested Samuel.

"I've heard that he did," said Matt.

"It ain't true!"

"Samuel, I—"

"That's why you want my pa, isn't it? You *are* gonna put him in jail!"

"Samuel, if he burned down the loan office—"

"He didn't!"

"But, Samuel, people here say—"

"I know he didn't!"

"How do you know, Samuel?"

The boy's lip quivered and tears rolled down his cheeks.

"'Cause I did!"

Matt was stunned and sat bolt upright in his chair. The woman gasped. Matt ran his hand through his hair. He could tell Samuel was scared. Then he remembered the boy's blistered fingers.

"It's okay, Samuel. Calm down. Now, tell me what happened."

The boy was quivering. "I don't know. Are you going to put me in jail?"

"No, of course not. Why would you think that? Did you do it on purpose?"

The boy shook his head several times fast.

"Okay, then, I wouldn't arrest you for an accident." Matt was beginning to understand. "Samuel, your parents probably don't know you did it. The whole town thinks your pa did it, and he got scared and ran away." *That still doesn't explain why he left his son,* Matt thought. "Tell me how it happened, Samuel."

"I . . . I . . . was playing . . . There was an old mattress out in back . . . It caught on fire—"

"You were playing with matches?"

Samuel nodded.

"Is that how you got them blisters? You burned yourself?"

Samuel nodded again. Matt sighed and looked at the cafe owner. "I'm gonna need some help."

"What can I—"

"I have to find his family and bring them back. Someone needs to watch Samuel and let the town know what happened. Can you watch him?"

"No, I'm here by myself. I—"

"What about the church? You have a preacher here in town?"

"Yes. Reverend Hinkle and his wife live in the parsonage behind the church, far end of town." She pointed north.

Matt stood and slid his hat on. He paid the bill and thanked the woman, then took Samuel to the rear of the loan office. The charred remains of an old mattress were leaning against the building.

Matt squatted and sifted through the ashes with his fingers, finding that below the surface the ashes were still soaked from the bucket brigade. He glanced over at Samuel, who stood with his hands in his pockets and his head down, shifting his feet nervously.

"Is this where you were playing?"

He nodded, then pointed a few feet away. Matt moved there, searched through the ashes again, and pulled out a soggy, burned matchbox.

He got up and led Samuel back to the Morgan. Together they rode to Reverend Hinkle's house, where they were greeted out front by the minister and his wife. After Matt explained the situation to them, Mrs. Hinkle gathered Samuel to her and took him inside. Matt gave the preacher the matchbox and shook his hand.

"Pray for me, Reverend. I need God to guide me."

"I'd say He already has," the minister observed, smiling.

Matt mounted Blister, tipped his hat, and rode off toward the DeCamp property while Samuel waved from the window.

CHAPTER

————— ✦ ✦ —————

TEN

S arah was awakened by the groaning of one of the men. She opened her eyes slowly, at first uncertain where she was. When she moved her head she found out her neck had stiffened. She stretched it, rubbed her eyes, and looked around.

Oh, yes, she recalled. She stood slowly and went to check on the men.

Clyde was asleep, but his face was not relaxed. She lifted the blanket and inspected the dressing on the stump. There was very little blood. The cauterizing had worked. She shuddered when she thought of spreading the gunpowder on the freshly sawn stump and lighting it; the flash, then the smell of burnt flesh; and her own reaction, which had not been pretty. She just couldn't hold it down. When she recovered she folded the flaps of skin she had left over the raw flesh and wrapped the bandage snug, then turned away and cried. Luke tried to comfort her, and she quickly composed herself.

Replacing the blanket over Clyde's body, Sarah stepped to the other man. He looked peaceful. His breathing had improved, and Sarah was elated. It appeared he'd be okay.

Jacob Page was snoring. She smiled. He was fine. The problem she was going to have with him was keeping him down long enough for his leg to heal.

Charlie Jack and Billy were asleep in the corner. Billy had a room here, naturally, but decided to rough it with all the other men. Sarah had a great respect for him already, based on what she had heard from her father and Matt. Now she knew that what they said was true.

Sarah retired quietly to the kitchen and put on a pot of coffee. She made a large bowl of biscuit dough and lit the stove. As she rolled the dough and cut out the biscuits, she realized how easy cooking was compared to what she had endured yesterday. She longed to be a wife and a mother . . . Matt's wife.

For the first time, she realized she loved him.

The door opened and Billy padded in. He was barefoot.

"Mornin', missy," he said smiling.

Sarah beamed at him. "Good morning, Mr. O'Hara."

"Please, honey, call me Billy. All mah friends do."

"All right, Billy. Coffee?" She lifted the pot.

"You was readin' mah mind."

Sarah poured a cup and handed it to him. Billy drank the burning liquid without flinching, then exhaled happily.

"That's wonderful! Do Ah smell biscuits? You know, Sarah, if you feed these men too good they won't eat mah cookin' no more. Maybe you oughta throw a little dirt in the food or somethin', anythin' to make it not taste so good."

Sarah laughed. "Not on your life, Billy!"

Billy looked at her with a knowing grin.

"What?" Sarah asked.

"Huh? Oh, Ah was jus' thinkin' what a lucky fellah Matthew is."

Sarah blushed but didn't get a chance to answer. They were interrupted by a cry from the parlor.

"Hey!"

Sarah ran out of the kitchen. Jacob Page was sitting up, supporting himself on his elbow.

"There y'are!"

"Good morning, Mr. Page. How are you feeling?"

"I'm hungry, that's how!"

"And a little testy, perhaps?"

"Oh, and I s'pose when *you* wake up with a broke leg you're all peachy and pleasant?"

"Probably not," Sarah admitted. "But I wouldn't chew out the doctor and the cook."

"Oh, yeah." He smiled. "Sorry. I'm still used to wakin' up and talkin' to Bonehead, my mule. I dreamt 'bout him last night, thought he had stepped on me."

Billy came out of the kitchen with a plate of biscuits and a cup of coffee. He gave it to Jacob, then saw that the other men were stirring, awakened by Page's outburst. He retreated to the kitchen.

"Ah'll take care of breakfast, Sarah," he told her as he left. "You check your patients."

She nodded and went back over to Clyde. His eyes were open, and he turned his head to her when she took his hand.

"Good morning, Clyde."

"Mornin', angel," he said. "Thanks for givin' me my life. I know what gangrene can do." He squeezed her hand. "Thanks."

Sarah smiled. "Feel like eating?"

"No, not quite yet. It still hurts awful bad."

"Doctor Smithson from Bridgeport should be here soon. He'll have something for you."

John was groaning. She went over and felt his forehead. Her touch apparently registered; he opened his eyes.

"Well, hello, John," Sarah said. "Welcome back." His gaze was blank. "Do you remember what happened?" No reaction. "You were in a cave-in. You were injured by falling rocks. Your arm's broken, maybe some ribs, but you're going to be okay. Your head hurt?"

He closed his eyes, then opened them again, which Sarah took as a "yes." She put her hand gently on his face. "You're going to be okay. Just get some more rest." He closed his eyes, and they stayed shut.

One by one the men woke. Those who could got up and filed into the dining room. Those who couldn't were served by Billy and Sarah. When Charlie Jack got up he went straight for Billy's stash of piñon pine nuts. He also took a couple biscuits and ate them dry with his hands.

Most of the men recovered from their exhaustion after sleeping and eating and cleared out of the boarding house. There was work to be done in the mines, especially the one that had collapsed. Luke stayed around and helped Billy take out the cots and clean up. It was his day off from the mine anyway. Every now and then men would come in to check on their friends' progress. At noon a larger than normal group plodded in for lunch, having heard others speak of the virtues of Sarah's cooking.

The injured men continued to improve. By late afternoon John had spoken his first words. He didn't remember anything since he sat down in the tunnel to eat his lunch. He took in some bread and milk and went back to sleep.

Clyde was finally able to sit up. When he did he looked at the blanket where his leg should have been and lost control. He broke down in great spasms of sobbing, punctuated by sorrowful moaning the likes of which Sarah had never heard.

She felt his loss sharply and fled the room. Billy gave her a few minutes, then followed her outside. It was cold and dark because of a heavy cloud cover, but Sarah was unaware of it. O'Hara found her leaning against the wall of the building, her fists in her mouth and arms tucked tightly against her as she cried silently.

Billy put his arm around her but didn't say anything. She turned and smothered herself in his chest and cried for a few minutes while he stroked her hair, then sniffed, swallowed, wiped her eyes, and went back inside.

That evening Doc Smithson finally showed up. Sheriff Taylor had dispatched him to Bodie as soon as he returned from bringing the Hendricks' baby into the world.

He brought laudanum and morphine and gave Clyde and John what they needed. His examination of the men was watched in silence by Sarah and Billy. When he was done he turned to Sarah.

"Young lady," he said.

"Y-yes?"

He smiled. "Best doctorin' I've ever seen outside of a hospital or my own office. Considering what you had to work with, I couldn't have done any better. You have every right to be proud of yourself. These men probably would've died without you."

She blushed and smiled. "Thank you."

The doctor looked at Charlie Jack's arms. "How come this man didn't get a poultice or something?"

"He said he'd take care of it himself," Billy defended.

"I no have Paiute medicine," Charlie Jack said, shrugging.

Dr. Smithson scraped the wounds clean, then bandaged the

Indian and told him to stay in bed for at least two days to keep the infection from spreading. "Too much activity will give you all kinds of problems, maybe even blood poisoning."

When the doc finished, Billy set him up with a room. He would stay a few days to make sure they were all going to heal properly, then leave Billy in charge. Billy also gave Sarah a room. She needed a good night's sleep and, though she tried to turn it down, he wouldn't hear of it.

After she finished cleaning up the dinner dishes she wandered into the parlor. Jacob Page was sitting up in bed, holding an old, beat-up guitar and plunking the strings awkwardly. They buzzed and howled in protest.

"Where'd you get that?" Sarah asked sitting down beside him.

"It's Billy's. I saw it in the corner, asked 'im fer it. I'm bored." *Plink, buzz, clunk.* "A little hard to play, though, with jes' one arm."

"May I?"

"Shore." Page handed her the instrument. She strummed it once, tuned a few strings to her satisfaction, and sang "Amazing Grace" while thumbing the basic chords. When she stopped, the room was silent and all eyes were on her. She blushed.

"Mighty purdy," Page said. "When you and Matt have me over once a year fer my birthday you kin sing me that."

"What do you mean, me and Matt?"

"You know . . . you, and Matt . . . together."

"Aren't you being a little premature? Matt and I have hardly spoken to each other since we first met."

"Oh, really? He's tol' me a lot about you. I figgered he and you'd gotten to know each other. That's part of the reason he went to Bridgeport th'other day, was to see you. Did he chicken out?"

"Not exactly. My pa—Sheriff Taylor—said he could come over for supper on Sunday after church."

"Hmmm. On Sunday af—say, now that you mention it, where is Matt? I completely forgot about him in all the excitement."

"Father sent him to Coleville for something."

"Hmmm. Listen, Sarah, tell me somethin'. I been thinkin' 'bout it, and I meant t'ask Billy but seein's how yer here I'll ask you. When I met Matt on the trail—he was chasin' me, you know, I stole his horse. 'Course, I didn't know who he was, and he didn't know who I was, and—anywho, he was lookin' at me and I was

lookin' at him, and we both suddenly realized who we was, and
. . . well, he . . . hated me like the dickens. I don't blame him, mind
you, he had a right. I was selfish and deserted him and his ma when
he was jes' twelve or so."

Page shifted his body on the bed, grimacing slightly. Sarah
remained silent and Page continued talking. "I un'erstood that. But
something happened to him after he rode off. The next time I saw
him his whole attitude was different. He asked *me* to forgive *him*.
I don't git it. Do you know what happened to him?"

"All I know is what Billy told me. Finding out your father is
alive when you thought he was dead is a pretty big blow. He had
to deal with that, plus the resentment that caused. You didn't die
like he thought, you ran out . . . or so they say." Her cheeks reddened. "The way Billy explained it to me, Matt realized he had to
make things okay between you and him, and between him and
God."

"What do you s'pose made him think a that?"

"Something his mother told him. There is no peace in life without Christ."

Jacob Page looked away from Sarah. He had heard his wife say
those things, too. He hadn't paid much attention to her, though.
He was a good man, what did he need Jesus for? Sure, he was
happy for Matt. But Matt was young, had his whole life ahead of
him.

"I'm plenty peaceful," he told the young woman.

"Yes sir," she said politely. "Mr. Page, may I ask you something?"

"Go 'head."

"Do you think meeting Matt out here, after all those years,
under such strange circumstances, was an accident?"

"I hadn't really thought 'bout it, to tell the truth. What do *you*
think?"

"I think God had a hand in it. And when God does something,
it's always for a good reason."

"Like what?"

"I don't know, but I'll bet if you think on it, you might just
come up with an answer."

She stood and bent over him, planting a kiss on his forehead,
then walked away. His face reddened, but he said nothing.

Sarah entered her first-floor room and closed the door behind her. Although it was still early in the evening she had decided to go back to Bridgeport now that Doc Smithson had arrived, and she wanted to get an early start in the morning. Rain had been threatening for several days, and she didn't want to get caught in it. The longer she waited the more likely that was.

Sarah climbed between the clean sheets with many thoughts on her mind, but before she could consider any of them she drifted into a deep, well-earned sleep.

CHAPTER

ELEVEN

Matt found the DeCamp cabin with little difficulty. The land office agent had provided good directions, the landmarks were easily spotted, plus the road went right past it and DeCamp had painted his family name on the fence. But what Matt saw was not what he was expecting.

He slid off the Morgan and tossed the reins over the fence rail, then walked slowly up to the charred pile of lumber and debris that had been the DeCamp residence.

"The good citizens of Coleville," Matt muttered. He walked through the black skeleton of the doorway and gazed slowly around at the mess.

The DeCamps apparently hadn't taken much with them. It looked as though all of their possessions were still here: furniture, dishes, knickknacks, toys, even some clothes. Matt guessed they hadn't taken the time to stop, perhaps only just long enough to grab a few important things.

Except Samuel.

Matt wandered back outside. The ground was covered with footprints, the residue of the vigilance committee. He stepped to the fence and Blister snorted at him, then he picked up the reins and walked the horse up the road, carefully inspecting the wagon tracks. There was more than one set, and at times they overlapped, making it hard to tell one from another.

Pulling himself into the saddle Matt decided to keep riding and not worry about which track was which, at least not for the moment. He figured the DeCamps were headed for Oregon and were in a hurry. They weren't likely to try to cover their tracks or attempt any trickery. Once they were sure the people of Coleville were no longer following them they would probably slow down so their horses didn't keel over. With a woman and a young girl, they should be easy to find.

Page shook his head in disbelief. What could they have been thinking? How could they leave Samuel behind? Were they planning on coming back for him? Maybe they thought someone would take the boy in. The boy's mother would never go for that. Matt couldn't imagine a father who would desert his son . . .

Yes, he could, he realized suddenly. He still couldn't understand it, though. What goes through a man's mind when he rides off, thinking he'll never see his family or his kid again?

Angered by his stirred-up old feelings and his disgust at DeCamp's actions—all so unnecessary—Matt dug his heels into Blister's flank and urged the Morgan down the road at a good clip. He almost had to force himself to remember that DeCamp *hadn't* burned the loan office.

Matt couldn't help but admire the countryside as he rode. Although less dramatic than Bridgeport or Bodie, it was still beautiful and inviting. Every turn in the narrow road revealed a new place where he wouldn't mind settling down; and thinking of settling down reminded him of Sarah, the woman he wanted to do all this settling down with. He urged Blister on.

A fork in the road several miles away caused him to pull the Morgan up sharply. He followed the various wagon tracks with his eye, trying to determine which set might be DeCamp's.

Think I'm just gonna have to guess. Let's see. That there set is covered by that one. There's some off to the right, kinda slide as they make the corner. Hmmm, they seem to be the newest, nothin' goes over 'em.

He put both hands on the saddlehorn and leaned forward. "Okay, God, I guess I need Your help. Best I can figure, I need to go that way . . ." He nodded his head toward the right-hand fork so God would know what he was talking about. "And I hope that's right."

He paused a second, seeing how his decision felt. When he felt nothing he shrugged, kicked the Morgan into life and took the right-hand fork.

He rode for several hours, not stopping to eat. There were only two, maybe three hours of daylight left, and he didn't want to waste them. DeCamp had quite a head start on him, and Matt needed to make up ground fast, so he rode well past dusk, finally stopping only when he and Blister were too tired to move safely in the dark.

They bedded down for the night by the side of the road, Matt stretching out under the stars with his saddle under his head and a blanket thrown over him. He stared up at the stars, amazed at the number of lights in the Milky Way, and thought about the God that created them all. How expansive the universe must be, he thought, yet God cared for him as an individual. But He cared for Samuel, too, didn't He? Then how could this be happening?

The thought disturbed him, and Matt didn't sleep well, waking well before dawn. Blister pawed the ground nearby, sensing his master's urgency. Without even taking the time for coffee, Matt saddled his horse and picked up the trail once more. He rode for most of the day, hoping to close the gap significantly. He figured he was making much better time than DeCamp, staying on the move more than a family in a buckboard could, and traveling faster.

It was nearly noon when he pulled Blister to the side of the road for a break. Matt slid off and stepped behind a convenient bush. He stood there daydreaming, staring off into the valley below, when he realized the road he was on wound down into it. He could see something moving slowly on the road below.

Matt hurried back to Blister and pulled a pair of binoculars from his saddlebags. He focused the glasses and tried to hold them still so he could make out what was raising a cloud of dust on the road.

It was a horse and rider. Matt lowered the glasses, disappointed, and started to turn away when he caught a glimpse of a second dust cloud, quite a distance behind the first. He raised the binoculars again.

A buckboard, with two people on it, one smaller than the other.

Moving back to the horseman, Matt saw that he had stopped and seemed to be waiting for the buckboard. The rider appeared to be a small, stocky man. That's all Matt could make out at this distance, but it appeared to be DeCamp and his family.

So, DeCamp brought a horse and let his wife drive the wagon. Matt was surprised he had caught up with them so fast. They had had almost two full days' head start, but with a child and a buckboard, the feeling that they were out of danger, a potentially reluctant mother who didn't want to leave her son: it all made sense that Matt could gain so much ground.

Besides, Matt realized, he hadn't actually caught up to them yet. He was still high on the mountain and the road down was full of time-consuming switchbacks. He was several hours behind them and wouldn't make it up before dark.

Matt decided to cut the gap between them, then stop for the night and catch up to them at first light. He didn't want to confront them in the dark. That was too dangerous, especially since DeCamp would likely think he was going to be arrested and his survival instinct would kick in. No, daylight would be safer—for both of them.

Matt trotted back to Blister, who was enjoying some wild grass at the road's edge. He put the binoculars away, gave himself and the horse a drink, then climbed on.

The Morgan responded to Matt's heels digging into his sides, shook his head, snorted, and took off. Once away from his roadside rest area Matt could no longer see his quarry. He wanted to be at the bottom of the mountain by dark so that the treacherous and slow part of the ride would be behind him. The switchbacks were steep and tight and a wagon would have been forced to drive slowly and with great care. It was easier on a horse, but he couldn't allow the animal to build up too much speed. One slip could be deadly.

Blister cooperated on the downgrade, although it was taxing. The sky had not cleared and there was no wind, but the air was cold. Matthew knew the horse would need a rest soon, and so would he.

They rounded a slow curve in the roadway, around a large rock outcropping, and almost suddenly the road stretched out ahead of him, across the grass valley. Matt guessed he had gained another hour or two. It was dusk, and there was only an hour left before it'd be too dark to find a suitable place to camp.

Reluctantly, Matt reined up and walked Blister off the road to look for a soft spot to bed down. He found it not far from the road: a level spot under an overhanging rock. The night sky was ominous, and Matt felt rain in the air. That it had not already rained was a little surprising. Perhaps it wouldn't, Matt thought as he led Blister to a tree to tie his reins. Perhaps the weather had turned and the storm would pass over.

A bolt of lightning abruptly ripped through the sky, followed seconds later by deep, rolling thunder. Blister pulled back against Matt's lead nervously and jerked his head. "Maybe not," Matt conceded as he struggled to hold on.

The deputy won out, and his mount settled down after Matt secured him and gave him a little sugar and a hatful of oats. Matt collected some deadwood and kindling and built a small fire, careful to do so on the south side of a large rock so it wouldn't be seen, just in case DeCamp was smart enough to keep a wary eye behind him.

Hunger wasn't a factor tonight, and Matt didn't feel like going to the trouble anyway. He knew, however, that he'd need energy in the morning, so he took some sourdough and jerky and washed it down with canteen water.

He fed and watered the horse, which nuzzled Matt's hand with his soft, warm nose. Matt rubbed it affectionately.

Sleep came easily. Matt left his heavy coat and his gun on, and used his slicker for a blanket, just in case the rains came.

They did and with a vengeance. The first few drops woke him before dawn. He gathered his belongings and put on the slicker just before the deluge hit, then took cover to wait it out. The rain fell in sheets at times, saturating the ground and removing any hint of a trail his quarry might have left. There was little he could do but wait it out, at least until it subsided, and he had plenty of time to think: about Samuel, Sarah, and his own future. What would it hold? What did God have in store for him? He wished he knew, and yet, on second thought, that would take all the fun out of it. Besides, if it was bad, he'd just as soon not know.

For all its ferocity, the storm passed quickly, moving to the south. The rains stopped as suddenly as they started, leaving a clean, fresh aroma in the air. It was invigorating, and Matt searched for enough fuel to boil a pot of coffee. The brew was strong and good.

The clouds had thinned but still blocked the sunlight. It was past time to move on. He wondered how DeCamp and his family had reacted to the brief storm.

With the slicker rolled up and lashed to his saddle, Matt hit the trail one more time. He thought about how he loved the out-of-doors, the California countryside, his job as a deputy, his horse.

What about Sarah?

The thought was involuntary. How would she take to this kind of life? Would he have to give up the cross-country treks? After all, this was only his second. He'd like to get in a few more before settling down.

But was there anything he wouldn't give up for her? He couldn't think of it.

I wonder if she can cook? It didn't matter. He'd eat jerky. She could—"Hey! I've got to get back! Supper at the Taylor's is in two days!"

He pounded his knees once onto Blister's sides. *"Yeehaw!"* The horse took off, and Matt was on the hunt again.

The hunt didn't last long. An hour after he started Matt had picked up their trail in the muddy road. Yesterday's tracks had been washed out by the morning deluge, but the obliging DeCamps gave him a new one, making Matt's job easier.

He could see where they had made camp. They had probably taken shelter under their buckboard and built a fire this morning as Matt had, only theirs was bigger. There was still some firewood piled where the wagon had been.

Again the nagging question returned to Matt's consciousness. Why had they left Samuel behind? Was it only to keep Fred from getting caught? Matt couldn't believe that. Samuel was their son, their flesh and blood.

The coals were wet, but the wood wasn't all burned. The rain had put the fire out. They were close, maybe an hour ahead. Matt could make it up in no time.

Then what? he wondered. *Then what?*

CHAPTER

TWELVE

Sarah's eyes flickered open. She lay there, not moving, her brain numb, trying to figure out what time it was. The room was still dark, so the sun must not be up yet, she thought. Should she go back to sleep? No, she was anxious to get home.

She sat up in bed, the quilt wrapped around her, and peered out the window. No, it was early morning. The sky was dark because of the clouds. Sarah swung her legs over the side of the bed and set her feet down on the cold floor. She picked them up immediately and chirped her displeasure, then eased them down again.

Standing slowly, she padded over to the window, parted the curtains, and put her nose to the chilly glass. Before her breath fogged the window she saw the dark clouds moving in. Miles away to the north, it looked like rain, and it was headed this way.

The young woman dressed quickly and ran out to the kitchen. Billy was already up, making coffee.

"Sarah? Ah thought you was gonna sleep in a while. You was plenty tired." He poured her a cup of scalding coffee, which she accepted gratefully.

"I need to get home, and the weather doesn't look good."

"No, it don't. Been threatenin' rain for some days now. Likely to deliver today. You sure you want to start out?"

"If I don't leave now, when?" she asked. "This storm could stay for a month, you know that. Then turn to snow. It's not that far, and the road's good." She took another sip from her steaming mug. "I'll hurry."

"Okay, missy, if you're determined to go Ah'll git you some food for the trip and hitch your wagon."

"Thanks, Billy, you're a dear."

Sarah returned back to her room and collected her things, then hurried outside. She had bundled up in her greatcoat, knowing by her touch on the glass that it was cold outside. She opened the door to the porch and was met with a blast of frigid air that made her breath fog.

"*Brrr.* But thank God it's not cold enough to snow." She walked across the street to the stable where Billy was tightening the horses' harnesses.

Her food basket was on the seat. It was full of bread and salt pork and pine nuts. She'd never had pine nuts. Charlie Jack always ate them, and he was in good shape, so they must be okay. She wondered what they tasted like.

"She's ready," Billy announced, and lumbered over to the woman. He took her by the shoulders and held her at arm's length. "Mah, you are a fine specimen! It's no wonder Matt feels 'bout you like he do. And when he finds out you're a great cook and can doctor and play the guitar and sing like a robin, why . . ." He smiled. "You done good, girl, you done good."

She smiled. "Thank you for all your help, Mr. O'Hara."

"From now till the Good Lord takes me I'm your Uncle Billy, y'hear?" She nodded and he wrapped his arms around her. He smothered her with a hug, then picked her up and set her on the buckboard seat.

"Charlie Jack can't come along. Doc's orders," Billy said. "You want someone else to ride with you? Them horses is actin' a mite nervous."

"No, I don't think so," Sarah declined. "I'll be fine. The road's clear, and I know the way."

"Sky looks awful mean," Billy observed, looking up. "Hope we can get the mines operatin' again today. Men need to work. Be nice to hear that stamp mill again. Kinda lets you know ev'rythin's all right with the world." He gave Sarah a serious look. "You be careful and don't dawdle none."

She gave him a reassuring smile and shook the reins. "Giddap!" She shook them again and the horses moved reluctantly, but her persistence won out and they came together, pulling the now empty buckboard with ease. She sped them up, even more anxious now that she was actually on the way home.

As she bounced down the road, Sarah glanced over her shoulder at Billy, who was still standing there, watching her. He gave her a wave.

She was jostled noisily by the buckboard down the Bodie road, the springs under the seat reacting to every rock and hole the wheels rolled over. The dark clouds that had moved in slowly were now picking up speed, with no hint of breaking. With one hand on the reins, Sarah pulled her greatcoat tightly around her and shivered but did not slow down.

Alone with her thoughts she tried to suppress the memory of Clyde's leg by thinking of Matt: his strong hands, kid's grin, shy ways, and unceasing pluck. She was glad he had shaved his mustache. He was handsome with a mustache, but it made him look so much older. Besides, her father had a big shaggy one, and it always smelled of tobacco.

I hope Matt doesn't pick up that habit, she thought. *Oh, a pipe wouldn't be too bad, I guess. They smell good, but he won't smoke it in my house!*

She laughed at herself. Now *she* was being premature. Yet it all seemed so natural. The sheriff (that's what she called him when he wasn't acting like a daddy) would adjust have to relax a little and let them spend more time together. Sunday dinner was fine, but both he and Ma would be there, and, knowing the sheriff, he'd dominate the whole conversation.

The buckboard suddenly hit a small chuckhole and she bounced off the seat, landing with a thud that made her cry out involuntarily. Irritated, she slowed the team to flatten the road some.

After going several miles without a hitch, she thought she'd give the animals—and herself—a rest. She slowly pulled the reins back.

"Whoa, whoa," she called. The animals responded, pawing the ground and shaking their heads, sensing they were headed home. They whinnied and blew and moved in place restlessly while Sarah stood and stretched, and peered at the oncoming clouds with a furrowed brow. Her hair was blown back by the wind, and she pulled up her collar to try to keep out the cold, although it didn't have much effect. There was no time to waste. She could see that the rain was closer, much closer than it had been that morning.

She picked up the reins again and called the horses into life. The road grew narrower and more winding the farther she went from Bodie. She knew there was a canyon up ahead eight miles or so and wanted to clear it before the rain hit.

For an hour she drove the horses, subjecting herself to constant buffeting and bouncing, until her backside was numb. She was near the beginning of the shallow, twisting canyon and wanted the team to traverse it without problem, so she stopped again to let them rest. Once through the canyon she'd come to the main road that connected Bridgeport with Bishop to the south. From there, it would be mostly downhill and clear sailing all the way home.

She stopped next to a hill, which blocked the wind some. It was almost noon, she guessed, but wasn't sure as the sky was dark with rain-sodden, black clouds. She eased herself down from the wagon, rubbed her backside to restore feeling, then took her basket down to see what Billy had put in there for her.

Thunder roared in the distance, and a single drop of water hit Sarah on the nose, then another on the arm, and a few on the top of her head. The sprinkles increased and Sarah saw a magnificent, jagged lightning bolt flash several miles away, followed shortly by a peal of thunder that she also felt.

The incredible power of God, she thought.

Sarah climbed into the back of the wagon and hunkered down under the tarp, determined to keep dry as long as possible. She started to open the basket to have a bite to eat when, without warning, another bolt of lightning struck close by, so close that even under the tarp she could see the light from it.

That was enough for the horses. One of them bucked, and they both took off; unevenly at first, causing the wagon to whip wickedly from side to side, tossing Sarah around helplessly. Without someone on the reins, the horses wouldn't synchronize, and the wagon followed recklessly, bouncing out of control.

Then the thunder that accompanied the lightning ripped, almost deafening in its intensity. This frightened the horses even more, and at the same time, the skies opened and rain peppered the countryside.

Sarah couldn't get control of herself. Even if she could manage to climb into the seat, she doubted the reins would be within reach. She'd have to hold on and ride it out.

Easier said than done, she thought. No sooner did she find something to grab than she was shaken loose. Her head was bumped repeatedly as she was thrown from side to side and from front to back, losing all sense of direction and wondering how the wagon would hold together. She understood for the first time the concept of chaos and called on God loudly for help. She felt the bruising of her body, struggled to gain control of herself, and finally, after a large jolt, found herself suddenly airborne.

She flew blindly through the air, screaming, still covered by the tarp, and landed in a heap on wet, muddy prairie grass. It was pitch black and something was pinning her down. It took her a few moments to realize the tarp had landed on top of her.

Frantically she fought her way out, gasping for the air she felt she was being deprived of. She stumbled on her basket nearby, finding it intact, and the food Billy gave her still wrapped. She hoped it would still be edible. Bumped and bruised, but with nothing broken, Sarah struggled to her feet.

As she stood, she became instantly dizzy, aware of a sharp pain in the back of her head. Gingerly she felt back there, finding a goose egg. When she checked her fingers, there was blood on them.

Undaunted, Sarah tried to get her bearings. She realized she wasn't on the road but didn't know which way it was. The team must have run off of it. She turned and started walking down a sloping incline toward a meadow she couldn't see, hoping to find at least one of the horses.

She was fair game for the rain now. Her coat, although warm when dry, was soon soaked, and the water began seeping through the material. The dirt she walked on was quickly a muddy sea.

Sarah found the going difficult, stepping in ankle-deep water several times. Once she fell face-first into a puddle, and as she turned over and sat up, she cried until she laughed, then cried some more, finally picking herself up and continuing on her way. She had to get home. Hoping the horses had gotten tired and stopped, she refused to think about the other possibilities, not yet. No sense getting unnecessarily upset.

The clouds were so thick and the rain so heavy that she

couldn't see more than a few feet, and when she looked up, it beat hard on her smooth face forcing her to put her head back down and shield herself with her hands. Then another bolt of lightning crackled. She was startled but saw what she was looking for.

The wagon was on its side about a quarter mile away. At first she couldn't make out the horses, but as she drew near, she saw one of the animals on its side next to the wagon, struggling to get up. The other was nowhere in sight.

Sarah yelped and ran headlong toward the wagon. The ground wasn't level, and as she ran down an incline, she felt herself losing her balance. Before she could slow down, she again fell face first, hit the mud, and slid several feet into a large thicket of prickly sage.

She rolled over, groaning, then came up to a sitting position, spitting out mud. She took inventory of herself, decided she was okay, and picked herself up. Looking down, she was appalled at her ragged and muddy dress and coat. Her hair was a dripping, tangled mess.

Will I ever get clean? Sarah was immediately aware how silly that thought was and refocused her attention onto the wagon. She walked to it slowly.

As she feared, it was of no use. Two wheels were broken. She stepped gingerly to the horse. The animal was caught in the harness and unable to get up, no matter how much he struggled.

If I can free him maybe I can ride him home. She moved over to see what she could do, then noticed it wasn't the harness keeping him down.

The animal's leg was broken.

"Oh, no!" she complained out loud. She stood awkwardly, considering her predicament, then realized she couldn't let the horse continue to suffer. *What can I do? What can I—?*

She remembered her father's rifle. Walking around the wagon, she searched the landscape for the gun. She hoped it hadn't bounced out. . . No, there it was, just a few feet away, caught in a sagebrush. She grabbed it and shook the water off.

"Daddy always keeps his guns oiled," she told herself. "I hope it still shoots."

Working the lever action as she had been taught to do, she fed a round into the chamber as she walked back to the horse. She pointed the muzzle of the carbine at the horse's forehead, turned her

face away from the animal and pulled the trigger. She was nonetheless surprised when it fired, and the recoil knocked her down.

When her vision cleared she gazed at the horse. It was still, rain-
water diluting the blood that flowed from the hole in its head. The
sight brought her to tears and she held her face in her hands until
a spasm shook her senses and she recalled her predicament.

The rain hadn't let up, so her tears were inconsequential, and
she quietly stopped. She knew she needed to get moving and forced
herself up as she tried unsuccessfully assessing her location. She
was in some pain and had a headache, and the rain and dark still
limited what she could see. She wanted the tarp, but when she
started to get it, she realized that somehow she had gotten turned
around. She didn't know where the road was and had no sense of
direction, and even the tracks made by the runaway wagon had
already been obliterated.

Looking at the useless buckboard and dead horse, she could see
she'd get no help from them. The wagon had rolled and the horse
was next to it, nothing to indicate the direction from which they
had come.

Sarah scanned the area for a landmark but didn't recognize
anything. Disoriented now and almost in a panic, she began talking out loud, as if someone might hear her and answer.

"I can't stay here," she shouted. "But which way should I go?
Which way is Bridgeport, or would Bodie be closer? And which
way is Bodie? Where is it?"

She looked up into the driving rain. "Lord, help me!"

She stumbled about blindly, falling several times. Frustrated,
she finally took some deep breaths, said a quick prayer, and put
her hand down to raise herself. Rather than feeling something
mushy and slimy, however, the ground was coarse and stiff. She
recoiled instinctively, then looked closer. She had accidentally
found the tarp.

But that meant she had gone in a circle. She had heard that people lost in a forest would do that, but this wasn't a forest.

Nonetheless, she was encouraged. She folded the wet tarp as
best she could to a manageable size and tucked it under her arm.

With the rifle and food basket in one hand and the folded tarp
in the other, Sarah threw caution to the wind, picked a direction,
and started walking. She was cold, soaking wet, bruised from her

bumpy ride, and still had a headache, but she couldn't just stand there.

"I hope it's the right way, Lord," she muttered.

The tarp was especially cumbersome and kept slipping from under her arm. She'd stop, adjust it, pick the rifle and basket back up, and start out again. She hadn't gone a hundred yards when it fell for the sixth or seventh time.

Crying, she plopped down beside it in a puddle, more frustrated than anything else.

I can't go on like this. Something's got to give, she thought. She beat the ground beside her, sending a splash onto her dress, which was already so wet that it didn't make any difference.

She looked from the tarp to the rifle to the food basket to the tarp again, wondering what to give up. The tarp was the hardest to carry, and she needed the food, but the rifle, what could she use that for?

This is wild country . . . you never know . . .

Sarah stood and unfolded the tarp, spreading it out completely and draping it over some sagebrush. She folded two adjacent corners under, checked her work to make sure it was satisfactory, then picked up the rifle and food basket and continued walking.

CHAPTER

THIRTEEN

Matt pulled himself once again into the saddle and urged on Blister. They moved as one, Matt confident on top of the animal and the Morgan comfortable under him. Matt was anxious to be done with this. Once he caught up with DeCamp he still had to get him to listen, something DeCamp might not be inclined to do. Matt didn't know what kind of welcome he would get, but any man who would desert his son to save his own neck was desperate and might not feel bad about killing someone he thinks is trying to put a noose around him.

There was another reason for Matt's anxiety—his supper date with Sarah and her folks! The last thing he wanted was to miss that because he was chasing an innocent man across the countryside.

"Blister, I hope you're up to the return trip!" he said, patting the animal on the neck. "I'm probably gonna push you pretty hard."

Blister snorted a response.

"Oh, good. Glad to hear it." Matt dug his heels in, and the Morgan responded obediently.

The lull in the storm didn't last. A half-hour after it stopped, the rain started again, accompanied by wind, thunder and lightning. Matt's steed didn't like it but trusted his rider and didn't slow or bolt at the flashes.

Rain dripped constantly from the front and back of the brim of Matt's hat. The wind and Blister's speed made the rain seem as though it was falling sideways, and it stung Matt's face. He held his head down and would have continued without letup, but he saw something out of the corner of his eye that pulled his head sharply back to his left.

There was a small cabin back off the road a ways, smoke curling out of the chimney.

Not an odd sight, this, but there was something behind the cabin that made Matt pull up his horse. A buckboard with a tired-looking horse still hitched to it was partially hidden on the far side of the single-room structure. Another horse, this one saddled, was tethered nearby.

The cabin was made of split logs from trees felled to make the clearing it stood in. The few windows it had were glass, poor quality mail-order that let in little light. The roof was hand-split shingles, the chimney made of local rock. But as quaint and rustic as it was, it looked warm and dry.

Matt dismounted quickly and led Blister to cover, some fifty yards north of the cabin. He squatted under the trees, pondering his next move.

"DeCamp's taken shelter with his family," he told Blister quietly. "He don't know for sure he's being followed, but it wouldn't surprise him none, neither, I'll wager. What should I do, huh, fellah? Storm the place? Naw, don't want nobody hurt. Don't know who else is in the cabin. Maybe it was empty when he came up on it, maybe not. Could be some other family inside that let them in out of the rain. Could be anything."

He idly picked up a stick and pushed it around in the mud.

"Well, I gotta do somethin'." He threw the stick down and began circling the cabin in a crouch, looking for a window to peek through. He left his horse tied in the trees.

With the ground as soggy as it was he didn't have to worry about being quiet, or stepping on a dry twig. The rain on the cabin's roof was probably deafening inside. There was a window on the back side of the cabin but no cover between it and the trees. He'd have to cross open ground. He hoped that they weren't watching.

Keeping his torso bent at the waist, Matt advanced quickly. He kept to the side of the window, then leaned over an inch at a time and peeked. There he was! DeCamp sat near the fireplace, wrapped in a blanket. Huddled nearby in blankets of their own were his wife and daughter.

Matt was considering bursting through the door and taking them by surprise when another man walked into view inside the cabin. He was fully dressed and handed DeCamp a steaming mug. Then a second man appeared and handed something to DeCamp's wife. Two men! Were they peaceable? What were they doing here? They didn't look like prospectors.

And they were wearing six-guns. How many men wore their six-guns in the house? The young deputy tried to see more, but it was difficult to do through the rain-spattered, cheap glass. The first man wore his pants tucked inside knee-high boots. His mustache was long and his face stubble several weeks old. He wore his gun in a large holster that hung limply in front of his left leg. His clothes were baggy and dark. He looked familiar.

As he turned Matt recognized him. Bart Monroe, the robber Matt shot during the holdup attempt at Harvey's store.

What's he doing out of jail?

Matt retreated back to the woods. This complicated matters. Matt's mind was nearly overwhelmed considering all the possibilities. Were DeCamp and Bart compatriots? No, not likely. Surely even DeCamp wouldn't bring his wife and child here if he was. Wasn't Bart in the state prison doing ten years? How'd he get out? Who was the other man? Did DeCamp know these men were criminals? Were the DeCamps being held captive? What were Bart's intentions? Would he let them go?

Even as he was trying to formulate a plan he heard the distinct sounds of a tussle inside the cabin, then a woman's scream. Matt ran carefully back up to the window and looked in. DeCamp was on the floor, still wrapped in the blanket. He appeared to be unconscious, or at least groggy. The mug was on the floor beside his empty hand, tipped, the contents soaking into the dirt floor. There was a small stream of blood running down his temple. While the second man held the girl with a hand over her mouth, Bart advanced on Mrs. DeCamp. She cowered in the corner, keeping the blanket tight around her.

"No, please, leave us alone!" Her voice cracked as she pleaded.

"Ha! I bin locked up for a month now," Bart shouted, "and I'm sittin' here and a pretty woman comes to my door all wet and says kin she dry off and git warm, and I'm s'pose to leave you alone?" He moved forward. "You cooperate and I'll let you live. If'n you don't, well . . ."

The woman whimpered, tears rolling down her cheeks. She looked at her terrified daughter and unconscious husband, then closed her eyes.

Bart smiled. "That's better." He unbuckled his gun belt and let it drop.

Now or never! Matt thought. He ran to the back door, gun drawn, and threw himself into it. It splintered and flew open. Matt slid into the room and drew a bead on Bart.

At the first distraction, the young girl kicked her captor in the shin. He yowled in pain, relaxing his grip. She sprang out of the blanket in her bloomers and dove. As the other man went for his gun, Matt turned and shot him in the chest. He fell hard onto the floor and didn't move as Matt watched him, stunned by his own actions. Without even a thought, he'd killed a human being. He'd tried before, yes, but had never succeeded. And this time there hadn't been any thought behind it. He'd just wheeled and fired.

But now was not the time to lament. At the same time, Bart bent over to pick up his gun and the woman kicked him in the behind, sending him sprawling toward Matt. Bart fell into the deputy, knocking the gun out of his hand as both of them went down. They grappled on the floor, and Bart managed to slug Matt in the face.

Stars exploded in Matt's head. He threw his fists out wildly, but the blows were weak and easily deflected. Still in his slicker, his movements were restricted. Bart was on top of him now and through foggy eyes Matt could see another blow was coming. At the last second he twisted his head away, and Bart's fist glanced off Matt's cheek. Matt brought his knee up as he shifted his weight and knocked Bart over. He scrambled up, but Bart was quick to recover also, and both men now faced each other. Matt's head was thick and his vision blurred. He was sure he was bleeding from somewhere.

Bart quickly assessed Matt's predicament and swung his leg out, sweeping Matt's feet out from under him. Matt went down

hard, knocking the wind out of him. His mind reeled as he struggled to suck in air, and uncontrolled thoughts flashed through his
mind. *I'm done for. I'll miss Sunday supper. What about Samuel?
Sarah!*

Suddenly there was a shot followed by a scream, and Matt
jerked. He felt pain and heard a woman crying hysterically, then
wondered why he was still able to think at all. The pain wasn't
sharp like he expected getting shot to feel; instead, he had the sen-
sation he'd fallen a great distance and landed hard. But that
couldn't be it, he was already on the floor. Something had fallen
on him. It smelled bad.

*Is the fight over? I must've lost. Maybe I'm dead. Something
heavy's on me. It's dirt. I'm being buried! Lord, I'm coming—*

"Are you okay?" The voice was female, and the weight on his
chest was slowly lifted. Someone was patting his cheek. He opened
his eyes, but one was swollen and didn't open far. Through
blurred, misty vision Matt saw the face of a woman. He recognized
her. It was Sarah! No, no, it couldn't be. The vision in his good eye
cleared a bit more. This woman was older, and tears streamed
down her face.

"How are you feeling?" She was speaking to him again.

"I—I'm okay, I—ow!—I guess." She helped him sit up, and he
saw Bart laying next to him, face up. Blood trickled from the man's
nose and mouth and was thick on his chest. Curious, Matt lifted
Bart's shirt to see the shoulder wound he'd inflicted that day in
Harvey's store. The scar was there, red and ugly, but the wound
apparently hadn't been serious. Didn't matter much now, Matt
thought.

He sat up and turned his head slowly around. Standing next to
the fireplace was a short, stocky man with dark hair, red face, and
a nicely trimmed mustache. He was wrapped in a blanket and held
Bart's gun in his hand.

The woman helped Matt to a chair. She was wearing her damp
dress that had been hastily buttoned. Her undergarments still hung
over a rope stretched between nails on two walls. She wet a rag in
a bucket of water and dabbed at his face. He flinched at the sharp
pain over his eye.

"Sorry," she said. "It's swollen, but I think you'll be okay."

Matt groaned his response.

"We're much obliged to you," the red-faced man said coldly. He wiped his mouth to remove the dried blood and walked over to Matt. He poured Matt a cup of coffee and handed it to him.

"Thanks," Matt said weakly.

The woman stepped away and moved over to check her clothes.

"You came along at a real good time," the man said. "In fact, it was near perfect. If you'll forgive me for sayin' so, it was almost *too* perfect. Who are you?"

Matt was beginning to think more clearly now. DeCamp was suspicious and Matt was unarmed. "Name's Matt Page."

"How'd you happen by?"

"Just ridin' by, saw the smoke comin' from the chimney and thought I'd see if I could borrow some heat. When I walked up I heard the trouble and looked in. These men looked like bad news."

"Sure enough, they was," the man agreed.

"Is that how they got in? Wantin' to sit by the fire?"

"It's their cabin. We were the ones out in the storm," said the woman.

"What were you folks doin' out on a day like this?" Matt asked, hoping to buy himself some time by playing dumb.

"Going to Oregon," the woman said.

"Be quiet, Annie. This stranger don't need to know every detail of our lives."

"I'm sorry," Matt said. "I didn't mean to pry. I'm just tryin' to clear my head out." He started to peel off his slicker but found it difficult because he was wet.

"Here, let me help you with that," the man said. He set the gun down within Matt's reach as he helped him off with the raincoat. Matt thought about going for it but remembered he wasn't here to arrest DeCamp. Matt felt a little pain in his arm as he pulled the sleeve off and complained. The man eased up and allowed Matt to slip his arm out on his own.

"Thanks, Mr. DeCamp," Matt said absentmindedly.

Instantly DeCamp picked the gun back up and pointed it at Matt. The deputy silently berated himself for the slip-up.

"Just happened by, eh?" DeCamp said. He carefully pulled back the lapel of Matt's leather coat and saw the star.

"Get outta them duds!" he ordered the deputy. "I owe you for helpin' my family, but I ain't goin' back!"

"Listen, you don't—"

"Shut up and start strippin'. You're wet anyway, and I'm gonna make sure you don't follow me."

"Why don't you kill me?" Matt challenged as he began pulling off his jacket and shirt. It was a calculated risk, but he had to get the man to talk.

"Like I said, I owe you. But I didn't do nuthin' back there, so I can't kill a lawman. It'll satisfy me just to get outta the state."

"If you didn't do nuthin' why are you runnin'?"

"'Cause them people in Coleville think I did somethin', and they want to string me up."

"You tellin' me you didn't burn down the loan office?"

"No, I didn't."

"You were in town that day."

"Boots and pants, Deputy," DeCamp said, wagging the gun. "I didn't need to burn down the loan office."

"They foreclosed on you."

"I was bringin' 'em this." He leaned over and dug in Bart's pocket, keeping his eyes and the gun trained on Matt, who pretended to struggle with removing his wet boots.

DeCamp found what he was looking for and held it up. Matt was staring at a quartz nugget the size of a child's fist. It was heavily laced with gold. "I went in to pay off the mortgage. Found it the day before."

"Then why'd you run?"

"They was gonna hang me. Them people been hatin' us since day one. I doubt they'd've stopped long enough to listen."

"How'd you know they thought you started the fire?"

"Someone shouted and pointed at me, the crowd got stirred up . . . I didn't wait around to discuss the matter."

"That's apparent," Matt said, somewhat sarcastically.

"What's that supposed to mean?"

"What about your son? Why'd you leave him behind?" Matt's question was sudden and point blank.

DeCamp remained expressionless.

"I ain't got no son."

CHAPTER

FOURTEEN

Matt was stunned, but before he could respond, DeCamp's wife spoke up.

"Frederick, that isn't true. That boy is yours. We both know it. Don't think you're protecting me. For six years you been denying that boy his heritage. He knows it, you know it, and I know it."

DeCamp remained stoic. His wife turned to Matt and continued.

"He thinks I don't know. A wife knows. Samuel isn't mine, but he's Frederick's. He's never admitted it. Always denies it. Says he doesn't know why that woman's been following us. She just wants a father for her son." Mrs. DeCamp looked at her husband but spoke to Matt.

"When she caught up to us in Coleville she dropped him off, then disappeared. Fred's been taking care of Samuel, pretending he was just helping out a little lost boy. But I could see it in the boy's eyes."

She paused to take a breath. DeCamp's eyes were beginning to water, but he didn't interrupt.

"You're a good man, Fred. You been a good husband and father to me and Ruth. I don't know why or how this happened, and it doesn't matter any more. What matters is we've got to give your little boy a home—and a daddy. I'll love him like he was my own because he came from you . . . and I love you."

DeCamp was crying freely now, oblivious to Matt. "I'm sorry, babe. It was one of them things, I didn't plan it . . . I felt so guilty about it, I—I guess I thought, if I denied it, eventually she'd give up and stop followin' me."

"And that's why we've been moving so much and keeping to ourselves, so it'd be harder for her to find you?"

DeCamp nodded, and Annie put her arms around him. She held him tightly as she spoke low in his ear. Matt couldn't hear but suddenly felt very much like an intruder. After a few moments DeCamp, who still held the gun, looked at Matt. "How'd you know about Samuel?"

"Met him in Coleville. He knew you were runnin' because of the fire and got real upset when he thought I was gonna arrest you."

"Of course." DeCamp smiled. "He didn't want his ol' man in jail."

"Oh, there's more to it than that," Matt assured. "He knows you didn't set the fire." DeCamp thought about that and gave Matt a questioning look. Matt continued, "Because he did." He let that sink in. "It was an accident. I checked it out. His fingers were burned a little, and he showed me where he dropped the matches he was playin' with."

"So you knew all along I was innocent."

"Yep."

"Then how come you're chasin' me?"

"For one, to tell you don't have to run; two, to bring you back to Samuel. He's bein' looked after by Reverend Hinkle and his wife, who are also gonna set the people of Coleville straight. If you run to Oregon, things would never change for you. You'll always think someone's lookin' for you, and Samuel would always wonder where his family is."

"I don't know what to say."

Matt looked down at himself. "How 'bout puttin' down that gun and lettin' me get dressed?"

DeCamp lowered the gun, and Matt picked up his clothes.

"You want to dry out first?" DeCamp asked.

"If it's all the same, I'd like to get back as soon as possible." He paused and looked at the dead men on the floor. "Frankly, I'm gonna need your help haulin' these men back to Coleville for proper disposal."

"I don't know . . ."

"Frederick!" Mrs. DeCamp scolded. "This man risked his life just to help you put yours back together. The least we can do is help him out. Ruthie, get your father's clothes."

Matt dragged Bart outside as DeCamp dressed. In a few minutes DeCamp came out dragging the other man. Together they loaded them both into back of the buckboard and covered them with blankets.

As they readied to leave, though, something in Matt's brain clicked, and he hailed DeCamp.

"This ain't your place, and I don't think it's theirs," Matt said, jerking a thumb toward the back of the wagon.

"No, likely it ain't if they just escaped from prison."

"Then whose is it?" Matt asked. DeCamp shrugged and Matt stood next to his horse thinking. Then he spied a small barn off in the trees. The door was open a foot or so. Matt dropped the reins and walked tentatively to it, easing the door open with his foot while standing to the side and drawing his Peacemaker.

As soon as he leapt into the barn in a crouch, gun at the ready, he knew there would be no need for it. In the middle of the barn was a man sprawled face down in the straw, a red stain in the center of his back. He wore only suspendered pants and a cotton shirt, no shoes or hat. He was stiff.

A soft moan reached Matt's ears as he stared at the body. Jerking his head up, he peered slowly around the dimly lit outbuilding, finally making out something in the far corner. He approached it cautiously, then recognized it to be a woman. She did not move, but Matt could discern shallow breathing.

Her simple calico dress had been ripped, and her face was bruised and bloody. Matt pulled a horse blanket off a stall wall and gently covered her, then shouted for the DeCamps.

"It ain't very pretty," he warned Annie. "But she needs help."

Annie nodded hesitantly, then moved over to the woman, arranging the blanket so she could be picked up. With a wet cloth Ruthie had retrieved from the house, Annie dabbed the woman's face. She revived somewhat, remaining groggy, and tried to struggle, whimpering pitifully. Annie spoke to her and her woman's voice calmed the injured female, who clung to Mrs. DeCamp sobbing, inconsolable and unable to answer questions. She mumbled a man's name and Annie looked up at Matt.

"Probably her husband," the deputy said.

Annie took in a deep breath and whispered to the woman while caressing her head, and the woman howled. Annie held her and rocked her while Matt and Fred removed her husband's body and buried it behind the house.

When she was aware enough to sit up, they loaded the woman—who finally gave her name as Bessie Travis—into the buckboard seat between Ruth and Annie. DeCamp saddled his horse.

Matt tied the remaining horses to the back of the wagon and mounted Blister. The rain stopped, and in a few minutes, the clouds broke. A brilliant sun peeked through and warmed them.

"It won't last," Matt observed.

"Don't matter, Deputy," DeCamp said. "I'm anxious to get back, and Mrs. Travis needs to be looked after. We'll be fine."

Matt smiled through his swollen face, gave Blister a *tch tch* and started back toward Coleville at a walk, followed by the wagon and DeCamp on his mount.

Hours passed as Sarah trudged over soggy ground, but the rain did not let up. The golden prairie grass sunk beneath her feet, the depressions filling with water as she left them.

As she tired from the hard walk and relentless storm, she grew more frustrated. Her body ached and her shoes—not made for such a hike—soon raised blisters on her feet.

After crossing several small hills and valleys, she came to a rocky area. The going was treacherous and difficult, and she was exhausted, so she decided—somewhat reluctantly—to rest for a spell. Sarah scoured the cliffs and found a shallow cave, just a short climb up the sloping face to her right. She crawled in out of the rain and collapsed.

Sarah slept, unaware of the passing of time. When she woke she sat up, leaned back against the hard granite, and closed her eyes. She couldn't find a place on her body that didn't hurt.

The relief from the torturous rain was joyful. Sarah didn't move for several minutes but finally forced herself to reach down and unbutton her shoes. Painfully pulling them off she saw raw skin under popped blisters. She rubbed her swollen feet tenderly, trying to work out the stiffness. Night would be coming, and Sarah knew it was bound to be cold. If she didn't dry out her clothes, she'd freeze.

She looked around the mouth of the cave. There was no fuel to start a fire.

Lacking a better plan for the moment, she opened the basket to see what Billy had prepared, hoping, praying it was dry. There was a small loaf of hard bread, a knife to cut it, some jerky, pine nuts, and dried fruit. She wondered how many days she could make it last.

"At least I won't go thirsty," she said with a weak laugh.

Sarah took the knife and cut small pieces off the end of the loaf, then pushed it into her mouth and chewed. She held her open mouth under the rain that dripped from the overhang of the cave opening, washing the crusty sourdough down her tightened throat. A few pieces of dried apple and some pine nuts were followed by more water.

Slipping out of her coat was difficult, as it was heavy with water and stuck to her arms. Sarah wrung it out as best she could and set it on the ground next to her, then did the same with her petti-coat, thinking it would make a good pillow.

Now more comfortable, Sarah stared out from her hide-a-way, seeing an occasional bolt of lightning and hearing the thunder echo up the canyon. She began singing a hymn, almost inaudibly at first. Her voice cracked and her throat was sore, but she did not stop. When the song was over she prayed, leaned back against the rock, and fell asleep.

Her teeth were chattering when she woke. It was pitch dark and no stars or moon showed, but the rain had stopped. Sarah didn't know what time it was but knew she was cold. The petticoat and her greatcoat had dried somewhat and she pulled them over her and curled up in a ball, wondering if she would make it through to morning.

Sarah stayed awake most of the night, afraid to go to sleep for fear she'd die. She finally did so in spite of herself, waking with first light. It had not rained much during the night, and the morning clouds were broken, with blue sky showing in patches.

Her feet were numb, which she realized was probably a blessing. They were still swollen and raw and would have hurt terribly if not deadened by the cold. She couldn't stand—her legs hurt too badly to support her weight—so she crawled to the mouth of the cave to survey the landscape.

Occasional golden shafts of sunlight reflected off flat, wet rocks, their surface twinkling silver-like. This contrasted nicely with the golden patches of prairie grass that shimmered as they waved casually in the morning breeze. Sarah reached for the basket and ate some of the jerky and bread, not bothering to cut the loaf but tearing off hunks and stuffing them into her mouth.

She ran her fingers through her matted, tangled hair.

"Oh, how I wish I had a hairbrush!" she told herself. She fussed with her locks, not realizing how hopeless it was, quitting when she was satisfied she had accomplished something.

It was only then, having run out of diversions, that Sarah came face-to-face with the reality of her situation. Not knowing where she was, unable to walk very far, and with precious little provision, her eyes began to fill. She was tired of crying but didn't know what else to do. Cry and pray. What else was there?

Maybe I'll be missed. By whom? My parents aren't expecting me any particular day, not knowing what was going on in Bodie. The folks in Bodie think I've gone back to Bridgeport. Matt's not even anywhere nearby. He'll come to the house Sunday for supper, and I won't be there! She sobbed openly and began to talk out loud. "I'll never be there! I'll never see—"

Her lamenting was interrupted by a sound outside, near the entrance to the cave. *Footsteps! Could it be someone?*

"Hello?" Sarah called hopefully. There was only silence.

The young woman's heart pounded. Footsteps again, closer now.

"Hello?" She retreated as she spoke, sucking in air and still fighting the spasms from her crying. She wiped her face with her hand and pushed herself backward on her behind. Help would have answered. Her hand landed on the rifle she had forgotten about.

Picking it up Sarah worked the lever, chambering a round. "I hope you still work," she told the Winchester, fearing the rain had ruined it. She could still smell her father's gun oil.

"If I've ruined you, Daddy will skin me," she whispered. The footsteps resumed and were right outside the cave. Something was stalking her. It wasn't human, too many steps. *A wild animal.* Her mind raced. *What could it be? What's out here?*

She raised the shaking rifle to her shoulder. *Steady, girl . . . easy now.*

Slowly it advanced. The low sun cast a menacing shadow that darkened the opening. Sarah closed her left eye, sighting down the barrel, and held the rifle tight. Her finger pressed back on the trigger, anticipating the creature, but in her agitation, Sarah fired accidentally and too soon. The gun boomed, thumped Sarah hard in the shoulder, and the bullet hit the cave wall, ricocheting harmlessly into the air outside. The animal was missed and fled unseen, surprised and frightened by the noise.

Smoke curled up from the barrel and receiver, and Sarah, on her back looking up at the ceiling of the cave, choked on it. Still coughing, she pushed herself back up to a sitting position and rubbed her right shoulder. She scooted toward the mouth of the cave and cautiously peeked out. Nothing was moving except what the wind blew. The clouds seemed to be building up again. The air grew colder by the minute. Soon it would rain again, perhaps even snow. Up here it could snow most any time of the year.

She needed fire.

But how? I don't have anything to start one with, and nothing to burn. Sarah looked at her feet. They wouldn't take her far, not without some protection. And they were too swollen to force into those high-button shoes. She glanced back at her things and her eyes fixed on the petticoat.

Taking the small knife, she cut the petticoat into pieces. She wrapped thick clumps of material around her feet and tied them in place with thin strips, knotting them at the top.

Tentatively she stood, testing them out. Her legs shook as she put her weight on them and walked awkwardly out of the cave, rifle in one hand and knife in the other. In spite of her plight, she had to laugh at herself.

What a picture I make! The belle of the ball!

She stopped at the mouth of the cave and assessed things. There was dry sagebrush nearby—and plenty of it. There was no wood here, not a tree in sight. She knew she was at too high an elevation—her lungs told her that—and the weather was too harsh.

Sarah took a deep breath and hiked painfully out of the cave, then began gathering sagebrush and dragging it arduously back to her new home. She'd worry about starting a fire later.

It was the following morning before Matt and the DeCamps rolled into Coleville. Matt realized he'd never get back in time for Sunday afternoon supper in Bridgeport, and he was disappointed. He hoped the Taylors would understand.

As they reined up in front of the church, they were surprised to see a crowd of people filing out. It seemed the entire town was there. When the people saw DeCamp they stopped, milled around uneasily, but no one came forward. The last to emerge from the church were the minister and his wife. And a little boy. His eyes lit up when he saw his father.

"C'mere, son," DeCamp said quietly.

Samuel yelped and ran down the steps. He jumped into the wagon and threw his arms around his father's neck. Mrs. DeCamp stroked the boy's head and cried.

"Good morning, son," she said softly. He hugged her, then Ruth, then looked into the back of the wagon.

"Pa, why are those men sleeping in our wagon?"

The townspeople moved closer, curious about the bodies they hadn't noticed before, and Bessie Travis turned slowly to look. She had been silent the whole trip, her mind affected by her ordeal, and it would take a lot of care to bring her back.

"Those are mine," Matt said, riding up abreast of them. He revealed his deputy badge casually and asked several men to take the bodies to the undertakers. The minister walked up to him.

"I see God has protected you." Then he saw Matt's face. "Somewhat."

Matt grinned. "Lesson learned. Could you and your missus take care of Mrs. Travis? Her husband was killed by those men, and she was . . . you know. She's not in her right mind, might be a peck of trouble for you."

"No trouble at all," the preacher assured. "That's what we're here for, to represent Christ to the people." He motioned his wife over and she and Annie DeCamp took the distraught woman down from the wagon and into the house.

What's goin' on here?" Matt asked Hinkle, motioning toward the crowd that had emerged from the church.

"I called a town meeting," the minister explained. "Told them what you told me. There's some mighty lowly feeling people here. Of course, there's some that don't feel any different. But most of these people are good folk. They voted to rebuild the DeCamp place, if he and his family want to stay in Coleville. Until it's done, they can live with me and the missus."

"Glad to hear it. I think the DeCamps are gonna be valuable members of the community. They got a new life ahead of them. Tell me, Reverend, you got a justice of the peace around here?"

"The county swore me in for that, since Coleville is so small."

"Do you mind swearin' me out a statement 'bout these two? They're wanted—escapees from the state prison. Leastwise, one of 'em is for sure. The other, I don't know, but it's a good bet."

"How about we do it after supper? You come on in, you and the DeCamps. We've got plenty, the missus has a poultice for your face, and you can tell us all about it."

"Sounds fair, since I'm gonna be missin' a Sunday supper engagement back in Bridgeport."

"With a young lady?"

"And her folks."

The preacher winked. "There'll be more Sundays."

CHAPTER

FIFTEEN

It took Sarah several hours to gather a good supply of sagebrush, as she had to stop frequently to let her feet rest. The petticoat idea worked okay for walking far enough to collect a few clumps of sagebrush, but it wouldn't last long enough to attempt the walk home or back to Bodie. Sarah accepted the reality that she'd have to just sit it out until her feet healed enough to accommodate her shoes.

She vowed to never wear them again if she took a wagon trip, then vowed not to take any more extended wagon trips—at least by herself.

Real wood was what she needed, but there just wasn't any available. She wished the wagon was nearby. At least it would burn. But at this point she wasn't sure which way the wagon was, nor how far. So for now, although sagebrush burned too fast, it would have to do. At least it would smell pleasant enough, if she could ever get it lit.

With a large quantity of sagebrush filling the cave she leaned back and rested against the rock. Crying about her predicament was no longer an option. She was all cried out. Sarah knew that eventually someone would come for her. They had to. She'd prayed about it. Until then she'd just have to survive. She had shelter, her clothes were dry, there were plenty of water puddles she could drink from; what she needed was a source of fire and some food.

Even as the thought was passing through her mind, she noticed something out of the corner of her eye moving through the brush. It was a large sage grouse.

"I could eat that," she said softly. "If I could catch it—" She looked around and spied the rifle leaning against the opposite wall. As quietly as she could, she crawled over to it. Sitting with her back propped to keep her steady, she slowly cocked the gun and brought it to her shoulder.

The grouse moved into the open, unaware of the danger he was in—or unconcerned. *Maybe he's seen me shoot,* Sarah thought. She squeezed the trigger as her daddy had taught her, this time holding the rifle butt tight against her shoulder so the recoil didn't slam it into her.

The rifle roared, and the grouse fell.

Sarah jumped up, dropping the rifle. Cheering for herself, she hobbled to retrieve the bird, oblivious to her pain, and brought her prize back triumphantly.

She sat in the cave mouth to clean the animal with Billy's little knife, humming unconsciously as she always did in the kitchen. *Prairie chicken,* she thought. In her mother's kitchen she had cleaned and cooked many domestic chickens, and she found this bird much the same.

As she worked, the clouds overhead began to thicken, and the blue patches of sky gradually disappeared. She had been hearing thunder for the past several hours getting closer and closer, first in front of her, then from somewhere else.

The lightning returned as well, and it started to sprinkle. Now that she wasn't out in it, Sarah almost enjoyed the weather. She watched as the valley lit up in a flickering flash, causing motion- less objects to look alive.

She thought about her family, what they might be doing now— probably snuggled up in the parlor by a roaring fire, her mother quilting and her father smoking his pipe quietly. They wouldn't miss her yet; she wasn't due back. They would have no idea she was huddling in a cave in the middle of nowhere, with no real hope for rescue and soon to face a cold night without heat or food. She thought of Matt, so handsome and kind, and how she might never see him again . . .

Her eyes began to tear, and she buried her face in the folds of her skirt as she drew her knees up.

Suddenly a blue, undulating flash filled the cave as a large, ragged lightning bolt reached down from the low clouds about a quarter mile away. Sarah looked up as she sucked in her breath, surprised and a little frightened, and saw the last split second of the bolt as it struck the ground and set some dry sagebrush on fire. She let out a sigh of both relief and awe, then came to her senses.

Fire! Sarah jumped up. "Thank You, Lord!" she cried. She dropped the grouse and ran toward the burning bush, heedless of the light rain. It was enough to get her wet, but she hoped she could retrieve some and bring it back before the rain put it out.

Frantic, Sarah arrived at the bush and grabbed the largest stalk. She took off running back, careful not to let the fire get too close to her hands. It was burning fast. Her feet hurt. The cave wasn't getting any closer, it seemed.

Finally, with very little of the bush left, she made it in and ignited some broken sagebrush she had already arranged in a small circle of rocks. It flared up and crackled hot, just as the sky let loose. Sarah collapsed onto the floor of the cave, exhausted but victorious.

By evening she was in relatively good spirits with her stomach full and her body warm. She had kept the fire going and managed to cook the grouse, and now that it was all eaten, she tossed the carcass clear of the cave entrance so a passing animal wouldn't be attracted to the cave by the smell of the remains. Sarah felt her strength renewed and she was warm for the first time in several days. There was enough fuel for her small fire to last another day, so she moved behind the fire into the cave, curled up under her coat, and immediately fell asleep. Her last thought was of Matt, whom she imagined was probably resting comfortably in Harvey Boone's parlor by now.

Deputy Page rode south out of Coleville. His face was still swollen from the beating but much improved, thanks to the minister's wife. She and her husband were remarkable people.

Matt left with mixed emotions. He had made new friends and wanted to spend more time with them; he was happy about DeCamp's decision concerning Samuel, but he desperately wanted to see Sarah.

The weather had held for two days, with broken clouds and cold and wind, but no rain. But the snows were coming soon, and more foul weather was imminent. Even as he left town, Matt saw the rain to the north.

With Sunday supper already as good as missed, Matt held Blister to an easy pace. The air was clear and clean and smelled fresh and invigorating. Blister had enjoyed the rest and the oats and ran without complaint.

Matt's signed statements were folded and tucked safely inside his saddlebags. One cleared DeCamp of the arson charges; the other certified the death of Bart Monroe and his as yet unidentified accomplice. The preacher, acting as justice of the peace, had notarized both. Matt could get a judge to sign them in Bridgeport.

As the day wore on, the clouds began building again, and toward evening Matt began looking for suitable shelter. Not too far from the still-muddy road he located a large overhanging rock, big enough for both himself and Blister to get under.

He led the horse in and took off the saddle, then brushed the lathered animal carefully and gave him a good portion of oats. As Blister supplemented his dinner with prairie grass, Matt gathered some wood that wasn't too wet and built a fire. He opened a package of food Mrs. Hinkle had provided and enjoyed the cold ham, biscuits, and fruit. As he ate, he sat with his back to the fire and surveyed the darkening countryside contentedly.

It soon began to rain, and Matt's thoughts turned to Sarah. He longed to see her, to smell her lilac water, to hear her melodic voice and touch her small, soft hands.

He sighed and settled his head down onto his saddle, thinking of Sarah, picturing her knitting and rocking by the fireplace as he drifted off.

The next day Matt rode into town about four in the afternoon. It was a typical foul-weather day in Bridgeport. The rain followed Matt in, but the folks weren't surprised to see it. They'd cleared the streets early and just a few of them were running last-minute errands. They scurried down the boardwalk, holding their hats on their heads.

Matt passed the Argonaut and glanced through the glowing yellow windows. Harvey Boone sat at his usual table, but this time

Mary wasn't serving him. She was sitting across from him with a plate of her own, listening to him talk with rapt attention. Matt noticed the window sign read CLOSED and smiled.

"'Bout time, Harvey. 'Bout time."

The sheriff's office was dark so Matt kept riding, headed for Taylor's house. The coal oil lamps glowed inside the residence and smoke curled up and out the chimney. As Matt slid off his mount, he hoped Taylor would let him hang around with Sarah for a while, even if supper wasn't included.

Matt stepped through the gate and strode up the walk, then onto the porch. He knocked firmly on the door, which was opened by Mrs. Taylor.

"Evenin', ma'am."

"Why, Matthew, come in." She stepped aside. "We missed you at supper."

"Sorry, Mrs. Taylor. Turned into quite an affair." He moved into the light as he took off his hat.

"Oh my, look at your face!" she said. "Run into trouble?"

"It kind of ran into me. I'll be okay."

"You must be tired. Come, sit down." She led him into the parlor where the sheriff sat, nursing his pipe and contemplating. Matt sat where directed, then looked about the room. Something—or rather, someone—seemed to be missing.

"Prisoner all locked up and tucked in?" the sheriff asked his deputy without looking at him.

"Well, sir, not in so many words."

"Oh?" The sheriff turned and saw Matt's face. "Ah. Got the better of you, did he?"

Matt touched his face. "Oh, no, Bart Monroe did this."

"Bart Monroe? I got a letter on him just yesterday. He broke from custody at the jail in Sacramento several days ago. He was being taken out to stand trial for some robberies committed there before we caught him." Matt noticed the *we*, even though Taylor hadn't been in on the capture, but let it go without comment. Taylor continued, "The other man was Jake Chandler, a stage robber and all-around horse's behind."

"Ohhh, so that's his name." It was Matt's turn to be coy.

"You meet up with him, too?"

"They was together."

"Let me get this straight. You meet two escaped convicts by yourself and get beat up but ride home, and you ain't dead? What happened to them?"

Matt took out one of the letters from his inside pocket and handed it to Taylor. While the sheriff read he *hmmm'd* and *ohhh'd* and nodded, then looked at Matt sideways. "By yourself again?"

"No."

"Praise be the Lord!" the sheriff said, looking skyward. "So, who helped you?"

"Fred DeCamp and his family."

"*What?*"

Matt gave Taylor the other letter.

"So he's innocent, eh?"

"Yessir."

"Well, I got to hand it to you, Page. You done what I sent you to do and more. You done a fine job. I always knew you'd prove to be worthwhile." Mrs. Taylor rolled her eyes, but no one saw it.

"Thank you, sir. Uh, excuse me for askin', but . . . is Sarah here?"

"No, she ain't." He relit his pipe. "She went up to Bodie a few days ago, took some medical supplies. They had a cave-in in one of the mines. She hasn't come back yet."

"Do you know who—"

"No, but it weren't your pa. Charlie Jack was the one rode in with the news. He'd a said so if your pa was hurt."

Matt stood up.

"Where you goin'?" Taylor asked.

"To Bodie," Matt said, leaving out the *of course.*

"It's a mite late," the sheriff said. "It's been four, five days. They probably have it all under control. Why don'tcha just wait till morning. You hungry?"

"Yessir."

Mrs. Taylor got up and went to the kitchen.

"You sure Sarah's okay?" Matt asked the sheriff.

"We ain't heard otherwise. Say, there's your dinner. A little late in the day, but it'll taste just as good. When you're done you can bed down here if you like."

"Thanks, but I'll sleep in your office tonight, if that's okay. I gotta take care of my horse."

"Suit yourself, Deputy, suit yourself."

Matt walked into the kitchen and found Mrs. Taylor setting out a plate of hot food. Smelling it, his stimulated stomach juices responded, and he remembered how hungry he was.

He ate in silence, concerned about Sarah. *Aw, she's okay,* he convinced himself. *Charlie Jack or somebody'll bring her back, if I don't get there first.* He wondered about the cave-in, who was hurt, how it happened; and he worried about his father. Matt reminded himself to turn his interest in the mine over to him, in exchange for enough gold to buy some land and build a cabin.

Not in Bodie, though. He didn't want to settle there. He'd rather go someplace where the weather was moderate, someplace where summer was more than the two-week period between the end of one winter and the beginning of the next.

He'd serve in Bodie as long as Sheriff Taylor wanted him to serve. Then he'd transfer to Coleville and reopen the office there—after all, he still had the key—or he'd quit and take up some other job. Heck, he might even farm. Goodness knows he knew how!

When he'd cleaned his plate Matt said good-bye to the Taylors and rode Blister back up the street to the livery. Harvey and Mary were still sitting in the Argonaut, talking. This time they noticed him, and he waved. They waved back but didn't invite him in.

This must be serious, Matt realized happily.

He fed, watered, and rubbed down the Morgan, then tucked himself in on the cot in the sheriff's back room. His fatigue caught up to him, and he was asleep within minutes.

CHAPTER

SIXTEEN

Matt rose early and wasted no time getting himself on the road. The sun was not yet completely up and the sky, a dull yellow fading up to blue, was pocked with scattered clouds. This storm had all but passed, but there would be another—and another. Matt was anxious to get home, see his father and his friends, Billy and Charlie, but most of all, Sarah.

The road was still damp because very little sun had shone since the rain had stopped, and Blister occasionally walked through puddles, kicking up drops of mud onto his irritated rider.

Blister didn't break cadence all the way to the Bodie Road turn-off. As Matt reined him around the tight left turn, he glanced up to the top of the cliff, half expecting to see Charlie Jack standing up there, watching him as he had done the first time they met. Matt didn't look long, though, and gave Blister a hurry-up kick with both feet.

Just a few miles out of Bodie, Matt pulled the Morgan up sharply. In the gradually sloping grass field to his right, he could see a roan horse grazing. It looked odd to him, and as he rode closer to take a look, he realized it was wearing part of a buckboard harness and dragging a piece of lumber.

"Blister, this don't look good," he said quietly, leaning forward to pat the Morgan on the side of the neck. He urged his horse off

the road and toward the grazing animal. Its head jerked up when
it heard the loping horse, and Matt saw a wild look in its eyes.
Skittish, it backed up and turned to run, but the lumber it dragged
was as good as a tether and kept it from getting away. Matt caught
hold of a leather strap and spoke softly to the frightened beast,
then slid down from Blister's back and undid the buckles of the
harness, freeing the roan.

It whinnied and trotted off.

"You'll be okay, boy," Matt said, "Go on now."

But in this unfamiliar pasture, the horse had nowhere to go and
just stood there, eyeing the human suspiciously.

"Have it your way," Matt said, pulling himself astride his own
horse. "Now, where's the rest of your wagon?"

He turned Blister around and scanned the countryside, knowing something was nearby. That horse couldn't have gotten far
dragging that piece of wagon tongue behind him. Yes, there it was,
maybe a quarter mile off—an overturned wagon hitched to a dead
horse.

He turned the Morgan and led him carefully off the road and
down to the broken buckboard, then dismounted and walked
around the wagon slowly. There was nothing on or near it to identify its owner. The horse had an obviously broken leg and a bullet
wound in its head.

The rain had been severe here. He couldn't find any type of
trail, no footprints, no markings, no—*Wait, what's that?*

Something was out of place beyond the wagon. It didn't look
natural. Across the valley, in the midst of the sea of golden prairie
grass and brown sagebrush was a large, dark green—*arrow?*

Matt whistled and Blister sauntered over to him. He hoisted
himself into the saddle and rode over to the strange phenomenon.
It was only when he was on top of it that he realized it was a tarp,
draped across the sagebrush, with two corners folded under to
form the arrow.

Pointing the way to what?

Matt didn't know, but if this wasn't accidental then someone
must be in trouble.

"It ain't a bent blade of grass or a footprint, but if I don't follow that arrow I best open a dry goods store," he said to Blister.
He scanned the countryside ahead, shading his eyes with his hand.

"C'mon, Blister, let's go. There's some canyons up ahead that I've been in before. Let's see what we can find."

He rode with a combination of apprehension, excitement, and plain old fear in the pit of his stomach. There was no trail to speak of, no prints or other signs of human disturbance. People had little reason to go into these canyons, considering they led to the same place the road did. Whoever had dumped that wagon didn't know where they were going, Matt reasoned. They apparently had a firearm, since they shot the horse.

With the sun finally out and the air warming, Matt was almost sorry he couldn't enjoy it more. It had been awhile since the weather was this nice.

He came upon a large expanse of prairie grass. The ground underneath it had been softened by the volume of water it had soaked up, and Blister sank with each step across it. Matt noticed something odd. There were small tracks across the grass. They seemed to be tracks, at least. They didn't appear to be footprints— the shape of each imprint was too irregular. But the spacing between prints was very human-like. Or bear. No doubt the rain had distorted the tracks.

"We're on to something, Blister. Somebody's been by here. Looks like they were headed yonder." He stared out at the hills in front of him. "They may have been on their way to Bodie, unless they're lost."

He goaded the Morgan across the valley floor. As the miles swept under him, it became more apparent that the person he was tracking was indeed lost. The trail began to meander.

"Maybe I'm getting my trails confused," Matt suggested to Blister. "Either that or this person was having a time of it. Maybe they were drunk—or injured."

Matt was abruptly struck with a frightening possibility: he could think of only one person who had recently gone to Bodie in a buckboard who wasn't very familiar with the territory, someone who would be determined to get to Bridgeport regardless of the weather, and had small feet.

Sarah.

Could he be tracking her? What's she doing out here, where's she going, how long had she been out here?

Is she still alive?

Matt rode into the canyon, wanting to hurry but forced to take it slow because of the terrain and the need to locate a trail. He scanned left and right as he made his way methodically down the slope. Had she gone the other way she could easily be back in Bodie and safe; there was no point going that way, so he chose the direction that led nowhere.

Sarah sat in her cave, wrapped in her coat and comfortable despite the fire having gone out during the night. Despair had set in the day before, and her face was blank. She knew she had missed supper with Matt, which for a time bothered her more than the prospect of not being rescued, but another night had passed. She had lost her source of heat for warmth and cooking, and all her food was gone. Although her feet were better, she knew she was too weak to get far, and she still didn't know which way to go.

Forlorn and sleepy, she curled up and closed her eyes. Unaware she was doing so, she began singing softly.

> *O God, our help in ages past,*
> *our hopes for years to come,*
> *Our shelter from the stormy blas—*

She heard something. She listened. *Another animal come to attack me.* She grabbed the rifle and cocked it.

Matt allowed Blister to pick his own path over the rocky terrain. The sun had not been shining long enough to evaporate the water standing in the crevices and hollows, and the water sparkled in the sunshine like the glint of placer gold in a miner's pan.

There was a dark place off in the distance, a small patch of ground charred black. *Lightning,* Matt thought. He jerked Blister to an abrupt stop. *What was that?* It sounded like singing. Matt strained his ears.

"I must be crackbrained," he admitted to his horse. "I coulda swore I heard something."

Immediately a shot rang out close by. The bullet kicked up dirt and rock about twenty-five yards in front of him. He worked to control his startled horse and moved in a full circle in one place before getting Blister to break and run.

I think it came from over there! He tried to focus on the cliffs to his right. *There! Is that a cave?* He yanked the horse hard to the right just as a white specter stepped into the open in the mouth of the cave and raised a rifle to fire again.

Sarah recoiled from her first shot, which she had fired blind. She stood up and crept to the mouth of the cave, saw the beast coming toward her and prepared to fire again.

"Sarah!"

It had called her name. *Animals don't talk!* She tried to focus her tired eyes. A horse and rider. Could it be . . . ?

"Sarah!"

"Matt?" She said it to herself, unbelieving.

He came closer, riding hard.

It's her! He waved, and she lowered the gun. She looked lost. *What's that on her feet?* She looked like she was standing in two little clouds. Her hair was a matted and tangled mess, her face pale and drawn.

He tugged Blister to a halt and jumped off before the Morgan could come to a complete stop. He ran up the slope to her, slipping on the loose rocks but not slowing. She just stood there, helpless and crying. When he reached her he grabbed her waist, and she flung her arms around his neck.

"Sarah!"

"Oh, Matt, it *is* you! You're real!"

"I found you, Sarah. It's okay."

She looked up at his face with tears glistening on her white cheeks. With cracked lips she said, "Oh, your face." She touched his swollen eye gently. He leaned down slowly until his lips were next to hers. She didn't move but closed her eyes as she felt his breath on her mouth. Then he kissed her softly. She relaxed into his arms.

They cried together until they both sat down, exhausted.

"I knew you'd come," she said. "The thunder, it won't stop. Will it rain again?"

"There's no thunder," Matt said softly.

"Listen, can't you hear it?"

Matt tried but shrugged. "No, Sarah, the only thing I hear is the stamp mill in Bodie, just over that bluff." He pointed north. "C'mon, Sarah, let's go home."

"Not yet."

"Huh?"

She put her head on his shoulder. "We're finally alone."

"Oh, yeah," he said, putting his arm around her. "Alone at last. The hard way."

CHAPTER

SEVENTEEN

B illy O'Hara rocked on his porch, his chair creaking against the boards, listening with satisfaction to the steam engine and the stamps at the Empire Mill start up again as he drank his morning coffee. There was a chill in the air that the sun wouldn't abate, what with winter fast approaching, but the air smelled fresh and pure following the two-day rain, and Billy drew a lungful.

"This is the life," he said to himself. "The town's back to normal. Deputy Matthew'll be back soon. His pa and the others are on the mend. The mill and the mines is back in business, and all's right with the world." He paused. "Well, maybe not that last part." He glanced over at the Indian in the other rocker. "What say you, Charlie Jack?"

The Paiute grumbled as he wrapped his blanket tighter and pulled his hat down lower. He held a steaming mug of coffee—heavily laced with cream and sugar—and drank, the bandages on his arms making life a little difficult for him.

"Rather be on horse," he mumbled.

"Ah know," Billy sympathized. "Ah don't blame you none. Must be terr'ble to have to sit around on the porch, all cozy and comfortable, drinkin' your sweet brew and eatin' mah pine nuts instead of ridin' the open range on a smelly horse, fightin' flies and cold and rain."

The Indian nodded. "Yes. Is hard."

Billy laughed. "Well, ol' friend, you'll be fine enough to ride in a day or so. Until then you'll jus' have to sit here with me. Or you can go in and listen to Jacob Page beller about everything that ain't to his likin'."

Charlie Jack didn't even take time to think about it. "Stay here."

Billy chuckled again, but a wary look down the street to the south from the Indian stifled the man's laughter and prompted him to follow the Paiute's gaze.

Riding slowly into town on a black horse was a lone rider. Except for his white shirt and gray striped vest, he was dressed all in black, with a long black coat and a small-brimmed hat pressed low over his eyes. He pulled up easily on the tired animal as he reached the boarding house and gazed down at Billy, his eyes shaded by heavy brows and his upper lip obscured by a thick handlebar mustache.

He opened his mouth to speak, but a cough rose up his gullet and he turned his head away to let it run its course, then, after wiping his mouth with a handkerchief, returned his attention to O'Hara.

"I say, suh, is there a hotel in town?" he asked, his gravelly voice quiet and respectful, the accent deep South.

"No. This here boardin' house, that's all there is," Billy explained. "But we welcome overnighters."

The stranger reached into the pocket of his satin vest and flipped Billy a gold coin.

"I'll take a room, suh. Be back later to check in. Does this town have an establishment?"

"A saloon? Over yonder." Billy nodded in the direction of the place. "Jus' follow the crowd."

The stranger nodded his head once and touched the brim of his hat. "Obliged," he said, relaxing the reins and moving on up the street at the same slow pace.

"Don't get many gamblers here in Bodie," Billy commented to Charlie Jack when the man was out of earshot.

"Look mean," said Charlie Jack.

"Yep, that he does." Billy bit the coin. "But his money's good."

Matt and Sarah sat for an hour in the mouth of the cave, a good part of it spent letting her cry it out, Matt doing his best to comfort her. Then they exchanged tales of the past few days, and sympathized with each other over their injuries. When all was said and done, Matt put his arm around Sarah's shoulder and drew her to him. She yielded willingly, letting a spasm shake her as she nestled on his chest.

With a dirty, callused thumb, Matt gently brushed her wet cheek, leaving a streak of dirt, then undid the knot on his neckerchief and wiped her face with it. Sarah was oblivious to his actions. Her eyes closed, her breathing regular, she was soon asleep, exhausted from her several-day ordeal.

Matt grinned like a man who just laid down four aces, enjoying the feel of her against him, the warmth of her soft skin. He could have sat there with her forever, could have died happy in that cave, but the practical side of him won out. He moved her gently.

"Come on, Sarah. We need to get back. It ain't far."

Her eyes flickered open and she raised her head.

"Huh? What did you—where—who are . . . ?" Then she focused on him, and remembered. "Oh, yes," she said sweetly. "My knight in shining armor, come to rescue me."

"Can you get up?"

"I don't know. My legs are awful tired, and my feet burn."

"Let me help you." Matt stood and lifted the young woman to her feet, but her legs, quivering from lack of nourishment, wouldn't hold her. Matt grabbed her waist, then changed position and caught her up in his arms, carrying her out of the cave and down the slope to where Blister stood, munching contentedly on a patch of moist prairie grass.

"That's enough of that, old boy," Matt told the horse as he lifted Sarah into the saddle. "All that green'll stop you up like . . . well, like you don't ever want to be stopped up. It'll kill you. When we get back to town you can have a whole bucket of grain."

With Sarah securely in place holding the pommel, Matt led Blister by the reins and headed home, Sheriff Taylor's Winchester resting in his left hand.

An hour later the canyon opened up into Bodie's valley, not a mile from the first building. Sarah looked around, amazed.

"I was going in a circle," she muttered.

"More or less," Matt agreed. "Mostly you were just headed back the way you came, only not on the road. If you had kept going you'd have been home yesterday. But, of course, you didn't know that," he added, not wanting to increase her bad feelings. "And your feet, they couldn't have gone a step more. You did the right thing, leaving those directions and stopping in the cave, makin' a fire and everything. I must say, though, I don't know why you didn't follow the sound of the stamps back to Bodie in the first place."

"The mill was shut down because of the cave-in," Sarah explained. "I didn't hear them until this morning."

"Oh, yeah. Very many hurt?"

She hesitated. "A couple men. One dead and one knocked on the head who might still die. The third broke his leg."

"Anyone I know?"

"Uh . . . your pa was the one who broke his leg. He'll be okay though."

"Pa? What was he doin' in the mine?"

"He got hurt during the rescue. You'd have been real proud of him, Matt."

"He's only got one arm. What was he doin' helpin' with the rescue?"

"He isn't helpless, Matt. Besides, all the other men were exhausted."

"I wish I'd been there to help, instead of traipsin' all over the county lookin' for a man who hadn't done anything wrong. Well, anyway, no point in grousin' about it now. Pa will be fine. So you were headed back to Bridgeport when the storm hit, is that it?"

Sarah nodded. "Lightning rattled the horses." She closed her eyes, remembering the soulful, pleading expression on the face of the horse she had destroyed, and her lip began to tremble. She bit it, choking her sorrow back down and swallowing her self-pity.

Matt had his eyes on the way ahead and didn't notice, caught up in his own thoughts . . . thoughts about the DeCamps and Samuel, how the little boy had gotten a father, just like himself after all those years. Matt hoped his pa wasn't hurt too bad. Life was tough enough with just one arm, now having only one leg to boot.

They traveled on in silence, Bodie just over the next rise. As they crested the hill and it came into view, Matt stopped for a second to drink in the sight of the small town, then continued on.

"It's good to be home," Sarah said softly as they broached the edge of the town proper.

It took Matt a couple minutes to click on what she had said—
her home was Bridgeport, not Bodie—and then to try and figure
out what she meant. Did she just mean civilization? Was she still
a little disoriented? Or was she thinking of moving to Bodie, and
if so, why?

The answer came to him, but it was more than he dared hope
for and he kept silent, afraid speaking about it would make Sarah
change her mind.

Matt shouted and waved as the Empire Boarding House came
into view. Billy pushed himself slowly out of the rocker, not believing his eyes.

"Matthew? That you? And you got Sarah with you? What in
the world are . . . ? What's the problem with her feet?" He lumbered down the steps without waiting for a reply and lifted Sarah
from the horse without help. He carried her directly inside, shouting for Charlie Jack to heat some water.

"Find my salts! They're in the cabinet in the corner." He set
Sarah on a soft chair and unwrapped her feet gingerly. "What's
this, your petticoat?" he mumbled. Her feet were red and swollen
and blistered, and Uncle Billy sucked in his breath. As soon as the
water was ready, he eased her feet down into the salty concoction.
At first the mixture stung, and Sarah jerked her feet up, splashing
Billy in the chest.

"Don't do that, Miss Taylor," he scolded. "It don't do no good
if they ain't in the water. Don't make that face at me, I know it
hurts, but it'll stop after a few minutes." She put her feet down
slowly and clenched her teeth. "There you go, honey. That's right."

While Billy took care of Sarah, Matt spent a few minutes tending to his horse. He removed the saddle and blanket and tossed
them onto the porch, then gave Blister a quick rubdown and a
bucket full of water. He asked an idle man to get the horse some
oats, and he finally responded after Matt flipped him a coin.

Only when Matt boarded the steps did he notice Charlie Jack,
sitting quietly after returning from the kitchen.

"Charlie Jack! What are you—say, you okay? What'd you do
to them arms?"

"Charlie Jack okay," the Indian said. "Matt father hurt." He
jerked his head toward the front door of the boarding house. "He
glad to see you."

"Thanks, Charlie. I'll talk to you later."

The Indian nodded and Matt entered the parlor of the boarding house as Sarah was nursing her feet into the hot, salty water. Billy stood and turned to the deputy.

"You try getting in with her?" Matt said, looking at Billy's shirt.

"No, but I considered dunking her when she done that," Billy said. "Now, don't you worry none. She'll be fine in no time, no time at all. Say, you don't look too good yourself." He gently took Matt's bruised and swollen jaw in his beefy hand, turning the lawman's head from side to side.

"Ouch," Matt said when Billy pressed a little too hard. "You ain't fixin' to soak my head, are you?" He pulled back from Billy and reached up to rub the side of his face.

"What's the matter?" Billy asked. "You got more than a bruise?"

"Teeth hurt," Matt said.

"Someone musta clobbered you good," Billy concluded. "You need to have a dentist take a look at that."

"Is there one in town?"

"Not hardly. Bridgeport or Aurora, take your pick."

"I'll give it a few days," Matt said. "I never liked dentists much."

"Ain't never met no one who did," Billy observed.

"Where's my pa?"

"In his room."

"Thanks." Matt went quickly down the hall before Billy got any ideas about trying to tend to his teeth, leaving the man to fuss over Sarah, and knocked on his father's door.

"Who is it?"

"Matt."

"Come in, boy, come in. Don't stand out in the hall makin' a scene."

When Matt did so he saw his father stretched out on the bed, his leg in a splint.

"S'cuse me if'n I don't jump up to greet you," Jacob Page said. "I done busted my leg, like a fool."

He told Matt the story, embellishing it heavily to make it interesting, but soon tired.

"I'll talk to you more later," Matt said. "Glad you're okay."

"Yeah," Jacob said quietly. "And you can tell me what horse kicked you." Matt's father grinned as he rubbed his jaw self-consciously and gently traced the swelling on his bad eye. "Now go on, let me git my rest."

Matt grinned back at his father and backed out of the room.

In the parlor, Billy poured the deputy a mug of hot coffee from the ever-present pot on the stove.

"She's gone to bed," Billy said, explaining Sarah's absence.

"She was in pretty sad shape."

"You're not so hot yourself," Billy noted.

"A little tired, maybe. And hungry."

"Ah got some hot soup and warm cornbread in the kitchen. You sit yourself down, Ah'll get it."

He hurried out while Matt grabbed the nearest chair and eased himself into it, but the deputy hadn't even gotten settled when the door to the boarding house burst open and a breathless man rushed in.

"Deputy!" he called. "Deputy! Oh, there you are."

Matt didn't get up. "What's all the fuss?"

"There's been a killin'!" the man told him.

"Calm down, fellah," Matt ordered. "Now what's this about a killin'?"

"Down in Aurora. Dub Crenshaw was killed in a alley, shot from behind."

"In Aurora, you say? That's a mite far away to concern me."

"Yes sir, I suppose. But the constable, he said to come and tell you, because he thinks the man that done it may have rode this way."

"When did this happen?"

"Early this mornin'."

"Then he'd already be here if he was coming this way," Matt surmised. Billy had wandered in from the kitchen to see what the commotion was all about. Matt turned to him.

"Any strangers in town?"

"Just one that Ah saw," Billy told him. "Rode in a few hours ago, reserved a room, then sauntered over to the saloon. Looked like a gambler to me."

Matt again addressed the messenger. "Tell me, who is the man who shot Crenshaw? What's he look like?"

"We don't rightly know for certain. Long black coat, that's all I can say."

"What? Then what makes you so sure he came this way?"

"I ain't sure 'bout nuthin'. I'm just deliverin' the message for the constable. He says it's so, and I didn't question him none. I do know no one seen the shootin'. Just a shadow running out of the alley in a long black raincoat. It was still dark. Hear tell he got on a horse and rode south. Ain't nuthin' that direction 'cept Bodie."

"Is Palmer mounting a posse?" Matt asked, still sipping his coffee.

"Oh, yeah, I'm sure he is. He sent me on ahead to give you fair warnin', in case the man came here."

"We appreciate that," Matt said. "Thanks. Here, get yourself something for your thirst." He handed the man a coin.

"Yes sir. Thanks."

"After that you can go on back or stay, it's up to you. But it might be a good idea to hang around until the constable arrives. You took enough chances by yourself on the road already."

"Don't I know it," the man said. He started to turn, but Matt called him back.

"You, uh, didn't happen to see anyone on the road, did you?"

"No sir, not a soul. This ain't the time of year to be makin' no unnecessary trips."

"Okay. Well, thank you, friend."

The man nodded and left the boarding house, a slight limp in his gait as he led his animal across the street to the saloon.

"Ne'er-do-well," Billy mused, setting a tray on the table next to Matt. "Probably the first money he's earned all month, and he can't wait to get rid of it."

Matt set his coffee cup down and dragged himself out of the chair.

"Well, I guess I better go over there and have a look at this stranger."

"You should eat first," Billy said.

"If I do that, I'll want to go to sleep. I'll have some later."

"You gonna need help bringin' him in?" Billy asked. "He looked awful mean."

"No, I ain't bringin' him in," Matt said. "We don't know that he did anything. It ain't against the law to come to Bodie wearin' a black raincoat. Lots of folk wear black raincoats in weather like this. I just want to size him up, keep an eye on him until Constable Palmer gets here."

"You be careful."

Matt ran a hand through his hair, heaved a large sigh, and stuck his hat on. "Thanks, Billy, I intend to. I'm too tired to do anything else."

CHAPTER

EIGHTEEN

The saloon was quieter than usual. The reopening of the mines and the mill had drained the customer pool, along with the added burden of shoring the cave-in site, cleanup, and the depletion of men due to injuries and exhaustion.

Matt had no trouble spotting the stranger, even though he'd removed his coat and hat. He sat with several other men—all locals without jobs—playing poker. The largest pile of money seemed to be in front of the stranger, who eyed his opponents with confidence and a smirk, and a twinkle in his eye.

The man was pale, not sickly so, but indicative of a man who slept during the day and played all night. Red around the eyes, his forehead glistened. He coughed lightly now and then but still smoked cigars incessantly and maintained a bottle of whiskey in front of him, pouring from it whenever his glass emptied. He also kept his opponents' glasses full.

Matt stood by the end of the bar, drinking a glass of water and munching pine nuts.

"Sorry I don't have any *koochabee* for you," the bartender remarked, wiping a glass out with his towel.

Matt angled his head slowly toward him and gave him a stare. Word had apparently gotten around.

"I'm extremely disappointed," Matt said, then gave the man a little grin. "Perhaps you could find some jerked beef for me."

"Sorry. All out. How about some pickled eggs?"

"Good enough."

He handed the deputy a jar and went back to his wiping.

While Matt chewed on the eggs he watched the stranger win hand after hand, although his take was small in this low-stakes game. He lost once to a pat hand, a local do-nothing who was dealt a straight right off, but the stranger seemed amused by it and won the remaining games.

He didn't appear to be cheating, and no one questioned him. Perhaps the pearl-handled revolver sticking out of a shoulder rig prevented any arguments.

It wasn't long before the men lost interest.

"Must not be planning on staying long," Matt mumbled to the bartender. "Word'll get around. He won't have anyone wantin' to play him."

"Probably just needs a stake and then he'll move on. Bodie ain't a real jumpin' place, after all, just bein' a bump in the road."

Matt considered this, watching as the stranger got up and stretched and drew his coat on, followed by his hat, but Matt's further considerations were interrupted by gunfire outside.

He barged out through the batwings and stopped on the boardwalk to see what was happening. More shots were fired and men were hooting and hollering. This wasn't a fight, it was a celebration, and it was coming from in front of the Empire hoist house.

"Yee haw! We found it! We found us a mother lode!" The man punctuated his joy with more shots as Matt and others converged on the celebrants, pouring out of every building and alley in all states of dress to find out what the ruckus was.

Matt snatched the gun from the miner's hand and ordered the others to put theirs away.

"Someone's gonna get hurt!" he shouted, all but unheard above the din. "Now what's this all about?" He caught the miner by the throat to get his attention. "What's going on?"

"We found it! A vein a foot wide, three inches deep! Pure and clean as a baby's bottom!"

"What's this?" a man barked, pushing his way through the throng. It was Thomas Wellman, foreman of the Empire Mine.

"Ben, what's all this about a vein? Have you been drinking? You're not even mining today. You're on the cleanup crew."

"It was the cave-in!" Ben explained at the top of his lungs. "It exposed a vein. We quit that crosscut too soon." He pulled a rock from his pocket and shoved it at Wellman, who held his lantern up. The sight threw an awed hush over the crowd as the lantern's glow revealed a nugget the size of a fist, almost fifty percent pure gold.

The silence was broken by a whoop, and men all around began cheering and hugging and dancing in the street, alone and with each other.

"They been without women too long," Matt muttered, as he was jostled by the celebrants.

But they had a right to be happy. This meant more jobs, more money for everyone; this meant a boom for Bodie, more mines to be opened, more claims filed. Good times had come at last.

Matt watched with mixed emotions as the party continued, handing the six-gun—once he'd emptied it—back to Ben. Wellman retreated to the hoist to go down to see for himself while a group of men headed for the saloon. Matt followed their progress, noticing the stranger standing outside, looking not a little disappointed at his poor timing. The visitor saw the deputy, touched his hand to the brim of his hat, and stepped off the boardwalk onto the street. He untied the black horse and led it across the street to Billy's.

Uncle Billy watched also. He had come out at the first shot, afraid Matt had gotten into it with the stranger, and was relieved to see the deputy striding down the street toward the boisterous miners. He waited until all was clear, then made his way to the lawman.

"Well, this is good news," he said to Matt.

"Yessir, Billy, it is," Matt said wistfully.

"What's a matter, Matthew? Ain't you excited?"

"Oh, I suppose. This means a lot to Bodie. It'll be growin', people comin' in from all over creation, families . . ."

"Yep, that's true," Billy agreed. "They'll be comin' in droves, if that vein's as good as he thinks, especially with Aurora dwindling now that the Esmeralda district is tappin' out and windin' down. What's wrong with that?"

"I'm not sure, Uncle Billy. I just don't have a good feelin' about it. We'll start seein' more bad folk, too. Profiteers, gamblers, more saloons, fightin', killin', prostitutes, the Chinese with their opium . . . Bodie'll never be the same again."

"You was expectin' somethin' else?"

"No. Hopin' maybe. I like Bodie just as it is, nice and quiet and manageable."

"Yeah, but it ain't so good that way. Why, jus' look at the past couple days. We didn't have a doctor in town—or a dentist, for that matter. There's no church. People can't buy what they need most of the time. We don't even have but a single restaurant, and it's none too good. Ol' James Finster's a miner what give up, and now he's makin' everyone eat what he knows how to cook: beans and sourdough. Bodie could use a boom, yes sir. It'll be good for us, make life better. Yeah, there'll be more problems. Always is. But we gotta take the bad with the good."

Matt felt his jaw and winced. "Yeah, I suppose."

"Still hurtin', eh Matthew?" Billy said. "You gotta get that taken care of, son. Very least you need to take some whiskey, deaden the pain. It'll work on your eye, too. She's goin' down some, though. Lookin' better."

"I don't drink," Matt reminded him.

"Neither do Ah. This ain't drinkin', this is medicine. Come on, Ah got a little set aside, jus' for this. Besides, you need some sleep, too. Our stranger's goin' to bed, looks like. You can watch him tomorrow. The whiskey'll help you sleep through the pain."

Matt followed Billy back to the boarding house. Inside they found the stranger seated by the stove, his feet on a small table, his coat and hat still on. His saddlebags occupied an adjacent chair.

"Ah, there you are," he said, unfolding his lanky legs and standing as Billy walked over to him. "I thought you'd be cele-brating with the rest of them."

"Not me," Billy said. "Ah saw you go in, knew you'd need your room. Step over here, if you don't mind. You can sign in and get your key."

"Thank you, suh." He followed Billy to a rolltop desk in the corner and signed where Billy indicated, paying cash for the room and a bath.

"You already paid some," Billy reminded him, fishing the double eagle out of his vest pocket.

"That's for you, for your trouble," the man said. "And I'm obliged."

"Well, thank you." Billy handed him the key. "Up the stairs on the left. Ah'll be up in a bit with your bath water."

The stranger nodded and turned, noticing the deputy seated in an upholstered chair in the corner, eyeing him thoughtfully while he stroked his swollen jaw.

"Evenin', Sheriff," the man said.

Matt nodded just as his tooth sent a stab of pain through the root and into the jaw. He winced.

"Got a medical problem there, Sheriff? You don't look so good."

"So I've been told," Matt acknowledged. "By just about everybody. I'll be fine. Thanks just the same."

"All right, suh. Good night then." He advanced up the stairs.

Matt nodded and slouched back into the chair.

"Where's Charlie Jack?" he asked Billy, who was bringing out Matt's dinner one more time.

"Asleep out back," Billy replied. "You know, Matthew, he's a doctor."

"Charlie Jack?"

"Course not. The stranger." He nodded toward the stairs and set the tray down on the table next to the young lawman. "Says so on the ledger. Maybe he could look at your tooth."

"If he's the killer from Aurora, I sure don't want him messin' inside my mouth," Matt protested.

"He don't act like a killer."

"Because he's so polite?"

"No, he just don't seem to be in no hurry."

"Maybe he ain't. Maybe he figured we wouldn't know anything about it. After all, Aurora's in Nevada. Which way did he come from?"

"From that way," Billy said, pointing south. "Course, it'd be no trick at all to circle around town and enter from the opposite way, jus' to throw us off."

"But why stop here at all? Why not just keep ridin'?"

"He needed a stake. Figured he'd stop long enough to clean out a few men, get some grub and some sleep, and leave again in the morning, no one the wiser."

"Maybe," Matt agreed. "Still, it seems like an awful lot of trouble. I wonder what happened to Dub Crenshaw."

"Probably won the stranger's money gambling, so he shot Dub the first chance he got," Billy theorized.

Matt shook his head. "If that's so, why wouldn't he have taken his money back? He wouldn't need to stop here to gamble. If it was me, I'd be halfway to Sacramento by now. Besides, this fellow don't lose much at the table. It's his profession."

Billy shrugged. "You got me. Ah ain't no detective. Ah still think you ought to have him look at your tooth."

"Did I hear someone say 'tooth'?" The voice came from the stranger, who had just reached the bottom of the stairs. "I didn't mean to intrude, but I left my saddlebags on the chair."

"Matthew here's got a bad tooth. Someone gave him a round-house."

"Struck an officer of the law? I can't abide by that. Point out this fellow to me, and I'll see that he's soundly chastised."

"He's dead," Billy informed the stranger.

"Ah. As it should be. Well, perhaps then I can take a look at your tooth, since I can't provide your attacker with my opinion of his deed. It just so happens I'm a dentist, though I don't practice any more. I've found there's more profit in men's pockets than in their mouths. And, quite frankly, more people dislike their dentist than dislike their dealer." He smiled and picked up his saddlebags. "I'd be honored, Sheriff."

"I'm just a deputy," Matt corrected.

"Never say *just* a deputy, suh," the stranger said. "It is an honorable position."

"Still, I'd rather not—"

"Matthew!" said Billy sternly. "Stop bein' a baby and let the man at least look. You don't have to let him do nuthin' if you don't want."

"I'll be gentle," the stranger said. "Could be there's nothing wrong that a few days won't fix."

"Oh, all right," Matt relented. "Just so everyone will stop harping on me."

The dentist set his saddlebags down and grabbed the lamp. "All right, Deputy, tilt your head back. Looks like he slugged your eye so hard it rattled your teeth." He chuckled at himself while Matt glared. "All right, open wide now. That's it. Ah yes. Um hmm. I see. That one there, is it?" He touched it lightly and Matt howled, the doc pulling his finger back just in time.

"Sorry, my friend. It's cracked. It's begun to die already. Best we take it out."

Matt groaned and sank back into the chair.

"I'll get the whiskey," Billy said.

"Just so happens, I have my tools," the stranger said. "Cheer up, Deputy. This will only take a second."

CHAPTER

NINETEEN

Matt woke the next morning at first light, still sprawled in the chair in the same position as when he went to sleep. As best he remembered, that is. His head ached from the whiskey, his jaw from the extraction. His mouth felt as if it was full of cotton, then he realized it was. His cheek, at least. Blood-soaked cotton stuffed in there to fill up the hole. He marveled that he hadn't choked on it during the night.

He got up tentatively, bracing himself on the arm of the chair until his head cleared, then made his way slowly to the kitchen. Over the basin he pulled out the cotton and tossed it into the stove to burn, swirled some water around in his mouth and spit it out, then rinsed again with some of Billy's medicinal whiskey. He considered swallowing but had second thoughts and got rid of it, after letting the alcohol soak into the tender gum for a minute.

He was still leaning over the basin when Billy entered.

"Oh, Matthew. You're up. How's the mouth?"

"Sore!" Matthew said, glaring.

"Soak some more cotton in that hooch, keep it numb. You'll be fit as a fiddle in a day or two. Ah don't suppose you want some breakfast."

Matt shook his head. "Just need my canteen filled."

"Goin' somewheres?"

"Out ridin'. I can't stand to sit around when it hurts like this. Gotta keep busy. Thought I'd take a ride north toward Aurora, see if I could pick up a trail. I could use the fresh air, too."

"Well, you be careful," Billy cautioned. "You ain't a hunnerd percent."

Matt waved and stuffed a whiskey-soaked wad of cotton into his cheek, then left via the door off the kitchen just as Sarah hobbled into the room from the other direction.

"You shouldn't be up," Billy chastised.

"I couldn't sit around all day," she explained. "I've got to keep busy."

"Ain't you a pair," Billy said, shaking his head.

"Who?"

"You and Matthew."

"Why do you say that?"

"You both oughtta be off your feet, takin' it easy, and you both are up and at 'em."

"What's the matter with Matt? Is he okay?"

"Oh, yeah, he's fine. Doc Holliday pulled his broken tooth, that's all."

"It wasn't in the front, was it?"

"No, honey," Billy chuckled. "It wasn't in the front."

"Who's this Doc Holliday?"

"Tell you what," Billy said. "You get off your feet, I'll make us some tea and sit with you, tell you all about it. Go on now." He shooed her out into the parlor.

Blister was refreshed, having had a rubdown and a bucket of oats and a night's sleep, and was ready for another day's ride. He stepped lightly and Matt scolded him, and held a tight rein to keep the animal from moving too fast. Reading sign was hard enough without doing it from the back of a bounding, frisky horse.

Several miles out of town a narrow path split off from the main road. It was marked PRIVATE PROPERTY on a hand-painted sign and had the name *Wm Bodine* painted underneath. The path led over a hill, but Matt could see smoke curling up over the crest of the ridge, several miles deeper into the country.

"A mighty secluded place to live," he said to Blister. He checked the ground and saw no evidence of recent travel into the property, and continued on his way, confident no one had gone up the path recently.

Another mile was behind him when he pulled Blister to an easy halt. Up ahead, off the road a few feet, lay a horse—still saddled. Matt dismounted slowly and approached on foot, leading the Morgan. The animal snorted and shook his head, uneasy at the smell of dead horseflesh.

First he scanned the countryside, then, keeping a wary eye out, Matt knelt by the animal and examined it. Its leg was broken, and it had fallen in the ditch in such a way that the saddle would have been difficult to remove without damaging it. The beast also had a bullet wound in its head.

The horse was covered with the residue of dried sweat. Whoever had ridden this horse had ridden it hard. It probably stumbled due to exhaustion or might even have broken the leg when it fell after its heart began giving out.

Matt rose slowly and pushed his hat back on his head, giving the countryside the once-over again but seeing nothing. He was glad the air was still cool; heat made tracking more tedious. The day had dawned clear, but clouds were building, and it looked like the rains would return by dusk.

He spat out a wad of whiskey-saturated saliva and rinsed his mouth from his canteen. He then filled his hat with water and let Blister drink. Mounting the Morgan, the lawman reined him off the road and urged him up the sagebrush-covered slope to give himself a better view.

Near an outcropping he jumped off the horse and scampered up the rock, then stood and peered at the ground below. After he spotted what he was looking for, he put his binoculars up for a closer look.

"Yep," he said out loud, "there he is." He jumped down and let Blister take him back down the hill, then steered the horse to what he had seen in the brush.

A dead man clad in a black coat lay in the heavy growth, all but invisible from ground level. He was near the horse but not so near he could have been thrown that far. That he might have tried crawling before he died was something Matt considered, so he turned him over.

"Look at this, Blister."

There was an angry bruise on the man's forehead, and his open eyes were locked in a surprised gaze that had seen his fate a split-second before he died.

"I do believe old Dub Crenshaw's killer came south from Aurora after all." Matt said to his horse. He checked the man's pockets but found no papers or money. His sidearm was still stuck in his belt. Matt pulled it out and found four loaded chambers, one empty, and one expended cartridge.

He hoisted the body onto Blister's rump, tied it on so it wouldn't slip off, then took another sip of water, swallowing this time. Matt hung the canteen over the pommel of his saddle and lifted himself up, but, instead of heading back to Bodie, he rode slowly in the opposite direction at the edge of the road, scrutinizing the tracks in the dirt down the center. A hundred yards down the road, he stopped.

"Things may not be as they appear," he said softly to Blister. "Let's go, boy." He turned back toward Bodie and let the Morgan move at an easy lope.

Sarah accepted her tea and smiled at Billy.

"I never made it home," she explained.

"Yeah, Ah figured that. Ah see you walked a ways. It's a good thing Matthew found you."

"Yes, it is. By the way, speaking of Matt, was that his bottle of whiskey on the counter? Was he drinking?"

"Yes and no, Sarah. He used it to deaden the pain, but Ah don't think he drank much. Not for thirst, anyway."

"Good," Sarah huffed. "I don't like the smell of it on a man's breath."

"Well, Sarah, Ah got to tell you, your nose is a mite too sensitive. There's a lot a smells in this world that are gonna give you a turn. The odor of liniment, ceegars, a man who ain't had a bath all summer, fresh cow pies, the outhouse . . . but they's all part of life and you're gonna smell 'em. Now Matthew, he fought me about the whiskey, but couldn't hardly keep from takin' it when he had that tooth pulled. Besides, if Ah remember rightly, the Apostle Paul told Timothy in the Bible to take a little wine for what ailed him. If Matt wanted to drink a little whiskey to keep the pain down, Ah don't think he'll be delivered to hell for it. You know, bad smells is jus' God's way a reminding us about sin, and how much we need Jesus."

Sarah dropped her head contritely. "You're right, Billy, I was being selfish."

"And you got to learn to trust your man, too," Billy went on. "Matthew's got a good head on his shoulders. He won't let you down none. You look up to him, put yourself in his hands, and he'll take care of you. God won't let him fall into waywardness . . . and neither will Uncle Billy, as long as Ah'm around. You trust God and Matthew, and you'll be fine."

Billy took a sip of tea. "Sorry for goin' on so. How's them feet of yours?"

Sarah smiled. "Thank you. I needed to hear those things. And my feet are much better. I'll be back to normal in a couple days."

"Then you'll be ready to go back home?"

"I suppose," she said wistfully.

"You sound as if you ain't too anxious."

"Oh, I want to go home. Don't think I don't. I just would rather stay here with Matt."

"You afraid a losing him to someone else?"

"No . . . and yes. I suppose I am a little, though I don't know why."

"It's because you love him so, that's why. It's natural to feel that way. If he means that much to you, Sarah, why don't you stay here? In Bodie?"

"What would I do?"

"Same as you would in Bridgeport, Ah guess. Laundry, baking, canning . . . Let me tell you, there will be plenty to keep you busy real soon. Bodie will be booming in no time."

"I hope so too," she began, "but—"

"Hope, nuthin'!" Billy said emphatically. "There was a big strike last night. I'm surprised all the shootin' and shoutin' didn't wake you."

"Oh, then all the commotion was real? I heard it but never really woke up all the way. I thought it was part of my dream."

"Weren't no dream. The cave-in exposed a real nice vein. Soon's word a this gets out people will be streamin' in. They'll need places to live, supplies, food, clothing, jobs . . . We don't even have a decent place to eat—'cept mah kitchen of course."

Sarah's face brightened, and she looked at Billy with a gleam in her eyes. She jumped up and gave him a hug and a kiss on the cheek. "Billy, you wonderful man!"

"What'd Ah say?"

Sarah pulled her chair close and laid out her plan.

Matt slowed the horse when he reached town and walked it to the small shack he called his office. He lifted his leg over the pommel and slid down, tying his horse to the rail and untying his passenger. By this time he had been seen, and several men began to gather around, murmuring about the dead man and trying to get a look at his face. One of the onlookers finally stepped up to help the lawman.

"Thanks, Mr. Tate," the deputy said. "Can you see he gets taken care of?"

"Sure, Deputy. Who is it?"

"Don't know, but I reckon he's got something to do with a killin' in Aurora."

There was more murmuring, and one man gave Matt a congratulatory slap on the back, but the deputy was not encouraged—he hadn't done anything. Disregarding them, he turned on his heel and put his office to his back, deciding on a direct course of action, and strode across the wide street to the Empire Boarding House, where he found Billy lounging in the kitchen.

"Is he up yet?" Matt inquired.

"Who? Your pa?"

"No, the doc."

"He ain't been down. Who was that you brung in hanging over your horse, Matthew? Did you . . . ?"

But Matt didn't hear the rest. He was headed up the stairs. He reached Holliday's room and held up a fist to knock, but before he could he was hailed from inside.

"Come in, Deputy. Door's unlocked."

Matt hesitated but went ahead and turned the knob, pushing the door slowly with his left hand, his right resting on the backstrap of his pistol.

"It's all right, Deputy," Holliday coughed. "I'm just resting on the bed, my hands are in plain view."

Matt swung the door open all the way and stepped in.

"Good morning, Deputy. How's the tooth?" Holliday held open a hand. Don't tell me, I can see it on your face. It hurts bad, and you didn't sleep a wink. Well, before you shoot me, let me say in my defense that it'll feel better in a couple days. It always hurts right off."

"It's not the tooth I'm here about," Matt said. "And how did you know it was me?"

"Well, for one thing, them gum-soled boots of yours are quieter than most and not too many men wear 'em. You took the stairs two at a time and stopped outside my door. I assumed you were anxious about something or upset, and, well, since I pulled your tooth last night I figured that's what you were sore about."

"Oh." Matt relaxed. "That's good figuring. Everything but the tooth part. That's the least of my concerns right now."

Holliday sat up. "Well, then to what do I owe this visit?"

"Tell me straight, Mr. Holliday—"

"My friends call me Doc."

"Okay, Doc. Where'd you ride in from?"

"San Francisco. Left there a few days ago."

"So you didn't come through Aurora."

"Heavens no, Deputy. That's the opposite direction. Fact is, that's my next stop."

Matt slumped into a chair next to the door, partly relieved Holliday wasn't involved. He didn't look like someone with whom Matt was prepared to tangle. But he was also disappointed. There was still a mystery to solve. "That's what I suspected," the lawman said.

"What's the problem, Deputy?"

"There was a shootin' in Aurora yesterday. Messenger said they thought the killer was headed south."

"And you thought I did it."

"I thought it an odd coincidence, you ridin' into town the same day."

"Ah, yes, I suppose it could look bad that way. I would suspect me as well."

"I rode out this morning to see if I could pick up a trail, any sign that he rode this way."

"What'd you find?"

"One fresh set of tracks into town. That would have to be the messenger's. And several miles out a dead horse with a dead man nearby. Horse had a broken leg, the man had hit his head on a rock. The horse had been running hard—"

"Broke his leg and threw the rider," Holliday finished. "So what's the problem?"

"The horse had been mercy shot."

Holliday understood immediately. "Takes a live man to put an injured horse out of its misery. I'd say someone else was involved in that little scenario. You think so too, I see. You back to me, then?"

Matt shook his head. "No. Only one man I know of coulda done it. Had to be the messenger."

"The man who rode in with the news?"

"Yep." Matt pushed himself out of the chair. "Had to be. He'd a rode right by that dead horse. The man was in the brush and hard to see from the road, but that animal was as plain as day. I'm sure, if he was a legitimate messenger from the constable in Aurora, he'd a stopped to check it out and told me about it. The way I figure it, he kills the man in Aurora, hightails outta town, riding hard. His horse breaks a leg somehow, so he shoots him without thinkin'. Then this other rider comes by, and our man thinks he's trailin' him or goin' to Bodie to alert us, so he takes him down, hits him in the head with the rock, then rides in on his victim's horse."

"Why stop here? Why not keep riding?" Holliday asked, getting up and walking to the mirror to admire himself. He slicked back his hair and twirled the ends of his mustache, then walked over to the window.

"That part bothers me, I admit," Matt said. "Maybe he didn't know Bodie didn't have a telegraph office, figured we'd already be lookin' for him, so he . . . shoot, I don't know."

"You've almost got it. If you were looking for him, he'd have to come into town as someone else. What better ruse than to report directly to you and warn you, then sally over to the saloon for a casual drink? He hoped you'd do exactly what you did and find the dead man, thinking him to be the killer. It was too late to unshoot his horse, so he just hoped you wouldn't notice. In the meantime, he's tired and hungry. Thinking he's got some time, and not wanting to hurry out of town the wrong way and attract attention so soon after bringing you the news, he waters himself, has a plate of food, relaxes with a few hands of poker, then goes to sleep in the corner of the saloon."

Matt cocked his head and viewed Holliday askance. The gambler saw the deputy's odd look out of the corner of his eye and turned to view the lawman full on.

"That's an awful detailed speculation," Matt observed coolly.

"Wasn't speculation. The last part, at least. Is the man you're referring to short and dark, with baggy gray clothes and walked with a touch of a limp, like maybe he fell off a horse?"

"Yeah, that's him." Matt was wary. "How'd you know?"

"I observed that man's actions last night. He was none too pleased when I cleaned him out. In fact, he was downright rude when I won his watch." Holliday held it up. "But I suspect my companion, Mr. Colt, talked him out of trying something foolish." Holliday opened the cover on the pocketwatch. "What's the name of the man killed in Aurora?"

"Dub Crenshaw."

Holliday handed Matt the watch. "This might be his." Inside the cover were the engraved initials *D.E.C.* in fancy script. "I got witnesses," Holliday added, just in case Matt was planning on suspecting him again.

"He's our man, all right. I wonder if he's still in town."

The gambler turned back to the window and leaned on the sill. "I half-expected him to look me up this morning, but instead he chose to ride out, heading south."

"How do you know that?"

"My good deputy, there he rides, even as we speak."

Matt ran stumbling to the window, almost falling through it, and saw the man who had brought the news of the killing to town riding hard, leaving Bodie behind him. Matt turned and ran out of the room and down the stairs without a word, leaving a smiling Doc Holliday in his quarters.

"Good luck," Holliday said quietly.

CHAPTER

TWENTY

Matt left the boarding house at full clip, not acknowledging either Billy or Sarah, and leaped onto Blister's back. The horse caught his master's excitement and spun around, whinnying and snorting, his mane flying wildly. At last, a chance to run.

Matt heeled him, though it was hardly necessary. Blister flew over the road, his thundering hooves kicking up dirt and small rocks. Matt reached up and pressed his hat down on his head to avoid losing it, to no avail. His hair now flapping like Blister's mane, Matt crouched and leaned forward, standing slightly to smooth the ride, and let the Morgan have its head.

A mile out of town he sighted the suspect, who happened to glance back and saw the charging deputy at about the same time. The man hesitated, turned to get a good look, then slammed his heels into the animal's sides, and the wild-eyed horse broke into a gallop. The chase was on.

Blister was blowing hard, but his pace never slackened. His powerful muscles tensed and flexed beneath his rider, and his hooves hardly seemed to touch the ground. Were it not for having to think about what he'd do when he caught the man, Matt would have whooped in delight at the magnificent beast under him. He made a mental note to do this again sometime for no good reason, so he could enjoy it.

Though the road was dry, the surrounding countryside was still heavy with the water that had drenched it the past few days. Still pools stood in the low spots, reflecting the blue sky and white, puffy clouds that dominated the landscape. In the distance, to the southwest coming up by way of Mono Lake, gray storm clouds gathered. Animals scurried away from the edge of the road, frightened by the pounding of Blister's hooves they could not only hear but feel. Birds suddenly took flight from the sagebrush at the side of the road, squawking their displeasure.

Matt was oblivious to it all. He was focused on his quarry and was gaining. Another mile and he'd have him.

The man rounded a hill and disappeared. As Matt followed half a minute later, the road stretched out before him, straight and empty. He pressed the Morgan's flanks tight with his legs, leaned back, and pulled the reins hard, forcing Blister on his haunches like a cow pony and skidding to a stop. Matt threw one leg over, but before he could dismount, a gun discharged and the bullet whistled past his ear, even as the sound of the shot echoed off the nearby canyon wall on the far side of the road behind him.

Matt dove for the gully, slapping Blister on the rump sending him away, and rolled in the grass to safety but ending in a shallow stand of cold water. His Peacemaker was in his hands, although he couldn't consciously remember grabbing it, and he fired a round blindly out of sheer terror and frustration.

"This is Deputy Page, Mono County! I order you to throw down your gun and surrender!"

There was only silence for a response. Matt wasn't expecting obedience from the man, he was just hoping the fugitive would shout something back so the deputy could locate him.

"You don't have a chance!" Matt said. "There's others know it's you. You get away from me, someone else'll follow. It's just a matter of time."

Still no answer. Matt crept along the gully, keeping down and hoping he couldn't be seen, mindless of the pain that still plagued his mouth. He ventured a quick look and, from his new position, saw the man's horse behind a rock outcropping on the opposite side of the road. There was no other cover nearby.

"Listen to me," Matt called. "Give up now and you won't be hurt. You have my word. I'll take you back to Aurora where you'll get a fair trial. There'll be no lynching, I guarantee. You've killed two men, don't make it—"

A single gunshot interrupted him. Matt jerked and pressed himself into the ground. He waited. As thunder pealed in the distance, a plan came to him. He crawled down the gully about fifty yards, checked the man's rock and found there to be sufficient cover, then waited.

Finally, it happened again. A bolt of lightning flashed across the darkening sky followed by thunder ripping through the valley.

Matt climbed out of the gully and ran across the road, using nature as cover, hoping his opponent would keep his head down long enough for Matt to cross open space, the thunder canceling out his footsteps.

The lawman dove behind a clump of sagebrush and prayed, his breathing heavy. The wind picked up. The dark clouds moved in more quickly now until there was no more blue sky showing. Matt advanced again, circling wide around the rock and wondering why his adversary hadn't tried anything. Maybe the man was doing the same thing, he considered.

Less cautious now that he'd circled to the man's flank, Matt spied a small rock on the up slope behind the killer's rock, took a breath, and drew his gun. Running for it as fast as he could, jumping stones and sagebrush and keeping low, he finally slid in behind it and hunkered down to catch his breath, then peeked around the side and down the hill. There his quarry crouched, leaning into the rock, still and silent, waiting.

Excited because he hadn't been seen, Matt knew he had the man. He cocked the .44 and leveled it, then called to the fugitive.

"It's over! Hands up! You got nowhere to go!"

The man didn't move.

"You heard me! Drop the gun and stand up slow! Don't make me use this!" *Please,* he thought. The gun shook slightly as he squeezed the stocks. Still, the man didn't respond.

Matt squinted as a few sprinkles struck his unprotected face and craned his neck, then began a slow and careful walk down the slope, keeping the blade of his front sight on the man's back and his finger on the trigger, ready for any sudden moves.

It soon became evident the man would never move again, at least on his own accord. Suddenly nervous, Matt prayed it wasn't true. What if the man was innocent? What if his theory was wrong, or Holliday had lied? What if the man ran because he believed Matt was a robber? Matt thought back . . . Had he identified himself as a law officer?

Maybe the killer was Doc Holliday after all, and he'd tricked Matt into chasing an innocent person so he could make his escape.

The deputy holstered his gun. It had to have been a lucky shot. He never even saw the man . . . no, wait. The man fired first. Matt had fired only once, and the man had fired again after him. Matt couldn't have killed him.

He reached the dead man, and the mystery was solved. Seated on the ground, the man leaned awkwardly against the rock, his head hanging down. His pistol was still in his right hand. Matt put a hand on the man's head, turning it for a look at his face, then was sorry he had done so. Matt turned away, sickened, his breath suddenly short.

Shaken by the suicide, Matt turned and stepped away as a torrent was unleashed, quickly dowsing the already saturated ground. Matt fought down his emotions, trying to make sense of it, hoping and praying he hadn't made an error. Fear stuck in his throat.

But he had work to do. Whistling for Blister, he took his rope off the saddle and returned to the dead man. He grabbed the collar of the man's coat and pulled it over the head, then looped the rope around the neck, keeping the coat in place, hiding the face from anyone in town who might see Matt ride in—and hiding it from himself. Then he dragged the body to Blister and left it lying while he mounted his horse and retrieved the dead man's mount.

He led the horse and draped the corpse over the animal's saddle, securing it with the remainder of the rope, only then retrieving his slicker and putting it on.

He ignored the rain and rode home slowly, stopping just once to fetch his hat. When he made town the streets were deserted, and he breathed a sigh and shivered, realizing only then how cold and wet he was.

He rode directly to the mortician's shack—Lark Woodrow, an engineer for the Queen Anne, had worked at a funeral parlor back

East before gold fever yanked him out West—and took the man inside.

Matt thanked Woodrow, asking him to keep the man's state to himself, and rode directly to his office, locking himself in. Only after prayer and comfort from the Holy Writ was a slightly older but significantly wiser and more-seasoned Deputy Matt Page ready to come out.

The rain had ceased, and the clouds were breaking up by the time the sun began rising over Bodie Bluff.

It's first yellow-orange rays streaked over the town and across the valley like a circus canopy, stretched tight and tied down to the tops of the hills on the far side. The wood buildings basked in their glow and the promise of a warm day, but looks were deceiving as the chill in the air, cold enough to steam the breath, foretold the season's first snow, and the smoke from every chimney and stovepipe in sight provided sufficient witness to this reality.

Doc Holliday braved the morning, stepping off the Empire's boardwalk with his possessions in hand and securing them to his mount. Matt came out to the porch to see him off.

"Thanks for fixin' my tooth, Doc," he said after Holliday eased himself into the saddle.

"My pleasure, Deputy."

"My friends call me Matt."

"I'd be honored to be included in that exclusive circle, Matt," Holliday said graciously. "I'm glad it worked out to the good for you. I take it that was the constable from Aurora I heard come in last night."

"Yes. They positively identified the suicide as the man who shot Dub Crenshaw. Apparently there had been a witness after all. Thanks for your help, Doc."

"It was nothing, Matt, but you're welcome. If you're ever in the Arizona Territory, look me up. I'm sure you'll have no trouble finding me."

"Why there?"

"I hear the weather there is good for the lungs." He hacked into his fist, as if punctuating the sentence.

"You ought to get that checked. It doesn't sound too good."

"Too many of these, is all." Holliday took a cigar from his

inside coat pocket and stuck it between his teeth. "I probably ought to cut down."

"Well, you be careful, Doc."

The Southern gentleman and former dentist, now a roving gambler, tipped his hat and smiled, then turned his horse and left town.

Sarah limped outside and joined Matt on the porch, a shawl wrapped tightly around her against the chill. She hooked a hand in the crook of Matt's elbow and leaned into him, gazing up at him with an adoring smile.

"How's your tooth?" she asked.

"Gone," Matt replied glumly, still peering down the road. "How's your feet?"

"A little tender, but I can get around okay."

"That's good." Matt finally looked down at her and grinned, his first smile in days. He slowly pulled his arm from her grip and draped it around her shoulder.

She sighed and closed her eyes, enjoying the moment, then looked back up at Matt with a smile. "You want to help me look?" she asked.

Matt's expression was blank. "Look for what?"

"A good location for the Quicksilver."

"Beg pardon?"

"You've been so busy I haven't had a chance to tell you. Come on, we'll talk."

She led him off the porch as the sun crested the hill and bathed them both with its light: the light of a promise of a new day, an end to the rain, and the warmth of times to come.

PART

THREE

CHAPTER

ONE

APRIL, 1872

Deep inside a small private mine, several miles east of Bodie near the Nevada border, two young miners toiled in the thick, dusty air. Their faces were as chiseled and angular as the rock they mined, caked with dark red dirt, streaked by slow-moving drops of sweat. The two miners stood at the face of the crosscut deep inside the mountain. One of them held the steel shank of a star drill steady while the other hefted a large wood-handled steel hammer. The miner holding the drill stuck it into a deep, two-inch diameter hole in the rock, pushing it until it stopped.

"Another three inches," he told his partner. He gripped the steel rod tightly and prepared for the blows.

The young man with the hammer was spent. This was the seventh and last hole that would be drilled for the dynamite they would use to loosen two feet of gold-bearing rock in the face of the crosscut. It had taken almost eight hours to bore those seven holes, and their exhaustion was nearly complete.

He took a deep breath and brought the hammer up, then swung hard and hit the end of the drill. Again he swung, and again the drill bit into the rock. One slip and the twenty-pound sledge hammer would continue past the drill and strike the hands of the man holding the shank, pulverizing his bones. Only complete faith in his partner kept the man from breaking his hands away just before the hammer struck. But a loose drill wouldn't cut, just bounce off the rock, so he held fast, trusting his partner.

In another thirty minutes the hole was deep enough. They set down their tools and the younger of the two, twenty-year-old Joshua Bodine, inspected the work. He checked the depth of the holes, their angle into the rock, and pronounced them ready.

Bodine and his brother, twenty-four year-old Jefferson, moved the heavy steel plate onto the floor next to the face they had just drilled. When the dynamite was set off, the loosened rock would fall onto the muck plate, and they would shovel it into the ore car to be transferred out of the mine to the small two-stamp mill.

Satisfied that the muck plate was in place, Josh left the mine. When he was clear, Jeff pushed his dynamite into the holes, set the blasting caps, and connected the wires. He worked alone now. It wouldn't do for William Bodine to lose both his sons just because one of them made a mistake.

Once on the surface Jeff set the charges off, and they could hear the rumble deep inside the mountain. A blast of air and fine debris whooshed out of the mine entrance moments later.

The first time Josh had experienced this—he was ten—he got right up and started toward the tunnel to go in and begin mucking, but Jeff grabbed his arm. "Relax," Jeff had said. "You go down there now, and you'll suffocate. The fumes from the nitro displace all the air. We need to give it some time."

So Josh had learned at an early age about one of the many dangers of the mining business.

As he sat outside the shaft now with his brother, waiting for the air inside to clear, he looked off down the side of the bluff at the road in the distance. He wondered what was beyond the hills around their claim. He could just see the peaks of the Sierra Nevadas with their year-round snow cover and wished he could ride over to them. There were towns at the feet of these mountains . . . Bridgeport, Bishop, Independence . . . and he longed to experience them: the laughter of the people, the tinkling of the pianos in the saloons, the perfume of the dance hall girls, the restaurant food, the soft hotel sheets or the warmth of the water in the bath house, the pleasure and excitement of the big city.

He sighed—resigned to his lot and frustrated by it—but said nothing.

After an appropriate wait, he and Jeff trudged back into the mine, shoveled the loose rock off the muck and into an ore car and winched it out, and repeated the entire process.

This was the routine in the Rebecca Mine, which was owned by the boys' father, William Bodine. He had prospected these hills for years, placer mining here and there, trying some hard rock mining on the slopes of sagebrush-covered hills, walking over miles and miles of the California and Nevada mountains and plains, until he finally found an outcropping of gold-bearing quartz that led to a vein inside the mountain large enough that required help. He sent for his family, who came by wagon from South Carolina: his wife and two small boys.

Rebecca Bodine had taken ill during the trip, however, and had died shortly after arriving. Undaunted, Bodine raised his sons by himself, training them in the ways of mining and teaching them reading and writing. They grew up in the mines, never knowing another way of life.

But there was more to mining than getting the gold-bearing ore out of the mountain: The gold had to be separated from the rock. This was done by crushing it into powder and mixing it with water, then adding quicksilver to leach the gold out. At first, they had no way of crushing their ore on a large scale and had to haul the ore by the wagon-load to an *arastra* in nearby Nevada. For a percentage of the assayed value, the Mexican who owned the *arastra* would crush Bodine's ore and deliver the bullion to Carson City.

The high cost of paying the Mexican forced William Bodine to invest in his own mill. He built it himself, with the help of his sons, ordering the stamps from a forging company in San Francisco. It was now a seven-stamp affair, the original battery of five stamps and another battery of two stamps that he got second-hand from the Empire Company in Bodie the year before.

The stamps were driven by a steam engine. Because it wasn't practical to start the engine every day—it took too long to get it up to running speed—the Bodines mined for a month, crushed all the ore they had mined until they were done, which took several weeks, then returned to the mine for another month.

The boys' father did his share of the work, but it was his job finding the ore and prospecting the land, which took so much time that his sons ended up doing most of the mining and milling without him.

Jeff, being the oldest, ran the mill and treated his task as though the operation was solely his own. He had learned the business from the ground up, as had his brother, and wasn't afraid to tackle any task. Under his watchful eye the mill ran smoothly, and the Bodines turned a good profit.

Jeff stood on an observation deck elevated above the stamps supervising the operation. The ore was crushed by the eight-hundred-pound stamps into powder, mixed with water, and forced through a fine screen onto the sloping amalgamation table. A copper plate on the table had been coated with quicksilver, and as the sludge rolled over it, the gold and silver stuck, the rest of the mixture sliding down to the end of the table for release into a tailing pond.

Periodically Josh would scrape the amalgam into a bucket and hand it up to Jeff, who put it in a safe. When the safe was full, the mixture would be boiled in a retort, vaporizing the quicksilver and leaving just the precious metals. This mixture was then poured into a bullion bar and stored, the accumulated bars occasionally shipped to Carson City, while the quicksilver was reliquified and used again. Milling, like mining, was a never-ending process.

Tending the stamps was probably the most dangerous job in the mill. The pistons fell onto the rock with enough force to crush it into a fine powder and would certainly crush a man's hand if it got in the way. Jeff had almost learned the hard way once and was more than grateful when his father decided to let Josh handle that chore. William thought that was only fair since Jeff had to handle the explosives.

Jeff looked forward to the day his father would turn the whole operation over to him. The mine and the mill were his world, and he had no desire seeing what was outside his domain. He was content.

After they had finished with their work for the day, the brothers stepped outside for a breather. While Jeff splashed water on his face, Josh wandered off toward the house. It would be dinner soon, and he had something to do before then.

Catching his breath after rinsing the dust off his face and arms, Jeff walked down the hill toward their home, anxious to see his father and report on the activities of the day. As he approached the white-washed, two-story structure, he heard several gunshots nearby. Not at all alarmed, he nonetheless stopped and looked over his shoulder at his brother. Josh was wearing a holster and firing his six-gun at a row of bottles propped on a fence rail.

Jeff walked over slowly, watching his brother practice. Josh stood with his knees slightly bent, his body erect, his arms at the ready by his sides. On an unheard cue his hand would slap against the holster and pull out the gun, cocking it at the same time, then point and shoot, all in one smooth motion. He was so fast it was a blur, and six out of six times a bottle exploded.

"Pretty good shootin'," Jeff said dryly, "but what will it ever get you?"

"What do you mean?" Josh asked, opening the breach and dumping the spent cartridges onto the ground.

"What I mean, little brother," he said, emphasizing *little*, "is that practicing your quick draw with that pistol and rig of yours serves no purpose. We're miners, and when we need food we buy it. We ain't feudin' with no one, and if we was, we'd prob'ly sit down and talk it out."

"That may be your thinkin', but it ain't mine." Josh reloaded and squinted at his brother. "I may be doin' miner's work, but I ain't no miner. I don't plan on spendin' the rest of my life here, eatin' rock dust and waitin' for a cave-in. There's a big world out there, and I want part of it."

"Pa wouldn't be very happy hearing you say that. He's worked his whole life buildin' this for us. It'd be a slap in his face if he thought you didn't care none."

"I appreciate what Pa's done, but I got my own life. I'm twenty-one tomorrow, and it's time I set out on my own. I ain't cheatin' Pa none. He got a good twenty-one years outta me. I weren't no slacker."

"Leavin' him is a fine show of appreciation. Least you could do is stick it out until he passed on."

"He ain't even sickly!" Josh protested. He trotted out and set up more bottles while Jeff leaned against a fence post. When he came back he said, "He's got ten, fifteen good years in him still. He'll understand."

"Maybe. But I don't. What's this hankering for moving on that you've got? Where'd it come from?" Josh didn't answer but shot three bottles with one draw and reholstered. "You read too many of them dime novels," Jeff continued. "Them ain't true stories, don't you know that? That ain't the way life is out there. You're a dreamer!"

Josh drew again and fired twice, then wheeled toward Jeff and fired again before his older brother could react. The bullet slammed into the fence rail under Jeff's arm, the impact driving small splinters into his shirt sleeve.

"Hey, you—!" He reacted to the scare while Josh laughed. "You coulda killed me!"

"I hit what I aim at," Josh countered. "Let that be a lesson to you. Leave me alone!"

Josh holstered the weapon and strode to the house.

Jeff watched his upstart brother walk away, hate and anger in his heart, but he would do nothing. He would not displease his father.

The three Bodines were quiet around the dinner table: Josh acting as if it was his last meal; Jeff, although hungry, toying with his food, wondering what Josh was up to; William watching them both thoughtfully, unaware of the conflict.

"How's the mill running?" the elder Bodine finally asked Jeff.

"Just fine, Pa," he answered, shaping his mashed potatoes with his fork into a swirling mound. "Our ore is real heavy with gold. I think the vein must be gettin' thicker."

"Josh?" William said, turning to his other son. "How 'bout it?"

Josh looked up. "What's that, Pa?"

"The vein. Is it gettin' bigger?"

"Oh, yeah. I suppose." He went back to his plate.

"What's the matter, son? Something troublin' you?"

Josh didn't answer, and William looked over at Jeff. The eldest son only shrugged. *He* wasn't going to bring it up.

"Joshua?"

Josh glanced up at his father. "Uh, it's like this, Pa. I think it's time I . . . uh, went out on my own. I want to see more of the world than the inside of a mine all my life. There's a lot to see out there and a lot to do. I want to experience it for myself."

"Go ahead, son, you can have a week off. We'll get on okay." He looked at Jeff. "You too. You both been workin' hard. You could use a rest. The mine, she isn't goin' anywhere."

"I ain't tired," Jeff said. "And that ain't what *he* meant," he spat out.

"Huh?" The elder Bodine was puzzled, and he looked to Josh for an explanation.

"Uh . . . that's right, Pa. I ain't talkin' 'bout a holliday. What I mean to say is . . . I'm leavin'. For good."

"Well, I can't say as I'm surprised. I seen that look in your eye ever since you had that gun mail-ordered here. And spendin' all your time makin' that holster and practicing. But tell me, son, why do you want to leave for good?"

"I told you. I want to see the world, have some fun, meet people, make my own way."

"How you gonna get by?"

"Eventually I'll find work if I need it. But the way I figure it, a good portion of this place is mine. I figured you could give me my inheritance now, in cash. Then I can make my own start."

"*What?*" Jeff said, incredulous.

"I don't have that much cash," William said. "How about some gold dust. You can cash it at any bank."

Jeff couldn't believe what he was hearing. "You're gonna do it?" he complained to his father.

"It's his right," the elder Bodine stated with a tone of finality. He pushed himself away from the table. "Joshua, I wish you'd reconsider. I don't think you're gonna find out there what you're lookin' for. But you're a Bodine, and I know your mind's made up. Think about it tonight, and if you still feel the same in the mornin', you can go with my blessings."

Jeff complained: "But that leaves me to do all the work by myself!"

"I'll help you, son. I did it before, I think I can remember how to handle a star drill and hammer. Besides, I think we can hire a man full-time to give us a hand, not just part-time like before. We're not big, but we're big enough for that."

He left his sons at the table, Jeff with his brow furrowed at his slightly amazed but excited little brother.

CHAPTER

TWO

Josh woke before sunrise but stayed in bed, staring up at the ceiling. He had waited for this day a long time and wanted to savor every second. Slowly he swung his legs over the side and put his feet on the braided oval rug that covered a small part of the wood floor. He stretched and stood, and lit the oil lamp on the dresser, taking in the sounds and smells of his first day on his own.

He looked carefully around his room, trying to decide what to take with him. He grabbed a pair of blue jeans out of the drawer along with a beige cotton shirt, and rolled them up, then put on a clean pair of gray, wool pants, his Sunday shirt (never needed on Sunday yet) and his best wool socks, the ones with the fewest holes.

The only boots he had were miner's boots, but they would have to do for now. When he got to town he could get something else. Josh stuck his black felt, flat-brimmed hat on his head and admired himself in the mirror. Running a hand over his chin he thought about getting a shave in town at a real barber shop and smiled. A bath, too. Life would be good.

He buckled his gunbelt around him and felt the grip of his six-shooter, then eased the gun out of the holster. He opened the loading door and dropped the second set of spent cartridges from the day before onto the bed. The gun was dirty, so he carefully broke it open and ran a solvent-soaked rag down the barrel and cylinders. He followed with a dry rag, then another, and wiped the gun down carefully. He put a few drops of light oil in strategic places and worked the action several times. A final wipedown, another inspection, and he was satisfied.

Returning the gun to its holster after reloading it, he took one last look around the room, then stepped out, closing the door behind him. As he made his way to the kitchen, he passed his brother's open door.

"I see you're goin' through with it." Jeff was awake, sitting in a chair in his long underwear.

"What'd you expect?" Josh stopped by the doorway but didn't go in.

"Oh, I expected you to go through with it, all right. You're insensitive and selfish, don't care about Pa and me, just yourself. It's no skin off your nose what happens here."

"Is that a fact? Look, Jeff, I don't expect you to understand this, but there's more to life than makin' money diggin' gold outta the mountain. There's a whole world out there. Fun people, good times . . . you oughta try it. You'd see! I ain't gonna get old inside the earth. It ain't natural."

"And what *is* natural? Is that gun you're totin' natural? What do you need that for?"

Josh glared at his brother before answering. "Protection."

"From what? Good times? Fun people?"

"Don't be stupid. I know that ain't all there is out there. There's robbers and criminals, we all know that. That's why I've been practicing. A fast gun hand'll give me the protection I need so I can enjoy the good times."

Jeff looked down and shook his head but said nothing.

"Look, I know you don't agree with me," Josh continued. "That's obvious. But I'm right, you'll see."

"I wish you were, Josh, I wish you were." He studied his brother for a moment, then said, "Well, I guess this is good-bye."

Josh stood at the door momentarily. "Good-bye." There was nothing else to say. He turned on his heel and moved on down the hall.

Josh went into the kitchen and grabbed a canvas sack, filling it with cured ham, jerked beef, and bread, then reconsidered and put it all back. He could eat in restaurants.

He moved to the parlor and saw his father sitting in silence, only one lamp lit.

"You're leaving then, son?"

"You know I am, Pa."

"Yeah, I know." He held out a small but heavy-looking sack, tied at the top with a cotton cord. "Here. This is your share of everything. Take whatever horse and tack you need."

"Thanks, Pa. You won't be sorry."

"I already am."

"Well, don't be. This is just what I have to do. I want to see what's it's like out there."

"I don't s'pose it would help if I just told you . . . No, I reckon not. Tellin' someone how apple pie tastes ain't the same as eatin' one."

"I'm glad you understand."

"Oh, I understand, son. But that don't mean I agree with it, I just know you're gonna do it anyway. You're twenty-one, you have a right to go, and if you want your inheritance, I guess I can go along with that, too. I just want you to be careful. And don't be reckless with that iron."

Josh slipped the sack into the saddlebags he had packed his gear into and slung them over his shoulder. He walked to the door.

"Bye, Pa. I'll write."

"You do that. It'll help me not to worry."

"I'll be fine," Josh assured his father, slapping his holster to indicate why he thought so.

"You're welcome back anytime."

"Thanks, Pa, but that won't be necessary."

He stepped out and shut the door behind him.

"That's what I'm afraid of, son," the elder Bodine said quietly to himself. "That's what I'm afraid of."

Jeff stood with his arms folded across his chest, silently watching from the hallway door, a scowl cutting lines into his forehead. His father turned and saw him, reading his undisguised attitude.

"He's your brother, Jeff, and he's gone. Don't you have work to do?"

"Yessir," Jeff acknowledged without moving. "What're you gonna do when he comes crawlin' back?"

"The same thing I'd do if it was you."

End of conversation. William Bodine walked out, leaving Jeff alone.

Josh strode confidently to the barn in the cool of the early-morning spring dawn. He saddled their newest horse, a calm bay with a white spot on its forehead and white feet, and climbed into the saddle, then walked it out of the barn and down the trail toward the main road.

The young man rode slowly, his whole life ahead of him. He basked in his newfound freedom and independence, savoring every step of his mount away from the mine and toward tomorrow. He listened to the pounding of the stamps, enjoying it for the first time.

As he moved away from them and the sound receded, he smiled, feeling relief as if a burden had been lifted. He vowed never to set foot inside a mine again.

At the road, he eased the bay to a stop. *Which way?* he wondered. To the right, toward Nevada just a few miles down the road? Or left, toward the Sierra Nevadas? The nearest town was Bodie, a small gold town that in the past few months had experienced a growth spurt. Beyond that was Bridgeport, a regular, non-mining town with all the attractions and pleasures he was expecting. Not that Bodie didn't have them, it had them in spades, but Bodie also had big loud stamp mills, and that's what he was trying to get away from. And once Bridgeport became boring he could move south to Bishop or north to Carson City.

Aurora, the nearest town in Nevada, was a mining town like Bodie. Too many miners for his liking. Josh turned the bay to the west, deciding on Bridgeport as his destination. A day or two in Bodie, though, might prove amusing. It undoubtedly held many "opportunities" for a young man with money to occupy himself.

Bodine rode easily, not pushing the bay too hard this early in his trek. The scenery was boring to him, and he paid no attention to it. He had grown up surrounded by rolling hills and sagebrush, grouse, jackrabbit and rocks. And no trees.

Bridgeport had trees, he knew. And saloons, bath houses, restaurants, gambling parlors, dance halls . . .

It was located at the foot of the Sierra Nevadas, and from there, he'd be able to travel into the mountains and do whatever he wanted. He could chase Paiutes, sleep under the stars, shoot deer.

No more dark, smelly mines, working with superstitious Cornish miners. He laughed at their practice of leaving food out for the tommyknockers, little elves who'd play tricks on them, like stealing their tools and causing accidents if they weren't fed regularly.

Wide-open spaces, pine trees, maybe even an outlaw or two, shooting the six-gun from a running horse: these are the things he had read about and wanted to experience for himself. Gambling in a smoke-filled room, watching girls dance, buying a round of drinks for the house.

"Fire in the head!" he shouted, practicing the call he would make after winning a bundle at the faro table. The men would cheer and fill their glasses, then he would pay the tab, and it wouldn't bother him because he had so much.

If he was really lucky some rowdy would cheat at cards, and he'd call him on it. The man would reach for his pistol, but Josh would outdraw him and rid the town of the roughneck!

It's gonna be great!

Several hours into his ride, when he was near enough to Bodie to hear the distant thunder of the stamp mills, he chanced upon two men resting on a rock just off the trail. Their horses wandered nearby, nibbling on the new growth of prairie grass in the gully by the side of the road.

He slowed up his bay.

"Mornin'!" he greeted.

The men eyed him suspiciously, then one spoke.

"Mornin'." He was rough-looking, with a shaggy mustache and stubble-covered face, skin like leather and a weathered holster worn nearly in front of him that caressed a Navy Dragoon in need of bluing. The wood grips were cracked and chipped but otherwise smooth from years of use. His dark pants were baggy, tucked into knee-high riding boots with a pointed toe and high heel, and he wore a dark gray shirt under a long, black coat. On his head was a limp old Texas hat with a hole through it.

The other man was cleaner, but his clothes were tattered and greasy and his brown Montana Peak hat with a concho band was sweat-stained. He had a long, curly tangled beard, and his hair hung over his ears and collar. His blue jeans were faded and worn, and his gun was stuck in the waistband without a holster. He was squatting by the rock, chewing tobacco. His whiskers were stained dark brown below his mouth. He was obviously not a member of the genteel set.

"Where you two gents headed?" Josh asked.

"What's it to you?" the squatting man asked, punctuating his question with a large gob of brown spit, some of which dribbled down his whiskers.

"Shut up, Shag!" the man with the mustache said. "The man's jes' bein' neighborly."

"Mmmmmm," the man called Shag growled.

"Excuse my pardner, there, friend," the mustache said to Josh. "He's kinda shy around strangers. My name's . . . Smith, Ezra Smith." He stepped up to Bodine and extended a dirty hand. Josh took it, somewhat tentatively, but the man's handshake was boisterous and seemed sincere. "This here's Ezra Shagsley."

"You're both named Ezra?"

"Huh? Oh . . . yeah. Ha ha. Funny coincidence, eh? We calls him Shag after his last name so's there's no mix-up."

"Pleased to meet you gents," Josh said. "You brothers?"

"What's that?" Smith looked puzzled. "Uh, no we ain't. Why'd y'ask?"

"Same name and all."

"Oh, I . . . uh—" Then he caught on and laughed. "Say, that was a good one, thinkin' we 'uz related 'cause we're both named Ezra. Warn't that a good one, Shag?"

"I don't git it," Shag answered, looking at Smith vacantly.

"Well, you and me is both named Ezra, see, and this guy sez— aw, fergit it." He waved Shag off and turned his attention back to Josh. "What's yer handle, friend?"

"Josh Bodine."

"Josh Bodine, eh? That's a right friendly name. Where you headed, Mr. Josh Bodine?"

"Oh, I don't know, just ridin' down the road a piece."

"Seein' the sights, eh?"

"Yeah. But I thought I'd stop in Bodie and take in a bit of what they have to offer before I move on, though."

"That so? Why, me and Shag, we 'uz fixin' to do the zact same thing, wasn't we Shag?" The bearded man grunted. "We 'uz headed north. Wouldn't mind if'n you tagged along with us. In fact, we'd be right honored." *And happy to relieve you of yer money if'n you got any.*

"Mount up, then," Josh said. "I don't aim on lettin' no grass grow under my feet."

"Sure thing, Mr. Bodine," Smith said.

"Call me Josh."

"Okay. Josh it is." Smith smacked the still-squatting Shag on the shoulder, raising a small cloud of dirt. "C'mon, Shag. Josh is anxious to git to town. We don't wanna keep 'im waitin' now, do we?"

Shag grunted, then stood up and whistled. His horse came immediately over to him, and he swung himself up into the saddle. Smith walked to his animal, a ragged-looking sorrel, and mounted. His old, worn saddle no longer creaked.

Josh, happy that he'd already made some friends, started off down the road.

Smith hung back and rode close to Shag. "We'll give 'im a mile, just till he's comfortable, then take his money."

Shag glared at Smith. "Ezra?" Shag spat. "That's bad enough, but why did *both* of us have to be named Ezra? Couldn't you think of another name?"

"It slipped. 'Sides, he don't know. Anyway, Ezra's a name right outta the Good Book. He 'uz one o' them apostle fellers, followed Jesus aroun', passin' out food and dunkin' people in the river and stuff. It's a good name."

Shag just shook his head. What's done was done.

Josh slacked his pace and let the men catch up.

"So, you been to Bodie before?"

"Oh, yeah, lots of times," Smith lied. "How 'bout you?"

"Not even once," Josh said. "I've spent my entire life on my pa's claim, workin' his mine."

"Got a mine, does he? What kind? Copper, coal?"

"Gold."

Shag almost swallowed his chew.

"Oh, gold," Smith said. He tried to sound disinterested, but his voice cracked. He cleared his throat to cover up. "S'cuse me, my throat's kinda dry. Long dusty trail and all."

"It is a mite thirsty out here at that," Josh conceded.

"When we git to town we'll buy you a drink," Smith offered. "Won't we, Shag?"

"If'n I have to," Shag muttered under his breath.

"So you and yer pa got a diggin's?"

"Oh, we got more'n that. We got us a real mine and a seven stamp mill!"

This idiot's rich! Smith thought, smiling inwardly. He glanced at Shag who raised his eyebrows knowingly.

"So, what're you doin' out this way?" Shag asked. "Takin' a little holiday?"

"No, I left for good. Got my share and said 'good-bye', wanted to see the world."

"Well, yer seein' it," Smith said. "But be careful. There's some bad people out there—" Shag quietly kicked him in the shin. Smith ignored it. "Bad people who'll steal you blind if'n y'ain't careful."

"Well, I ain't worried much," Josh said. He patted his holster.

"That's a strange-lookin' hunk a leather, boy," Smith observed. "Barely covers your piece. And it angles back funny. Where'd you get that?"

"Made it myself."

"Do tell. Why's it look like that?"

Josh abruptly wheeled his bay around, drew his gun with blistering speed and fired into the sagebrush twenty-five yards behind him and to his left. A jackrabbit had been darting and bounding, but as Josh fired, the animal landed on its side, bounced, and flopped, then remained motionless. Josh twirled his gun and dropped it into the holster in one swift motion before turning once again toward Bodie.

Smith whistled low. "Nice shootin'," he said slowly. He looked at Shag as if to say, *We'll hafta think of another plan.*

CHAPTER

THREE

The three drifters rode the rest of the way into Bodie as if they had all been partners for a long time. Three astride, Smith and Josh chatting and trading yarns while Shag just listened, grunting every now and then. As they sauntered down Main Street, Smith and Shag dropped back a few paces to discuss strategy. The trio was an odd sight to those citizens of the gold camp who gave them a second glance: two dirty, scroungy, unshaven trail tramps slouching in their saddles, fronted by a pale, smooth kid in clean clothes with a neat, polished leather holster and shiny six-gun, sitting erect. The two weathered men rode well-traveled horses that hung their heads most of the time; the kid's was as curious and excited as he was.

One of the people most interested in this odd trio was the town constable, Mono County Deputy Sheriff Matthew Page. He had watched the town grow since the big strike by leaps and bounds from a small mining camp with three mines, one stamp mill, a boarding house, one saloon, a bad cafe, a store, and a few dozen miner's shacks to a bustling town with hundreds of citizens, numerous mines scattered around the bluff, three mills and a variety of services for the townsfolk, including butchers, lawyers, dance halls, a Chinese laundry, and even a new restaurant, the Quicksilver.

Following her ordeal in the wilderness, Sarah had moved to

Bodie and opened the cafe, following the example of her friend Mary from Bridgeport. It made sense. Sarah loved to cook and wanted to be near Matt, and Bodie needed a cafe.

Page found himself with little to do this particular morning. He was sitting on his office porch, waiting for lunchtime, when he first saw the three men ride into town. They were all strangers to him.

The office with its jail was near the north end of town. It had been in the center of town before the boom, but all the growth was into the valley to the south. Eventually, Matt figured, Bodie could have a main street two miles long if it kept growing like it was.

The men passed the deputy, not seeing him. Matt leaned back on the rear legs of his chair, his feet on the porch rail and his hat low on his forehead. He appeared to be asleep. The jail wasn't marked by a sign. It didn't need to be; everyone knew where it was.

There's a strange group, Matt noticed. He examined the two surly drifters riding behind a clean, fresh-faced kid, regarding them with more than an idle curiosity.

"I wonder if they're together," he muttered. "Those guys bear watchin'."

Traffic on Main Street was busy. Several buckboards were moving about, some laden, some empty. Men on foot hurrying to the mines or mills for work, or dragging their feet with shoulders hunched, having just gotten off. The saloons were in full swing. Because of the twenty-four shifts at the mines and mills there were always thirsty men wanting to dampen their parched throats or anxious to contribute their wages to a needy faro dealer.

Matt watched as Josh and the Ezras reined up in front of one of the watering holes, a hastily constructed joint named the Highgrade, in honor of the illegal practice of some miners of stealing nuggets when they left work in extra long pockets or false bottoms of their tin lunch buckets.

They got off their mounts and tied the reins to the rail. Josh took his saddlebags off the horse and tossed them over his shoulder before walking in, an act that did not escape the eyes of Smith and Shag. They nodded at each other behind Bodine's back.

Josh stopped suddenly at the door and turned to the men. "I'll be back in a minute. I need to attend to somethin' first."

Smith shrugged and pushed his way through the batwings. Shag didn't react at all but followed Smith into the saloon. Josh looked up and down the street, then said something to a passing man, who pointed. Josh tipped his hat and walked up the street, turning into the Bodie Bank. In a few minutes he was back out and hurrying down to the Highgrade.

Through the batwings and up to the bar he strode, excitement coursing through his veins. A banjo player in the corner was strumming his heart out but could hardly be heard over the din of glassware clinking and voices raised as men competed with each other to be heard.

Most of them miners, the men wore the usual clothing Josh was so familiar with: blue jeans or baggy woolen trousers tucked into heavy boots, long coats, unkempt mustaches and dark hats. Shag blended right in, except for his cowboy-style riding boots and range hat.

The bar along the left wall was long and massive, highly polished with large columns at the corners, a well-worn brass foot rail and several brass spittoons on the floor in front of it. Black blotches dotted the floor around them.

Behind the bar was a mirror, hung from the top corners and tilting down, with bottles lined up on the shelf in front of it. Nearby was a painting of a nude reclining female. The bartender stood behind his bar with a towel, wiping the top of it when he wasn't pouring whiskey or dime beer. In the back of the room were the faro tables. They were covered with green felt, and the dealers sat at a small notch cut out of the table, laying down cards and raking in other people's money.

Josh spotted Smith and Shag at the bar and took his place next to them.

"So, Josh Bodine. What do you think of this?" It was Smith. He put an arm around Josh's shoulder.

Josh was wide-eyed. "Looks like a lot of fun."

"That it is. That it is," Smith admitted, sounding almost melancholy. Shag was already downing a beer. "Let's join our friend Shag in a libation, shall we?"

"A what?"

"A drink, boy, a drink," Smith said fatherly. "Oh, barkeep." He slapped on the bar.

The bartender came over. He wore his hair slicked back, an

attractive silk shirt, brocade vest, long sideburns, and was clean-shaven. "What'll it be, boys?"

"A couple beers for me and my friend, here." Smith patted Josh on the back.

The bartender drew the mugs full of the warm, frothy, amber liquid and set them on the bar. Smith laid down a coin and took a drink. Josh picked his up carefully and inspected it. He was fascinated by the bubbles that rose inside the glass and the foam on top of the liquid. Smith glanced at Shag who was watching Josh with a looked of amused disgust.

Josh smelled the foam.

"You gotta drink it, Josh," explained Smith. "It ain't lilac water. Ain't you never had a beer before?"

"No. Pa don't believe in drinkin'."

"Don't believe in drinkin'? What kinda pa don't believe in drinkin'? Why, my pa not only taught me to drink, he said I was the reason he started in the first place!" Smith laughed loudly. "C'mon, son, drink up!"

Josh took a hesitant sip. All he got was a mouthful of bitter foam, so he tipped the glass farther back and filled his mouth with the warm brew. At first he thought it was terrible and wanted to spit it out, but he forced himself to swallow and try another. The taste was pungent, almost nut-like, and left him thirstier than he was when he started.

He tipped the mug a third time, taking several gulps before Smith pulled his arm down.

"Whoa, cowboy, slow down. You got to go slow with this stuff when yer new. You need to appreciate the flavor. Drink too fast and it'll knock y'over. It's like gettin' too much sun. You feel okay while yer out in it, so you stay out in it and don't know yer burnt till you gone and burnt yerseff real good."

Shag smiled through a foam-covered mustache to himself but did not let Bodine see it.

"Thanks, I'll remember that," Josh said. He took another small drink, then looked around the room. "Say, where's all the dance hall girls?"

"In the dance hall, I reckon," Smith said.

"Why aren't they in here?"

"Huh?"

"You know, wearin' them frilly dresses and hangin' around with the customers until they get up on the stage and do a cancan."

"Where'd you get an idea like that?"

"I read about it."

"Well, them stories ain't what you call accurate."

"They ain't?"

"Nope. See, this here place and all saloons, they's men's territory. Wimmin don't come in here for the most part. I seen a couple wimmin twenty-one dealers, but they's an exception."

"Then where are the women?"

"Well, you see, Bodie bein' a minin' town, there just ain't many. The good ones is all married, and the others, they's on one a the back streets, and I betcha we kin find one a them at the hurdy-gurdy house."

"Hurdy-gurdy house?"

"Yeah, you know, dance house. Where you buy a ticket, then dance with a gal, then buy her a drink and git another dance ticket. You kin dance with her agin or if'n she smells bad or has a mustache, you kin dance with someone else. And if'n you feel real foolhardy, you kin dance with one o' them señoritas, if'n you don't mind wakin' up with a knife in yer back!" He and Shag laughed.

"I'd like to go there," Josh said.

"Later, son. There's plenty a time for that," Smith said. "It's still early. We need to get us some grub, maybe do a little gamblin' . . ." He raised his eyebrows enticingly at the greenhorn and smiled, showing all the brown teeth he had left. "Whaddya say, friend?"

Josh emptied his mug and wiped his mouth with his sleeve. "Not now. I think I'll have another," he told the bartender. "And one for both my friends here." The bartender nodded and drew the beers.

"Cain't argue with that, can we, Shag? If he don't want to gamble right now, that's okay by me." He laughed. "Long as he's buyin'!"

They drank their beers, then Smith led Josh out of the establishment, holding him by the arm. Josh was operating on an empty stomach, and the beer was working on him quickly, although he was unaware of it.

"You know, Ezra," he said slowly to Smith on the way out, "I'm feelin' a little . . . funny."

"It's the altitude. Bodie's pretty high up. The air's thinner, or somethin'. Shag gets the same way, don'tcha, Shag?" Shag glared at him, but Smith continued without taking a breath. "You'll feel better when you git somethin' under yer belt."

They took him to the nearby cafe they had seen earlier. Smith looked at the sign. "The Quicksliver Cafe. That's a funny name."

"Quick*silv*er," corrected Josh. "It's what we use to leach the gold outta the quartz after it's crushed."

"Oh. Well I never done much minin'," said Smith. "I been on plenty of cattle drives, though." He opened the door, and they tromped in, finding a table near the sidewall. As they sat down, Smith reached up to take Josh's saddlebags off the young man's shoulder. "Here, lemme help you with that."

Josh put his hands on the bag. "No thanks, I've got them just fine."

Smith moved his hand away nonchalantly. *Not fer long,* he thought. He immediately changed the subject.

"So, what looks good?" he asked no one in particular, looking at the menu.

A young woman in an apron came over to their table.

"May I help you boys?"

"Well, now, ain't you a right purdy thing! I'm a wishin' you wuz on the menu!"

"Sorry, boys," she said with a serious face. "I suggest you choose something else."

"Oh!" laughed Smith. "In that case, how 'bout some fried chicken with corn on the cob, mashed potatoes and gravy, cornbread, hot coffee, and apple pie for dessert?"

"Sounds fine," agreed Bodine. Shag just nodded.

"Three specials," the young woman said. "I'll be right back with your coffee and cornbread."

"Thank you, ma'am," said Josh.

"Oh, yeah, thanks," repeated Smith. Josh noticed that, as rough and unrefined as Smith and Shag appeared, they were not uncivilized. This was a common characteristic among rowdies and roughs: No matter how vile and foul they were, they usually held a civil tongue in the presence of good women. With the soiled doves, it was another matter, of course.

She returned shortly with three steaming mugs of dark coffee and three plates of moist cornbread covered with butter.

Bodine thought he might begin drooling. He had eaten only his father's or brother's or his own cooking for as long as he could remember. It was okay, but it was nothing like this.

They ate greedily, none of them saying an intelligible word during the entire meal. Shag grunted frequently, and every time he opened his mouth to stuff in something, half the previous bite fell out. Undaunted, he returned it to his mouth and eventually cleaned his plate. He leaned back in his chair, shutting his eyes and awaiting dessert, oblivious to the food all over the front of his shirt.

"Good eatin's," Smith said to the woman when she came back with the pie.

"Thank you," she acknowledged as she set the golden wedges down in front of them.

Smith looked at the slice. "Hoowhee! That looks grand! Did you make that?"

The young woman smiled. "As a matter of fact, I did." She was genuinely pleased that they had enjoyed the meal.

"I got to hand it to you," said Josh, who by now was beginning to feel better, "you're a right fine cook."

"Thank you." She turned to wait on someone else. The door opened and in strode a man just a few years older than Josh. The sun was behind him, beaming through the windows and making it hard to make for Josh to make out his features. He wasn't a miner and didn't appear to be a drifter, either. Shag ignored him, giving full attention to his pie, and Smith started to look away, but a momentary glimmer on the man's chest attracted his attention.

It was a silver star.

Smith chewed slowly, watching the lawman out of the corner of his eye, and gave his head a slight flick to alert Shag. Shag peeked, then shrugged and went back to eating. Bodine didn't notice Smith's caution, though, because he was also staring at the new arrival. Josh was intrigued, almost thrilled. A lawman! Just like the novels.

Deputy Page was unaware of the attention he was being given. He had his eye on the young woman waiting on tables. She saw him, her face breaking into an instant smile, and Matt walked up to her and gave her a hug.

"Matt!" she scolded.

"What?"

"Not here, in front of everybody."

"Why not? Everyone knows we're—"

"I'm working!"

"Oh. Well, in that case, how 'bout some lunch?"

"I'll be right back with it."

"Thanks, Sarah." Matt found an empty table near the kitchen door and settled into it, setting his hat on the farside of the table. Josh and the Ezras were finished, and Smith was anxious to leave. When he stood, Josh volunteered to pay, and not being one to argue about a thing like that, Smith beat a hasty retreat, followed immediately by Shag. They waited outside, out of the deputy's sight.

Josh laid the money on the table just as Sarah came out with Matt's food. She saw him and nodded an acknowledgment of his payment. Matt looked to see what Sarah was doing and recognized the clean-cut kid he had seen ride into town. He looked around the room but didn't see the other two men. The kid walked out.

"Reminds me of you, not too long ago," Sarah commented.

"He is a handsome fellah at that," Matt said with eyebrows raised.

"I didn't mean that. I'm talking about his whole . . . attitude, I guess you could say. Seems innocent."

"Humph."

"Don't *humph* me, Matthew Page." She set the food down. "Here, eat it all."

"Even the vegetables?"

"Even the vegetables."

Sarah walked away to assist other patrons leaving Matt with his peas and carrots.

When Josh walked outside Smith and Shag were nowhere to be seen. He was puzzled and decided to go on without them, but no sooner did he start up the street than they appeared behind him.

"Wha—? Where were you guys?"

"Oh, jes' waitin' fer you in th' alley, outta the way," Smith explained. "Well, you ready fer some more drinkin', mebbe some gamblin'? I gotta feelin' yer a lucky man."

"I s'pose."

"Great! We'll go—wait a minute, lookee here." They were passing the side of a tobacconist shop. When they rounded the corner they were suddenly confronted by a large, brown, scowling Indian. Josh drew his gun quickly, but Smith grabbed his arm. "Hold up, there, Josh. He won't hurt you."

Josh looked up at the Indian. He was holding a clump of cigars. "It's wood," Josh said.

"No kiddin'," Smith said, giving it a knock with his fist. "You really haven't been anywhere, have you?"

"I said I hadn't."

"Yeah, I know. I thought mebbe you was exaggeratin' a mite." He peered inside the store. "C'mon, let's go in here fer a minute."

They stepped inside the store and were greeted by the tobacconist, a pudgy little man with a handlebar mustache, smoking a crooked beige pipe that had a white bowl. Blue smoke curled up from it as he puffed.

"May I help you gents?"

"Uh, yeah, just a minute . . . say, what's that thing yer smokin' from?"

"Why, this is a Calabash, imported from England, with a German meerschaum bowl and a hand-carved bone stem."

Smith gave him a funny look. "Hmmm . . . interesting. You got any chewin' tobacca?"

"Certainly. We have several varieties."

"Jes' gimme a clump a the reg'lar stuff."

"Very well." The tobacconist took a handful of dark cut leaves from a jar, stuffing them into a small linen sack with a drawstring. He handed it to Smith. "That'll be two bits, sir."

Smith reached into his pants pocket, came out empty and tried his shirt, also without success.

"Uh, Josh, kin I borry twenty-five cents?"

"Sure." Josh handed him the coins and Smith gave them to the storekeeper, who thanked them and put the coins in his drawer. As he did, Shag gave a little peek into it, but there wasn't much there. Too many two-bit customers, like themselves.

Smith walked outside, followed by Shag and Bodine, and greedily opened the sack. He reached in and pulled out a handful of the leaves and stuffed them into his cheek. His chew was the size of a small mouse—and about as appetizing—and several cut leaves dangled out over his lip. He handed the sack to Shag who took an even larger wad, then passed the sack to Bodine.

Josh looked inside. "Smells kinda like licorice."

"Yeah. Tastes like it, too," Smith replied. He looked at Shag and rolled his eyes.

"I used to watch some of the miners do this," Josh went on. "Never tried it, though."

"There's a first time fer everythin'."

"That's why I left home," Josh said. He took a small clump of leaves, surprised that they were moist, and tucked them hesitantly into his mouth.

"It'sh shweet," he said with difficulty.

"Take it easy," Smith warned. "It's called chew but you gotta have done it fer a while before you kin mash it 'tween yer teeth. Jes' tuck it in there and let it sit, and spit when you need to."

Bodine stopped chewing and looked around.

"In the street," Smith said.

Josh spit into the street. Some of the thick brown ooze dribbled down his chin.

"Whenever yer inside, find a spittoon," Smith said. "It's the civilized way." He took the sack from Bodine and stuck it into his pocket. "Let's go wet our whistles again and check out the tables."

He and Shag took off down the street. Bodine spit again, wondering why his head was feeling a little woozy, and followed.

They went back into the Highgrade and ordered at the bar, then took their beers over to a table. After the chew and the beer, Bodine was dizzy and loose. He decided to try his hand at the faro table.

"Go git you a chair," Smith said. "I'll be right over." Josh obeyed but kept his saddlebags with him.

"Keep an eye on him," Shag said quietly to his partner. "Don't let him lose too much."

Smith nodded. "I might jes' help 'im win."

While Shag sat across the room, nursing beers and watching, Josh learned the game of faro, and enjoyed a little beginner's luck. Once, after several beers and a few winning hands, he even lived out his fantasy of buying a round for the house, much to Smith's chagrin.

Josh stayed too long, though, and soon lost all that he had won and more. Four beers to the bad, he was getting irritated.

"C'mon, Josh, that's 'nough fer t'day," Smith whispered. "We oughtta be goin'. There's a lot more fun to be had in this town."

"No, I gotta win it back," Bodine protested. "I'm catchin' on now. I can do it."

"Leave the man alone," suggested the faro dealer to Smith.

"Mine yer own biz'ness," warned Smith. "Yer takin' advantage a the boy."

"It's his choice, pal."

"He's drunk!" explained Smith, becoming agitated.

"No, he ain't."

"C'mon, Josh." Smith tugged on Josh's arm, but he wouldn't budge.

"No!"

"I told you to leave him alone!" The dealer cautioned.

Smith turned his head to the dealer and cut loose a string of profanity. " . . . And that includes yer parents!" he concluded.

As Smith finished, there was a sudden movement across the table and men near the dealer scattered. He had pulled a small nickel-plated derringer out of his vest pocket and pointed it at Smith. Bodine saw it and switched sides, recognizing the need to protect his friend. His reaction was automatic from all his practice and in a split-second his own six-gun leaped into his hand, and he fired.

As the patrons heard the shot, there was an abrupt and perilous stampede for the door. The saloon all but emptied, and Shag was swept out with them. Smith grabbed Bodine and jerked him up, careful that Josh still had the saddlebags. He needn't have worried; Josh had them in a death grip.

Bodine, Smith, and Shag made their way down a back alley. Josh, feeling a little unsteady on his feet, forced Smith to drag him by the arm.

"That was good shootin', wasn't it?" Bodine asked.

"Oh, yeah, real fine," said Smith. "Jes' a little too quick, though. I coulda taken 'im easy."

"Not the way I saw it."

"Well, yer judgment wuz colored by yer drink."

"D'ya think I killed him?" Josh was at the same time fearful and hopeful.

"Naw, he ducked. You only murdered his chair." Smith's comment drew a snort from Shag. "An' it's a good thing," Smith went on. "We ain't lookin' fer no trouble!"

"Think they'll be lookin' for us?"

"Fer you, mebbe. You oughtta lay low fer a while."

"Where?"

"I gotta plan, boy. One you'll really like."

CHAPTER

FOUR

They led young Josh Bodine down the alley—Shag keeping a lookout over his shoulder—then around the corner to a two-story building. It looked to Josh like a house, but when he walked inside he saw that what should have been a parlor was instead a large room, the full width and depth of the building. The room had bare, wood floors, and chairs lined the walls on three sides. At the back of the room was a small bandstand upon which a lone piano player tinkled out a waltz. Several men spun around the floor with young ladies of all descriptions.

One of the women was a young, dark Spanish maiden with deep-set brown eyes and thick, black, long hair. Her brightly-colored skirt swirled as she moved to the music, and she flung her hair about on purpose, mesmerizing the miner dancing with her.

Josh looked around the room wide-eyed. There were three or four women standing or sitting idly on the fringes of the dance floor, and they all gazed expectantly at the new arrivals.

Smith leaned over to Bodine. "Close yer mouth, boy, yer catchin' flies." He left Josh and Shag standing inside the door and sauntered over to an older woman nearby. She was overweight and didn't look to be a dancer, but, out here, who could tell?

Another woman caught Bodine's eye. This one was young, about his own age, Josh figured, and sat by herself in the far corner. Her short, red hair was piled up on her head, and she squirmed in her low-cut dress, obviously none too comfortable. Plain-looking, wearing too much makeup, Josh was nonetheless taken by her.

She saw him stare and looked away, embarrassed. Soon the plump woman accepted something from Smith and made her way to the redhead. She spoke to the young woman briefly, then the redhead got up and made her way slowly toward Josh. Smith glanced at Shag and nodded once.

The young woman held her hand out for Josh to take, but he was transfixed and just stared at her. She reached out and took his hand and led him gently to the dance floor.

"I . . . uh . . ." was all he could say. It was obvious to her that the young man with the shiny gun and saddlebags over his shoulder had never danced. She tenderly moved him into position and moved close, but the saddlebags were in the way.

"Sorry," Josh said. Without taking his eyes off hers he pulled the bags off and tossed them onto a chair. She moved next to him, and his breathing quickened.

She's so . . . soft! Josh couldn't believe it. He hadn't known what to expect. He danced clumsily, but she kept smiling and didn't speak, and when the tune was over, she led him to the bar for the required drink. She requested wine for both of them. Josh paid for the drinks and downed his quickly without taking his eyes off of her.

The piano player started again and off they went, Josh enthralled by the young woman who seemed to be as taken with him as he was with her.

Two more dances and two more drinks later the young woman whispered in Josh's ear. His eyes grew wide, then he agreed with her proposal, almost reluctantly at first, but after she stroked his arm, he lost all resistance. He retrieved his saddlebags and followed her out the rear door, oblivious to Smith and Shag.

Outside, she took his hand and walked to a row of attached shacks, called *cribs* by the locals, and pushed open the thin, wood door, stepping lightly inside and pulling Josh in behind her. The room was sparsely furnished with a rickety bed, a small dresser, and an unpadded chair. There was precious little space in which to move around, although that usually didn't matter in the cribs.

She opened the top drawer of the dresser and took out a bottle. "Thirsty?" she asked sweetly.

Josh swallowed hard and thought about it. "My throat is kinda dry."

Pouring Josh a drink and smiling she said, "Set your things on the chair. You're gonna be needin' your hands." With his back turned momentarily as he stacked his belongings nervously on a chair, he didn't notice that she dumped something into his glass.

Taking his drink from her small hand, he downed it in one gulp, then poured himself another, which he drank just as quick with shaking hands. When he turned, she was standing by the bed, wringing her hands, her face shrouded with anxiety. Josh's brow twisted in perplexity at the girl's demeanor, but before he could question her, his vision blurred, and he grew dizzy and nauseated. He staggered to the bed and collapsed.

A short time later Smith and Shag conferred in the alley behind the cribs.

"You know," Smith said thoughtfully, bouncing Bodine's bag of gold in the palm of his hand, "we could git a lot more outta this town if'n we want."

"You still thinkin' of robbin' the bank?" Shag asked suspiciously. "I thought when we stumbled across this rich kid we'd settle for him. No risk."

"This is a gold town, the mines have payrolls to meet . . . I reckon there's a lot a money in the bank."

"I know that's what we planned, but . . ."

"Don't worry. There won't be any way we kin git nailed fer this."

"How's zat?"

"We'll git Mr. Josh Bodine to rob it fer us."

"You got me this time," Shag said, scratching his head. "You come up with some hairbrained ideas sometimes. Both of us named Ezra?"

"Would you stop with that already? It's possible, you know."

"Still, I don't know how you're gonna git this kid to rob a bank fer us. Ain't it enough to take his gold? There's a ton a money there."

"No, it ain't enough. Not when there's so much available for the takin'."

Shag wiped his hand down over his face slowly, stopping, then rubbing his chin. "What the heck, let's hear your plan."

A one-armed, bearded miner in his best clothes stepped up to the teller window and passed a small sack and an assay slip through the hole in the grate to the teller.

Moving to a small scale nearby, the teller weighed the miner's gold, compared the results with the assay slip, then counted out the money. The bank manager, seated at a nearby desk going over some ledger sheets, looked up and watched the transaction with no particular interest. He glanced at the clock, hoping no one else would come in before closing time.

He was disappointed when the front door opened, but his disappointment became fear when he saw that the incoming customer wore a bandanna over his face and had a six-gun in his hand.

"Git 'em up!" the robber yelled as he turned the lock on the door. He walked over to the bank officer at the desk and motioned for him to get up. When the manager complied, the bandit waved him over with the gun to where the other men were.

When the robber's attention was elsewhere, the miner slowly began dropping his arm, thinking he'd try for the gun in his coat pocket.

"All the money, now!" ordered the bandit. The teller emptied his drawer and stuffed the bills into a bank bag. He started to push it toward the bandit.

"The safe!"

The teller moved obediently to the safe and spun the dial. It opened with a heavy *click click*, and the teller pulled out several bags of cash and gold.

The miner moved suddenly, reaching into his pocket and pulling out the gun. The bandit saw the motion out of the corner of his eye and turned, quickly firing twice. The first shot struck the miner in the arm, the second thumped him solidly in the chest. His gun clattered to the floor where he crumpled, moaning, beside it.

The bandit grabbed the heavy sacks from the startled teller and fled to the door. Still locked, he didn't waste time fiddling with it, instead kicking it open. The wood splintered, and the glass shattered. He raced out and jumped on the waiting horse. The white-footed bay protested the harsh kick to his ribs, then galloped down the street toward the edge of town.

Inside the bank the men rushed to help the fallen miner. The miner groaned as they turned him onto his back. His wounds were serious, and they hoped he was as tough as people said.

"Mr. Page!" the teller shouted.

"Arnold, get a doctor!" the manager ordered.

"I'm okay. Git the deputy." The miner coughed as he spoke.

Arnold ran out into the street where a few people had started to gather cautiously, hearing the commotion and seeing the masked man ride off.

"Bank robbery! They robbed the bank! Someone get a doctor! A man's been shot!"

People began to converge on the bank now that the danger had passed for a look at what all the fuss was about. A few ran the other way, and in a few minutes Deputy Page emerged from one of the saloons at the far end of the street where he had been conducting a routine check. He saw people running and heard the yelling.

"What is it?" he shouted to no one in particular. He trotted after them and noticed everyone converging on the bank. He sped up and put his hand on the butt of his gun.

Near the bank an old man with only a few teeth ran up to the deputy. "I saw it, Sheriff, I saw him git on his horse and ride off."

"You see everything, Noah," Matt said, not slowing down.

Noah struggled to keep up. "But I did! He come outta the bank with his gun blazin', jumped on a big ol' horse with a new saddle and took off."

Noah was known for seein' things he couldn't have seen. He was there when James Marshall discovered gold at Sutter's Mill. He was there when Lee surrendered to Grant. He even claimed to have been there when the Alamo was overrun by Santa Anna down in Texas. ("He must've been one of the Mexicans," someone once mocked.).

"Well, okay, Noah," Matt said, stopping. "You wait in my office, and I'll talk to you later."

"Yessir, sheriff!" Noah padded off happily.

Matt followed the crowd to the bank, then pushed his way onto the boardwalk, grabbing the bank teller by the arm and dragging him up to the front of the place.

"It's your pa!" Arnold said.

"Huh?"

"Your pa. He's the one got shot!"

Matt let go of the man and plowed through what was left of the door. Jacob Page was sitting up, leaning against the teller's kiosk below the window while the manager tried to control the bleeding.

"Oh, son. It's good to see you."

"You okay, Pa?"

"I think so. It's bleedin' pretty good, but I don't think it hit nuthin' important."

"Your arm—"

"Yeah," lamented Page, looking down at it. "That's what ticks me off."

The town doctor, Clarence Madsen, rushed in with his black bag.

"Move aside, boys, so I can—oh, it's you, Deputy, I—Mr. Page! Whatever happened to you?" He knelt down and pulled Jacob's clothing out of the way so he could see the wound.

"We're gonna have to get that bullet out, Jacob," Madsen said. "I'll have someone get a stretcher and carry you to my office."

Jacob started to push himself up. "I don't need no dang stretch—" He fell back, unable to support himself with his injured arm.

"Don't move, you old goat!" ordered the doctor, who was Page's senior by at least fifteen years. "I know you're tough. We all know you're tough. But you need to be still so you don't bleed to death." He noticed the blood on Jacob's sleeve. "Let me see that," he said, cutting the cloth away. "Doesn't look broken . . . bullet went clean through . . . isn't bleeding much . . . Your arm should heal okay."

Madsen got up. "I'll be right back, Matt. Keep him awake . . . and still."

"Yessir." Matt squatted by his father. "So what happened?"

Jacob Page told his son the story and gave him a good description of the robber.

"Wearing fairly new clothes, huh?" Matt reviewed the information while his groggy father nodded. "Nice hat, blue bandanna, his gun and leather gear were well taken care of . . ." It sounded like the kid he had seen ride into town. "Was he with someone else?"

"N-no one that I saw." The pain was getting worse. "He came in alone, I didn't l-look outside. He acted like he was alone."

"No, there was no one else," said the bank manager. "I saw a horse outside, but just one. He was alone."

That kid just didn't look the type, Matt thought to himself. Couldn't have been him.

"How old was he?" Matt asked.

"Hard to tell," said the bank manager. "His face was all covered and his hat shadowed his eyes. His hat was black, flat brim and no band."

"Do you remember anything else?"

"Well, he was about your height and build, brown hair, quick with a gun, had this fancy rig like I've never seen before."

"That all?"

"No. If memory serves me correct, he was in the bank earlier in the day. Cashed some gold dust."

"Think he was checkin' the place out?"

"That would be my guess, Deputy."

Two men came in with a stretcher followed by Doc Madsen. They carefully lifted the wound Page onto the canvas and took him away. Matt talked to the bank manager a few more minutes, then headed back in the direction of his office. No one who had been outside the bank when Matt arrived had seen anything important.

Matt stopped in at the Quicksilver to tell Sarah. She immediately took off her apron.

"Where're *you* goin'?" Matt asked.

"Doc Madsen's going to need some help."

"He knows how to dig out a bullet."

"Yes, but he doesn't know about your pa. I doctored him before, remember?"

"He can be a pain, can't he?" Matt admitted.

Sarah gave him a little smile. "I'm not worried about your pa as much as I am Doc Madsen."

Matt had to smile. Sarah put the CLOSED sign in the window and locked the door behind them. She patted Matt on the arm. "Be careful."

The deputy watched her walk up the street, his heart full of admiration for the young woman.

CHAPTER

FIVE

After Sarah disappeared into the doctor's office, Matt wheeled around, strode to the jail, and prepared a battle plan. He was surprised to see Noah sitting at his desk. The old man was playing with a pair of handcuffs.

Noah looked up, startled, and jumped off the chair, dropping the cuffs with a metallic clatter onto the desk.

"I . . . uh . . . what took you so long, Deputy?"

"Noah, what are you doing here?"

"You told me to wait here for you."

"I did?"

"Yeah, when you was runnin' to the bank. I tried to tell you I saw the man in the blue bandanna git on a horse and ride outta town."

"Oh, yeah, I guess I remem—you mean to say you actually *did* see the bank robber?"

"I said I did, didn't I?"

"Well, yeah, but you . . . Okay, Noah, what did you see?"

"Well, you see, I was walkin' up the street—Main Street, that is—I was goin' to the general store to git me some airtights of peaches—I really like peaches. They're easy on my stomach 'cause they pack 'em with sugar water, like it says on the label—you ever play 'know yer cans?' I useta win all the time. I really read them labels. You need to know what's in them cans. And I needed some lye soap and—"

"Do you suppose you could get to the point?"

"Huh? Oh, yeah. So anyway, I'm walkin' up the street, past the bank, when I see this guy walkin' in—"

"The robber?"

"No, no, I don't think he was a robber. You're pa ain't a robber, is he?"

"So you saw my pa go in?"

"Yeah, I did. And then a minute or so later—'course I'm way up the street by now, but I happened to look back an' seen a cowboy go in."

"Cowboy?"

"Well, yeah, you know, nice new gunbelt—no one wears gunbelts but cowboys, everyone else just sticks their iron in their pocket or waistband, or hangs their holster on their pants belt—'ceptin' you, of course—an' he had a black hat, blue bandanna around his face—"

"You saw the bandanna on his face?"

"Yep."

"Didn't you think something was wrong?"

"Nope. Cowboys wear them things on their faces like that to keep trail dust outta their noses and mouths."

"Noah, there isn't a cattle drive anywhere near here."

"You and I know that, but I figger this cowboy, maybe he don't know that. Cowboys ain't that smart, you know."

Matt rubbed his hand over his face, trying to maintain his composure. "Noah, did you see his horse and which way he went?"

"Yep."

"And?"

"It was a real nice bay with white feet and a white spot on his forehead in the shape of a state."

"A state?"

"Yep, you know . . . a state. Like Virginny is a state, New York is a state—"

"So the horse had a spot on his forehead that was shaped like a state."

"That's it."

"Which state, Noah?"

"Which state?" Noah scratched his head and looked off into the distance. "I don't rightly know. I just thought when I saw it, 'now that looks like a state.'"

"Which way'd he ride, Noah?"

"South. He rode south."

"Thanks, Noah." Matt started to usher him out. "You've been a big help."

As the deputy was pushing him through the door, Noah kept talking. "Yep, he rode south. Now if you want to know what his horse looked like, there's one just like it out behind the cribs."

"What?" Matt stopped pushing.

"Oh, yeah. 'Bout a half-hour later I was waitin' here for you, I had to run out to the squat—I got this stomach problem, you know—and I decided to go walk around a bit, and out behind the cribs was a horse just like the robber's tied to a nail stickin' outta the wall. I think it was a sixteen penny nail, it was pretty big—Hey! Where you goin'?"

Matt left Noah talking to himself in the doorway and ran out to the alley where the cribs were located. There wasn't much foot traffic out. Although the sky was nearly dark, most of the night owls hadn't emerged yet.

Moving silently behind the row of attached shacks, Matt tried to make out the shape of the animal. There it was, standing patiently—a saddled bay with white feet. The deputy moved closer to get a look. He was surprised to see Illinois on its forehead.

Matt counted down the row of cribs, noting the number of windows so he wouldn't kick in the wrong door. He stole quietly around front, counted the doors, and took a deep breath. Drawing his Peacemaker and slowly cocking the hammer, he walked quietly up to the crib.

Josh Bodine woke up hard, his head in a vise, his eyes watering. It was dark, and he was alone.

As his eyes adjusted, he tried to figure out where he was. His memory was clouded. He recalled pieces of the day. Drinking. Oh, he remembered drinking. What else? *Think!* Faro. He lost some money at faro. Money? *Gold!* Josh jerked his head toward the chair. The saddlebags were there, and he breathed a sigh of relief in spite of the throbbing behind his eyes.

Josh struggled to sit. He swung his feet over the side of the bed and put his head in his hands. Rubbing his eyes he turned his head slowly in all directions to stretch his neck. His mouth was full of sagebrush. Relaxed again, he opened his eyes and stared absentmindedly at his gear on the chair. Slowly he realized it didn't look right.

He flipped the cover back on one of the bags and reached in, but instead of pulling out his bag of gold, he held a canvas bank bag. Puzzled, he opened it. The bag was full of currency.

"What this?"

He set the bank bag on the chair and noticed his gun. It looked different. He pulled it out of the holster. It was dirty, as if it had been fired. He opened the loading door, cocked the hammer back two clicks and slowly turned the cylinder. Three of the rounds were dented instead of just the one he remembered firing at that faro dealer.

"What in the—?"

Splintering wood and the crash of the door as it flew inward caused Josh to bolt backwards on the bed. He was so surprised he didn't have a chance to use the gun he still held. The man who kicked in the door jumped in and drew a bead on him.

"Don't move!" he shouted. He stepped over and relieved Josh of the weapon. "Get your hands up where I can see 'em, nice and easy."

"Wha—?"

"Now!"

Josh put up his hands. Matt shot a glance at the chair. "And there's the bank bag. This is nice and tidy. What's your name?"

"J-Josh Bodine. What's go—?"

"Josh Bodine, you're under arrest for bank robbery and attempted murder."

"Huh?"

"Get your clothes on! Let's go!"

Josh stood slowly, keeping his shaking hands in the air. Confused and afraid, his head pounding, he was too groggy to understand completely what was going on. It was obvious the deputy thought that he had robbed a bank. And there was the bank bag full of money on the chair. But beyond that, Josh was lost.

"Whatever you think I did, I don't know anything about it."

"That's not the way I see it," Matt said. "Put them pants on slow."

Keeping one hand in the air Josh pulled his trousers up awkwardly. He had no intention of doing anything to get himself shot. This lawman meant business. Josh was too scared right now to remember that he took off from home in search of adventure. It had found him but not like he imagined.

He buttoned his shirt, stuffed his bandanna into his pocket, and pushed his hat onto his head.

"Can I sit down to pull on my boots?"

"Slow and easy."

"Don't worry, Sheriff. I ain't gonna do nuthin' stupid. I'm innocent, and you're pointing that hogleg at my chest. I'm scared, I don't mind sayin'." He pulled on his boots, tucking his pant legs into them. "Listen, I don't know where that money come from. I been here all afternoon, sleepin'."

"Alone?"

"Well, it didn't start out that way, as you might imagine. I don't know when she left."

"What's her name?"

Josh paused. "I don't know," he said quietly.

Matt motioned with his gun for Bodine to stand, then handcuffed the young man behind his back, picked up the saddlebags and his prisoner's gunbelt. Matt told him to head out and followed him out the door.

After locking Bodine up, Matt went back for the horse and tied it to the rail in front of the jail. Noah was there.

"Yep, that's it. That's the horse I seen. And the boy you got in there, that's the one was ridin' it. Ev'rythin' but the face, you know. I didn't see the face, he had that bandanna coverin' it. A blue one. Made it difficult to see his . . . no, made it impossible." He guffawed. "No, it were right impossible to see through a blue bandanna. 'Course, he was—"

"Thanks, Noah," Matt said. "I'll write out your statement, and you can sign it later."

"I'll have to ex it, if you don't mind. I never learnt to read and write so good, and I—"

"Okay, Noah. No problem. See you later."

Matt left his eyewitness and trudged up the street to Dr. Madsen's. He stepped inside quietly. Sarah was taking off a smock the doctor had given her to keep her dress clean.

She smiled. "It went well. Your pa's out now. We ethered him. The bullet went through the muscle and hit a rib. It broke—the rib, that is—but the bullet didn't hit anything vital."

"Sounds like he's really lucky."

"Sounds like God's really watching over him, you mean."

"Yeah, that's what I mean. How about his arm?"

"Not too bad. It'll heal okay. He won't have use of it for a while, though. Someone'll have to take care of him."

"Uncle Billy'll probably be able to help with that. I know he'd want to." Matt smiled at the young woman. "C'mere." He reached out, put his arms around her, and drew her close. She pressed against his chest and shut her tired eyes.

"Say," she said after a moment, looking up at him, "how come you're not out after the robber?"

"I already caught him. He's in the jail."

"No! Where'd you find him?"

"Holed up in one of the soiled doves' cribs. When I busted in he was sittin' on the bed, countin' the money and gettin' ready to reload his six-gun. He gave up without a fuss."

Doc Madsen came out from the back room where he did his surgeries, drying his hands on a towel.

"Ah, Matt. Glad you're here." He reached into his pocket and handed a small gray object to the deputy. "Looks like a .44."

Matt turned the lead bullet over and over in his fingers. The tip was distorted from hitting bone, but the caliber was unmistakable.

"Thanks, Doc."

"My pleasure. Did I hear you say you caught the man already?"

"Yeah."

"Good work. Who is he?"

"Don't know, really. Drifter, I guess. Says his name's Joshua Bodine. Musta just left home recently. Everything of his looks kinda new. At least it doesn't have that trail-worn look to it, know what I mean?"

"Very well."

"I saw him ride in this morning." Matt was struck by a sudden thought and turned to Sarah. "In fact, he was in the cafe this mornin' when I came in to eat."

"Oh?" Sarah said. "Maybe I'll remember him. May I see him?"

"Well, I really don't know what that'll prove. I got his gun with three empties. His description matches. The horse is the same. I got the bank bag with some of the money—"

"Not all of it?" interrupted Madsen.

"No, just some of it."

"Where do you suppose is the rest?"

"Don't know. Maybe he hid it somewhere. Maybe the woman he had been with took it. Who knows? She's long gone. I'm gonna get the bank people to do an identification, then take it all to Judge Wadell."

"Looks airtight to me," Madsen concurred.

Sarah's brow furrowed slightly. "I'd like to see him."

"Why?" Matt asked.

"I don't know, I just do."

Matt shrugged. "Whatever. Why don't you fix him some dinner? You can take it to him when I get back." He paused and looked her directly in the eye. "Don't go in there alone."

"Yes sir, Deputy," she said smiling, a slight trace of mocking in her tone.

Matt grinned. "Please."

"Okay. I'll see you later."

Matt moved toward the door. "Thanks, Doc. I'll come back later and check in on Pa. We'll take him over to Billy's as soon as he can be moved."

Madsen nodded and Matt slipped out the door.

An hour later the deputy sat at his desk, writing his account of the incident. Both the bank manager and the teller identified Bodine as the man who had robbed their bank. Josh protested vehemently but without avail. Despite not having seen his face during the robbery, they were convinced.

Matt looked up as the door opened. Sarah came in holding a

tray, which she set on Matt's desk. She put a plate of food in front of him and headed back to the cell with the other. Matt got up intent on going with her.

"Sit down and eat, Matt," she chided. "I'm just a few feet away, and he's locked up. I'll just push the tray under."

Matt thought a moment, then slowly turned without comment and returned to his desk.

Sarah looked at the man on the bunk, then slid the tray under the door. "Here you go, Mr. Bodine. Dinner."

Josh was curled up on the cot with his arm over his face. He moved the arm slightly at the sound of her voice so he could see her, then sat up. Sarah was surprised he was so young. His eyes were puffy and red, not at all the picture of a trigger-happy bank robber.

"Th-thank you," Bodine said. He got up and retrieved the tray, then sat on the bed and held it on his knees. "Oh, this smells good," he said. He tore into the food, then glanced up with his mouth full, surprised the woman was still there.

"Oh," he said, wiping his face with a sleeve. He swallowed hurriedly, then furrowed his brow. "You look familiar."

"You ate at my restaurant this morning. The Quicksilver."

"Oh, yeah." He took a bite of her fried chicken. "Are you the sheriff's girl?"

She thought about that. Did he mean was she the daughter of the sheriff, or the deputy's girlfriend? Didn't matter, really. The answer was the same.

"Yes, I suppose you could say that."

"Thought so. I saw the way you two looked at each other."

Sarah blushed.

"I never had a woman look at me like that—and mean it. The girl at the dance hall, she—oh, I'm sorry, I probably shouldn't be talking about this with you."

"No, it's okay. Please go ahead, if you want."

"Sarah?" It was Matt, calling from the other room.

"I'm fine. We're talking."

"You sure?"

"Yes, Matt. I'm sure." She turned back to Bodine. "You were saying?"

"Are you here to try and get me to confess without me knowin' I'm doin' it?"

"No. I just wanted to talk to you, that's all."

"Why?"

Sarah shrugged. "I don't know. Woman's intuition."

"What's that?"

Sarah smiled. "No one knows. Sometimes we just feel like something might be important, only we don't know why."

"Oh."

"So you were saying . . . ?"

"About the girl? Well, she looked at me like she thought I was special."

"Maybe she did."

"No, she was just bein' paid to do it. Them girls don't like anybody. Not even themselves."

"I've always thought that," Sarah lamented.

"You know," Bodine said with his mouth full of mashed potatoes, "the funny thing is, I was so drunk I don't remember anything about it. I recall goin' in there with her, watchin' her get un—oh, sorry—you know, get ready. Then the next thing I know, I'm wakin' up, seein' some odd things, my head bustin', and suddenly he's breakin' down the door, accusin' me of robbery and shootin' someone." He jerked his fork in Matt's direction.

"You know, the man who was shot is Matt's—the deputy's—father."

Bodine looked up. "That explains why he was so hard when he took me in."

"He didn't hurt you, did he?"

"No, he just wasn't too kindly is all."

Sarah didn't answer. She knew Matt hadn't treated Josh any different just because Matt's father was the victim. Bodine knew it, too, he was just being defensive.

"I understand the evidence against you is very strong," Sarah ventured. "People have identified you, and you have no alibi."

He looked straight at her. "I can't explain it. All I know is, I didn't do it." He pushed the tray back under the door. "Thank you. That was very good."

"You're welcome," Sarah said, picking it up. "Do you have any family that can help?"

"None that I can ask. I left home for good. Can't go back. Can't ask for help."

"When did you leave home?"

He put his head in his hands and shook it slowly. "Early this mornin'."

CHAPTER

SIX

Judge Horatio Wadell rapped his gavel sharply the next morning promptly at ten.

"This court is now in session. This is a preliminary hearing to decide whether the defendant, Joshua Bodine, sitting over yonder with Deputy Sheriff Matthew Page, should be held answerable to the charges of bank robbery and attempted murder. Has he been provided with counsel?"

"Yessir, Your Honor," said a man in suit standing near Bodine.

"State your name," the judge ordered.

"It's, uh, me, Your Honor. You know, Pete Jensen." The spectators, which included just about the whole male population of the town, murmured in derision. Jensen was new at this and didn't understand the rules of court conduct.

"Yes, Pete, I know. That was for the benefit of the official record."

"Oh."

"Take a seat by your client. Deputy, you sit over there." Wadell pointed to a nearby chair, which Matt quietly moved over to and sat down.

"Who is here to prosecute?"

A heavy man with large, gray sideburns and a gold watch

chain hanging from his vest pocket rose from a creaking chair at the next table.

"I, Patrick Kelly, Your Honor, have been so designated."

The crowd was excited and anticipated a short, one-sided match. Bodie did not have a prosecuting attorney, but attorneys-at-large who represented whatever side got to them first. Kelly, who recently had moved to Bodie from Aurora, was a master who had never lost—whether prosecuting or defending—and Jensen was a beginner with no track record.

"Very well," Wadell intoned, "is everyone ready?"

All nodded.

"Mr. Kelly, have you prepared an opening statement?"

"Yessir, Your Honor."

"Okay, men, let's get this show on the road. Remember, gentlemen," his voice rising as he addressed the whole room, "this is just a preliminary hearing. There's no need to ramble on and on. Just tickle me with the high points. And you men in the gallery, try maintaining yourselves—in other words, keep quiet."

Matt smirked to himself. It was obvious Wadell was all too familiar with the carnival atmosphere some judicial proceedings could lapse into if the judge let them get out of hand.

"Mr. Kelly, you may proceed."

"Thank you, Your Honor. Yesterday, just at closing time, the Bodie Bank was robbed. Mr. Jacob Page, a leading citizen of the community, was gunned down by the robber, fortunate that his wounds did not prove fatal. Said robber then took thousands of dollars from the bank and fled. We will produce ample witnesses who will prove, beyond any doubt, that the robber was one Joshua Bodine." With high drama, he flung his arm and pointed an accusing finger at Bodine, while every head in the courtroom turned to look at the young defendant, as though this was the first time they'd heard he was the one accused of the crime.

"That it?" asked the judge, yawning.

"Yes, Your Honor," Kelly said, and he retracted his arm and sat down.

"All right, Mr. Jensen. Your turn."

Jensen stood hesitantly. "Thank you, Your Honor. The defense ha—" His voice cracked, and he stopped to clear it. "The defense has the unenviable task today of attempting to cast doubt on the prosecution's case—enough doubt to cause the court to release Mr. Bodine—which we admit will be most difficult." A wave of whispers swept through the room. Jensen continued, undaunted. "The fact is, Mr. Bodine is innocent. Because he was asleep, apparently alone, when the crime occurred, he has no alibi. The evidence against him is circumstantial, as you will discover. If Mr. Bodine was guilty, he would have prepared an ironclad alibi. The fact is, Mr. Bodine has no alibi because he was unaware he would need one. He was spending the afternoon with one of our fallen angels, not robbing banks and shooting people." Jensen sat down.

The judge banged the gavel, quieting the crowd, then spit into a brass spittoon at his feet. "Okay, Mr. Kelly. Let's get your witnesses up here."

Kelly started his prosecution by calling the bank employees, who recounted the event and explained that they based their identification on Bodine's physical appearance and clothing. Jensen's cross-examination of them was ineffective. They were positive that the clothing worn by Bodine and the robber were the same. Jensen made some notes.

The prosecution then called Noah to the stand, much to the delight of the crowd. Wadell knew Noah and hoped Kelly could control him.

"Noah, were you near the bank when it was robbed?" Kelly asked.

"Say, now, I didn't do it!" Noah protested.

"I'm not trying to imply that you did, Noah. Just answer the question, please."

"Okay, yep, I was in the vicinity."

"Were you—"

"At least I assume I was in the vicinity. I didn't know the bank had been robbed at the time. If I did, I'da yelled 'bank robbery!' or somethin', but since I didn't I—"

"Noah, excuse me. Did you see someone come out of the bank and get on a horse, then ride off?"

"Oh, sure, yep. This feller comes outta the bank and jumps on a nice bay—real purdy horse, nice shiny mane, white feet, a white state on his forehead—"

"A *what*?" Judge Wadell interrupted.

"You know, a white spot on his forehead in the shape of a state, like on a map. I didn't know what state. Just looked like a state to me. I heard people say it looked like Illinois to them, but I never been to Illinois so I wouldn't know. I ain't studied maps none either so—"

Wadell groaned and cut him off. "Go ahead, Mr. Kelly, and can you get to the good parts?"

"We shall, sir. Noah, did you see this horse again later? Please just answer yes or no." Someone in the gallery groaned in disappointment. Wadell rapped his gavel and glared at the unseen culprit. Two or three men behind the offender pointed him out playfully.

"Yep, I did," Noah answered.

"Where did you see the horse?"

"Out back of the bawdy houses."

"In the alley?"

"Yep.

"No further questions," Kelly said.

"Can I go?" Noah asked.

"Not yet," said Wadell. "The defense gets to ask you some questions, too. Go ahead, Mr. Jensen."

"Thank you, Your Honor. Mr. Porter—"

"Call me Noah."

"Okay, Noah. Have you ever told a tall tale, you know, a yarn?"

"You mean, like a lie?"

"Well, in a manner of speaking, yes."

"No, not that I know of. But then, if I had, you don't think I'd admit it, do you?" He laughed at himself.

"Did you accompany Lewis and Clark on their trip west?"

"Only partway. I went on ahead and—"

"Were you present at Appomattox?"

"I handed Grant the ink pen."

"The Alamo?"

"Beside Davy Crockett the whole time!"

"No further questions."

Jensen sat down, unsuccessfully surpressing a grin, obviously pleased with his attempt to discredit Noah.

Judge Wadell rapped his gavel. "Lunchtime! Be back in an hour." The crowd immediately broke out in loud conversation as they filed out of the room. Matt led Bodine back to the jail where Sarah had lunch waiting. They ate together at a table, Bodine remaining unshackled. They did not discuss the proceedings.

The hearing resumed at one o'clock when Kelly called his next witness.

"Deputy Matthew Page."

Matt stood and walked to the stand, was sworn in, and sat in the witness chair. It was his first time, and he fidgeted nervously.

"Deputy Page, by whom are you employed?"

"Mono County. I'm a deputy to Sheriff John Taylor, assigned to Bodie to function as town constable."

"Can you tell us in your own words about the events of the day in question?"

"I was in one of the saloons when I heard a commotion and went outside. People were running to the bank, so I followed them. I saw Noah. He told me about the horse and rider—"

"This was outside the bank?"

"I saw Noah outside the bank. I had him wait in my office, and he told me later about the horse and rider he saw."

"Wasted a dang good bit of time, too!" shouted Noah from the gallery. The crowd laughed, Matt flushed, and Wadell banged.

"Knock it off, gents! Noah, you shut up or I'll have you removed. Go ahead, Patrick."

"Thank you, Your Honor. Then what, Deputy?"

"I went in the bank, helped my pa—uh, the victim, Mr. Page—got statements, and that's about it."

"And later in the day, what happened?"

"Noah told me where the horse was. He described it down to the spot on his forehead."

"The spot that looked like Illinois?"

"Yessir."

"And you found this horse?"

"Yes, right where Noah said it would be, behind one of the cribs. I went around front and arrested Mr. Bodine inside. His clothes matched the description given by the bank people."

"Anything else?"

"His gun had been fired three times and the caliber was a .44, the same as the slug Doc Madsen removed from my pa." He took the bullet out of his vest pocket and handed it to the judge. "And

the bank bag was on the chair, with the bank's money in it." A
murmur ran through the room. How much more obvious could it
be? Heads began nodding.

Kelly sat down, and Jensen took his turn.

"Deputy Page, is there anything about this whole case that
bothers you, that just doesn't add up?"

"I'm not sure what you mean."

"How much money did you find in the bank bag?"

"Five hundred dollars."

"How much was taken?"

"Upwards of five thousand."

"How do you explain that?"

"I don't know that I have to. I think that's something the bank
robber should explain."

"Mr. Bodine, in your opinion."

"I didn't say that, but that's sure how it looks."

"Why wouldn't Mr. Bodine have all the money?"

"Objection!" Kelly interrupted. "Calls for a conclusion."

"Save it for the trial," snapped Wadell. "I want to hear the
answer. Go ahead, Deputy."

"I don't know why not. Perhaps he lost it, buried it, gave it to
someone, or it was stolen while he was asleep."

Jensen moved around the table. "And why would Mr. Bodine,
after robbing a bank and shooting a man, leave town, then come
right back and bed down with a prostitute, just a few blocks from
the bank? Why would he risk capture?"

Matt shrugged. "Who knows? Brave, stupid . . ."

"Innocent," suggested Jensen. "Could it be that Mr. Bodine
was in town, with a prostitute, asleep in her crib because he wasn't,
in fact, the bank robber?"

Matt shrugged.

"Did he look like he'd just woke up?"

"Well, his hair was stickin' out every which way, and his eyes
were puffy. I'd say he did. But what about the gun and the
money?" Matt challenged. "And the witnesses?"

"Ah, the witnesses. Did any witness describe the robber's face
to you?"

"No, it was covered with a bandanna. A blue bandanna just
like Bodine had when I arrested him."

Jensen walked over to the crowd behind him. He spotted a man with a bandanna around his neck, cowboy-style.

"Your Honor, may I . . . ?"

"Only if you make your point in a hurry."

"Thank you." He pointed at the man. "You, sir, may I see your bandanna?"

Puzzled, the man untied the knot and handed the bandanna to Jensen. The attorney took it and gave it to another man, while hiding him from Matt's sight. "Would you be so kind as to put this around your face?"

The man took the bandanna hesitantly, and smelled it. The crowd laughed. Smiling at his sudden entrance into the spotlight, he tied it over his face with a flourish.

Jensen turned to Matt and stepped aside. "Deputy, would you describe this man's face to me?"

"I can't. He's got a bandanna covering it."

Jensen retrieved the bandanna and thanked the man, who was congratulated by the men near him.

"Okay, Deputy Page, say someone just committed an offense, but all you saw was a bandanna. Would you, in all honesty, be convinced that this man was the other man? Would you be able to tell the difference?"

"There's more to it than that. We had other things to go on."

"Yes, we've heard those other things. Clothing, a horse, a bank bag and a gun with three empties."

Jensen turned to the gallery again. "Anyone here have a gun with three empties?" The sound of weapons being checked filled the room, then two men raised their hands slowly.

Jensen turned to the judge. "No further questions, Your Honor."

Wadell spat. "Okay, Deputy. You can step down. Mr. Kelly, who's next?"

"Mr. Lars Bjorgen."

A tall, blond-headed man stood up and walked nervously to the platform. Jensen looked at Bodine questioningly, but Bodine just shrugged. Bjorgen was sworn in and took his seat.

"Mr. Bjorgen, what is your occupation?"

"I'ym a myner," he answered with a thick Scandinavian accent.

"Were you in the Highgrade yesterday morning?"

"Yah. Aye vass haffink uh beyer."

"Did you see Mr. Bodine in the saloon?"

"Yah."

"What was he doing?"

"Oh, drinkink und gamblink."

"Faro?"

"Yah."

"Was he winning?"

"Oh, no, he vass not."

"He vass—I mean, he was losing a lot?"

"Yah, und gettink plenty angery."

"What did he do?"

"Vell, anudder man treaten him, und reach fer a goon, und Mister Bodine draw und shute, very fast und gude, then roon away."

The room buzzed.

"One spent chamber in the saloon. Two during the holdup. By my count, that makes three empty chambers. No further questions." Kelly interlaced his fingers across his stomach and leaned back in his chair, pleased with his apparent coup. Jensen and Bodine whispered, Bodine nodded, then Jensen addressed the judge.

"We have no questions of Mr. Bjorgen at this time."

"Okay, Mr. Jensen. It's your call. Mr. Bjorgen, you may stand down, but it's possible you'll be recalled later."

"Tank you, surr," he said, nodding timidly as he stood.

"Any more?" Wadell asked Kelly.

"Mr. Page, *Senior*, could not make it here due to his wound, but it is our understanding that he would have nothing additional to add that the bank employees haven't already covered."

Jensen's face lit up.

"Very well, then," said Wadell. "Mr. Jensen, would you like to call your first witness?"

"Yes, Your Honor, I would. I call Mr. Jacob Page." The spectators reacted with gasps and a few chuckles. Poor Jensen, what an amateur!

"Didn't you hear Mr. Kelly just say that Mr. Page is unavailable?"

"Of course, but I also heard him say that Mr. Page could offer nothing additional. It is our contention that we have the right to find that out for ourselves. Mr. Page was there, and we believe he may be able to exonerate the defendant. I stand by my right to call him."

Wadell sighed. "You're right, dang it." He spat. "Deputy, when will your pa be able to talk?"

"Day after tomorrow, at the soonest."

"Mr. Jensen, can you call someone else in the meantime?"

"Your Honor, it is our contention that Mr. Bodine was framed. Our purpose is to show that sufficiently so that he will not be bound over for trial. To do so, to see that justice is served, there are some people we need to locate. In addition, this introduction by Mr. Kelly of testimony regarding my client's alleged conduct in a saloon earlier in the day seems irrelevant, and we would like to assess what he is up to. The prosecution shouldn't be throwing us surprises like that. After all, a man's freedom is at stake here. A few hours delay in the interest of justice seems reasonable."

Wadell leaned back in his chair and spat. "I have to admit it, Mr. Jensen, you're right. This court will reconvene at 9:00 A.M., day after tomorrow. Come prepared to finish, gentlemen, as finish we will, God willing and the creek don't rise."

He stood, spat, and walked out. Jensen leaned toward Bodine and whispered in his ear. "I'll see you at the jail in a few minutes." Bodine nodded.

As the onlookers filed out, noisily discussing the progress of the case with each other and offering opinions, Matt led a shackled Josh Bodine back to the jail.

CHAPTER

SEVEN

"Can I get you to close the door, Deputy?" Jensen asked.

"Sure, no problem." Matt shut the heavy, wooden door that led to the cells of the jail giving Jensen and Bodine the privacy they required. Sarah was rocking next to Matt's desk in the chair she had brought in for the purpose. A quilt she had stitched herself covered her legs.

"So, how goes the hearing?" she asked.

"I don't know. All right, I guess." Matt shrugged and pretended to be interested in something on his desk.

"Will he have to go to trial in Bridgeport or not?"

"Hard to say. The defense hasn't started their side yet, although I can't say what they could possibly do or say. Jensen even insinuated in court that my pa had something to say that would clear Bodine. I don't think that's too likely. There's too much evidence against him."

"Not the way I understand it."

"What do you know that the rest of us don't?"

"All the evidence you have makes him *look* guilty, but none of it actually proves anything."

"One or two coincidences I could accept," Matt said, "but not five or six."

"That's just the point," Sarah explained. "There's too many coincidences. Someone planned this."

Matt shook his head. "I don't know. But I get the feeling you think he's innocent."

"No, I'm just saying it's *possible* he's innocent."

"So it's possible? So what?"

"Do you want an innocent man to go to prison while the guilty man goes free?"

"Of course not."

"It seems to me you should look at all the pieces of the puzzle. There's still some missing, you know."

"Like what?"

"The girl he was with. Why wasn't she there when you kicked in the door? How does she figure into this? Where is she now?"

"Okay, okay. You're right about that. I'll look for her."

"Good. And what about the other two men?"

"What other two men?"

"The men that were with Josh in the Quicksilver yesterday. I served breakfast to three men at the same table. They were walking out when you came in."

"I only saw Bodine."

"You were pie-eyed—which, I must say, I appreciated."

"You know," Matt said thoughtfully, "now that you mention it, I saw all three of them ride into town at the same time. They looked so different, I couldn't see how they could all be together. Of course, that could mean they were in on it somehow. Maybe they were supposed to meet him and didn't show, or he got too involved with the—with the young lady and lost track of time." He looked at Sarah who was smiling, pleased with herself.

"Tell me, Sarah, what made you get interested in this?"

"Well, in the first place I don't want you possibly making a mistake." She stopped rocking. "In the second, I just don't think he's the bank-robbing type. He's too . . . innocent. You know, inexperienced."

"There's a lot of unanswered questions, I'll grant you that much."

"Why don't you go talk to him while Mr. Jensen's in there?"

Matt stood. "Thanks." He leaned over and gave Sarah a peck on the cheek. "Deputy's best friend." Sarah blushed.

Matt stuck his head around the door.

"Mr. Jensen, may I have a word?"

"What is it, Deputy?"

"I was wondering if I could ask Mr. Bodine something, with you here of course."

Jensen turned to his client. "Josh?"

Bodine shrugged. "Sure. What have I got to lose?"

"Thanks," Matt said. He stepped all the way in and let the door close behind him. "Do you have any idea how I can find the girl?"

Bodine shook his head but answered, "Try the hurdy house. That's where I met her."

"Okay."

"You're going to look for her?" Jensen asked.

Matt nodded. "If Bodine's innocent, I don't want him going to prison. I want the real culprit."

"So you think he may be innocent?"

"I didn't say that, Mr. Jensen. I'm not afraid of it, though. I guess you could say I'm a realist. I believe what I can see, for the most part, but I know enough about God to know some things aren't always obvious and some things have to be taken on faith. I'm interested in truth."

"We're mighty glad to hear that."

Matt had a sudden thought. "By the way, Mr. Jensen, what do you think my pa has to say that will clear Bodine?"

Jensen grinned sheepishly and hunched his shoulders. "I don't know that he does. I wanted to buy us some time, and that looked like a good way to do it. For all I know, your pa will say the same things the bank people said. If you can find the girl, that might clear it all up."

"Hmmmm." Matt's brow furrowed in thought. "What about them two men you were with?" he asked Josh.

"You know about them?"

"Saw you ride in with them. Sarah—the gal that brought your dinner last night—she served you all in her restaurant."

"That's right!" Bodine turned to Jensen. "They did it! They set me up!" Josh started to get mad and excited. "They're the ones that stole my gold, set me up with the girl, got me drunk—"

"What gold?" Matt asked.

"*My* gold! My father gave it to me when I left. It was my stake. Those guys robbed my future—"

"Calm down, Josh," Jensen cautioned. "We still have a problem. Even if we can convince the judge there are two other men, we still have to make him believe you didn't rob the bank. If it wasn't you—and I'm convinced it wasn't—then who was it? Don't forget, we've already said you have no alibi, that you were sleeping. We're gonna have to do more than cast doubt on your guilt. We're gonna have to *prove* theirs! Is that how you have it figured, Deputy?"

Matt nodded. "Pretty much. But first things first. Describe the girl to me. We'll start by finding her."

Leaving Jensen with Bodine and the attorney's promise to keep Bodine secure, Matt walked the few blocks to Bonanza Street. Even before he reached the hurdy house he could hear the piano, as well as the tramping of feet on the wood dance floor. The other sounds of the area, which bordered Chinatown, assaulted his ears: the uncontrolled revelry of the drunks, the high-pitched shrieking of two Chinamen in debate, the scuffling of feet on the dirt road, the barking of an unseen dog.

Matt strode to the door of the dance hall and pushed it open, then slipped into the crowded room as unobtrusively as possible, which was quite a trick considering the shiny star on his shirt.

He glanced around the room trying to pick out the girl from Bodine's description. They came in all sizes, races, and ages; some pretty, some ordinary. They were dressed, for the most part, like any other woman would be dressed to go to a dance. They were not here to entice the men into sin—that the men were here was evidence they had already been enticed by their own lusts. The girls were here to make the sin easier for the men to commit.

Bodie had been growing too fast. Matt couldn't keep up with all the new arrivals. Why, half the men in here he didn't know, not even by sight. Every day a stage arrived with new passengers clinging to it like dead flies on flypaper. It was all Matt could do to check those people out when they came to town. There was no way he could keep an eye out for those who arrived under their own power.

The young deputy was a little uneasy. He recalled his first night in Bridgeport, walking around town wondering about the women in the dance halls there. They didn't look like he had imagined they would. No flashy or cheap jewelry, no revealing dresses, just women who danced for money, some of them who would also—

"May I help you, Deputy?"

Matt was startled out of his daydream by a plump, attractive woman he figured to be about forty. She looked . . . experienced, well-traveled to him. She had a pleasant smile, large, brown, intelligent eyes under heavy brows, and wore heavy rouge on her puffy cheeks.

"Oh, uh, well, I'm looking for someone," Matt explained.

"They in trouble?" Her eyes narrowed.

"No. I just want to talk to her."

"Oh, it's a *her*. One of my girls? What's her name?"

"Don't know. I only know what she looks like."

"Maybe I can help you find her. What do you want to talk to her about?"

Matt smiled. "Official business."

"Humph. But she's not in trouble herself, you say?"

"I shouldn't think so." Matt was smart enough to know that if he let on that the girl could be in trouble, this madam wouldn't help him find her. Truth is, he didn't know. Maybe she was, maybe she wasn't.

"Very well, then, I'll do what I can to help the law. Just remember this later. What's she look like?"

"Thin, freckled, red hair piled up, lots of rouge."

"That's kind of a broad description, Deputy. There's lots of girls that fit. We can eliminate the Spanish girls, of course." She craned her neck to look around the room. Matt felt she was stalling. Just how many skinny young redheads coule there be?

"Okay, well thanks anyway. I'll find her." He touched his hat brim. "Nice to have met you, Miss . . . ?"

"Rosa Bailey. Miss Rosa. That's what I go by here."

"Right. Miss Rosa." He tipped his hat slightly and started to wade through the crowd. Rosa clutched his sleeve.

"S'cuse me, Deputy, door's that way." She nodded in the opposite direction.

"Oh, I'm not leaving," he explained. "I came here for a young lady, and I ain't leaving till I find her. If I have to I'll thin out your crowd some, get rid of the people I don't need—like the men. Make it easier to spot her." He turned away from the madam, pulled his sleeve free, and started off. She lurched toward him and grabbed his arm.

"Wait!"

Matt stopped and looked at her with raised eyebrows.

"Okay," she relented. "I'll help. But I don't like the idea."

"I told you, Miss Rosa, she's not in trouble with the law, not unless she's done something wrong." He looked around. "And I ain't talkin' morally wrong, I'm talkin' about things like stealin', stuff like that."

"Okay, Deputy, you win. I'll tell you who she is."

"What's her name?"

"Nellie."

"C'mon, Rosa. Half these girls name themselves Nellie when they take up the business. What's her real name?"

"What difference does it make?"

"Rosa, where is she?"

"Gone."

"Whaddya mean, 'gone'?"

"You know. Good-bye, departed, left."

"Where'd she go?"

"Don't know. She got on a stage yesterday, just a few minutes after she . . ."

"After she what?"

"After she took that young greenhorn over to the crib for his first time." She looked around. "Deputy, can we go outside?"

"If you're gonna cooperate."

Rosa nodded demurely and brushed past the lawman. He followed her through the front door.

"Okay," Matt said, folding his arms and leaning against the porch rail.

"The truth is, Deputy, I don't know where she is. She took that kid to the crib, then an hour later she came through here with her bag packed, said good-bye, and got on a stage. She didn't tell me why she was leaving, and I couldn't stop her. She looked scared."

"Doesn't make any sense, unless she did something wrong."

Rosa sighed. "You're probably right, Deputy, but I don't know what it was. What's the deal with the kid? He claimin' she stole something from him?"

"He's in jail for robbin' a bank. He claims he was in Nellie's the whole time asleep. If that's true, why would she run off? Makes it look like maybe he did rob the bank, then Nellie took off with some of the money."

"Some of the money's gone?"

"Most of it."

Rosa began wringing her hands. "Oh, I hope you're wrong."

"Since when do you care if one of your girls steals from a customer?"

"Normally, I don't. But Nelda—that's her real name—Nelda means more to me than the other girls." She paused and sucked in a breath. "She's my daughter."

Matt walked to the stage office after letting the nervous Rosa return to her dance hall. Fortunately, only one stage left town around the time Rosa said Nelda fled. It was destined for Bishop, a two-day trip. Bodie didn't have a telegraph office yet, so he couldn't wire the sheriff there. He entered the stage office and moved over the dusty wood floor to the ticket window.

The look on Matt's face must have been strange because the stage agent asked, "What's troublin' you, Deputy?"

"Huh? Oh, I just need to get a hold of someone who left on that stage yesterday. I don't have time to ride after them, and we can't send a wire."

"Who is it you need?"

"A young woman, red hair, green eyes. Name of Nelda."

The agent thought, then shook his head. "I saw her in here yesterday. I surely did. But she didn't get on the stage."

"Oh?"

"No, never bought a ticket. She came in, stood around kinda nervous-like, shifting from one foot to the other, looking out the window. Then suddenly she sees somethin', runs out my back door, and that's that. Never saw her again."

The lawman thanked him and hurried back to the jail, wondering what it all meant, trying to reason it out. When the deputy arrived he found Jensen sitting at the desk. The attorney rose when the deputy walked in, but Matt waved him down. Sarah rocked. Bodine was stretched out on his cot in the cell, the door locked.

"Judging by your face, it looks like bad news," Jensen observed.

Matt pushed his hat back on his head and sat on the corner of the desk.

"Well, it ain't good, that's for sure. But just how it's bad, I haven't figured yet." Jensen looked puzzled and Matt explained. "The girl flew the coop. Disappeared. Although she may still be somewhere around. She didn't get on a stage, although she meant to." He rubbed the back of his neck, puzzled.

"She left an hour or so after Bodine went in there with her. Maybe she knows what happened, maybe she don't. Maybe she stole Bodine's gold. Maybe she took the bank money that's missing, maybe she didn't. Maybe she knows who robbed the bank. There's just too many questions that only she can answer."

"Matt, what do you think? Have you changed your mind about Josh? Do you still think he robbed the bank and shot your pa?"

Matt looked down. "I don't know, Pete. Part of me says he did, part says he didn't. My mind is less made up now than it was before, I'll say that. I'd like to believe him, but . . ." He looked up and caught Sarah's eye. ". . . but so far the evidence seems clear to me. I'm gonna try to find that girl, see what we can come up with, I guarantee you that."

"Thanks, Deputy," Jensen said. "We've got until the day after next. Do what you can."

Sarah followed Matt outside.

He turned.

"Matt, do you think you can find her?"

"I don't know. If she's still in town she may be hidin'. It sounds like she was gonna get on the stage but was scared off. That makes me think someone may have been after her. It could've been Bodine, could've been them other fellahs. If they caught up with her . . ." He left the sentence and her destiny hanging.

"What can I do to help you?" Sarah asked.

"I don't know, Sarah. I don't know. If you were her, where would you hide?"

"Someplace where no one could find me."

CHAPTER

EIGHT

Page walked through town as the last traces of daylight were replaced by the flickering yellow glow of the coal oil lamps. The buildings that had been whitewashed turned various shades of warm yellow, reflecting that light. The natural wood storefronts remained an earthy brown, displaying the ghostly shadows cast by Matt and the other pedestrians.

"She won't be in the cribs, that's for sure," he mumbled softly to himself. Speaking his thoughts kept his mind from wandering. "Naw, we'd look there. Rosa'd look there. Nellie was gonna take the stage, but something scared her off. So instead, she takes off and goes into hiding. But where? For how long? She'll need food, water. It'd have to be someplace where she could move without being seen, or if she was seen, no one would care."

Matt chewed on this awhile as he watched a little Chinaman scurry by in his black, silk pajamas, skull cap and wooden clog sandals. Matt watched him with curiosity. Most of the Chinese wore the clothing of the American West instead of their native garb. The Chinaman's queue flopped from side-to-side as he kept his head down, not looking anyone in the eye. He had no expression on his face, but Matt thought he saw the Chinaman scowl as he passed an old Paiute sitting cross-legged on the edge of the boardwalk. The Indian was wrapped in his blanket and snorted at the Chinaman, turning his head slightly to watch the Oriental out of the corner of his eye as the little man passed behind him.

Matt snickered at the drama, then was struck with an idea.

"Chinatown!" he said.

The girls' cribs were on the outskirts of Chinatown. As Bodie grew, more and more Orientals moved into town and set up shop. Few of them worked the mines or mills. They preferred the retail trade: laundries, meat markets, opium dens . . .

Matt shuddered. That's just what the people needed, something else to become addicted to. Booze, gambling, and loose women weren't enough. It wasn't the good citizens who frequented the dens, just the drifters and riff-raff, the rowdies and prostitutes. Matt didn't like the trend he saw developing. Soon he wouldn't be able to handle the town alone.

But, for right now, he had to put that aside. Nellie could be hiding in Chinatown, and he needed to start looking.

Matt sauntered up King Street, the entrance to the Chinese district. The sky was nearly dark, and the intricate red and yellow lanterns on the porches were being lit. As he passed Bonanza Street, the girls hanging around outside their places stopped to watch him. He smiled and waved, and they either ignored him or waved back hesitantly, not knowing what to think of him. There were quite a few of them out tonight, he noticed.

The Chinese district wasn't large, although it was growing faster than the rest of town. A hundred Orientals had moved into town in the last six months. They kept to themselves, mostly, and as a rule didn't venture into the other sections of Bodie except on rare occasions. Even then they didn't dawdle but hurried through their mission like the man Matt had seen a little bit ago.

The few Paiutes that hung around town didn't frequent Chinatown. There was a mutual distrust between the Indians and the Chinese, although Matt doubted either group knew why. It was probably just ignorance of the other race and their customs, and fear of the unknown—the same reason whites distrusted everyone else, Matt thought.

Matt passed a Chinese butcher shop, wrinkling his nose at the plucked ducks hanging by their necks in the window. The strange odors that wafted out the door assaulted him, driving him to hurry past.

If she's in there, she can stay hidden!

Next door was a joss temple, a center of worship for the Chinese. Matt lamented that the "yellow heathen"—as they were called in the *Bodie Gazette*—had built themselves a house of worship before the civilized, "Christian" whites, who met in the boarding house on Sunday morning—in pitifully small numbers.

Above every door in Chinatown was nailed a small, colorful box with Chinese writing. Matt was gazing at one with a furrowed brow when a nicely dressed Caucasian woman walked by. She saw his intent stare and stopped.

"Whatcha lookin' at, Sheriff, that's gotcha puzzled so?"

"Huh?" He turned his head toward her. She was short, pretty, with red-painted full lips and smiling green eyes. Her auburn hair was piled on top of her head. "Uh . . . I was just wonderin' what them little things are."

"They ward off evil spirits."

"They do?"

"Well, the Chinese think they do. They believe it protects their business or house."

"Hmmm." Matt glanced back up at the device for a moment, then returned his gaze to the woman. He figured her to be about twenty-five. At least, she looked that old. A hard life could have aged her.

"You familiar with Chinatown?" he asked.

"Some. This is where I spend most of my time. The good women of Bodie tend to dislike women like me frequenting their territory."

"Well, that ain't right," Matt sympathized, "but you know how they are."

"Yeah. And they ain't no different here than anywheres else. The Comstock, South Dakota. All gold towns is the same."

"I suppose."

"What brings you here, Sheriff? The Chinese don't have much use for white man's law. They take care of their own problems, mostly, unless their problem is with a white. The tong watches over 'em."

"I know. But this is still part of my town. Sometimes it's good to just walk around, let 'em see me, remind 'em that this is America, and we do have laws that apply to all people."

She put her hand on his arm and moved close, speaking in a whisper. "I been around, Sheriff. That ain't all you're doin' here."

Her touch surprised him, and she moved close enough that he could smell her perfume. "N-no, you're right, ma'am. Maybe you can help me."

She moved even closer and smiled.

"Now we're gettin' somewheres. Even lawmen need companionship. What can I do for you?"

Matt swallowed hard. "The first thing you can do is back up a little, ma'am, so I can move without disruptin' the parts of you I shouldn't disrupt." She looked disappointed and took a half-step backward. "Thank you," Matt said with a nervous grin. "I'm lookin' for one of Rosa's girls. She goes by the name of Nellie."

"What'd she do?"

"Nothin', far as I know. She's a witness."

"To what?"

"To whether a man we have in jail was with her when the bank was robbed."

"Why's she so hard to find? Just go to Rosa."

"I did. Nellie's run off."

"Sounds like she's guilty of somethin' or afraid. Which is it?"

"Don't know. But I don't think she's left town. She's hidin' someplace."

"And you think she might be in Chinatown."

"Seems likely. She'd be familiar with it, like you."

"But she's white, isn't that correct? The Chinese wouldn't hide her or protect her. They don't cotton to us workin' girls any more'n they do other whites."

"Is there any place in Chinatown where she might be able to hide herself and still have access to food and water? Someplace where the Chinese wouldn't care?"

"Mr. Sing's den, maybe. That's the only place where she could go without raising suspicion. She could stay there for days, as long as she bought a pipe now and then or took in enough trade to rent a room upstairs."

Matt thanked her and started to walk off, but she caught his arm. "A suggestion," she said. "Don't go in there like that." She nodded at his badge. "People'll scatter. They don't feel comfortable smokin' opium with the law standin' there."

"Thanks for the tip, Miss . . . ?"

"Jewel."

"Miss Jewel." Matt touched the tip of his hat.

"Number twelve, Bonanza Street. Stop in anytime," she said with a slight smile. She let go of his arm and watched him move down the sidewalk.

Boy, she was good-lookin', Matt thought. *And pleasant. Not the rowdy cat my mother warned me about. I can understand why they're so hard to resist. If I didn't know they talk that way to every man, no matter how dirty or smelly he is, I might . . . no, God probably wouldn't appreciate that . . . not to mention Sarah!*

Thinking of her snapped him back to reality. He shuddered, wiped the sweat off his forehead, and tried to dismiss the painted lady from his mind, though she was reluctant to leave.

Matt glanced around as he walked, looking for Sing's opium den. All the signs along the street were in Chinese, but Matt realized there probably wouldn't be any sign—in Chinese or English—proclaiming *OPIUM DEN: Come in, we're open.*

It turned out to be easy to find anyway, though. The smoke rolling out the door was a dead giveaway. All the windows had dark shades drawn, but, oddly, the front door stood open. Matt paused in the shadows across the street and pulled off his badge, pinning it inside the crown of his hat where it wouldn't be in the way. Passing Chinamen eyed him suspiciously, but he ignored them. Then one stood near him too long, and Matt gave him a hard look and growled low like a mad dog. The Chinaman recoiled, then turned, and scurried away.

Matt watched the front door of the den. He could see folks inside through the smoky haze, but the light was too dim for the deputy to make out what they were doing. He stepped into the narrow street and crossed to the den, entering only after taking a deep breath.

Once inside his senses were besieged. The odor of burned opium and incense. The noise of slurred Chinese and English from the drunken patrons. He was surprised seeing as many whites inside as Chinese. Some people were stretched out on cots, smoking or already passed out from the drug. Others were taking a break or waiting for a cot to open, playing fan-tan at small, wood tables in the center of the room. The only lights were candles scattered about the room.

A Chinese man of indistinguishable age padded up quietly and surprised Matt from his blind side.

"Yes, you need smoke?" He smiled ingratiatingly.

"Uh . . . no, thank you."

The Chinaman looked bewildered. "No smoke?"

"I'm looking for . . . a friend." Matt scanned the room to validate his comment. "Maybe later, okay?" He didn't want to get thrown out and be forced to create a scene.

The Chinaman walked off without comment and busied himself with paying customers. Matt shrugged and sauntered through the place, trying to be as discreet as possible as he checked out the female patrons. They all appeared to be prostitutes. Many of them were ragged, tired-looking creatures, with the look of experience far beyond their years and pale, drawn faces, their good years long since left behind. Whether it was their trade or their addiction that was at fault, Matt couldn't tell. Probably both. He wondered how they arrived at this sorry state. Did their desire for opium force them into prostitution? Or did their prostitution drive them to seek solace in the mind-numbing narcotic? He let out a long breath and just shook his head.

Most of the women ignored him as they puffed the opium. Some looked but didn't see. None of them looked like Nellie, yet they all looked alike.

An opium-drunk man staggered down the hall and bumped into Matt. The deputy stepped back without comment and let the man roll off and continue on his way.

At the end of the hall was a narrow staircase. Matt climbed it carefully and at the top was confronted by a small hallway of doors. He pushed the first one open slowly and saw a man draped over a chair, snoring. A second man was passed out on a bed. The room stunk.

The door across the hall was stuck, and Matt put his shoulder into it. He stumbled in as it burst open and a fat woman wearing only a look of surprise screamed. The thin man she was with ducked under the blanket.

"Sorry," Matt said sheepishly. "Wrong room."

He closed the door and moved to the third. It was opened by

an exiting woman with red hair, her eyes bloodshot and yellow, who staggered and tripped as she passed into the hallway and fell to the threadbare carpet. In the dim light, she matched Nellie's description.

Matt helped her up, and when she looked vacantly at him he asked, "Nellie?"

"What?" Her voice was harsh, spitting out hatred of life itself.

"Are you Nellie Bailey?"

She laughed. "If you want me to be, mister. I'll be anyone you want for a few dollars." Her breath was rancid and the lines in her face, now close to Matt's, betrayed her age. Matt let go, and she clomped awkwardly down the hall, guiding and supporting herself by feel along the wall. Matt felt dirty.

As he moved toward the next door, the lawman heard heavy footsteps on the stairwell. A large Chinaman, bald except for his long queue, appeared at the top of the stairs, filling the hall. The ancient man who had greeted Matt inside the front door was behind the big man, jabbering and pointing at Matt.

I think they aim to toss me out, Matt deduced.

He turned and faced the bouncer full on. The Chinaman pointed down the stairs. It was an order.

Matt held the man's gaze for a moment, then slowly shook his head and put his hand on the doorknob of the next room. The bouncer moved forward quickly. Matt squared off against him, momentarily forgetting he had removed his badge. The Chinaman drew a wicked-looking dagger from one of the mysterious folds in his clothing and advanced. He didn't like being challenged.

Matt looked down quickly and remembered where his star was. He pulled off his hat and held it up so the bouncer could see the badge pinned inside and held it near the man's face. This blocked the large man's vision briefly, and Matt threw a fist as hard as he could into his hat—and the Chinaman's nose.

The Chinaman staggered back, stunned, knocking the small proprietor down in a squall of Chinese that Matt was grateful he couldn't understand. Matt flexed and shook his punching hand as he stuffed his hat back on his head.

The bouncer growled and gave his head a shake, then glared at Matt. The imprint of Matt's badge was visible on the man's face.

Although momentarily stunned, he had completely recovered and was angry on top of it. He moved toward Matt with his knife at the ready. Matt backed up quickly and yanked his Colts Peacemaker from its holster, pointing it at the Chinaman. The man looked at it, sized up his chances, and continued moving toward the intruder.

Matt didn't expect this. Why didn't this ape retreat? Matt had no choice, he'd have to shoot. He'd already backed himself to the end of the hallway. There was nowhere to go.

Matt cocked the six-shooter, took careful aim, and fired twice into the ceiling. Immediately the doors flew open, including the ones Matt had not yet checked, and people poured into the hallway. They began a mad, confused rush for the stairs. Matt pressed his back against the wall at the end of the hall, out of the way of the stampede.

He strained to see if Nellie Bailey was among them as they rushed toward the staircase but did not see her. The mass of fleeing people swept the two Chinamen with them. Matt fired again keeping the rampage moving and followed them, checking every room to make sure they were empty. The large woman with the skinny man had remained behind. Matt tipped his hat again and shrugged his shoulders, and shut the door.

When the upper floor was clear Matt went down the stairs, cautiously keeping an eye out for his adversary, but found the downstairs empty also.

Nellie had not been in there.

Pinning his badge back onto his shirt, Matt made his way outside. Disoriented people were still running helter-skelter through Chinatown, many from adjoining establishments. Panic had spread like a disease, and the commotion emptied nearly a hundred people from the crowded dens. Unfortunately for some of them, in the darkness they had failed seeing the clotheslines that were strung across several yards and were suddenly tossed to the ground when their chins caught on the line as they charged from harm's way, finding themselves looking skyward with headaches and backaches and sore necks. A small price to pay for their iniquity, Matt thought.

The two Chinamen Matt had encountered, Mr. Sing and his bodyguard, had disappeared, lost in the network the Chinese had organized for protection of their own, but they would resurface. They always did.

Matt breathed an unsatisfied sigh and walked back to the jail empty-handed. But it had not been a total loss. He made a mental note to himself to come back and do this again sometime.

CHAPTER

NINE

The jail was silent when Matt returned and empty, except for Josh, who languished in his cell. The lawman stepped in and checked on him. The prisoner looked up from his cot.

"Evenin', Mr. Bodine."

"Evenin', Sheriff."

"I'm just a deputy," Matt corrected.

"It's all the same to me," Bodine said. "You're a lawman, and I'm jailed for a crime I didn't commit."

"I'd certainly like to believe you," Matt said, pulling up a chair as Josh raised himself on one arm. "But that leaves me with a problem. If it wasn't you, then who was it? And why does everyone think it was you? Help me out, Josh."

"I'd like to, Sher—er, Deputy, but it's like I said, I was asleep. I don't have any answers. You have any luck finding the girl?"

"Well, I know her name. Nellie Bailey."

"Nellie Bailey, eh? You're one up on me there, Deputy."

"And I know a lot of places she ain't hidin'."

Bodine settled back on the cot and looked at the ceiling. "This ain't how it was supposed to be."

"Beg pardon?"

"When I left home I wanted to have a good time, just like in the stories I read. I certainly didn't expect to wind up here, arrested for bank robbery—with no alibi—by a sheriff who's *nice* and not a snarling, no-nonsense gunfighter with a badge."

"Sorry I don't meet your expectations."

"I'm not tryin' to be critical. It's just not how I expected it to be."

"Maybe not, Josh, but this is how it *is*."

Bodine was silent, and Matt finally stood.

"You eat yet?"

"Yeah, Miss Taylor brung me somethin'."

"Okay. You get some sleep. I'll try again tomorrow to find that girl. You'd be well advised to think of anything you can that'd help prove your story."

"Do you believe me?"

"I don't know, to tell you the truth. If I just look at the facts— like a jury'd do if it gets that far—I'd have to say that they don't lie, and you did it. Unless one or more of the facts ain't what they appear."

Josh sighed as he settled back down on the bunk. "They ain't," he said quietly. "They ain't."

Matt blew out the lamp and locked the doors behind him as he left the jail, then crossed the street to the boarding house. His father had been moved there earlier in the day to recuperate in his own room under Uncle Billy's watchful eye. Matt nodded to O'Hara as he entered. The man was enjoying a cup of coffee by himself and smiled wide when he saw the younger Page.

"Matthew, how you doin'? Come, sit down. You wanna cup of coffee? It's real hot and real good."

"No, thanks, Billy but—you know, come to think of it, I will have a cup." He pulled up a chair while Billy took the coffee pot off the top of the pot-bellied stove and poured a mug of it for his friend. Matt accepted the cup and took a drink, then removed his hat and slouched down in the chair.

"You look a mite tired there, Matthew."

"I am. I been traipsin' all over Bodie, lookin' for one Nellie Bailey."

"Who's she?"

"A prostitute and a possible witness in the bank robbery case."

"How so?"

"The guy I arrested says he was with her all day, only she's nowhere to be found. She's hidin' out, and I don't know why."

"Was you perchance lookin' in Chinatown for her tonight?"

"Yeah. What makes you ask?"

Billy chuckled. "One a mah boarders come runnin' in here a few hours ago, all wide-eyed and opium drunk, said there'd been a major ruckus in Sing's den. Someone cleared the place out, there was fightin' and shootin'—you wouldn't happen to know nuthin' 'bout that, would you?"

"Maybe a little." Matt took another sip. "It wasn't all that exciting."

"Maybe not to you. But to everyone else it was."

"How's Pa?"

"Cantankerous."

"Like his mule, Bonehead?"

"Jus' like."

"In other words, he's—"

"Jus' fine."

"Is he sleepin'?"

"No. Miss Sarah's in with him now."

Matt raised his eyebrows, then leaned forward in his chair and lowered his voice. "Do you think I should say something to her tonight?"

"'Bout what?"

"C'mon, you know."

"Now's as good a time as any. You talk to you-know-who about it yet?"

"Yep. The last time I was in Bridgeport."

"Then what're you awaitin' for?"

Suddenly Matt heard a guitar being strummed and a female voice singing softly, coming from the direction of his father's room. He stood and walked softly on his gum-soled boots to the door, listening while drinking his coffee. Billy watched him silently, smiling a knowing smile, remembering when he had been newly in love.

Sarah finished singing and before Matt could move, the door opened. Sarah saw him, knew he had been listening, and blushed. Matt grinned.

"Evenin'. You sing very pretty, Sarah."

"Thank you." She nodded toward Matt's father. "He's still awake."

Matt went in but took Sarah by the arm and brought her back in with him.

"You two should be alone," Sarah said.

"Why? He dyin'?"

"No, I just—"

Matt caught a glimpse of Billy at the door, shaking his head and jerking his thumb toward the front of the building as he mouthed the word *outside*!

"Okay," Matt said, taking the hint. "But wait for me. I got something I want to talk to you about."

"All right, Matt." Sarah glided out of the room, casting Billy a puzzled look while he smiled and tried to act nonchalant.

Jacob Page was sitting up in bed, looking pale, but he brightened when he saw his son. Matt sat on the edge of his bed.

"I thought you fergot 'bout me, son."

"Been busy tryin' to solve your murder, only you're so stubborn you refused to die. Because of you a murderer won't turn out to be a murderer after all. How're you doin', anyway?"

Jacob rubbed his chin whiskers. "Well, let's see. I only got one arm an' I can't use it, had my leg busted so's I couldn't walk on it fer a few weeks, got shot in the chest th'other day . . . I'm fine. How're you?"

"I'll live."

"Glad to hear it."

"You gonna be up to testifyin' day after tomorrow?"

"Oh, I s'pose. You kin carry me in an' prop me up, an' I kin say my piece."

"I'm glad you weren't hurt more than you were."

"I'm glad he was such a lousy shot. A little more to the left an I'da been a goner." He paused and gazed wistfully at the door Sarah had just gone through. "Oh, Matt, I miss your ma."

Matt was stunned. It was the first time his father had mentioned her in that way. A tear came to Jacob's eye, and he turned his head to wipe it away. Matt said nothing, partly out of respect and partly because he didn't know what to say. In a few seconds his father, having composed himself, turned back toward his son.

"Well, if'n yer a done jawin', I want to git some shuteye!"

Matt got up. "Good night, Pa."

"Good night. Say, what is it yer gonna talk to Sarah about?"

Matt grinned. "Billy'll tell you."

"Humph!"

Matt strode out, found Sarah waiting patiently in the parlor. Grabbing her hand, he led her outside. As they stood in the dark under the stars and scattered clouds, she looked up at him dreamily.

"What is it?" she asked.

"I . . . I love you, Sarah." He grinned and blushed.

Sarah smiled but dropped her head to hide it, then looked back up at him with wet eyes and said, "I love you too, Matt. Have from the first day."

"By the pump? Nonsense. I was just a dirty drifter to you then."

"And I was just another girl by a well?"

"No, no. I could tell there was somethin' special about you."

"I felt the same about you," Sarah said.

They made eyes at each other for a moment then Matt got up the nerve to put his arms around her and give her a gentle hug. She yielded to him, relaxing her body against his, and put her cheek on his chest. After a moment of listening to his racing heart, she looked up into his face.

"Was that what you wanted to talk to me about?"

Matt unwound his arms, stepped back and watched the toe of his boot paw the ground, then examined something unusual under his fingernail.

"I . . . uh . . ."

"Matt? What is it?"

A sweat broke on Matt's forehead. Sarah noticed it, and her stomach tingled with anticipation. He took her hand. She noticed he was shaking. Just then a cloud drifted away from in front of the full moon, and its soft glow illuminated her face. Matt was nearly overwhelmed by the pale beauty of her skin and the deep blue of her eyes. He found himself staring at her.

"Matt?"

He took a deep breath. "Sarah . . . will you . . ." He paused and took off his hat, wiping his forehead with his sleeve. Sarah waited patiently for him to continue. "Will you . . . marry me?" There, he had done it. He exhaled heavily.

Sarah beamed, then threw her arms around him. "Yes, yes, I will, Matt. Oh, I love you." Matt just held her and smiled.

For a few luxurious moments they remained locked in each other's embrace, each having their own separate but intertwined thoughts about themselves, their prospective mate and their future. Matt recalled his mother and knew she would have been pleased with his choice. Sarah was everything his mother had been—in her own distinct way, of course—and the promise of a full life with her was more than a poor farm boy could have hoped for. He sent up a prayer of gratitude to God for blessing him with this woman.

Sarah loved him deeply. She had loved no other and knew that God had brought him to her. He was a good man, a strong man, with the courage of his convictions and an abiding sense of right and wrong. He had been brought up well, despite the absence of his father for so many years. Sarah hoped she'd meet his mother one day, in Glory.

Then a vision of her own parents broke through and startled her.

"Uh oh! What about my father?" she said suddenly, pulling away and looking up into Matt's face.

"What about him?"

"You should ask him about this. You know how he is."

"You're right, I do. That's why I asked him already."

"You did? When?"

"Last week. Remember when I took a ride to Bridgeport to deliver some papers?"

"I thought that was kind of funny, considering you could've sent them on the stage."

"Yeah, that was just an excuse. He said it was all right by him." He paused, then added, "You sure it's all right by you?" *Wouldn't hurt to make sure*, he thought.

"Of course," she said. "Of course."

Matt smiled and put his arm around her and squeezed. When he broke off he took Sarah's face in his hands.

"You're so beautiful!" he said quietly. He leaned toward her and kissed her softly. She kissed him back.

"Matt?" she said when they parted.

"Yeah?"

"What are tommyknockers?"

"Huh?" Matt shook his head to clear his ears, not believing what he had just heard.

"What are tommyknockers?" she repeated. "I heard some of

the miners in the boarding house talking about it earlier with your father. They were saying the tommyknockers were back."

"Oh, that's an old miner's superstition. The Cornish miners brought that with them from England. Tommyknockers are like . . . Oh, what are they? . . . Leprecauns, that's it. You know, little tiny men. Only they live in mines. They bang on things, cause accidents, steal tools, drop things down shafts . . . They're blamed for all the accidents in the mines. To keep them from causing trouble, the miners leave food and water for them. As long as they're happy, the mine is protected."

"But they're not real."

"No. The Cornish miners think so, but not many of the other men believe in them. But everyone plays along . . . just in case." Matt chuckled.

"So who eats the food?"

"What do you mean?"

"When the miners come back and the food they left is gone, who ate it? If the tommyknockers aren't real . . ."

"You got me," Matt admitted. "One of the miners probably sneaks back."

"Billy said they all swear they didn't."

Matt was perplexed. "Wait a minute. I thought we were speakin' in general. What're you talkin' about?"

"Billy said the tommyknockers have been eating the food and drinking the water and coffee they left. They all swear it wasn't them. But they refuse to post a watch. The tommyknockers won't come if they're being watched."

Matt suddenly looked as if he'd seen a ghost.

"Matt, what is it?"

"Where are these tommyknockers?"

"I don't know. Something about the abandoned section. They didn't say which mine."

"Only the Empire has an abandoned section. That's got to be it!"

"What?"

"Sarah, you're wonderful!"

Billy pulled up a chair next to Jacob's bed.

"What do *you* want?" Page asked. "Matt didn't mean you *had* to keep me company."

"Ah know. Ah wanted to talk to you."

"What about?"

"Well, Ah heard you say you missed your wife. Ah miss mine, too."

"What happened to her?"

"She got sick and died. The same thing that happens to all of 'em, I guess, sooner or later."

They were silent for a minute, then the big man spoke softly.

"Jacob, have you stopped and thought 'bout why all these accidents are happenin' to you?"

"Sure, I wondered 'bout it," Jacob admitted. "But I didn't waste a lot a time. They jes' happened."

"It don't bother you none?"

"Sure it bothers me. You know that. You hear all my complainin'."

"So what are you gonna do 'bout it?"

"What's to do? I can't stop 'em from happenin'."

"Maybe. Maybe not."

"Whaddya mean by that?"

"Don't you think someone's tryin' to get your attention?"

"Yeah? And who might that be?"

"Who brought you and Matt together?"

"Would you spit it out? I ain't in the mood for games!"

"Ah'm talkin' 'bout God, Jacob. He's been tryin' to git your attention since you and Matt met up."

"Why? What'd I ever do to God?"

"Nuthin'! That's the problem. It's high time you sided up with God so your son can have a good Christian father."

"What difference'll that make?"

"Well, Ah could tell you a lot a diff'rent things, but it all boils down to one. Where is Jacob Page gonna spend his eternity?"

"In Heaven, of course, if'n there is one. I lived a good life. He'll let me in."

"Well, Ah beg to differ with you, Jacob, but God don't keep score, weighin' the good you done against the bad. and it's a good thing, too, 'cause you'd lose. No suh, God only looks at one thing when he decides whose gettin' in and who ain't. Is Jacob Page covered by the blood?"

"Blood?"

"The blood a Jesus Christ. He died for your sins, Jacob. And now you don't have to go to Hell. You jus' have to give your life to Him."

"It's too late," Page said quietly. "That's somethin' I shoulda done a long time ago."

"That's the good part," Billy assured. "It ain't too late until you're pushin' up daisies. That's what Ah been tryin' to tell you. God has been workin' overtime tryin' to get you to understand that time is short. You could go any day. But you ain't dead yet. There's still a chance for you."

Jacob thought about that. "You say this Jesus Christ feller died for me, too?"

"Yep."

"Why?"

"I'm glad you asked, Jacob." He scooted his chair closer to the bed. "Let me tell you all about it."

CHAPTER

TEN

Matt ran off after escorting the bewildered Sarah to her room, telling her only that he'd explain the next day. He found Jensen at the attorney's home and quickly outlined his idea, then returned to the jail, checked on Bodine, and caught a few hours sleep.

When Matt got up it was still dark but wouldn't be for long. He met Jensen at the Empire Mine office per their arrangement, and they walked in together. Hiram Butler turned in his chair as they entered, surprised to see anyone so early.

"Deputy? Mr. Jensen? What's up? Kind of early, isn't it?"

"That it is," agreed Matt. He and Jensen both looked terrible, their eyes puffy from little sleep and their hair in disarray. "But I got a job to do, and I need your help."

"Coffee?" Butler asked, pointing to the pot on the stove in the corner.

"You betcha. Thanks," replied Matt. He walked over and poured two cups, giving one to Jensen. The lawyer still hadn't spoken. He wasn't used to getting up this early.

Matt took a long draw on the cup. "Great stuff, Mr. Butler."

"Thanks," Butler replied while lighting his pipe. "So, what's this job you got to do, and how can I help?"

"You know that fellah we have locked up for robbin' the bank?"

"*Do* I? He took my payroll!"

"Well, he claims he was with one of Bodie's doves all day, asleep."

"Likely story."

"All the same, I need to verify it. We don't want to send the wrong man to jail." He took another sip of his coffee. Butler waited patiently for him.

"Well," Matt went on, "I'm tryin' to find the girl. She took off, was gonna get on the stage, but somethin' scared her off. I think she's hidin' near town somewhere."

"What's that got to do with me?"

"She's layin' low, frightened, don't want to be found. I heard some of the miners are havin' trouble with a tommyknocker uprisin'."

"Let me get this straight. You think this gal's now a tommy-knocker?"

"In a manner of speaking. I think she may be hiding out in the abandoned section of your mine, acting the part of the tommy-knocker so the men would leave food and water."

"That's kind of a wild scheme!"

"It's all I got."

"But I suppose it can't hurt if we look," Butler relented. "What do you need?"

"Someone who knows the old, abandoned section to help us search."

"Thomas Wellman, he'd be the one. You remember Tom."

"Yeah. When's he comin' in?"

"He should be here anyti—" The door creaked open. "Here he is now, in fact."

Wellman came in, a little unnerved by the deputy's presence. He hadn't forgotten his part in the mine war and figured the deputy hadn't either.

"Now what'd I do?" he asked.

"Nothin' that I'm aware of," Page said. "We need your help."

Matt explained the situation to Wellman. When he finished Wellman shrugged.

"Be happy to help. Get me out of a day's work. Whaddya say, Mr. Butler?"

"Go ahead. I'm all for law enforcement. Especially if it gets my payroll back."

"Thank you," Matt said. He polished off his coffee and left the office with Jensen and Wellman in tow. As they made their way to the mine, Matt laid out his theory.

"That's interesting," Wellman said after Matt had finished. "If she could pull it off, she be able to live there for a long time. 'Course, she wouldn't be very comfortable, and she'd be plenty dirty. But if someone is scared, I expect they'd put up with a little discomfort."

"How many entrances to the old section?" Jensen asked, speaking for the first time.

Wellman laughed. "For a lawyer, you been awful quiet. I begun thinking you was a mute. There's only one outside entrance. It's boarded up. Inside, the crosscut connects to a new section about a hundred feet in. That's probably where the men are leavin' the food. They don't like venturing into the old section. A lot of the shoring has been removed, it ain't too safe." He turned to Matt. "Course, you and your pa know all about that."

Matt nodded. "So it's not blocked off inside?"

"No need," said Wellman. "We have no reason to go in there."

"So she could hide in there, sneak into the new section to take food and water left for the tommyknockers, then go back into hiding?"

"Easily."

"How could she see?" Jensen asked.

"She'd have to have a—wait a minute! One of the foremen asked for some additional lanterns the other day. Said a couple of 'em had disappeared!"

Matt considered the possibilities. They could stop the food and wait until she came out. No, that would take too long. Lying in wait for her would work, but he needed her today. The hearing would resume in the morning, and he wanted her there for it.

Wellman grabbed the deputy by the shoulder and pointed up the hill about two hundred feet.

"There."

Matt peered up the bluff into the shadows, trying to make out details. He could see a small, boarded-over opening in the side of the hill.

"How could she get up and down the shaft?" Jensen asked.

"There ain't a shaft in there," Wellman explained. "The old diggin's wasn't vertical. That's a drift, nice and level. There are some inclined crosscuts, but mostly it's pretty flat. We tapped it out horizontally before we started goin' down deep."

"Okay," Matt said. "Let's go."

They picked their way carefully up the rocky slope. The sun hadn't yet crested the ridge above them, but the hills to their backs were tipped in yellow, and there was enough light so they could see where they were going. Keeping off to the side in case Nellie happened to peek·out, they made their way quickly toward the opening.

"This may not be the time to tell you this," Jensen said, sucking in air, "but I'm not real big on crawling through confined spaces."

"Oh," Matt said. "Mr. Wellman, you got any ideas?"

"Yeah. We can leave him at the junction with the new section to make sure she doesn't slip away from us that way. That okay with you, Jensen?"

"Fine. Just make sure you pick me up on your way out."

"Stay put, then, and you'll be fine. We don't want you wanderin' off, gettin' hurt."

"Don't worry, I won't move an inch."

"What if she ain't in there, Deputy?" Wellman asked.

Matt shrugged. "Then I guess you've got real tommyknockers."

Wellman shook his head. "Miners," he muttered.

They crept up to the entrance. The boards were still in place, but several were loose and pivoted out of the way when pushed. Matt pointed to the soft dirt below their feet. There were shoe prints. Fresh, female shoe prints.

Wellman took the lead and whispered, "Don't say anything unless you have to. It echoes." He lit the lanterns they brought, pushed apart the boards, and stepped inside.

Jensen followed, Matt taking up the rear. The darkness engulfed them quickly, held off only by the dim glow of the flickering lanterns. Wellman picked his way carefully down the manmade tunnel, watching his step and feeling along the wall with his hands. When the ore car tracks had been pulled up for use elsewhere, the men doing the work weren't careful—no one was going to be here anymore, so they left the floor rough and debris-covered.

Matt checked the ground periodically, hoping to see some trace of the girl's footsteps. Every now and then Wellman would stop, hold his lantern aloft, and peer down a crosscut. Soon he came to one on his left. He motioned for Jensen to move in and stay put.

The deputy passed Wellman so he could inspect the floor before the miner tramped over it. He held the lantern at floor level so the light would cast shadows at the edge of the depressions in the dirt, making the footprints more visible. As he moved the lantern down, the young woman's footprints took shape almost magically. Matt pointed down the tunnel in the direction they led. Wellman nodded and once again took the lead.

They moved quickly now, the only sound the crunching of their shoes and the rustling of their pants. The lack of air circulation was stifling to Matt, an open-air man. The mine smelled pungent, moldy, and Matt imagined he was more out-of-breath than he actually was. The light from their lanterns was effective for only a few feet before the darkness swallowed it up. So short was its range that, if they ran, they could almost outdistance it.

Fifteen minutes into the mine from the junction, Wellman stopped abruptly and held his hand up, then motioned for Matt to move closer. He whispered in the deputy's ear.

"Her tracks go every which way. We'll have to split up or we could miss her. At the very least, it'll take all day."

"How can we know if the other has found her?"

"Try shouting . . . naw, that won't work. Besides, you might get lost." He paused. "No, we'll just have to keep going together. There's no safe way to do it quicker."

"Let me take a look," Matt said, kneeling. He inspected her shoe prints, then picked up a small object and peered at it closely in the dim light.

"What is it?" Wellman asked.

Matt handed it up to him. "A chicken bone. I think our tommyknocker is close by. Let's keep going."

Wellman nodded and let Matt move in front. Treading more slowly now, Matt saw that her tracks were less purposeful than they had been. He knew she had spent some time here and didn't just use this crosscut for travel.

They came to a fork. Wellman pointed to the right and gave Matt a hand motion indicating that there was no way out from there. Signaling Wellman to stay put, Matt went up ahead, only to return alone a few minutes later.

He nodded at Wellman. She had been staying there. She must be somewhere else in the mine at the moment, Matt reasoned, but he figured she was close. Unless she knew they were here.

They started up the main drift tunnel but hadn't gone ten feet when Matt stopped and crouched, and pulled the shade on his lantern closed. Wellman did the same, and they held their breath and listened. Footsteps. Then a faint glow from another lantern became visible, and she suddenly rounded the bend in front of them.

When she saw them she gasped and lost her grip on her lantern. It clattered to the floor and broke, and she was in darkness. Matt heard the rustling of her clothes and her retreating steps and quickly opened the shade on his lantern. She was gone.

"Wait!" Matt shouted. "We're here to help you!"

But there was no response.

Matt and Wellman, being taller than the girl, couldn't run in the low-ceilinged mine. They moved as quickly as they could and continued to shout.

"Nellie, please! Wait! It's Deputy Page. We won't hurt you. We're here to help. Please, no one will hurt you! Stop!"

Stooped over, he lumbered through the near-dark, trying to follow her and avoid the hazards on the floor at the same time. Once a loose stone sent him sprawling, and his chin raked the jagged floor, opening a wicked cut.

Wellman helped him up, and Matt ran on, oblivious to the pain and the blood. When they came to another fork, he stopped and got down on his hands and knees. Her tracks led into the smaller of the two passages. He listened. He could hear her. She was still within reach.

Wellman put his hand on Matt's shoulder.

"Be careful! This is a bad one. Lots of pits and debris. She can't go fast in here."

Matt nodded, but as he turned up the corridor he heard a faint scream, then silence. He moved forward suddenly, recklessly.

As he rounded a bend, he felt a hand on his arm. It gripped his elbow and abruptly jerked him back, pulling him down. Matt's lantern was knocked from his hand as he sprawled on the ground.

"Wha—?"

"Sorry, Deputy," Wellman said from the ground beside Matt. "I tried to call you, but you wouldn't listen. Look over there." Wellman held his lantern up. Just a few steps away was a rough pit that stretched across most of the floor. Matt crawled over to it, reaching for Wellman's lantern.

"Some men dug up the floor in here in a last-ditch attempt to salvage the tunnel and their work, hoping to find something."

Matt rolled onto his stomach and crawled to edge of the pit, holding the lantern while Wellman held the deputy's feet. The floor in front of the pit sloped downward and the rocks under the deputy were loose. The pit was a good eight feet deep, and on the rough, boulder-strewn floor lay Nellie Bailey.

She was not moving.

CHAPTER

ELEVEN

Let go and take the lantern!" Matt ordered. Wellman released his grip on the deputy's ankles, and he scampered over the edge, dropping into the pit beside the girl. Wellman held the lantern high, giving Matt as much light as possible.

Matt crawled quickly over to the girl.

"How is she?" Wellman shouted.

"She's still breathing!" He leaned down to her and patted her face. "Nellie!" He stroked her cheek and slowly her eyes flickered open. As Matt came into focus, a look of fear crossed her face, and her eyes widened.

"Don't be afraid, Nellie. I'm the deputy. No one's going to hurt you." He brushed the hair out of her face. "Where's it hurt?"

"M-my ankle." She had to force the words out.

Matt scooted down and carefully checked her legs. "The right one's a little swollen. Looks broke, but you'll be okay. You hurt anywhere else?"

She closed her eyes and opened them again. "I-I don't know." Matt felt her head. There was blood on his fingers when he withdrew them. Nellie's eyes fluttered.

Oh, no, I'm losing her! "Nellie! Stay awake!" She struggled to keep her eyes open and Matt moved closer to her face. "I'm gonna take you to your mother. Please, help me. Were you with a young man the other day?"

Her brow furrowed momentarily, then she nodded once, very slightly.

"Was he in your crib the whole day?"

She tried speaking, but Matt could not make out her words. He put his ear next to her mouth.

"A . . . cowboy paid me to . . . give . . . sleeping drink . . ." She stopped and took a breath. "Then he . . . come after me . . . I ran . . ." She struggled to breathe.

Matt was puzzled. If she gave Bodine a drug to make him sleep, how did she see him coming after her? Is that why she fled the stage office? He leaned down to ask her, but her open, glassy eyes told him he would not be answered.

"*No!*" he cried.

"What is it?" Wellman shouted over the edge.

Matt stared at her eyes as a tear ran freely down his dirty cheek.

"Deputy Page? What's going on?"

"She's gone."

"Gone? You mean dead?"

Matt sighed and looked up. "I'm afraid so. She hit her head when she fell."

Matt moved to a sitting position beside the girl, his arms across his knees and his head on his arms, remembering the morning he found his mother, cold and stiff in her bed. This was not what he had wanted. She wasn't supposed to get hurt. Why hadn't she stopped when he told her? What had he done? How would he face Rosa? He remembered the man who commited suicide rather than let Matt capture him. He felt bad, real bad, that day. But he got over it, realizing he had just been doing his job, that the man had made his own decision, taking the easy way out to avoid prison or the gallows. Matt wasn't responsible.

This time, though, he had failed. The one person who could solve the mystery was now dead, and it was his fault.

"C'mon," urged Wellman. "Let's get her outta here."

Matt didn't respond. He suddenly didn't have the energy to stand, much less climb out of the pit. He wanted to put off having to face the girl's mother for as long as possible. But a still, small voice within him told him to be of good courage, to take heart. Christ would be with him.

It wasn't really a voice, as such. Matt didn't hear anything. The words just seemed to pass through his mind of their own accord, and at first, he didn't know where they came from. Then the image of his mother presented itself, and he recalled hearing those words from her as she read the Bible the day they got word from the army that his father was dead, killed by a rebel bullet at Vicksburg.

"Matt? You all right?" It was Wellman again.

"Yeah, I'm fine."

Matt pushed himself up reluctantly, then looked down at the dead girl and up at Wellman to assess the situation. He stepped over her with his left foot and put his hands under her arms, pulling her limp body up as he stood. He propped her against the pit wall which positioned her face next to his.

Her unseeing eyes stared into his, questioning the unfairness of life. For the first time, Matt noticed how pretty she could have been without the ugliness of her lifestyle that had hardened her features. And so young!

Matt lifted her arms so Wellman could grab her wrists, then hoisted her by her waist. Wellman pulled her up and scooted back as Matt lifted, and in a few moments, she was out of the pit. Matt replaced his hat that had fallen off when he landed in the pit and stuck it down tight on his head. He looked for a way out.

"Get a runnin' start," Wellman advised. "When you jump I'll grab you, and you can swing you leg up over the side."

Matt tried, but Wellman's grip didn't hold. He tried again. The miner held fast this time, and Matt clambered out of the pit. Without comment, he picked up the girl and carried her, which allowed Wellman, carrying both lanterns, to lead him out.

They had covered more ground while chasing her than Matt had realized, and it took them a good half hour to reach Jensen's position. The lawyer saw their light and started to shout.

"Did you find—?"

Then Matt came into view, and Jensen knew something was terribly wrong.

"Is she . . . ?"

"Yes." Matt's reply was short and to the point. He kept walking. Jensen followed without further comment.

At the entrance, Wellman held the boards aside as Matt ducked through with Nellie. Jensen stepped out into the sun and put his arm up to shade his eyes. Matt stopped finally to get a rest and set his load down carefully. He sat next to her and looked up at the attorney.

"She ran from us, fell into a pit, and banged her head. Nothing we could do."

"I'm sorry." Jensen paused a proper length of time before asking, "Did she say anything before she died?"

Matt repeated her last words to Jensen. The attorney removed his hat and scratched his head. "If she gave him something to put him asleep, how could she see him a short time later, coming to the stage office?"

"You talkin' 'bout that kid that robbed the bank?" Wellman asked.

"Yes," Jensen answered.

"How do you s'pose she figgered he was headed to the stage office? Seems more likely she saw him headed to the bank, which is next door to the stage office, and just *thought* he was after her."

"You know, you could be right," Matt conceded.

"And not only that," Wellman continued, "I don't think you need to figure out how he could be there if he was unconcious."

"Why not?"

"Because he couldn't have been there if he was asleep someplace else. It just makes sense. It had to be someone else. Someone wearing his clothes."

Matt looked up at Wellman, thunderstruck. "By jiggers!" he shouted. "It's so obvious! Of course, that's it! Bodine didn't go to the bank. Someone else did and wanted us to think it was Bodine. He was framed!"

"That's what Bodine's been saying," Jensen pointed out.

"It was them two cowboys that rode in with—cowboys!" said Matt. "Nellie said a cowboy paid her to give Bodine the sleepin' potion. She'd know a cowboy from a miner or anyone else."

Wellman was thoughtful. "Say, Deputy, how'd you know she was in there? You know, hiding in the mine?"

Matt shrugged. "It was mostly a guess. Most of her clients were miners. I'm sure they did some talkin' when they were with her. She probably heard the men tellin' stories about tommyknockers."

Wellman nodded. The men were silent for a time before Jensen broke it.

"I'm gonna go talk to Bodine." He put on his hat and started down the hill.

"Do you need some help with her?" Wellman asked Page.

"No, Tom. Thanks. I'm gonna take her to her mother. Could you see that this gets boarded up once and for all? And give Mr. Butler my regards. I'm obliged to you both for your help. I owe you one."

Wellman looked Page in the eye. "Deputy, I never said anything before, but I owed you. You saved my bacon last year. I was ready to let that Reb incite me to do battle with the Queen Anne. I could have lost some friends' lives, maybe even my own. If I helped you today, I'm glad I could do it."

Matt extended his hand. Wellman took it.

"Thank you, Tom," Matt said. "I count you as a friend."

They broke off, and Matt bent over to pick up the girl, then carried her down the hill in silence as Wellman headed off to the Empire office. Matt paid no heed to the stares of the townsfolk as he walked down Main Street with the dead prostitute in his arms. A dog ran after him, barking, but was sent away by a nudge from the lawman's boot.

He turned up King Street and went directly to Nellie's crib. By the time he had pushed the door open with his foot and had laid her gently on the bed, her mother had gotten word via the grapevine and was hefting her bulk quickly up the street.

As she darkened the doorway, Matt turned.

"I'm sorry," he said, removing his hat. "She was hidin' out in an abandoned mine, and when we went in to fetch her, she got spooked. I tried callin' her, tellin' her it was okay, but she fell into a pit, bumpin' her head. There was nothin' I could do. I'm awful sorry." Matt's eyes and throat hurt from choking back the tears. It wouldn't do for the local constable to be blubbering. He could do that later, when he was alone.

Rosa moved slowly to the bed, wringing her hands. She cried as she stroked her daughter's waxen cheeks, wiping her own tears with bare fingers, then stood up straight and bit her lower lip as a spasm shook her body.

"Thank you for finding her, Deputy. I never wanted my daughter to grow up like I did, but I was desperate and couldn't help it. It's just as well that she's dead."

Another shadow filled the door. Matt turned to see Sarah. She walked quietly up to him.

"Mr. Jensen told me," she said, answering the question in Matt's eyes. "You go on. I'll stay here with her." She turned to the woman as Matt retreated.

"What about you, Rosa?" Sarah asked. "It's not too late for you."

"What do you know about it?" the madam spat at the young, virtuous woman. "You never endured hardship."

Sarah didn't defend herself. "God didn't send His Son to change your past," she answered quietly. "He wants to change your future."

As Rosa regarded Sarah with tear-filled, questioning eyes, Matt backed out of the room and walked to the jail, suddenly realizing how tired he was.

Matt dreamed he was being kissed, very lightly, on the cheek. He smiled in his dream, then the vision began receding, and he became aware of himself. He was groggy, still tired, and wondered why he was waking up. His neck was stiff.

As his eyes slowly opened and adjusted to the artificial light, he recognized an out-of-focus face near his, smiling.

"Sarah?" She kissed him again on the cheek, and Matt remembered he was in his office.

"I guess I fell asleep."

"Poor dear," she sympathized.

"How's Rosa?" he asked, taking his feet off the desk and twisting his head to extremes, relieving the tension and working out the kinks.

"It hit her hard," Sarah said. "But she listened to what I told her about God. She has something to think about in her grief, a little hope for herself. I told her I'd help her with the funeral arrangements."

"How'd she react to that?"

"Suspicious. The prostitutes don't get much consideration from the *good* women in town, as a rule. Especially when it comes to burials. It's not right to treat people like that."

Matt took Sarah's hand and inspected it closely. It was pretty and smooth, but the palm was callused. He didn't care. She was a hard worker, and that was good. He rubbed the back of her hand absentmindedly.

"You're on the right track to change all that," he told her

"Well, I'd like to, but the married women won't listen much to me. They don't want the doves mixing with them."

"Understandable, I suppose," Matt said. "They've got to figure some of their men been with 'em. And no sense danglin' temptation in their face, anyways."

Sarah sighed. "Maybe Rosa will at least change her ways."

"I'll tell you, Sarah, you better have some idea what to replace it with. She needs an income. And don't get too vocal about reforming all of 'em. Half the men in town'll be mad at you."

Sarah laughed. "I'll work quietly. It's more effective that way, anyway. And I need some help in the Quicksilver. If she can't cook, I'll teach her." She leaned down and kissed Matt on the forehead. "Why don't you go get some sleep. You need to be ready for tomorrow. I'm going to see your pa before I go to bed myself. I'll say hello for you."

Matt grinned proudly as she left.

CHAPTER

TWELVE

The echo of Judge Wadell's gavel resounded throughout the courtroom.

"Let's have some order in here, gents. Sit down and be quiet!"

The spectators simmered down and settled into their seats. Wadell rapped a couple more times, silencing the humming and hissing, then spoke to the two attorneys.

"Is everyone ready, including Jacob Page?"

Pete Jensen, with Bodine seated beside him, nodded. "Yes, sir, Your Honor. We're ready. Mr. Page is here."

Pat Kelly echoed, "Us too, Your Honor."

"Good. Let's get started. I want to finish this hearing today. Mr. Kelly, since we delayed Mr. Jensen's first witness until today, and his witness was someone you were going to call, if you gents don't mind, I'll go ahead and give Mr. Kelly first crack at him. Okay with you, Pete?"

"Certainly, sir."

"Go ahead then, Kelly."

"Thank you, Your Honor." Kelly looked around the room until he saw the elder Page. "I call Jacob Page to the stand."

Page stood hesitantly, helped by Uncle Billy, and hobbled slowly to the witness chair. He was sworn in and took his seat, falling rather heavily into the chair, wincing in pain. Everyone in the room held their breath, and when Jacob sighed momentarily, the rest of the room exhaled with him.

"Mr. Page, would you state your occupation?"

"Mining superintendent and owner."

"Does your mine have an account at the Bodie Bank?"

"Does Bonehead have big ears?"

Page smiled, the crowd laughed, and Judge Wadell banged on the table.

"Do me a favor," the judge told him. "Try answering the questions without your usual wit. I'd like to get out of here before first snowfall."

Page shrugged. "Sorry, Judge. It was a dumb question. Bodie only has one bank."

"You'll find that lawyers ask a lot of dumb questions. It's their job, and they're good at it." He smiled so everyone could laugh, and everyone did, except Kelly and Jensen. Wadell cranked his head toward the attorneys.

"Gentlemen, let me remind you, this ain't a trial, just a hearing. Indulge me a little and just get to the good parts. Go ahead, Mr. Kelly."

"Thank you, Your Honor. Mr. Page, when you were in the bank the day of the robbery, did you get a good look at the man who shot you?"

"Well, mostly."

"What do you mean 'mostly'?"

"I saw everything but his face."

"It was covered?"

"Yep. By a bandanna. Jes' like the one that feller's wearin'." He pointed at Bodine who still wore his bandanna around his neck. A murmur passed through the spectators.

"Mr. Page, can you tell us what happened when you were first shot?"

"Well, I tried sneakin' inta my pocket fer my gun, and the man turned and plugged me a coupla times."

"He tried to kill you?"

"Oh yeah. But he was a lousy shot."

Bodine tugged at Jensen's sleeve and whispered something to him. Jensen scratched out a note while Kelly continued and passed it to Matt, who read in disbelief.

"So he was trying to murder you, but you were saved only because the robber was not an experienced marksman."

"I don't believe I said that, Mr. Kelly. What I said was, he's a lousy shot."

"What's the difference?"

"One's quality, the other's quantity. You can be a good shot and never kilt a person, or you can be a fair-to-lousy shot and git into lotsa scrapes. Course, you'd have to be lucky, too." He grinned.

"All right," Kelly said, perturbed. "Thank you for clarifying that. The point is, though, that he meant to kill you."

"Yep. No doubt about it."

"Mr. Page," Kelly said as he moved slowly toward the witness chair, "please take a good look at the defendant, Mr. Josh Bodine, then tell me: Is he the man who robbed the bank and shot you?"

Page peered at Bodine, looking him up and down. Tension was high in the room as everyone waited for Page to do what three others had already done: identify Bodine as the robber.

"Well?" Kelly prompted.

"That's why he's here, ain't it?"

"Mr. Page," interrupted Wadell, "we're trying to determine that. It hasn't been decided. All we're asking is for you to tell us if Mr. Bodine is the man who shot you in the bank. Don't pay no mind to what anyone else says."

"Okay. No, he ain't the man."

There was stunned silence in the courtroom. Kelly's sardonic smile had turned into a gape. Slowly heads began bobbing and mouths started flapping, until the crowd was talking out loud, and some men even moved around. Wadell rapped his gavel repeatedly.

"Quiet, men, quiet down!" He rapped more and Matt got up and waded through the gallery, sitting the men down and shutting them up. Finally, when things were settled, Kelly was allowed to continue.

"Mr. Page," he said almost sternly, "are you telling us that Josh Bodine, the accused, is not the man that robbed the bank and shot you?"

"That's what I said."

"Others have testified that he is."

"I heerd from my son that they identified his clothes and his horse and some other stuff," Page said indignantly. "But nobody has identified *him*!"

"How can you be so sure it wasn't him?"

"See them boots?" He pointed at Bodine's feet, and those who could, craned their necks to look at them. "Them are miner's boots. And small ones at that." With much difficulty Page raised one of his legs so all could see it clearly. "They's jes' like mine, see? Miner's boots."

"So?" Kelly asked.

"So," Page continued, putting his leg down, "the man what shot me was wearin' cowboy-type boots. You know, pointy toe, high heel worn way down on the outside, lots of stitchin' all over it. And they was big. He had big feet, what couldn't a fit in that feller's boots."

As another murmur coursed through the onlookers, Kelly sat down, defeated. "No further questions."

"Mr. Jensen?" Wadell asked.

"I have no questions of Mr. Page, Your Honor."

"I waited two days so you could have no questions?"

"Mr. Kelly asked them all for me, Your Honor."

The men in the gallery that had been so sorry for the beginner Mr. Jensen a few days before, now completely enjoyed this turnaround as the young attorney had bettered his more experienced counterpart and did so without asking a single question.

"Very well," Wadell sighed. "You may step down, Mr. Page." As Matt moved forward to help his father, Wadell kept talking. "Mr. Kelly, do you have any more witnesses?"

"No, Your Honor. The prosecution rests."

"Okay, Mr. Jensen. You're on."

"Thank you, Your Honor. I'd like to ask the court's indulgence, if I may—"

"Not another delay, Counselor."

"No, sir. I want to call the defendant, not to give oral testimony, but to give a demonstration, one that will prove his innocence."

"This is highly irregular. What is it you want him to do?"

"You recall that Mr. Page referred to the robber as a lousy shot. I recall Mr. Bjorgen calling Mr. Bodine a good shot. I want to give

Mr. Bodine the chance to prove who's right, while proving himself innocent at the same time."

"You aim to give him a gun?"

"Three shots, Your Honor. That's all we ask."

"I object!" shouted Kelly. "We can't give a loaded gun to a man on trial!"

"How else are we going to prove the point?" Jensen countered.

The crowd began arguing both sides, and Wadell nearly broke his gavel, he was pounding so hard.

"Deputy!"

Matt jumped up. "Yessir?"

"Can you control him?"

"Yessir. If he does anything he ain't supposed to, I'll shoot him."

"Okay," relented Wadell. "Kelly, you're overruled. Let's do this thing outside in an orderly fashion. Matt, you stick to Bodine like mud on a boot."

Matt took Josh outside while Jensen ran to the jail and retrieved Bodine's gunbelt, which was locked in Matt's cabinet. The men from the gallery filed out the side door into the alley and followed Wadell out behind the building. The judge set three bottles on a rock about twenty feet behind the building.

Matt positioned Bodine, and Jensen ran up with the gun.

"Okay, Deputy. That's a bit farther than the robber was from your pa. At my signal, Bodine will draw and fire three rounds."

Matt handed Josh's gunbelt to him. He strapped it on, then checked the gun. It was fully loaded. He slid it back into the holster then nodded, somewhat apprehensively, to Matt.

"We're ready, Your Honor," the deputy declared.

Wadell took out a handkerchief and held it in the air. "When I drop the handkerchief, you draw and fire before it hits the ground. That should give you more than enough time."

Bodine nodded, then fixed his eyes on the bottles. He flexed his hand. The crowd was silent. Matt watched Bodine's hand closely. A sweat broke out on Jensen's face. The handkerchief was released.

Immediately Bodine drew and fired three successive rounds. All three bottles exploded into a small rain of glass, and the spectators to a man hunched their shoulders or jerked their heads at the noise. Before the handkerchief had touched the ground Josh had holstered the gun, unbuckled the gunbelt, and handed it to Matt. The onlookers exploded in a cheer.

Jensen's voice rose above the din of the crowd. "No further questions, Your Honor!"

"Mr. Kelly?"

Kelly just waved off the judge and plodded back to the courtroom.

"Very well," shouted Wadell. "Shall we go back inside and get this finished up?" He moved quickly back to the courtroom followed by the chattering crowd.

Once they were all settled, Wadell spoke to Jensen. "Any more witnesses, Counselor?"

"Just one, Your Honor. I'd like to recall Deputy Page to the stand."

This prompted a murmur from the spectators. The defense was calling the man who arrested Bodine to testify in his behalf! What could this mean?

Matt stepped up and raised his right hand.

"No need for that," Wadell said. "You were sworn in the other day. I reckon it's still good."

Matt eased himself into the chair. Jensen stood.

"Deputy Page, this hearing is to determine whether or not the man you arrested, Mr. Josh Bodine, should be held for trial for robbing the bank and shooting your father. Is that your understanding?"

"Yessir."

"Do you have a personal stake in the outcome of this hearing?"

"What do you mean?"

"Are you determined that Mr. Bodine end up in prison?"

"No, sir."

"Why not?'

"I'm concerned that justice be served. I want the true robber brought to justice. If it's Mr. Bodine, fine. If not, then I'll have to keep lookin'."

"And if it's not Mr. Bodine, will you lose face for having arrested him by mistake?"

"Why should I? Nobody here would have done any different under the circumstances, including you and Mr. Bodine."

"You've heard some testimony, including your own, which paints a pretty bleak picture for the defendant."

"It's not as bleak as it used to be."

"No, that it isn't. But there are still some circumstances that point the finger at Bodine. Would you agree with that statement?"

"Yes, I would."

"With that in mind, you being the law officer in this town, what have you been doing the past couple days to find the answers to the questions that have been raised?"

"I've been trying to check out his story."

"How?"

"I've been lookin' for the girl he says he was with that day."

"The prostitute?"

"Yessir."

"Did you find her?"

"Well, yessir."

"And what did she say?"

"I object!" Kelly interrupted. "That's hearsay. The girl can testify for herself."

Judge Wadell started to rule. "Objection sust—"

"She can't!" interrupted Matt.

"What do you mean?" Wadell asked.

"Uh . . . she had an accident. She fell and hit her head. She's dead, Your Honor."

"You were there when it happened?"

"Yessir. So was Thomas Wellman from the Empire."

"And you talked to her before she died?"

"Yes, Your Honor."

"Well, I want to hear what she had to say, if it'll help me make a decision on this matter. I'm going to overrule your objection, Pat. Dying declarations are gospel in a court of law, as you know. Go ahead, Deputy. Answer the question."

"Well, she told me that a cowboy paid her to give Bodine something to make him sleep."

Bodine jumped up. "That's why I don't remember!" he shouted.

Wadell rapped his gavel as the room buzzed. "Sit down, Mr. Bodine. You men in the gallery, clam up or I'll clear the room!"

He spit, not even trying to hit the spittoon. "Anything else, Deputy?"

"Only that when she was in the stage depot, preparing to skip town, she saw him through the window, thought he was headed after her, so she ran and hid."

"But you found her."

"Yessir."

"So Mr. Bodine *wasn't* in the crib all afternoon," Wadell concluded.

"Well sir," Matt said slowly. "There's the problem. The man she saw through the window is the man who robbed the bank, and if Bodine was drugged, it had to be someone else . . . wearin' his clothes."

"Except, as your pa said, not wearin' his boots."

"Because the bank robber couldn't fit in Bodine's boots."

Jensen had sat down. Wadell was doing fine without him.

"Mr. Kelly, do you have anything else to add?"

Kelly just slumped in his chair and shook his head.

"Well, then," Wadell said. "If Mr. Page is certain that the defendant is not the robber, and this young woman said, just before she died, that she drugged Bodine, I can see no reason to hold Mr. Bodine any longer. It is the opinion of this court that Josh Bodine did not rob the bank and did not shoot Jacob Page—for which Mr. Page should be greatful. Sir, you are free to go. Deputy, you've got your work cut out for you." He rapped the gavel and got up. "Let's retire to the Highgrade. First round's on me."

The men in the gallery let out a simultaneous whoop and scattered, clearing the room in a minute. Josh slouched in his chair and closed his eyes while Jensen beamed and slapped him on the back.

"You're free to go, son!"

Bodine looked sick. "Go where? I'm broke. You got my horse and saddle and gun as payment for defending me."

Jensen looked at his hands. "You can keep them, son. To be honest, when I made that deal I didn't think I had a chance of saving you. I thought you wouldn't be needing them."

"I figgered the same thing, Mr. Jensen, but a deal's a deal. I don't want to owe you. If it's all the same, maybe I'll buy them back from you someday."

"Have it your way, Josh." He stood. "Come on, I'll buy you

lunch. Matt!" Jensen shouted to the deputy who was across the room talking to his father. "Meet me at the Quicksilver in fifteen minutes. Bring your father, if he's up to it."

Matt nodded and waved, and helped his father out the side door while Bodine watched them in silence.

Jensen went over to Kelly and extended his hand. Kelly took it with a wry grin.

"Good job," the experienced attorney told Pete.

"Sorry I had to be the one to break your string."

"You didn't."

"No? How do you figure that?"

"I'm prosecuting the case of the Bodie bank robbery. When young Page brings in the real robbers I'll begin round two. This was just a warm-up. My record is intact."

"Sir," Jensen said, plucking his bowler from his head, "any lawyer who can turn defeat into victory that easily is an honor to his profession."

CHAPTER

THIRTEEN

That night, at the suggestion of Sarah Taylor, Uncle Billy sponsored a celebration dinner for Josh Bodine. Josh had hung around the Quicksilver much of the afternoon after lunch, not knowing what to do. She'd had a good talk with him, but he couldn't be convinced to return to his father's house.

"I burned my bridges," he had told her. So she left him with some words of encouragement, and he hiked up Bodie Bluff to think.

The mood around the dinner table that evening was joyous, for the most part. Josh was relieved to have been exonerated for the robbery, and he was more than a little perplexed to find that he had a friend in Matt Page.

Sarah listened intently as the men retold the tale of the trial and the adventures of the past few days. Uncle Billy marveled at Josh's prowess with a gun, and Sarah and several of the men cried when Matt told the tale of Nellie Bailey. Jensen was congratulated heartily for a successful beginning to his career.

O'Hara had given Bodine a room for the night after talking him out of leaving town on foot. He told the young man, "You ain't the first man to get free room and board, and you'll not be the last. Stop bein' so proud."

While they were enjoying Sarah's peach pie, Jacob Page, with his mouth full, put a question to Josh.

"So, whatcha gonna do now, boy?"

Bodine stared into the steam swirling across the top of his coffee. "I don't know. I just don't know."

"I understand you have minin' experience. You could put in a application at one a the mines. Course, no one can guarantee you gettin' a job. There's a lotta men outta work here. They started streamin' in a few months ago, and they never stopped. Every mornin' there's a line a men, waitin' fer jobs."

"Naw, I don't think so, Mr. Page," Josh replied. "I swore to myself I'd never set foot in a mine again. I'll head north, get a new start somewhere. That's what I set out to do in the first place. Only difference now is, I don't have any money. Don't go takin' that wrong. I ain't lookin' for a handout."

"You could stay here in Bodie," Sarah suggested. "I'm sure there's something you could do. Someone'll hire you."

Bodine shook his head. "Thanks, but I just don't feel like Bodie is for me. Too many bad memories, if you can understand that."

"Makes sense," Matt agreed.

"Too bad," Billy offered. "Ah think you'd do well here, but if you got to move on, you got to." He said it with finality then turned to Matt. "Where d'ya s'pose them cowboys went?"

Matt shrugged. "I don't have a clue. Josh told me they said they were headed north. I'm guessin' they'll head to Reno with all their loot, or maybe San Francisco, or Lake Tahoe."

"Sounds reasonable," agreed Jensen. "But they've got several days' head start on you. You'd have a tough time catching them even if you knew where they were headed."

"I got their names," Matt said. "I can send out wanted posters."

"Them are prob'ly aliases," Billy pointed out. "Two men ridin' together, one named Smith, both with Ezra for a first name. Think about it, Matthew. Here's two men, former cowboys by their dress, hangin' around on the Aurora to Bodie road, waylayin' lone riders. Sound familiar?"

Matt looked at Billy, startled. "You mean the Reb? They're the ones?"

"It's likely. No one was onto them. Ah think Ah seen 'em before, the way Joshua described 'em. They finally made their haul, and now they gone north, like you said. Ah think you're right about that."

"Well, then I'll just have to go north and play it by ear."

"Do you have to go?" It was Sarah. "I know I'm being selfish, but maybe . . . maybe the sheriff can send someone else."

"No, Sarah. It's my responsibility. It happened in my town."

"Y'ain't gone' alone, are you?" Jacob Page asked.

"If I have to. I'll stop in and see the sheriff. Maybe he can send someone—"

Matt was interrupted by a man bursting through the boarding house doors.

"Deputy! Nixon and McDougal are at it again! They're gittin' ready to fight over to the Highgrade!"

The man ran back out, not wanting to miss any of the fun, and Matt pushed himself away from the table. He started toward the door but stopped to question Billy.

"I thought Nixon was in jail in Bridgeport."

"He got out yesterday," O'Hara explained. "Come into town peaceful enough but realized it had changed a mite since he was here last. He come here lookin' for a room, found out Ah didn't have one for him, and he didn't have no job, neither. Sorry Ah didn't tell you, but you was so busy . . ."

"That's okay, Billy. No problem." The lawman walked out, sighing.

"I guess I'll get on over there, too," Jensen said, downing his coffee as he stood. "Someone'll need me."

Matt could hear the shouting and cheering as he neared the saloon. The windows were intact, so far. He pushed open the batwings and waded through the crowd, raising howls of protest from the men he jostled. The spectators had formed the usual circle around the combatants and were placing their bets.

Nixon and McDougal had squared off against each other, their fists raised. Neither had a weapon. They moved about, circling each other warily and challenging each other to throw the first blow. The spectators cheered them on.

Matt was closest to McDougal, but the wiry Scotsman hadn't seen the deputy, his gaze fixed on his opponent. Matt grabbed

McDougal by the shoulder, and the small man abruptly wheeled and threw a hard left blindly into the deputy's jaw, decking him.

Too late, he recognized his victim and stood immobile, suddenly afraid for his rash act. Nixon saw his opportunity. With McDougal's attention distracted, Nixon ran forward and tackled him. They fell hard to the floor, their fall broken by the body of the stunned deputy who was already there.

The blow to Matt's face had surprised him, and he lost his balance and went down. He was angry now, for although his tooth problem had long since healed and stopped hurting, the memory was still fresh, and he didn't want the loss of another. But no sooner had he hit the wooden, sawdust-covered floor than a ton of bricks was dropped on top of him. He flashed back to the fight with Bart Monroe, and the deputy's survival instinct took over. He twisted his body and pushed, and the two combatants rolled off and continued grappling with each other.

Matt was mad now, and as his head cleared, he hefted himself to a kneeling position, fire in his eyes. Nixon and McDougal rolled in an embrace, coming to rest finally with Nixon on top. McDougal had Nixon's lapels in both his hands, and Nixon grabbed McDougal by the throat and brought his arm back to deliver a blow.

Page lunged and grabbed Nixon's arm. McDougal slithered out from under the Irishman and tried to take advantage of the deputy's grip on his foe. Matt saw it coming, though, and deflected McDougal's punch, then grabbed him by the neck. As the three struggled to stand, Matt placed himself between them and moved his grip on Nixon to the man's neck.

Matt choked them both in an attempt to end their struggling. They were so intent on pounding each other, it hadn't occurred to either of them to try escaping the deputy. When their pace didn't let up, Matt suddenly released his grip on them and stepped back. As he expected, they lunged toward each other. Matt quickly put his hands on the backs of their heads and gave their forward motion some help, knocking their heads together.

The spectators moaned in sympathy as the combatants' heads cracked like coconuts, and they crumpled to the floor. They did not move. Sawdust clung to their clothes. Large goose eggs formed on both their foreheads. Matt ordered several men to pick them up.

They hastily complied, fearing the same fate from the intense law-man, and carted them off to the jail.

Matt locked the front door behind him as he stepped out of the jail, both prisoners securely tucked into their private cells, nursing headaches. The lawman said a few words to Jensen, then heard a horse whinny behind him. He turned to see a familiar sorrel, ridden by his Paiute friend.

"Charlie Jack!" Matt shouted. "What brings you to Bodie?"

"Horse," said the Indian.

Matt started laughing, but his jaw hurt and he grabbed it. "C'mon down. Everyone's at Uncle Billy's."

Charlie Jack slid off the back of his mount and led it silently across the street to the boarding house. He left the horse beside the rail, untied, and followed Matt inside. The animal stayed put.

"How'd it go, son?" asked Jacob. "Anyone hurt—hey! Lookee here! It's Charlie Jack!"

When Josh saw the Indian come in behind Matt, he reached for his gun, remembering as he grabbed air that he had given it to Jensen. Instead, he jumped out of his chair, upended a table, and ducked down behind it.

Everyone stared at Josh, some of them snickering, then greeted the Paiute, who nodded once for the entire room. He wandered toward the kitchen, cast a puzzled look at the hunkering Bodine, and headed for the pine nuts.

Matt sat down after pouring himself a cup of coffee.

"That's an Indian!" Bodine said in hushed tones, as though the others hadn't noticed and were in great peril. He picked himself up and righted the table.

"Yeah? So?" Matt asked.

"You talk to him like he's your friend."

"That's 'cause he is," said Jacob Page.

"Didn't you notice the Indians hangin' around town?" Billy asked.

"No," answered Bodine slowly. "Just the one in front of the tobacco shop."

"They're all over," Sarah said.

Josh looked puzzled. "They in disguise or something?"

Matt laughed. "Most of them wear regular clothes and hats. Some wrap themselves in blankets."

"You don't worry about your . . . scalps?"

"Only when Billy trims my hair," laughed Jacob. "And he ain't no Injun!"

Charlie Jack returned from the kitchen with a handful of nuts.

"So where have you been, Charlie Jack?" Matt asked.

"Kitchen," he said. "Matt's memory taking slow ride."

"I mean in the past few months. We haven't seen you for a while."

"Oh. Charlie Jack visit family and digs in what you call Slinkard Valley."

"Slinkard Valley? Ain't that up west of Coleville?"

The Paiute nodded.

"I didn't know you had digs there," Matt said. "To tell the truth, I never thought about where you actually lived. I just figured you roamed around all the time."

"I live here." He swept his arm broadly indicating that his home was the countryside. "Have digs, family, Slinkard."

"I'd like to see it sometime."

"Someday."

"Oh, I—say, Charlie, could you ride with me tomorrow? I'm going north, trying to track a couple cowboys who robbed the Bodie Bank."

The Indian ate a handful of nuts. "Two men? Cowboy? Rob bank?"

"That's right."

"Have much money?"

"Yeah, and gold!" said Bodine. "My gold."

"They in Coleville," said the Paiute matter-of-factly.

"You saw them?" Matt asked.

"One moon gone. They whoop, holler, spend, act like wild Indian."

"That may be them. What did they look like?"

"Dirty. Long hair. Chew all time on leaves, do this." He pretended to spit.

"That's them!" said Bodine.

"We'll leave in the morning," declared Matt. "Charlie, will you ride with me? They robbed the bank and shot my pa."

Charlie Jack looked at Jacob Page. "You not dead."

"They didn't kill me, you dumb Indian," Jacob said good-naturedly.

"Too bad."

Everyone laughed at the Indian's betterment of the miner. When they stopped, the Paiute looked over at Matt.

"I ride."

"Great!" said Matt, genuinely excited. He was anxious to ride with the tracker again. "We'll get an early start. Billy, could you fix up some trail food for us? Don't know how long we'll be gone." He took another sip from his coffee mug, gingerly now because of the blow he'd collected from McDougal.

"Well, I need to get some sleep. Pete Jensen will see to it that the prisoners are taken care of in the morning."

"He'll probably let Judge Wadell yell at 'em, then let 'em go," Billy said. "Ah'll have your grub ready for you."

"Thanks, Billy. Good night Pa, Charlie, Josh." He nodded to them, pushed his chair back and stood. He grabbed Sarah by the hand and led her outside. In the shadows of the boarding house, he put his arms around the young woman.

"Good night, Sarah. I'll be off early. Be back as soon as I can." He kissed her forehead.

"You *better* come back." She touched his swollen jaw tenderly. "You're the only deputy I've got. You know, one of these days I expect you to win a fight."

"Don't worry, I'll be fine. Listen, this is all part of the job. You know that."

"Getting beat up?"

"No, I mean ridin' all over the country after bad guys. Good heavens, Sarah, your pa's been sheriff since before you were born."

"I know, but I still worry."

"Do what you always tell me to do. Trust God."

She lowered her head and fussed with a button on his shirt. "Okay, Matt." He put his hand under her chin, gently lifted her face and kissed her lightly. Then he quickly walked away toward the jail, leaving Sarah swooning in the darkness.

"Ain't love nice," said Jacob Page, his face pressed against the window.

"It shorely is," admitted Billy, fogging his pane of glass.

Charlie Jack moved next to them.

"What we look at?" He saw Sarah and rapped on the glass. She looked up in time to see Billy and Jacob bump into each other as they tried getting away from the window.

CHAPTER

FOURTEEN

When Matt woke at first light, Charlie Jack was already waiting outside. The deputy dressed quickly and stumbled across the street, acknowledging the Paiute with a wave. Charlie Jack sat erect on his horse and nodded patiently.

Matt entered the boarding house, finding Uncle Billy nursing a cup of hot tea. The younger man poured coffee from the ever-ready pot, downed it as fast as he could, then took the package of food Billy had prepared. The black man stood and gave Matt a handshake.

"Bring yourself back in one piece, Matthew," he told his friend.

"I'll sure try," Matt replied. He thanked Billy for the food and left.

Retrieving his horse and gear from the livery, Matt joined Charlie Jack, and they rode easily to Bridgeport. Managing the uneventful trip in only a few hours—unlike Matt's first trip there—and arriving well before lunch, they found Sheriff Taylor in his office.

It took Matt about a half hour to lay out the story for him. When he finished, Taylor stood and walked to the gun rack. As the sheriff unlocked it and took out a couple rifles, Matt noticed a familiar Winchester. He thought of Sarah, remembering how she stood in the mouth of the cave shooting at him, and smiled, but Taylor broke the trance.

"Huh?" Matt said. "I didn't hear you."

"I said, 'I'm riding with you.' Give me a few minutes to get Eli ready."

Josh Bodine rose early. Billy gave him a bundle of food for traveling. He had refused to let O'Hara give him any money, thanking him for what he had already done: the free room and food. Billy told the young man God would be with him.

"He sure hasn't been up until now," Josh replied. He turned to walk out.

"You ain't given Him much of a chance," Billy pointed out. "Every step a the way you done what you could to make sure God couldn't help you. Besides, I'd say the Good Lord has been with you, whether you realize it or not. Instead of fixin' to leave, you could be behind bars, wishin' you was still breakin' rock in your daddy's mine."

"Yeah, I suppose," he admitted quietly. "Well, thanks for all you done."

"You're welcome back, any time," Billy assured. "Good luck. And God will be with you, Joshua. You remember that."

Josh nodded and stepped out onto the porch, then stopped abruptly. There, tied to the rail, was his horse. His gunbelt hung from the saddle horn with a note pinned to it. Josh looked around. There was no one he knew nearby. He snatched the note and read it.

You'll need these. See you next time you're in town. Pete Jensen.

Josh looked around again, folded the note, and stuffed it into his shirt pocket, then removed the gunbelt and strapped it on. It felt good around his hips. He pulled out his iron, feeling its heft and opening the loading door and turning the cylinder slowly. Jensen had replaced the spent rounds with live ones. Josh dropped it back into the holster, slipped the small strap over the hammer spur to keep it in, and pulled himself up onto the saddle.

Anxious to leave Bodie behind, he turned the horse and kicked it, riding hard toward Bridgeport. Now that he had his six-shooter and horse, he could help the deputy find Smith and Shag. It was the least he could do to repay the lawman. Besides, those two galoots had his gold. His future.

Bodine kept a steady pace, stopping once, allowing his horse a drink from the shallow creek at the side of the road. He arrived in Bridgeport in the early afternoon, finding the sheriff's office locked. He rode to the livery to inquire, figuring the stable owner would know something.

"They rode out of town an hour ago, had that Indian feller with 'em," the man said. "Headed north to Coleville or Walker. There's only one road, so you should be able to catch up if you hurry. Just stay on the main road."

"Thank you kindly," Josh said, and urged his mount forward.

The lawmen and the Indian loped their animals, covering a lot of ground without tiring their rides out unnecessarily. When they stopped and rested their steeds at a rugged rock outcropping called Devil's Gate, Matt noticed a brief flash of light reflecting off something behind them. He took out his field glasses and stared into the distance. He could see a horseman, riding hard.

"Looks like Bodine," Matt said. "He's the kid that these buzzards framed for the robbery."

"I don't want no hothead gittin' in the way," Taylor said.

"He didn't strike me as such," Matt said, handing the glasses to Taylor.

"Not when he's sittin' in a cell, thinkin' his future is awful bleak. But now that he's free, he's out for revenge."

"He's good with a gun," Matt said. "And we may need him. Remember, it's just you and me. Charlie Jack don't carry a gun."

Taylor grunted. "Just so's he understands, he ain't to do nothin' we don't tell him to." He peered through the binoculars. "He'll be here in a half hour or so, but by then his horse'll be tired, and we'll have to let him rest. Let's put some more ground behind us. Let him catch up later, so we don't lose no more time. These jaspers ain't gonna wait around for us, and I ain't gonna chase 'em all the way to Oregon."

He handed the glasses back to Matt and, without another word, mounted Eli and rode off, followed by Charlie Jack. Matt packed the glasses in his saddlebags and hurried to catch up.

Josh saw the three riders on a distant crest of the ridge at the far end of the valley he was just entering. He pulled up his mount momentarily and took a drink from his canteen. Standing in the stirrups to take the weight off his numb hindquarters, he stretched. He had never ridden this far, and it was taking its toll.

He sighed and rode on.

At dusk, an hour after he had completed the climb out of the valley, someone off to the side of the road called his name. He wheeled around but saw nothing, then Matt popped up from behind a large rock.

"Over here!" he yelled, waving Josh over. "Tie your horse up there." Matt pointed to a stand of aspens.

Josh swung himself stiffly out of the saddle and led his mount to the trees, walking slightly bent over. Following the example of the other men, Bodine unsaddled his horse and gave him a hatful of water. He carried his food parcel over to the campfire and sat down in the dirt beside it.

"You're walkin' a little funny," Matt observed.

"Saddle sore," Bodine admitted. "I ain't used to this."

"Well, you can heal up tonight," Matt said. "I take it you're here to help us look for the robbers."

"They got my gold."

"Mmmm." Matt nodded toward the sheriff. "This here's Sheriff John Taylor. You met Charlie Jack already."

Bodine stood up gingerly and shook hands with the other men. "Pleased to meet you, Sheriff." He nodded to the Indian, still undecided about him.

"I hear you're good with a gun," Taylor said.

"I guess," Bodine said, shrugging.

"Ever shoot a man?"

"No."

"Different thing entirely. These guys are likely to be shootin' back, and they ain't gonna be sittin' on a fence holdin' real still for you."

"I can handle it," Bodine said, a little too forcefully. Taylor grunted. Josh opened his packet and took out a piece of Billy's jerky while Matt poured a cup of coffee from the pot on the fire and handed it to the youngster.

"Thanks," the former miner said as he took the cup.

"You can ride with us," Matt said, "if you remember that you're to do what we tell you. This is an official action, and if you get excited or go off half-cocked, well, I'll be forced to send you back—if you ain't already dead."

"I can follow orders," Bodine assured. "Been doin' it all my life." He took a sip of coffee. "Look, I'm out for my gold, not revenge. Besides this horse and gun, that's all I got in this world. You don't have to worry about me."

"Let's be sure that's the way it is," Taylor said harshly. He moved over to his saddle and spread his bedroll out. "I ain't slept on the ground for a while, and I'm liable to be cranky when I get up. Don't anyone cross me." He got comfortable and covered himself.

"We'll get into Coleville in the morning," Matt told Bodine. "From there, Charley'll take over while we track these guys."

"Can he be trusted?" Bodine asked quietly.

"Charley Jack? Completely. He saved my bacon several times. He's the best there is."

Bodine stared at Charlie Jack secretly. He had never seen an Indian close up before. All of his novels taught him that Indians were savages, out for scalps and blood—white man's blood—and that they wore little flaps of leather and nothing else, except maybe feathers in their hair. That Charlie Jack would be attired like a white man was a mystery to him.

The Paiute ignored Bodine as the Indian spread out a blanket next to the fire. He lay on top of it with his back to the flame, then looked over at Josh.

"Go sleep. Watch Charlie Jack tomorrow."

Bodine tried to act nonchalant, busying himself with his bedroll, but no one was fooled. Matt smiled in amusement at Charlie's knack for unnerving people. The Indian went immediately to sleep, and Josh tossed what was left of his coffee into the fire, causing brief hisses as the liquid was consumed.

An owl flew overhead, and as Bodine settled down under his blanket, he listened to the crickets, the rustling of the trees in the evening breeze, and the snoring of the sheriff. He soon gave in to his fatigue and was asleep.

CHAPTER

FIFTEEN

Josh was awakened by the clunk of logs landing on each other in the fire ring. Matt sat next to it, pushing the burning embers and aimlessly waiting for the coffee to boil. Sheriff Taylor was still asleep. Charlie Jack was gone.

The deputy nodded to Bodine as the kid pushed himself up off the ground stiffly. He wandered into the nearby trees in his stocking feet, and, when he returned, saw Taylor stretching.

"Didn't sleep a wink!" Taylor announced. He gathered up his bedroll and twisted out the kinks as Matt poured him a cup of coffee. "Thanks. We best be gittin' on the road. We're burnin' daylight!" He finished off the lukewarm coffee in a gulp and tossed the remains into the brush. The cup he tossed to Matt.

"We're ready," his deputy told him. "I fed the horses. Charlie Jack's gone on ahead."

"Mmmm." Taylor made his way haltingly to his horse, remembering why he gave more and more responsibility to his deputy, and lashed his bedroll behind the cantle of his saddle that someone had already cinched to Eli's back.

Matt tied the empty coffee pot to Blister's flank and pulled himself into the saddle. Bodine put out the campfire and joined the two lawmen as they rode in silence.

The road they traveled was well-worn and passed through several sagebrush valleys before descending into a narrow canyon. A stream rushed past them, cutting the gorge deeper, then leveled off peacefully, winding without apparent purpose through a meadow.

"Remind me to bring you fishin' up here sometime," Taylor said absentmindedly to Matt. It was the first time Matt could recall the sheriff acknowledging there was anything between them other than work. "The Walker River'll give up some nice trout," Taylor continued. Without waiting for acknowledgment, he kicked Eli in the side, and the animal loped in response.

They rode around a few more bends before Coleville came into view. Josh took in the little town with it's whitewashed wood and red brick buildings. At the far end was a pretty, little church, its steeple topped by a small but visible cross. On one side, about halfway down, a new building was just being completed, the roofers hauling their shingles up a stout ladder. Charlie Jack was riding slowly toward them down the middle of the otherwise vacant street.

"They go north, two hour," Charlie Jack said. "They not afraid. Think they not followed. Spend much money."

"Where do you think they're headed?" Matt asked. "Carson City?"

"Not go. Tracks turn. Pass."

"Monitor Pass?" Taylor asked.

Charlie Jack nodded.

"Shoot! If they get to Markleeville, we might never catch 'em!"

"Can you wire the sheriff there?" Matt asked.

"Good idea, son. I'll do that. You and Charlie Jack figure out what we're gonna do after that, how we're gonna set about catchin' up to them."

As Taylor rode toward the telegraph office, Matt sat in shock. *Son.* Sheriff Taylor had called him son. He wondered what that meant, but before he could decide, his thoughts were broken by the rumbling of an approaching buckboard.

Matt glanced casually at the driver and his family, who looked back. They recognized each other at the same instant.

"Deputy Page!"

"DeCamp! That you?" Matt tipped his hat at the man's wife. "Mrs. DeCamp. Oh, and Ruthie." Then a boy bounded out of the back of the wagon before it had come to a complete stop and ran to the deputy's horse. Matt slid down, and Samuel jumped into his arms.

"How are you doin', Samuel?"

"Real good!" the boy replied. "You should see the house they built!"

Matt looked up at the Dutchman, who smiled.

"It's a nice one," DeCamp said. Matt carried Samuel over to him. "What brings you fellahs here?" the farmer-turned-gold miner asked the deputy.

"Chasin' a couple bank robbers."

"Them two guys that've been hangin' around town the last few days?" Fred asked.

Matt nodded.

"I thought there was something fishy about them. I wish we had a regular deputy here in town."

"Tell your people to put a bug in the sheriff's ear. Maybe he'll station me here."

"You'd do that?"

"Sure. I'm already familiar with the jail. Ain't I, Samuel?" He winked at the boy who nodded knowingly. "Say, Mr. DeCamp, how's the gold minin' goin'?"

"Please, call me Fred. It's not too good, actually. I've found enough to keep us going. But I know there's a good vein around here. What gold I've found is jagged around the edges, hasn't been worn smooth by a long trip in the creek. The source is nearby. One of these days I'll be able to hang my sign." He passed his open hand in front of him. "The Golden Gate Mine. What do you think?"

"Sounds good. I hope it works out for you."

"Yeah. Me too. But if it don't, I'll go back to raisin' dairy cows and farmin'. That's what my pa and grandpa did, back in Holland."

"Nothin' wrong with that," Matt said. He turned to see Taylor returning. Matt set Samuel up in the wagon by Mrs. DeCamp. "Tell me," he said to her quietly. How's the woman?"

"Bessie? Oh, she's better. Much better. I'll tell her you came by. She'll be glad to know. Maybe someday you can pay her a visit. I think she'd like that."

"So would I," Matt said. "Well, we gotta git. Maybe I'll stop in and see you all when we're done, if I can."

"You're welcome any time, Matt," Fred told him.

The deputy climbed back on his horse as DeCamp whistled and shook the reins, moving off slowly. Samuel waved until they disappeared around a building.

"Who's that?" Taylor asked.

"Fred DeCamp and his family."

"Them that helped you with Bart Monroe?"

"The same."

"Well, whaddya know." He turned in the saddle to face Matt. "Sheriff Chance from Markleeville's gonna ride out this way with some men, cut them two off if they try to go up the pass."

"We can follow them up in case they double back," Matt said.

"Let's git." Taylor wheeled his horse around. "Charlie Jack, lead on."

Charley Jack nodded, and they urged their mounts swiftly up the road.

Bodine had watched all this in silence, somewhat in awe of the men. They were nothing like the stories he had read, yet these men were the real thing. Were the novels completely wrong? Here were lawmen and Indians, but they were nothing like he expected. They were human, subject to failure. They got cold, had bad days, made mistakes. The Indian didn't want to scalp him. Josh's head was in a whirl.

He marveled too at the scenery. Having lived most of his life in the desolate, sagebrush-covered hills near the Nevada border, he looked in awe at an immense, green valley. Running northeast from Coleville, it was miles of pastureland, seven, eight miles wide and a good thirty miles long. He guessed he could see clear into Nevada. This was Antelope Valley, he was told.

It was late in the morning when they reached the fork in the road that led up to Monitor Pass. The wind was picking up, and Josh pushed his hat down on his head to so as not to lose it.

The first few miles of the pass were through a narrow, twisting canyon cut by a small but swift stream. There was no way someone could sneak down past them. Ahead of the riders and on up to the right was Monitor Pass with its many, steep switchbacks. The road was the only way up or down the mountain. If the sheriff from Markleeville made it down without encountering anyone, then the robbers hadn't gone this way.

Charlie Jack rode ahead on the winding road, which was little more than a path, reading sign easily. Matt moved up behind him.

"So, what do you think? Did they go this way?"

"They ride slow. Horses tired."

"That doesn't make sense. They sat around Coleville for a couple days."

"Their horses are old and worn-out." It was Bodine, who had caught up to them. "I could tell that when I first met them."

Charlie Jack slid off his mount and climbed quickly up a rock to get a view of the trail ahead. Matt followed him, bringing his field glasses.

"Do you think we can catch up to them before they crest the ridge?" Matt asked the tracker.

Charlie Jack scanned the countryside ahead of them, then pointed.

"We catch."

Matt strained to see into the distance.

"There, near white rock."

The deputy shaded his eyes, then gave up and got out the field glasses. There they were: two weary saddletramps, halfway up the first set of switchbacks.

Josh climbed up, leaving Sheriff Taylor to sit with the horses. Matt handed him the glasses.

"That's them." he said, seeing the riders. His jaw was set, and he spoke through clenched teeth.

"Look up there!" Matt said.

Josh raised the glasses. There was a cloud of dust drifting over the top of the distant pass. Matt took back the glasses and looked for himself. The dust cloud increased until finally a group of riders appeared at the bottom of it. It must be Sheriff Chance with a posse. The deputy panned down to the robbers. They, too, had seen the Markleeville lawmen. The outlaws had stopped, apparently thinking about their next move. Matt saw one of them turn in his saddle and look back down the trail, then up again at Chance and his men.

The posse rode carefully but steadily down the steep trail. The two Ezras wheeled their mounts and retreated down the road the way they had come up, their long hair and overcoats flapping behind them.

Matt and the others scampered down from their perch and jumped quickly onto their mounts.

"Sheriff Chance is coming down the pass!" Matt told Taylor, "And the robbers have turned and are coming back this way!"

"We got 'em trapped!" Taylor shouted. "Let's go!"

They hustled their horses on up the winding trail. The road continued its climb, but the narrow gorge they were in and the trees by the stream made them lose sight of the switchbacks up ahead. Taylor wanted to confront them outside this canyon, out in the open where the robbers couldn't easily hide. They urged their horses on.

In about twenty minutes they broke out of the canyon. There was a valley spread out to their left, sloping upward, about fifteen miles long and a couple miles wide. It was surrounded by steep rock and tree-covered hills on three sides, and appeared to be completely closed in except for where they were standing. It did not appear to Matt to be a possible escape route.

The criminals came into view now and, seeing Taylor and his men, pulled up sharply. They were between a rock and a hard place, a posse on either side of them. They turned their animals around in a circle, surprising Matt when they took off toward the closed-in valley.

"They're goin' up Slinkard," Taylor shouted.

"Slinkard?" Matt said. "Where Charlie Jack has his digs?"

"The same," said Taylor. "C'mon. We got 'em now. There's no way out."

"Wait," interupted the tracker. "There is. Narrow pass, far end. Paiute use to get away when white man raid digs."

"I didn't know about it," Taylor said. "It must be well hidden. Do you think the outlaws can find it?"

"It hidden, but they desperate. They may find."

"What if they get through before we catch up to them?" Matt asked.

"We never find. Big country, many places to hide."

"What can we do?" Bodine asked, frantic. "We can't let them get away!"

"We'll just have to catch 'em," Taylor said.

"No, they too far," said Charlie Jack. "If make pass, they kill us easy. No chance."

"Can we get to the other side of the pass the long way before they get all the way through?"

"Yes. If hurry."

"Matt, you take Bodine and Charlie with you, get around to the other side to keep them from gettin' outta here. I'll wait here and force them to you with Chance and his men, but we'll hang back so we don't push them too fast, to give you a chance to make the other side."

"Okay, Sheriff. Charlie Jack, lead on."

The Indian raced his sorrel back down toward Coleville, followed closely by Matt and the saddle-sore Bodine. But the young man didn't complain.

CHAPTER

SIXTEEN

The alias Ezra Smith shot a glance over his shoulder at his pursuers. They were two miles behind them at the least, just starting their way down the slope into Slinkard. The trail under Smith and Shag had disappeared as the ground leveled off, and they were racing across the grassy, valley floor.

"This is a dead end, you idiot!" Shag shouted to his partner.

"It shore looks that way," Smith agreed, not slowing down. "But we may be able to find a way out down there, and if'n we don't, we'll shoot it out. It had to come to this sooner or later."

"If you didn't waste so much time in town lollygaggin' aroun' we wouldn't be in this mess now."

"Oh, shut up, would you? You bellyache like an ol' woman. I never heerd *you* come up with no ideas."

"Why'd you bring us down this valley? There ain't no way out."

"It 'uz this or stand there and git arrested. You kin stop and give up any ol' time you want. Jus' rein up yer hoss and throw yer hands up. Mebbe they won't shoot you."

Shag didn't answer but kept riding. Although the valley looked flat from a distance, the ground undulated, sometimes enough to shield them from view momentarily. But there was no place to hide. As they crested a ridge, Smith looked back again, but he didn't see anything. The posse was in one of the depressions, then rose to a ridge of their own.

"They ain't catchin' up," Smith said.

Shag looked back. "They ain't ridin' hard, neither. What's goin' on?"

"They think it's a dead end, too. They know they'll catch up when we hit th'other side."

"Say, ain't that smoke?" Shag pointed to their right, about two miles off.

"Looks like it. But no white people live in here."

"How do you know that?"

"No roads. White people like roads, so's they kin drive their wagons. That's an Injun camp."

"Don't make sense," Shag said, "Injuns livin' in a place where they could git boxed in."

Smith pulled his horse up. Shag did so too, then walked back next to him. "What'd you stop fer?"

"What you jus' said. Injuns wouldn't live in a place where they couldn't git away if'n they had to. There's gotta be a way outta this valley."

"Then let's stop jawin' and find it."

They ran their horses nonstop to the end of the valley, only looking back for a check on their pursuers when they reached the tree line. There they stopped, circling their horses and looking for some sign of a secret pass. Everywhere they looked was rock. Smith could read sign fair, but Shag was better, and he got off his horse.

He walked back and forth, looking at the grass for something that would tip him off, some indication that people had walked this way. Then he found it. A rock outcropping that looked to be sunk into the steep hillside actually hid a narrow path that led up the sagebrush-covered hill behind it into the trees. It was grown over and looked as if it hadn't been used in years.

The path was narrow, so Shag led his horse along it, pushing branches out of his way. He was followed by Smith, also on foot.

"This is perfect!" Smith said. "We kin wait at the end of this and pick 'em off one at a time as they come through!"

"I ain't keen on no killin'," Shag said.

"Well, they's gonna be a killin'," Smith assured. "The question is, who's gonna do the dyin', them or us? I'd jus' as soon it be them.

Once we're outta here we kin take this money and the gold and live like kings."

"Not out here, we cain't," Shag said. "I'm goin' back East where no one knows me and where they ain't no horses."

"Suit yerseff. But firs' we gotta git outta here, and killin' them lawmen is the only way we're gonna do that."

Shag grunted, but he knew Smith was right. Not knowing that the man Smith shot in the bank didn't die, they figured that, if they lived to be tried, they'd get hung anyway.

The path wound through a narrow but short rock canyon. There were places where there was hardly any footing at all, and the horses had to be pulled hard to make them follow. But follow they did, and in time, the pass opened up into a forest of aspen and pine trees.

"How'd you know 'bout this?" Shag asked Smith while they stopped to get a drink for themselves and their tired horses.

"What?"

"This hidden pass."

"Injuns always have 'em. They use 'em to sneak through after they raid a white man's homestead, or to drive stolen cattle through. If'n ya'd stayed with us on the cattle drive to Colorada you'd a knowd that."

"That little señorita in El Paso looked better to me at the time than the backsides of cows."

Smith laughed. "You got a point there." He put the stopper back into his canteen. "They'll be comin' to the bottom of the pass any time now. They'll find it easy, seein' us disappear like we done, so we better tie the horses up and go find a spot to drygulch 'em. Then we ride a few more miles up to the top a the ridge there, and we're home free."

Matt and Josh followed Charlie Jack back down the twisting road, then through the outskirts of Coleville. The Indian turned his sorrel up a path Matt thought looked familiar, and soon they passed a new cabin, built next to a charred spot on the ground. Matt recognized the DeCamp place.

This cabin was larger, and Matt admired the stone chimney. *I want a place like this someday,* he thought. *Me and Sarah, raisin' our kids, little Jacob and Molly.* He smiled.

They continued up the sloping hillside through the trees, not staying on a path. The way was steep in places, and the horses had to be led. Josh never said a word, and Matt could tell he was letting his anger grow. A word of caution to the young man would fall on deaf ears, so Matt said nothing.

Several miles above the house they passed through a small stand of apple trees. They bore no fruit now, not until later in the year. Matt made a mental note to return here with Sarah sometime. *I bet she could really make a fine pie with—*

"Here!"

Matt's thoughts were scattered by Charlie Jack's abrupt command. The tracker had reined up and pointed now to a stand of aspen at the far edge of a clearing. Matt took the lead and rode cautiously, followed by the Paiute and Bodine. When they reached the other side, they stopped.

"See rock?" Charlie Jack asked.

Matt nodded.

"Go there, turn right, find trail. It go down to valley."

"Ain't you goin'?" Bodine asked.

"Charlie Jack doesn't get into gunfights, Josh. He's a tracker, not a shootist."

"I thought all Indians were good fighters."

"This isn't his fight."

"Well, it's mine, sure enough." Bodine heeled his bay hard in the side and rode to the rock. When he turned right, the forest swallowed him.

"Matt hurry," Charlie Jack suggested. "He have hot head, no brain."

"You're right, as usual. Thanks for your help."

The Paiute nodded and watched as Matt followed Josh into the foliage.

The way was overgrown, and only someone looking for a path would notice it, and then only by looking down at the hoof tracks. It was less obvious than a deer trail and less well-traveled. Matt soon caught up to Josh who had stopped, lost.

"Follow me," Matt said.

He read the telltale signs as Charlie Jack had taught him and found the trail with no trouble. Bodine followed in disbelief. They hadn't gone far when a barrage of gunfire up ahead startled them.

Matt jumped off Blister and sent him back the other way. He

ran forward and took cover behind a tree. Josh did the same, hunkering down behind the same Ponderosa Pine.

"What was it?" Josh asked.

"I don't know. Maybe Taylor and the others caught up to them. I don't think anyone was shootin' at us. I didn't hear no bullets flyin' past."

Several more staccato shots made them instinctively duck, but there was no immediate danger.

"No, they ain't shootin' at us. Someone up ahead is shootin' the other direction."

The first shots sent the posse scattering all directions for cover. The man on the lead horse was plunked in the shoulder, and he tumbled off his horse. Another man's mount was shot out from under him.

Taylor climbed quickly off Eli—moving faster than he had in a great while—and dove for a nearby tree. He landed awkwardly, knocking the wind out of himself. He also twisted his wrist—his gun-hand wrist.

"Shoot!" he muttered when he regained his breath, wincing at the pain. "I ain't cut out for this no more." He sat with his back against the tree on the side opposite from where the shots had come. He knew they'd been ambushed by the robbers and wondered when Matt would show up. They were sitting ducks here.

He looked around for the others and saw Sheriff Chance with his gun drawn, peeking out from behind a tree of his own. A shot was fired, and the bullet slammed into the tree trunk, showering him with splinters. He pulled his face back to safety.

"Did you see where they are?" he shouted to Taylor. Taylor shook his head.

Sheriff Chance called out to his posse. "Bob? Fred?" At first there was no answer, then someone yelled back.

"They went back!" It was the injured man. "Said it weren't their fight!"

"Dang!" said Taylor. "Where's that blame deputy of mine?"

Matt and Josh crawled forward quietly. Another shot was fired, not thirty yards away. It too went the opposite direction.

"They got Taylor and the others pinned down," he whispered to Bodine.

"Let's call out. Let the sheriff know we're here."

"No! We can't give up our element of surprise. They don't know about us. We need to find 'em and soon. If Taylor and the posse start firin' back, they're likely to hit us."

He checked around. "I'll go ahead, you come up behind me, low."

Bodine nodded and drew his gun. *Finally,* he thought, feeling the heft of the six-shooter. He quickly put a round in the empty chamber and followed the deputy.

Taylor took off his hat and stuck it out from behind the tree to draw fire. It did and was immediately shot out of his hand.

"Did you see where it came from?" he asked Chance.

"No, it happened too fast. Do it again."

"I'm fresh outta hats."

"Well, you can—whoa, what's this?" He peeked out around the tree carefully, and Taylor strained to see what he was looking at without getting his own head blown off.

Matt and Josh finally saw them. They were forty yards ahead, hunkered down behind good cover.

"I'm goin'," Josh whispered.

"No!" Matt ordered, but it was too late. Josh left their cover and emerged from the trees behind the outlaws, crouch-walking fast.

"Drop 'em!" he shouted, drawing a bead on Smith.

Smith and Shag were surprised, but they didn't obey. They both rolled quickly and fired blind. Matt saw it happening but couldn't stop it. He ran forward as Bodine gave his command and watched in horror as the young man was dropped.

Matt fired as he charged, not really trying to hit anything but hoping to send the outlaws for cover, buying some time and space. He still didn't know where Taylor and the others were but knew they had a deadly crossfire set up.

As he neared Bodine, who lay writhing on the forest floor, he was spotted by Shag, who trained his six-shooter on him. Matt reacted immediately and fired again. Shag shot at the same time but flinched because of Matt's retort, and his bullet was off the mark—though not by much—going through the folds of Matt's shirt. Matt squeezed off a round as he reached Josh. His bullet fared better than Shag's, thumping the man in the chest. The outlaw looked down in disbelief as his gun slid from his hand and dropped softly onto the forest-floor blanket of dead leaves and pine needles. Then his body slumped and fell. His eyes remained open but could no longer see.

Matt grabbed Bodine by the collar and pulled him behind a tree. He was dazed but not badly hurt. The bullet had grazed his gun arm.

Matt wrapped Josh's bandanna around the wound, and it quickly was soaked with blood. Bullets from Smith's gun whizzed by.

Chance and Taylor watched the fight. With Smith distracted, Chance ran forward to a better position, one not in a crossfire. Smith, now realizing that Shag was dead and he was outnumbered, broke and ran, emptying his gun and keeping the lawmen down. Matt saw him.

"Keep your hand on this, tight. You'll be okay," he told Josh, placing the kid's good hand over the wound. "Wait here."

Matt sprang up and raced after Smith. The older saddle tramp was no match for the young deputy in his gum-soled boots, and Matt tackled the outlaw as he entered a clearing. Smith's empty gun was knocked out of his hand, and he cried out when Matt fell on top of him. The force of their landing knocked Matt's gun out of the holster, as he had not had time to secure the hammer strap.

Although Matt had the advantage of youth, Smith's ace was experience, and he used the deputy's own weight and momentum against him, flinging the lawman off. The outlaw scrambled up, saw Matt's gun, dove for it, and drew a bead on the deputy who was just now regaining himself. Smith cocked it and pulled the trigger.

The hammer fell on an empty chamber.

"So that's why you didn't shoot me." He tossed the gun aside. "Looks like I'm gonna have to teach you a lesson."

He advanced toward Matt, who jumped up and squared off, remembering his fight with Bart. But before any blows could be thrown, Smith suddenly ran off. Matt was momentarily confused but heard noises in the woods behind him as Taylor and Chance ran to help. After a second of hesitation, Matt gave chase.

Smith headed toward a rock outcropping. Over the top of the rocks Matt could see Antelope Valley in the distance. They were near the edge of the hill, and it was a sheer drop down to the valley floor below. Matt slowed just as the cowboy made it to the edge and realized his mistake. Having nowhere to go, he turned and charged the deputy.

Down they went, arms and legs entangled. Matt struggled to maintain a grip on the outlaw. Smith dug his fingers into Matt's eye, and the deputy realized the man's desperation. He was unable to dislodge the wiry cowboy's grip, so he brought his knee up hard.

This broke Smith's grip, and Matt pushed himself away, breathing a silent prayer. *Please, Lord, help me.* He didn't have time for more. Smith scampered up, surprising Matt with his agility, but turned and clambered up the rock. Matt followed but stopped when he saw Smith turn and sit down. He held something aloft.

Matt stopped, ten feet from the outlaw, and focused on what was in his hand.

It was Bodine's bag of gold dust.

"I'll make you a deal, Deputy. You let me go, I'll give you this. No one'll ever know. Whaddya say? There's a lot a gold in here."

"No deals. You come down, nice and easy."

Smith opened the bag, took out a pinch of dust, and let the wind carry it away.

"Whoops! That cost you a few hundred."

Matt was concerned about Josh's gold, and it showed on his face. Smith saw it but misread it, not realizing Matt wouldn't trade the gold for the outlaw's freedom.

"I told you, no deals," Matt repeated. Smith let loose a little more dust. "You're not in a bargaining position," Page told him. Then he heard something behind him. It was Josh.

"My gold!" he shouted. "Smith, that's my gold!"

"Why, Mr. Josh Bodine! Got any tobacca? How 'bout a drink?" He laughed and let a pinch more dust blow into the valley.

"No!" Bodine shouted. He suddenly raised his left arm and Matt saw a gun in his trembling hand. Before he could do or say anything, Josh fired. The bullet missed Smith but struck the rock near him, chipping off pieces that flew up into his face.

Stung by the debris Smith relaxed his grip on the bag, and it fell behind him. He twisted to grab it, lost his footing, and disappeared.

Matt scampered up the rock and leaned over the edge. He was looking into the face of the outlaw as shimmering gold dust drifted down into the valley.

"Hold on!" Matt said. He grabbed Smith by the wrists. The outlaw looked up at him defiantly and spat in Matt's face.

Fighting the urge to let go, Matt swallowed his feeling of hatred for the man and hung on. *Help me, Lord!*

But Smith would not be helped. He let loose with his fingers and gravity pulled at his body. Now only the deputy's grasp held him. Matt felt himself being pulled also and dug his toes into the rock.

"Why?" he shouted at Smith.

But Smith only looked at him and laughed as he slipped through Matt's fingers, falling and bouncing his way to the valley floor. He landed in a crumpled heap and did not move.

Matt stared at him, then felt himself being pulled back off the edge of the rock. Sheriff Chance helped him down. Matt dusted himself off and saw Taylor and Bodine standing together, the young miner grieving for a second time the loss of his inheritance. Matt knew exactly how he felt.

Charlie Jack met the men as they gathered their horses. He had followed Matt and Josh from a safe distance and, when the fight was over, moved in to do what he could.

"The bank's money is in here," Taylor said, going through Smith's saddlebags. "At least what they didn't spend." Taylor threw the saddlebags over Eli's rump and lashed them to his saddle, then thanked Chance for his help. The Markleeville sheriff handed Taylor his hat with the new hole, wheeled his horse, and returned to his town with his wounded deputy.

On their way back to Coleville, Sheriff Taylor stopped at Fred DeCamp's house and gave him the outlaws' two old horses.

"Matt tells me your younguns want to learn to ride," he told DeCamp. "These old nags oughta be gentle enough."

DeCamp thanked him and watched as they rode off, then saw Matt turn and ride back. The deputy spoke briefly to DeCamp, who smiled and said, "Don't worry. We'll be there."

Taylor, Page, and Bodine rode to Coleville in silence. There Taylor and Bodine were patched up and both fitted with slings. They were fed a hot meal by the minister and his wife and given beds for the night at the hotel. During the entire time, Josh had hardly spoken a word.

The next evening, as they neared Bridgeport, Matt tried to console the dejected Bodine.

"Cheer up. You're not dead."

"Might as well be."

"What do you mean?"

"All my money is gone."

"So?"

"Whaddya mean, 'So'? That's it! I'm broke!"

"I been broke before. It's no big deal. Get yourself a job."

"Doin' what? All I know is minin', and I vowed never to set foot in a mine again. Besides, your pa already told me there ain't no jobs available. Too many men are comin' in every day lookin' for work. I might as well get a job sloppin' hogs someplace. At least then I'd get somethin' to eat."

Matt watched a hawk circle lazily above them, drifting with the currents.

"Well," he said after a while, "pardon me for stating the obvious, but why don't you go home?"

Josh hung his head. "I can't," he said quietly. "Pa gave me my share. There's nothin' left for me there. And my brother, oh boy, he'd never let me hear the end of it."

"Ah, so that's it. You can't swallow your pride and admit you made a mistake."

Bodine didn't answer, but his face was flushed. Matt was silent for awhile, letting Josh chew on it, then offered a suggestion.

"Look, Josh, maybe you're right. Maybe your pa won't welcome you back. Maybe your brother will make life hard for you. But you'll never know if you don't give it a shot." He smacked Josh on the shoulder. "If you don't at least go back and give it a try, I'm liable to think you're a coward."

Josh bristled, but it faded quickly.

"You know," Matt said, "I read a story in the Bible about a fellah like you. Turned out okay for him."

"Yeah? Well, that was just a story, and nothin' in stories come out the same in real life."

"That so? Maybe you just been readin' the wrong stories."

There was a brief silence when Josh didn't respond, the only sounds the blowing of the horses and the crunching of their hooves on the dirt and the creaking of saddles under the weight of their tired and patched-up riders.

Matt looked off up the road. "There's Bridgeport. C'mon, Josh. I'll race you back to town. See you later, Sheriff!" Matt dug his heels into Blister's flank, and the Morgan jumped into a run, knowing that a rubdown and some oats were not far away. Bodine kicked his bay and took off also, hanging on with his good arm as best he could.

Taylor watched them and spoke to Eli.

"What's their hurry, ol' boy? They got a whole life ahead, both of 'em." He smiled and patted Eli's neck.

CHAPTER

SEVENTEEN

Three months later a new day dawned for Matt Page and Sarah Taylor. That day began as every other day had begun in Bodie. The thunder of the stamps in the mills preceded the rising of the sun because they hadn't ceased from the night before. They pounded the gold out of the quartz around the clock, heedless of the risings and settings of the sun and moon, not caring about the seasons, the weather, the heat, or the cold. The miners, millers, hoist operators, and powder monkeys walked to and from their jobs, toting their tin lunch buckets. Prostitutes slept, not able to arise for several more hours. Store owners began arriving at their businesses, ready for another day of service. Voices drifted out of the saloons, and wagons moved slowly up and down Main Street, the horses and oxen straining to pull the heavy loads of furniture and firewood, dry goods and people.

The air was crisp and cool, the deep blue sky free of clouds and tinted with the orange and pink promise of a new day. The future was bright for most of the folk of the camp; whether it would turn out that way or not didn't matter, it was the hope that it could and the expectation that it would that spurred them on.

As the sun reached its peak around noon, all was definitely not business as usual inside the Empire Boarding House. The parlor furniture had been rearranged. The tables had been removed and the chairs lined up in rows all facing the same direction with an aisle down the center.

Matt Page stood stiffly at the front of the room, his finger easing his buttoned collar away from his neck, and surveyed the crowd. His father, Jacob Page, and Irene Taylor occupied the front row, along with Billy O'Hara. Matt noticed with mixed emotions that Bessie Travis, the woman whose husband had been murdered in their barn by Bart Monroe and who had come to Bodie a few weeks before in hopes of starting her life over, had been eyeing Matt's father. Jacob Page was unsuspecting, but Matt didn't think that would last. Sooner or later, he'd notice her. The elder Page checked his pocket watch, and Mrs. Taylor straightened her dress. Uncle Billy caught Matt's eye and gave him a wink. The young man smiled weakly in return.

Harvey Boone and his new bride Mary held hands on the second row, more interested in each other than in the proceedings unfolding in front of them. Josh Bodine, his brother and proud father beside him, sat behind the Boones. Next to them, Fred DeCamp grabbed a squirming Samuel by the arm and shushed him while Mrs. DeCamp held Ruthie in her lap. Charlie Jack fidgeted in his chair near the back.

Even James Nixon and Red McDougal were there, sitting together, peace at last having been made between the two. The rest of the pews were filled with other miners and townspeople, all looking forward to the feed that was planned for later, piles of free food for all.

The door at the back of the church opened, and a spiffy, yet uncomfortable-looking Sheriff Taylor appeared, holding an angel on his arm. Matt was unaware of the grin that spread across his face as he gazed at Sarah, his eyes wide as if he'd just seen her for the very first time.

Sarah walked resolutely down the aisle, their eyes locked on each other until she was next to him. Sheriff Taylor cleared his throat, snapping them out of their hypnosis. Reverend Hinkley met the couple at the front of the church, smiled at Sarah, and winked at Matt before addressing the crowd.

"Good afternoon, gracious friends. We have gathered here today, in this God-forsaken gold camp, to join together these two young people . . ."

AUTHOR'S

NOTE

Bridgeport, Bodie, and Bishop are real towns. Bodie is now a well-preserved ghost town and a California State Park that you can visit and walk the same streets they did over a hundred years ago, left just as they were when the town was finally abandoned in the 1940s. Bridgeport and Bishop are still thriving communities.

Uncle Billy O'Hara is considered the godfather of Bodie. Most of the books that have been written about Bodie tell his story. He died in 1880.

The prison breakout of 1871 is a true incident, as are the names of the prisoners. The shootout at Monte Diablo led to the renaming of the mountain that looks down upon the lake to Mt. Morrison in honor of the lawman who was murdered. The lake itself was renamed Convict Lake and is an excellent place to fish for trout. It is about two miles off Highway 395, south of Mammoth Lakes, California.